Fake
GAME

Editor: Katie Krasne
Cover Designer: Cat at TRC Designs (@trcdesignsbycat)
Formatting: Alyssa at Uplifting Author Services
Interior Art: Alina Alilyushka

MADISON FOX

To Ethan.
For being the reason why I got into video games.

This book is for all the girls who were told that video games were just "for boys" and that liking anime was weird.

Fuck those people.

15 songs • 43 min 51sec • by MADISON FOX

FAKE
GAME

Reading Playlist

Name of the song	Time	Artist
Overstimulated	**3:23**	**Rival**
I'm Fine	2:39	Tim Frane
Remedy	3:34	Marin Hoxha
Go Ghost	2:21	Jackson Wang
Love Talk	3:52	WayV
Starry!	2:51	Viuk
Cravin'	2:53	Stiletto
In My Head	2:42	SVRRIC
Don't Wanna Be Famous	2:22	Despotem
stuck at 2	3:30	NO TIME FOR SILENCE
Freaky	2:00	Bryce Savage
Shibari	2:32	Featurette
Inhale	3:34	Moonfall
Anchor	3:28	Abandoned
Home	2:10	niko rain

GAMING GLOSSARY

Carry – when one person ends up being responsible for winning on behalf of their team or another player, normally because the team/other player is new, low-ranking, or just bad or lazy in comparison.

Co-op – cooperative; a type of gameplay where you play with other players on the same team to win an objective. Opposite is single player games.

Cozy games – a genre of games that are designed to be relaxing and feel good. Typically, they are nonviolent.

Dating sim – a subgenre of simulation games that are dialogue and choice based, where the objective is to use statistics to win over a love interest to complete the game in the allotted time frame. These games rely heavily on time management and building relationships. Not to be confused with a visual novel.

DLC – downloadable content. Refers to extra content that can be downloaded for the game that is separate from the main storyline.

Esports – electronic sports; a type of video game competition.

Easter eggs – hidden messages or features in a game.

Farming sim – a subgenre of life sim, where the player controls one or more virtual characters as they tend to a farm while going about their daily life and interacting with townspeople (e.g., Harvest Moon, Animal Crossing).

Gamertag – a player's in-game screen name. Players often go by their gamertag instead of their real names.

Glitch – a temporary error in the game system.

Lag – a delay between the input of an action and when the action is completed. Commonly, when you are lagging, your character will glitch.

Life sim – life simulation game; refers to a game where the player lives/controls one or more virtual characters as they go about life (working, dating, etc.) and are typically open ended (e.g., The Sims, Animal Crossing).

Lobby – an in-game waiting room.

Main – refers to a character/class you play most often or specialize in.

Merk/Merked – kill/killed.

MMO – massively multiplayer online. An online game in which many players play together on the same server.

Mod – a modification that is player made to a game. Not by the game developer.

Moderator – someone who oversees (in gaming: someone who oversees a server to make sure it is a safe and healthy environment for all users). Can be abbreviated to "mod."

Noob – refers to someone who is new at a game or lacks skill.

Otome game – a type of dating sim; a story-based romance game, normally geared toward women, with a female protagonist aiming to win the affection of one of multiple male love interests by the end of the game to receive a "good ending." Popularized in Japan.

OP – overpowered.

PvP – player versus player. A game where people play against each other (no computer-controlled opponents).

RP – role-playing. The act of playing an in-game character within the backstory you've assigned to them.

RPG – role-playing game. You create a character that you then level up through experience points.

Screen Peeking – the action of looking at another player's section of the television screen that they are playing on, when you are all sharing the same screen to play the game. Normally used to cheat during competitive multiplayer games.

Speedrun – the act of completing a game as fast as possible.

Swatting – the act of calling emergency services with a fake scenario to dispatch a large number of officers (typically, a SWAT team) to an address. In streaming, people will swat streamers while they are live streaming as a form of cyber harassment.

Subathon – subscription marathon; a livestream event when the streamer continuously streams for a long period of time (e.g. Forty-eight hours) without a break to gain an increase in subscribers. Normally there is a subscription goal to hit, and the streamer will stay online until they reach that.

Support – popularized by *League of Legends*, this is a support role in the game where the aim is to provide assists to the other players especially early in the game so they can gain experience points and level up. They are also known as the sacrificial hero role and are seen as the most expendable. Normally healers, shielders, tanks, etc.

Troll – a person who posts content online with the aim of harassing, irritating, and/or provoking others.

Villainess – the antagonist in an otome game.

Chapter ONE

DEER

66 **J**ACKSON, HE IS GOING TO KILL ME," my best friend Lee screeches.

"I don't know what you want me to do about it. I'm like three levels above you," Jackson's deep voice rumbles back through my headset.

"Jackson," she screams again.

"Lee, I swear to fucking God."

I let loose a laugh as I maneuver my own character through the dingy basement tunnels.

"Don't laugh at—" Lee's voice is cut off, signaling that her video game character did in fact get killed.

The audio in the horror game we are playing is based on character proximity. The closer you are to your teammates, the more they can hear you. But if you die, you can't hear each other at all, and you just end up stuck in an observatory role until the round ends or everyone else dies.

"She's going to be pissed," I muse.

As the top female video game streamer in the United States, Allison Lee—known by her gamertag LoveLee—is a force to be reckoned with. But while she might be a beast at RPGs and even has esports teams eying her, she is always the first of us to die when we play horror games.

Jackson scoffs. "I didn't see you rushing to her aid."

"She wasn't asking me."

Without Lee, there are pockets of silence between Jackson and me. When I first began playing video games with him, I used to get uncomfortable and thought he maybe didn't like me. Then I realized that that's just his personality; he doesn't really speak unless he has a reason to.

As one of the members of The System—the hottest group of video game streamers, made up of three stupidly attractive men—he is known as the broody, silent one. Jackson goes by the gamertag of Shield3d, a.k.a. Shield, and built his multi-million following playing horror games and streaming MMOs. His social media feed is filled with moody street pics, gym mirror selfies, and the occasional food post. Even when he goes out, he is always the one who keeps a level head, whereas his friends find themselves on the brink of getting arrested.

I spend more time thinking about him than I should, but it's because I can't seem to crack him. I'm friends with his publicist and his best friend's girlfriend, but Jackson and I never talk outside of gaming despite how often our paths cross.

I try not to read too much into it, but it does irk me slightly.

I've spent the last two years crafting my entire online video game persona, TheCozyDeer, as someone whom everyone likes. I'm supposed to be fun, cute and infectiously sweet—but this annoying grump of a man just won't take to it.

I sigh, bringing my mind back into focus as I walk my character down a corridor and come across a locked door. I pull out one of the keys I'd found earlier on in the game then open it.

A giant sludgy centipede creature sits in the middle of the room.

"Motherfuc—" my hands move like lightning over my keyboard as I try to exit the room. The creature begins to scuttle toward me, and I let loose another slew of curses— my Irish lilt slipping out from my practiced American accent—before I safely manage to get back out and close the door.

"You all good there, Deer?"

"Barely," I huff.

It's silent for a beat before Jackson swears.

"What?"

"I heard a noise I didn't like."

I snort, but I understand his unease. *Hunt Till Dead*, the viral co-op survival horror game we are playing, is based largely around sound. If you make too much noise, you can attract certain creatures to your location. The game is set during an apocalypse, and the aim is to scavenge around in the abandoned buildings of various cities for goods to survive. You rely on your team to help you collect enough goods to survive the night, but when your team member dies, you have to wait until the next day for them to respawn. Unless you don't collect enough goods, then you will all die when the clock hits midnight.

"I'm heading back to base camp," Jackson announces.

I chew on my bottom lip, calculating the value of the loot I've gathered. It is probably enough to get us through the night.

"Okay, I'm right behind you."

I begin running my character up a stairwell to reach him on the third floor, but the closer I get to him the more a distant noise begins to register in my headset. I spot Jackson's character, and my shoulders relax a fraction.

Until that distant noise turns into a very decipherable sound.

Nails dragging on the ground.

"Oh no," I whisper. "Oh no, no, no."

"Go, go, go," Jackson shouts, mirroring my dread. "It's just straight then left."

"I hate that sound," I hiss, running my character through the maze of corridors behind him. "I hate it. I hate it."

"Oh. I lied. It's just straight," he corrects when we come up to a dead end.

"Seriously?"

We backtrack, but the noise gets louder. My jaw clenches as my heart rate speeds up. Horror games and I have a love-hate relationship. They scare the crap out of me, but I live for the adrenaline. It's a nice change from my cozy games, and it's also helped boost my streams to a new level—people love to watch people getting scared.

"Fucking hell, I really hate this."

I continue to run down the hallway, but like a noob, I turn around for a split second to see how far behind me the creature is.

Its chalky white body instantly fills my screen, and I let out a short yelp as it kills me.

I lightly slam my mouse against my desk in frustration as my screen flips to the observer view, and I watch as Jackson continues to attempt his escape. Considering the creature just satisfied itself with my corpse, he should be able to make it out.

So annoying.

"Good try," Lee muses.

Since we're both dead, we can chat again.

"I should've survived that," I pout before grabbing a sip of water from my pink rhinestone tumbler. "What killed you anyway?"

"A Corpsewalker."

I can practically hear her lip curl as she spits out the name.

"Ew, I hate those things."

I turn my attention to my second monitor and browse the comments. It's hard to keep up with them whenever I stream with friends because I tend to get lost in the gameplay.

My eyes catch on the video of myself in the top corner, and I frown as I fix my curly pink hair under my headset.

"Fuck. What an L."

Jackson's deep timbre startles me, and I look back at my main monitor to see his character's body get dragged away by a giant fourteen-legged spider.

"That's rough, buddy," Lee consoles.

"You two need to stop dying," he grunts. "This is a co-op game for a reason."

My jaw pops open. "Excuse me? You're the one who led me down a dead end."

"Yeah, but you didn't see me die because of that."

My mouth opens and closes, but no words come out.

The audacity of this man sometimes.

It's to be expected though. If there is one thing I've learned about Jackson Lau, it is that he hates losing and has no issue blaming others instead of himself whenever it happens. Not that it stops me from playing with him time and time again.

"Are we playing another round?" Lee chimes in.

"Totally. I need to redeem myself." I give my wrists a quick roll.

"Yeah, I can knock another out," Jackson agrees.

We let the game randomize the city we land in and wait for our characters to spawn at the new base camp. It's almost pitch black when the screen loads, and my lips purse momentarily when I realize we've ended up in one of the cities with a higher difficulty level.

"Whoever dies last is the chosen one."

"Not funny, Deer," Lee huffs. "I hate this map."

"I mean, if you think about it, this game really helps you get over your fear of the dark."

"Or you could just bump up your gamma," Jackson drolls. "So the dark isn't that dark."

"You always take the fun out of things, Shield."

We each grab a flashlight from the base camp and start to make our way to the main entrance of the derelict building. Jackson and Lee make idle talk, but my eyes stray back to my second monitor where my chat seems to be glitching.

Scratch that.

It's being spammed.

DEERHUNTER19384099

I kn0w where u L1v3

I kn0w where u L1v3

I kn0w where u L1v3

I kn0w where u L1v3

I kn0w where u L1v3

I kn0w where u L1v3

I kn0w where u L1v3

I kn0w where u L1v3

I kn0w where u L1v3

I kn0w where u L1v3

I kn0w where u L1v3

I kn0w where u L1v3

I kn0w where u L1v3

I kn0w where u L1v3

I blink and they are gone, deleted by one of my mods. The user, no doubt, blocked as well.

I'm careful to keep my smile on my face and even

let out a short giggle as I force myself to breathe steady breaths and not freak out. There are over forty thousand people watching me right now. I will not have another panic attack.

I force myself to remain calm even though nausea roils in my gut and my heart beats with the force of a thousand elephants in my ear.

This isn't the first time this has happened.

I have no idea who this person is—and at this point, I'm starting to think it might be an entire group—but they seem hell-bent on trolling me and harassing me. It's been happening for months now, and this whole thing is eating me alive, like a zombie virus slowly taking over my system until I'm left as nothing but a skittish husk. They're all empty threats; nothing has come from their weird comments or ominous DMs. *Yet.* And that's the issue. With each passing day, with each stream, I get a little bit more paranoid.

What if they know who I am?

What if they do know where I live?

What if they do something?

A notification pops up on my phone, and I glance down to see a text from my main moderator, who is basically my personal assistant.

RICK

Blocked them and added the phrase to the list

Hope you're ok

ME

Thanks 😊 I'm hanging in there

RICK

ok. LMK if you need anything

Rick's a lifesaver. Without him, I'd be stuck monitoring and filtering through all my social media alone. I feel a little bad that he has to deal with a litany of dick pics, poems, and solicitations in my stead, but…better him than me.

"Shit."

I totally zoned out.

"Hey, guys?"

I swivel my character around but don't see either of them. Dammit. They seriously abandoned me? This map is hard enough as it is, let alone solo.

And after all that crap Jackson gave about being co-op. *Hypocrite.*

I head into the building and start calling out for them as I traverse the corridors. Yelling their names is a surefire way to get me killed if a wyrm is near, but it's a chance I'll take.

"Lee?" I shine my flashlight on and off, on and off, as I search for loot and my shitty teammates. "Leeeeeeee?"

"Just jump."

I still at the sound of Jackson's deep voice.

"If I miss, I'll die," she whines.

"If you stay there, you'll also die."

"Hey, guys?" I call out, continuing in the same direction.

"There you are," he sighs. "Come watch Lee die."

"Come watch me die? You bastard."

I walk through an archway to find Lee's character trapped on the other side of a broken bridge. She is perched on the railing and there's a round slime creature on the ground trying to engulf her.

"You're gonna need to jump, babes."

"I know," she grinds out.

"I'm giving you three seconds, then I'm leaving," Jackson flatly announces.

"Fine!" she huffs. "God. I don't know why I play these games with you two. If this was *FrozeLine*, you'd be eating your words."

"Three—"

"I GET IT." Lee's character leaps across the bridge and barely lands on the side Jackson and I are on. "Seriously."

"Come on. Let's keep moving. Did you get any loot, Deer?"

"Mm. I got a stop sign." I whip out the giant red sign I snagged on my way over and wave it around.

"Oh hey. Good shit."

I smile at his praise. "Thanks."

We start moving back down the corridor I passed through earlier, and Jackson stops in front of a locked door.

"Anyone have a key?"

"Yeah, I have one." Lee pulls out a silver key. "Good thing I'm not dead, huh?"

The door swings open, and we are immediately greeted by three turrets.

Fuck.

So not good.

"Close the door!" I yell.

"Crap, crap, crap," she chants as she scrambles to shut it right before the first bullet shoots out.

"Shit, that was close."

Light suddenly pours into my streaming room, drowning out the pink ambient glow I've been basking in. My arms jerk in shock, and confusion washes over me at the deafening noises shouting over my headset.

"What the—" The words become stuck in my throat as I crane my neck to look behind me.

My breathing stutters. Sheer, unbridled panic lances through my frozen body as my eyes bounce between the guns pointed at me.

So many guns.

"Deer? What's going on?"

I don't risk answering Lee.

"What's all that noise?"

Or Jackson.

Instead, I quickly raise my hands, careful not to spook the army of men filtering into my streaming room.

"Get on the ground," they start shouting.

"Face on the ground!"

I practically throw myself off my gaming chair. My bare knees crash on the floor, and I bite back a wince. My headset slips off as I crush my chest against my rug.

Everything gets louder.

All the yelling.

So much yelling.

"Hands behind your back."

"Hands behind your back, now."

I scramble to do as they say.

My throat becomes clogged.

It's getting harder to breathe, and my eyes begin to prick.

Someone grabs my wrist tightly and cold metal encloses it, but it doesn't stop my entire body from shaking.

Oh my Gods.

Oh my fucking Gods.

This can't be happening.

DEER

N ot safe.
I'm not safe.
    I hug myself tighter, digging my nails into my shoulders so hard that I'm shocked my pointy acrylics aren't breaking skin. My wrist aches from where the officer twisted, and it just serves as a brutal reminder.

Every single little noise has my head twitching and eyes darting around. I'm worried about inhaling too deep because it feels like something is going to pop out of the shadows any minute.

I haven't moved since the police left.

I don't even know how long ago that was.

All I know is that I was swatted.

I was actually fucking swatted.

My stomach churns like someone dropped a gallon of

sour slushie in it. I'm in danger of throwing up again even though there's nothing left in my stomach. I feel like such an idiot. Here I was, acting like Deer Hunter was just some nobody spewing idle threats.

I should've known to report it to the police. I should've alerted them that I was someone who was at risk of being swatted—that's what a smart streamer would've done. But no, I'd refused to believe this was an actual issue.

So damn naïve.

I'd been dead wrong, and I'd paid the price.

I bury my face in my knees, curling myself further into a little ball under my duvet.

THUMP.

THUMP.

THUMP.

My entire body jerks at the noise and my heart stops. I hold my breath, waiting for a group of men to come barging in again.

"Deer, are you in there?" Lee's voice filters through the cracks.

Crap.

"Deer, open up," Sydney calls out.

Double crap.

I don't want them to see me like this.

I can't. This isn't me.

This isn't Deer.

I panic, scrambling out of my sheets and almost tripping on my rug as I rush out of my room. My ankle twists, and I wince at the twinge but push past it with pure desperation flowing through my veins.

"I have a key," Lee reminds me. "If you don't open this

door in five seconds, I'm coming in anyway."

"Fuck the countdown, just open it," Jackson growls.

The anger in his voice shocks me as my fuzzy socks skid across the floorboards.

I hear the telltale snick of the lock and watch as my front door flies open. Four people come barreling into my apartment, and I see the moment a pair of cool gray eyes land on me.

"Oh, Deer," Sydney whispers as she rushes at me with open arms.

She squeezes me in a hug right before another small body slams into me.

"I was so worried," Lee's voice cracks as her arms wrap around my waist. "I called you like three hundred times, and you just weren't picking up. You freaked me out." She releases her hold on me and gives my shoulder a light shove. She's a little pissed at me, but I can see tears beading on her bottom lashes. One of them falls, trailing down her pale cheek.

Guilt wracks me, but in the aftermath of the police leaving, I hadn't been able to command my body to do anything other than crawl into bed.

"I'm sorry," I mumble as Sydney cradles me against her side. "I'm fine, really. Just a little shocked." I force a tense smile, and somehow, my voice comes out level.

Someone scoffs and I peek up to see Jackson glaring down at me.

I press my lips together as I avoid his gaze. I don't like that he can see through my lies so easily.

"What happened?"

Those two simple words pierce my bubble.

15

Syd feels me tense beneath her, and she gives my bicep a squeeze. She's been the publicist for The System for the last five years, and she is the mother hen of the group, always looking out for not only her guys but us girls as well. There's no one more protective than Syd.

"Come on, let's sit down for a second." She guides me over to the soft white couch, her arm never leaving me once.

"I was swatted." The words stick to my tongue like honey.

"Do you know who it was?" Parker Covington, British billionaire and resident joker of The System (known by the gamertag EnglishCoffee, a.k.a. English), follows his girlfriend's lead and crouches before me, placing a hand on my knee.

I shake my head. "No, there's—" I stop, clenching my jaw to prevent the words from leaving my lips.

What am I going to say?

Oh, there's been someone threatening me for months, and I brushed it off like a dumbass.

I let out a groan and press my palm to the space between my brows, rubbing away the tension.

"There's what?" Jackson pushes.

"There's nothing. I don't want to talk about it," I bite back.

His eyes narrow. "You're deflecting."

"And you're annoying me."

"Fine, whatever. If you don't want help, that's your issue. But don't forget that we've dealt with this shit before." He crosses his arms, drawing my attention to his strong biceps that are on full display with the muscle tee he has on.

Ugh. Gods. Why is he still hot when he is pissed?

"He's right. We can help," Lee calls out.

There's a loud crash, and we jerk our heads to my bed-room as Lee drops one of my pink Louis Vuitton suitcases onto the floor.

"That's custom," I whine, pushing out of Syd's grasp to check on my luggage. I run my hands across the leather, searching for any scratches. "What did you do that for?"

"I'm helping," she shrugs before walking into my clos-et. She begins to pick pieces off the hangers and heedlessly throws them at my suitcase.

"Lee," I grit out as a miniskirt narrowly misses my head.

"You can't stay here. You're coming home with me."

"Aren't your parents visiting soon?"

"There's more than enough space."

"Lee—"

"Someone knows where you live."

A chill breaks over my skin. I don't want to think about that. I just want to go back to ignoring it and everything else about tonight.

"I'm not imposing on your parents."

"Well, you're not staying here." She places her hands on her hips.

Lee is always so carefree that I sometimes forget how stubborn she can be. We're two sides of the same coin.

"She's right," Parker agrees as he comes to sit on my bed. "The security at this place is a wank."

"Exactly. Even you've said before that the security here is sucky," Lee muses as she chucks a pair of platform heels on the ground.

I press my lips together and stare at the growing mound of clothes and shoes.

I don't want to admit defeat, that I don't feel safe in my own apartment. Part of me thought that maybe if I just stayed here and pretended that nothing ever happened that I could remain in my little bubble of ignorance. That maybe the world isn't as scary as it feels.

The local police have my information now; they know I'm at risk of swatting, so they won't be as aggressive the next time it happens. *If* there's even a next time. Maybe this Deer Hunter person will give up now? They've had their laugh. They've traumatized me on stream, live for tens of thousands of people to see. That's normally the goal for these people. So, what more is there?

"Look, I get the concern, but I'm going to be fine. Really." I turn my head to stare at the big grump leaning on my doorframe. "It's like you said, you've dealt with this before. It's not that big a deal."

"That's not the point I was trying to make," Jackson sighs.

"Why don't you at least crash at one of our places tonight? Just for peace of mind. Aleks and Stevie are in New York again for the Hayes art show, so his room is free," Sydney says, referring to the leader of The System, Aleksander Knight (known by his gamertag NightBlade32, a.k.a. Blade), and his girlfriend, up-and-coming artist Stephanie Andwell.

I see the silent plea in her eyes, but I still don't give in.

"I'm serious. I'm fine." I stand up and walk out of my bedroom and to the front door, opening it. It's a touch rude,

I know, but I can't deal with any more of their smothering. I feel like I'm in the middle of a fire and someone is choking me at the same time.

It's making everything ten times worse.

"Fine." Sydney huffs, grabbing Parker's hand and leading him out of my bedroom.

Jackson has to practically pick Lee up and carry her to make her leave.

"I'm not happy about this," she hisses as he drops her by the door.

"I know you care, and I love you for that, but I just need some space. Please."

Her eyes soften and the pity swimming in them makes me feel guilty all over again.

"Call me in the morning, okay?"

"Okay."

She pulls me into a hug, and I squeeze her back, letting her know that I really do appreciate everything she's done. When I release her, Sydney takes her place and pulls me close.

"Call us if anything feels off."

"I will."

She lets me go, and Parker gives my hand a squeeze and throws me one of his classic winks before leaving with her.

Jackson starts to silently follow them out, but he pauses right after he crosses the threshold. I freeze as he looks at me over his shoulder.

"Don't be a hero."

And then he's gone.

I shut my door, locking it and then double-checking

that the lock is sturdy by twisting the knob an unnecessary number of times. Even then, it still doesn't feel safe enough.

I brace my legs and shove my armchair across the floorboards until it comes to sit flush with the door. That's a little better.

Numbly, I walk back into my bedroom and stare at the disarray of clothes and shoes on the floor that I can't be bothered to deal with right now. I barely even have the energy to make it into my bathroom to throw my hair up in a shitty bun.

I bug my eyes wide in the mirror and use my knuckles to remove my bright blue contact lenses. My natural hazel eyes stare back at me as I take the time to double cleanse and remove my layers of makeup before painstakingly cleaning my lash extensions. The monotony of my routine seems to calm the buzzing hive in my chest by a fraction.

Trudging into my walk-in closet, I peel off my signature pink dress and hang it up before grabbing an oversized T-shirt to throw on.

I stare at myself in the mirror and let out a self-deprecating laugh. If my hair was its natural strawberry-blonde color, you wouldn't even recognize me—but that's the point.

The wind howls outside, screaming into the silence, and I crawl into bed and draw my sheets tightly around myself.

I squeeze my eyes shut and will my mind to think calm, happy thoughts: my parents, video games, a fresh set of nails, those little Snorlax-shaped doughnuts from the shop downtown.

But no matter how hard I try, the tension never leaves. I just end up tossing and turning until my sheets become a tangled mess around my hot body. It takes another two hours before I admit defeat and slip from bed to grab my gaming laptop. Armed with a cup of warmed honey milk, I create a fortress under my sheets and load up a life sim, losing myself in a game where I can control the lives of others so I don't have to think about the lack of stability in my own.

Chapter THREE

JACKSON

God-fucking-dammit.

I eye the waifish woman with thinly veiled annoyance as she slides into the booth across from me and tosses me a shy smile.

"I take it my grandmother is not coming."

Her smile falters briefly, but she's quick to school it with a strained giggle. "It seems we've been set up."

I've been set up.

Her? I doubt it.

"I'm Jessica."

"Jackson."

Silence spreads out, and she presses her glossy lips together as she tucks a lock of black hair behind her ear. Her eyes dart around the restaurant, and I begin to feel like a little bit of an ass. It's not like it's this girl's fault she got sent here.

On second assessment, she's not bad looking. Her breasts are smaller than I normally go for, but her face is round and pretty.

I sigh and pour her a glass of water.

"Thank you." She reaches forward and takes a sip. "I'm sorry about this."

I wave her off, giving up on my frustration. "It's fine."

A waitress comes over and takes our order before popping a breadbasket on the table. Jessica dips a piece into some olive oil before taking a dainty bite.

"So, tell me about yourself. What do you do?"

"I play video games."

"Oh. Not hobbies, I meant for work. What do you do?"

Okay, now I legitimately feel bad for the girl. I understand that a blind date means you don't know anything about the other person, but this is just plain cruel. To both of us.

"I play video games, that's my job."

Her brows furrow. "Like you work for a gaming company?"

Maybe I should order a drink. This is going to be a long date.

"No, as in I live-stream online and post content to socials."

"Of video games?"

"Yeah."

"Oh." I see the wheels turning in her mind, and she course corrects, giving me a glass smile. "That's cool that you get to do something you love."

I hold back a sigh and offer her my attempt at a smile

instead. "What about you?"

"I'm a business analyst at Brock Meyers."

There is a clear glint in her eye and a warmth in her voice. It's obvious she loves her job and wants to talk about it, but I have absolutely no interest in hearing about what a business analyst does. There is a reason I dropped out of college and abandoned my economics degree.

"Nice."

I see a flash of disappointment at my monotone response.

It takes everything in me not to groan out loud. I didn't want to be here. I didn't want to be set up on a blind date. And yet, here I am, and now I have a girl who is getting all butthurt because I'm not interested in delving into her entire life story.

This is why I told my family I didn't want to do this. But did they listen? No.

No, instead, my *po po* seems to have colluded with my mom to subject me to torture.

Just great.

The waitress returns with our meals, and I busy myself by investing all my attention on the chicken piccata before me. La Sienna isn't the fanciest Italian restaurant, but they have pretty good food—and right now, it is my saving grace.

Jessica picks at her ravioli and continues to try to engage me in more small talk, but it's clear that we really don't have much in common outside of our families somewhat knowing each other. Which is the other reason why I can't just abandon this date or act like a dick—it'll get back to both of our families, and I'll get chewed out if I do anything that makes my family look bad or disrespectful.

I practically pounce for the bill when the waitress returns to clear up our empty plates.

"Thank you for paying," Jessica comments as I tuck my credit card back into my wallet.

I give her a shrug. "It's the least I could do."

"Yeah, I guess this was sort of a fail," she snorts, sliding out of the booth. She tries to mask it, but there is a bitterness in her tone.

"I hope the rest of your blind dates go better."

"You, too."

Not if I can help it.

"Thanks." I give her a nod as she walks away.

I wait until she walks out the door and then give it another few minutes before I exit the restaurant myself. The last thing I want is to bump into her and make this night even more awkward.

I'm already pulling up my mother's number and dialing it by the time I get into my Jeep and start driving home.

"*Wai*," her greeting filters in through my speakers.

"Ma," I return dryly.

"Ah. I take it dinner with your *po po* didn't go as expected."

"Unless she suddenly found the fountain of youth and turned into a twenty-something-year-old woman, then no. No, it did not go as expected."

She lets out a heavy sigh, "Jackson."

"I don't need to go on blind dates, Mom. I can handle my own love life."

"You don't have a love life."

"Yes, I do."

"No, you don't. You play around—that is not the same thing, and it's not respectable."

Shit.

I try to be discrete by conducting most of my activities at Cardinal Club, where customer confidentiality is key, and Sydney sweet-talks and bribes as many reporters as she possibly can to keep my sex life out of the press—but it's hard to hide everything when you're in the public eye, something always slips through.

Now it's my turn to sigh as Mom descends into a monologue of her own.

"*Po po* is just looking out for you. And your aunties are right; you are getting older, and you've yet to have a stable girlfriend in your life. When I was your age, I was already engaged to your father. And I know things are different for people your age nowadays, but that's not an excuse to not even try. Reputation matters, and it doesn't look good on the family for our son to not even have a girlfriend when everyone else we know is busy setting up weddings and celebrating their grandchildren. You're twenty-eight, time is ticking."

Why did I think calling her was a good idea?

"I've spoken to your father about it, and he agrees that we should pursue this. It's just a few dates. There's no harm in just meeting the women and seeing if they're a good match. You never know—auntie Lei met her husband that way, and they've been happily married for twenty years. So, just appease your grandparents and go on the dates."

"No."

"Lau Ka-yee, you will listen to me, and you will go on these dates, or so help me, I will come over there and force you to go on them myself."

I grimace. It's never a good sign when she switches to my Chinese name.

"I've let you do a lot of things in life that I was deeply opposed to, so for once, I'm telling you to do as I say and stop arguing."

Great.

She just had to pull the gamer card.

Even after all this time, she's still pissed.

Ten years ago, I helped my high school best friend, Aleksander, start his streaming career as the infamous masked gamer, NightBlade32, before eventually dropping out of college my sophomore year to join him—which my parents did *not* approve of. A few years later, we recruited one of our close online friends—Parker—to join us and formed a group called The System. The three of us rose to fame as masked video game streamers, accumulating millions of views and millions of dollars.

We are the most in-demand gamers in the industry, but that doesn't mean my traditional family understands what that means. To most of them, I'm just spending my days messing around online. Even with the rise of esports in China, it is still a foreign concept to them. It would be fair to say that my relatives are split in their support of me, and I am always fighting an uphill battle to win their approval.

It's exhausting never having anyone on my side.

"Fine," I grumble.

"Thank you, and don't forget your sister has another piano recital in a few weeks."

"It's already on my calendar."

"Good, I'll talk to you later."

"Okay, bye bye."

"Bye bye."

She hangs up, and I'm left in the silence of my car. I don't even bother turning my music on. I'm too annoyed to appreciate it. I just want to stew in my own frustration.

How many failed dates would I need to go on until they give up?

Too many.

Fuck. I wish there was a way out of this without having to actually get a real girlfriend.

I mentally accept my death sentence as I swing into the private underground parking garage at our apartment complex and park in my designated spot among Aleks' and Parker's luxury vehicles.

My mood stays sour the entire elevator ride up to the penthouse. I stop to grab a sparkling water from the fridge before heading into my streaming room.

The tension in my shoulders instantly loosens once I'm surrounded by nothing except the green LED glow of the room. I drop onto my gaming chair and crack open my can as I start my computer up. My PC whirs to life, and I admire it with a sense of pride. I built the entire thing from scratch. It had taken longer to build than planned because the graphics card I'd wanted was on backorder, but now it ran like a beauty with no lag. Custom PC builds can get pricey, but they are worth it if you're an invested gamer.

A notification pops up in the corner of my monitor, alerting me that Parker and Aleks are already online— which I gathered from how quiet the penthouse was when I came in. Even when we aren't live streaming, we are probably playing video games. When we stream, we have to be *on*, but on nights like tonight, we like to play just for the hell of it because it helps us destress and have fun. It's important for us to do both, otherwise we could risk losing our love for the games to the constant pressure.

I click on my friends list and scan to see who else is online.

Lee's playing *Gods League*, the most popular 5v5 MMO game and the top esport game, with Aleks, Parker, and two of our pro-gamer friends, Wylder and Ryder— twins who go by the gamertags WyldShot and Smooth-Ryde.

My eyes linger on the little round circle framing Deer's profile picture.

She hasn't been online in days, but I can see her racking up gameplay hours offline.

Not that I've been stalking her or anything, I'm just paying close attention. She's been quiet ever since the swatting, and it doesn't sit well with me.

The boys and I were swatted a few years back at the old warehouse we used to use for streaming before we moved into our current penthouse apartment. It had been a scary as fuck experience. Nothing prepares you for an entire SWAT team barging in, waving guns, and shouting at you out of nowhere.

Deer is still new to the gaming world compared to the rest of us, and I see the way the rise to fame unsettles her when she thinks no one is watching. I just wish she wasn't so stubborn. It pisses me off that she is still staying in that apartment when Parker has clearly pointed out its shitty security.

A notification pops up and I slide on my headset before

clicking on it to join the Discord server Parker's invited me to.

I'm instantly assaulted by him yelling, "What the actual fuck?"

"RIP, dude," Ryder laughs.

"You wankers could have saved me." Parker's London accent thickens the more frustrated he gets.

"You are literally support, English," Lee sighs. "That's your job."

"This is why I hate this game."

Parker kind of sucks at *Gods League* and avoids it when he can. He might be one of the best speedrunners to exist, but it doesn't matter how many years we've played, there is just something in his brain that won't let him get better at *League*. He's still ranked Silver class while Lee, Aleks, and I are all Ruby. Ryder and Wylder have God Master ranks, but as pros it would be embarrassing if they were anything less.

"How're we doing?" I finally chime in.

"Shield, welcome to the party, my man," Ryder drawls, addressing me by my gamertag.

"Parker's dragging us all down, per usual," Aleks grunts.

"I didn't ask to play, you all made me," Parker whines.

"No, we said we were playing, and then you got upset when we wouldn't join you in *FrozeLine* and complained you were lonely," Lee corrects.

"Yeah. Technically, you invited yourself," Wylder laughs.

"Whatever, I'm quitting. Jackson can take my place."

"Thank God."

I click to join their game lobby and then decide on which character to use for support. I don't mind the role; it just isn't my favorite. As support, my main job is to assist the lane player—Ryder in this case—until they amass enough experience and gold.

We start the game, and Ryder and I head down to the bottom lane of the map to begin working our way through the minions. Minutes pass as Ryder continues to farm for gold while I tap in for support and grow my XP.

A notification pops up on my second monitor, and my gaze darts to it.

I abandon my gameplay, quickly moving my mouse to click on the notification before it disappears.

Deer's profile loads, a little green dot appearing on the corner of her picture. But just as soon as it is there, it flicks away, turning gray again.

"Shield, the fuck are you doing?" Ryder bites.

I whip my attention back to my main screen just in time to see an enemy player blast him with a spell.

"Shit." I quickly throw a healing cast. "My b."

"You guys good down there?" Aleks checks in.

"Someone got distracted," Ryder grumbles before raining bullets down on the enemy and killing the fellow God champion. "We're fine now."

"Nice kill," Lee congratulates.

"Distracted? The great Shield?" Wylder taunts.

"Fuck off." I try to laser focus my attention onto the screen, my eyes darting between incoming enemies while keeping an eye on Ryder. We keep advancing down our lane to the tower we need to take down. Even with all the action, I can't stop that little niggle in the back of my brain that has me wanting to check on her status again.

She acts like the princess who doesn't need a knight to keep her safe, but that doesn't stop me from wanting to stand guard.

My attention continues to wane until I finally bite the bullet.

"How's Deer doing?"

My question breeds silence for a second before Lee chimes in. "Oh, are you asking me?"

"Yeah."

There's a loud sigh from her. "She texts me a pic every day as proof of life, but…I don't know."

"I've tried checking in, but she just sends me those little sparkly pink heart emojis," Aleks adds.

"You checked in?" My skin prickles.

"Yeah, like a decent human. What, haven't you?"

I grind my molars, focusing on blasting an enemy minion instead of on the fact that I now seem like the insensitive asshole. "I don't have her number."

"We're all friends on Discord, mate," Parker points out.

"Boys," Lee chastises. "It's fine. She should be coming over for Crime Night. I don't care if I have to go and drag her here myself. I'm making her leave that apartment and be a functioning member of society."

"I don't mean to sound like a dick, but I really need someone to help me take down this tower," Ryder drops in.

"Coming."

"That's what she said," Parker, as always, cuts in.

There's a soft round of chuckles, and it seems like everyone's instantly moved on from the heavy cloud I created. But I'm still stuck in the middle of the storm, my mouse moving to my second monitor to open Deer's profile.

I hover over the little envelope button, wondering what I should say.

"Shield, I need you here," Ryder warns.

I panic click out of her profile. "Got you."

Fuck, I need to get my head on straight. I'm sure she's fine. It's Deer, she's always saying she's fine.

Chapter FOUR

DEER

I'm not fine.

I haven't slept in days.

Well, technically, I've slept in random thirty-minute intervals, but that doesn't really count. The second my body begins to doze off, there will be some sort of tiny noise that rocks me right back to reality and sends my blood pressure spiking. It also doesn't help that every time I close my eyes, my overactive imagination conjures scenarios where the SWAT team actually fires off their guns, and I just see myself sprawled on my floor, bright red blood pooling against my pink hair.

I've clocked in over forty-two hours of *The Sims*, thirty-six hours of *Cherry Farm: Harvest Season*, and twenty-nine hours of *Moonstone Valley* in the last five days, and that isn't even counting the beta testing I'm doing for a new Kickstarter cozy game. It's not normal, even for me.

On the bright side, I have enough content filmed to last through the next month easily. On the negative side, it made me realize I need to upgrade my CPU because I've noticed a few of the mods lagging.

Some people—prejudiced, misogynistic people— think spending four grand on a setup to play simulators is excessive, but those people don't truly grasp the processing power it takes to run thirty-plus mods. In my baby gamer days, my laptop used to run so hot you could have tried cooking an egg on it.

I sigh, looking in the mirror that hangs on the back of my front door, and press the bags under my eyes, begging them to go away.

Today is the first day I'm leaving my apartment, and I've been standing at the door for fifteen minutes, willing myself to exit. My right hand is poised on the doorknob. All I need to do is turn the damn thing. But I just can't bring my body to function—a cloud of fear is cancelling out all rational thoughts.

My phone buzzes a few times, and I reach down to pull it out of my heart-shaped handbag to see a slew of texts in my group chat, which is aptly named "MURDER SQUAD."

LEE 🩶:
Where are you guyssss

STEVIE
literally in the elevator

SYD-BAE
coming

ME
that's what she said

STEVIE
nice

SYD-BAE
sometimes youre as bad as my boyfriend

ME

LEE 🤍:
Deer?

ME
on my way

I groan, clicking off my phone and dumping it back in my bag. I know there's no avoiding this. The girls would sooner come over here than let me skip out on Crime Night without a solid reason—and there is no way I'm letting them know just how much this swatting has been affecting me.

Pushing past the fear, I twist the doorknob and take my first step past the threshold of my apartment. My breath freezes in my lungs, and I strain my ears for anything that might sound off.

When no random assassin drops from the ceiling to murder me, I let myself take another step forward, and then another, until I make it all the way down the hallway and into the elevator. My body moves like a robot, but at least it's functioning.

It's only when I get down to the lobby that I stall again.

There's a man in a black hoodie and black face mask parked on one of the couches by the community pool table. Most people wouldn't give him a second glance, but I do. Because I recognize him just by his eyes.

My platform heels click softly on the tiles as I make my way to him. I force myself to calm and let my mask settle over me with practiced precision—no hint of anxiety leaking out. It's only when I stop right in front of him that he looks up from the mobile game on his phone. My skin heats from the intensity of his gaze, his eyes swirling pools of bottomless black framed by thick lashes.

"Why are you here?"

"You headed out?" He meets my bluntness tit for tat.

"Um, yeah. I'm going over to Lee's."

"'Kay, let's go." He stands up, his chest coming to rest mere inches from my nose.

I take a startled step back as he steps around me to head out of the complex. My brain glitches for a second as I stare at his retreating form.

"Uh…what?"

I jog to catch up to his long strides. The fresh outside air fills my lungs as I pass through the revolving door and into the late afternoon sun.

"I'll drive you."

"Did you come all the way here just to drive me to Crime Night?" I quirk a brow.

Jackson hands a ticket to the valet outside my apartment before turning back to give me a bored look.

"I was in the area and Lee asked."

I chew on my bottom lip, trying to determine whether he is telling the truth. It annoys me that he can read me like a book, while I struggle to even read his blurb.

An Army green Jeep comes to a stop before us, and Jackson opens the passenger door. "Do you want to be late?"

I let out a huff, hauling my ass into the passenger seat. "I could have driven myself," I mutter as he gets into the driver's side.

Jackson says nothing. He just removes his face mask and hood before putting the car in drive. I pull my phone out of my handbag to fiddle with it, but really, I'm just using it as an excuse while I stare at him out of the corner of my eye.

It's frustrating how attractive he is. His long black hair isn't tied in a bun for once, and the ends graze the top of his shoulders. My fingers twitch to rake my nails through it. This isn't the first time I've had the urge, and if the last year had taught me anything, it's that this urge isn't going anywhere soon.

My eyes trail down his arms to the strong hands gripping the steering wheel. Last Halloween he'd worn this super tight T-shirt that showed off every muscle on his perfectly sculpted body, and I'd spent more time than I'd ever confess to drooling over him. He is the kind of guy who could toss you over his shoulder without a second thought.

And I have thought about it.

There was a time when I harbored a tiny little crush on him. But *super* tiny and it was ages ago when I first met him. I'd quickly snuffed out that crush once I realized that he sees me as a by-product of his other friendships—an acquaintance at best. He's never made the effort with me before, this car drive notwithstanding. So, I've just accepted that while I find him hot as hell, it's just a physical thing. His grumpy personality has left more to be desired.

"What?"

"Huh?"

"You're staring." There's a glint in Jackson's eyes as he drawls out the words.

"So?" I can feel a flush creeping up my cheeks, but the amount of blush on my face hides any hint of it.

"Just making an observation," he muses, turning his attention back to the road. "You seemed preoccupied."

"I was just thinking about how they say men with big hands tend to have big penises."

The car jerks as Jackson's head whips to me, his eyes wide. I feel a sliver of satisfaction as his mouth opens and closes—even though I'm mentally kicking myself for saying that. I don't know why I say the randomest things when I'm around him...and now I'm thinking about his cock when I seriously don't need to be.

"Although, I'm not really sure there is any scientific evidence backing that statement. Not that I've Googled it or anything, but it's food for thought," I continue to babble, even though I wish I would just shut-up.

Jackson clenches his jaw. "You're spending too much time around Stephanie."

"I'm always like this." I shrug, pretending to clean under my nails.

Jackson doesn't say anything else for the rest of the ride, and I can't tell whether he is miffed with me or just embarrassed by my comment.

The car rolls to a stop outside Lee's opulent apartment complex, and I waste no time unbuckling my seat belt and popping open the door.

"Well, thanks for the ride. I'll be sure to give you a four-star rating."

"What time will you be done?"

I halt, one foot on the asphalt, and turn back to him. "What do you mean?"

"Your little Crime Night, when does it finish?"

I frown. "I don't know. Depends on how much we drink. Why?"

Typically, if we have a particularly tipsy Crime Night, I end up just crashing at Lee's instead of waiting to sober up and drive back. Occasionally, Syd will drop me off at home, but then I have to deal with getting my car the next day, and that always ends up being a pain. If it is a pretty sober night, I drive myself home, but there is never any telling how a Crime Night will turn out. That is the beauty of them.

"So I can drive you home."

"Why? I'll just have Stevie or Syd take me."

His eyes give me a quick once over before he turns away from me. "Fine."

"Okay, bye."

I shut the door, half expecting him to take off and leave me in a cloud of dust, but instead he just waits. When another second passes and he just stares at me through the window, I give up and turn around to walk into the building.

I really do not understand that man.

"Evening, Miss Deer," the doorman greets me when I walk inside.

"Evening, Bill," I smile back before making my way to the elevators. I come here often enough that I am practically an honorary resident. It is a stunning apartment complex, almost as nice as the one The System lives in.

I eventually reach Lee's floor and stand outside her door, taking a deep breath and centering myself before punching in the code and walking inside.

"Your favorite human has arrived," I chime in with a smile.

"Hi," Stevie's voice trills back.

Lee's head pops around the corner from her kitchen, and she gives me a massive grin before bounding over and crushing me in a hug.

"I missed your face."

"I missed yours, too," I say, squeezing her back.

"Come, I need help making a drink. I'm out of ideas."

"What would you do without me?"

"Dunno." She cocks her head. "Buy premades, probably?"

"Fair." I open her fridge and scan it before taking out a carton of watermelon juice, a can of club soda, maple syrup, and lime juice. One of our rituals for Crime Night is making different alcoholic concoctions; sometimes they are failures—like our coconut rum hot chocolate— and sometimes they are total wins—such as our peach schnapps-spiked boba.

"I didn't think you'd come for a second there," Lee whispers.

I glance at her out of the corner of my eye. "I considered it."

"Deer." Empathy fills her voice, and I give her a stern look.

"Don't. I'm fine." I reach for the vodka and begin to mix all the ingredients together before pouring the pink concoction into two glasses with some ice. I hold one out to Lee. "I just want to enjoy a little murder, okay?"

"Okay." She takes the glass from me with pursed lips, giving me a once over. "We decided on unsolved crimes tonight, by the way."

"Fun." I give her a wink before taking the lead and heading into her living room.

While my aesthetic might be e-girl pink, Lee's aesthetic is just *aesthetic*. Everything about her apartment is pretty, from the meticulously cared-for aquarium below her giant TV, to the opalescent coffee table, to the moon-shaped lamp. It gives lunar princess vibes.

I drop onto the couch, snuggling myself into the corner as I take a sip of my watermelon concoction. It isn't half bad.

"Syd's not here yet?"

"Nope. I think you were right, she was probably coming," Stevie smirks.

I snort and Lee lets out a muttered, "Oh my God."

"Let's start, and we can catch her up." I reach forward and grab the remote to flip to the right channel and pull up our show.

"I'm fine with that. To the murder," Lee cheers, holding her drink out.

"To the murder," Stevie echoes with her own wine glass.

"To the murder," I smile, finally feeling at ease.

Chapter FIVE

DEER

66 **T**he haunted house went up in flames and multiple dead bodies were found inside. All the deceased were graduated students from the local high school. However, upon closer inspection, it was found that the deceased did not die of smoke inhalation but instead murder."

"That's kind of a smart idea," Lee pipes up, "using the fire to hide your tracks." She tilts her head at the TV screen, causing her black French braids to sway as she scrutinizes the scene before us.

"Yeah, it's a pity it didn't work," Stevie laments, taking a large sip of her rosé.

"A bystander did note that three motorcycles were seen leaving the scene of the crime, and it was even believed that they were wearing Halloween masks not unlike those *of popular horror movie villains."*

"You know, those Ghostface masks are pretty hot," I chime in, reaching forward to grab a cookie from the table.

"Right," Lee hums in agreement, holding out an empty hand and twinkling her fingers.

I plop the cookie in her hand before going back to grab another.

"That's the same thought I had when I met Aleks the first time," Stevie nods.

"There's something incredibly wrong with all of you," a posh British voice scoffs.

All three of us girls turn to glare at the man camped out in the egg-shaped armchair in the corner.

"I can't believe you invited him." Lee shoots eye daggers at Sydney as she enters the room carrying a fresh bowl of popcorn.

"For the fifth time, I didn't invite him," the blonde huffs as she drops the bowl on the coffee table. "He invited himself."

"It's against the rules."

Lee, Sydney, and I have been meeting for a weekly Crime Night for two years now, and a few months ago we brought Stevie into the fold after she started dating Aleks. We alternate between watching true crime and haunted house investigations while snacking on baked goods, sipping on alcoholic concoctions, and sprinkling in a healthy dose of gossip. We rarely miss a week unless it's a holiday or there's some sort of gaming or work conflict.

There are only two rules when it comes to Crime Night. The first, no phones; we have to leave them in a bowl at the door. The second, no outsiders.

"Why would Parker voluntarily invite himself to Crime Night?" Stevie narrows her catlike eyes. "He hates scary shit."

"Maybe we're his only friends," I shrug.

"Or maybe it's co-dependency. He's too obsessed with his girlfriend," Lee nods.

"*He* can hear you." Parker rolls his baby blues dramatically. "And he expects you to be nicer to him because he brought expensive champagne as a peace offering."

"Babe, we talked about this. You need to stop with the third-person stuff," Sydney sighs as he pulls her onto his lap.

"The bubbles are pretty good," I hum, taking a sip of my champagne. I'd finished my watermelon drink an episode earlier.

"Thank you," he grins with a wink.

Parker Covington is an attractive man. He has a killer jawline and cheekbones that make everyone jealous, and paired with his dyed white-blond hair and impish grins, he looks like a sexy angel. It's no wonder Sydney fell for him even though she's his publicist.

"Champagne isn't enough to join the girl's club, sorry, English." I wrinkle my nose in feigned apology. "If we start making exceptions for you, we have to make exceptions for everyone."

As much as I try to remember to call Parker by his name, it still isn't second nature to me. I met him online through streaming videogames and tend to default to his gamertag even when we are in person. I have the same habit with all The System even though their identities are no longer a secret from the world.

"Oh, come on, don't kick me out," he pouts, flashing us all puppy dog eyes.

"Unfortunately, I don't think you have anything useful to add to Crime Night," Stevie shrugs, flicking her brown hair over her shoulder.

"My devilish good looks?"

Sydney throws a piece of popcorn at her boyfriend.

"Fine, fine," he huffs, bringing his hand up to fiddle with his cartilage piercings. "What if I offered you some gossip?"

Lee and I perk up.

"Gossip?" She grins.

"Do spill." I dramatically clasp my hands under my chin.

"Jackson's grandmother has been setting him up on blind dates."

"Wait, seriously?"

I couldn't imagine Jackson going on blind dates. He seemed like the kind of guy who only did what he wanted to do and not what someone forced on him.

"Tsk." Stevie rolls her eyes. "I knew this already."

"Yikes, I feel bad for him." Lee's eyes round with pity.

"Are they going well?" I don't know why I ask, but the question leaves my mouth before I have a chance to think twice. I don't really know that much about Jackson, and some part of me is drawn to the news like a magnet.

"No," Sydney scoffs. "But he is putting on a good act for the cameras at least. I'm just worried his patience is going to snap at some point. He's been in a foul mood all week because of them."

"How many has it been?"

"Only two so far, but there's definitely more on the horizon."

"Ugh." Lee wriggles her body in a feigned shiver. "That's my worst nightmare. I totally get how he must feel. Even my parents are putting the pressure on me. The perfect daughter should be getting married before thirty."

"I feel bad for those poor girls," Stevie sighs as she pours more wine.

"Yeah, he isn't invested at all," Sydney agrees.

"Negative percent interested. He's still sneaking out to see his hookups. I caught him coming back at like four a.m. the other day. I didn't even know the Club was open that late."

This isn't the first time I've heard about Jackson's active sex life, and like every time before, I find myself straining to hear more. He seems to be secretive about it but not enough that the rest of us don't know what he gets up to. I've never been one to shy away from good sex, but it's hard to find a partner when you've turned into a slightly paranoid recluse whose entire life is online. I haven't touched a dating app since the Deer Hunter stuff started up, which means I've been married to my vibrators the last few months—and as amazing as the Pleasure Core 3000 is, it doesn't exactly replace the kinkier desires I harbor that only a person can fulfill.

"He must be a good lay," I muse.

"Yeah. I mean, he is massive," Stevie agrees.

"Ohmigods, you've seen his dick?"

"What? No, I meant his body is massive." Then her eyes narrow, and a sly smile spreads over her perfect face. "Interesting that your mind went there."

Shit.

I scramble to backtrack.

"I'm just saying. It would make sense. He is tall."

Stevie cocks her head in thought. "You make a good point. He's only a little shorter than Aleks."

"Exactly, we could assume a correlation."

"Isn't Parker shorter than them both?" Stevie smirks, her eyes sliding to the blond.

"Hang on, I'll have you know I measure—"

"Parker," Sydney shrieks, cutting him off.

"What? I was just going to point out that I'm taller than Jackson." Honestly, all three of the men in The System were well over six feet tall, so by our assumptions they should all have pretty solid cocks. "So, does this mean I can stay?"

"Fine," Lee caves. "Just this once."

"Sweet." Parker pumps his fist in the air at the win.

"Now, hush up and let us get back to the murder at hand."

Four drinks, two dead bodies, and one screaming Parker later (turns out the visualization of a finger getting cut off didn't sit well with him), we're calling it a night.

"Can I get a ride from somebody?" I grab the empty bowls from the table and bring them into the kitchen to wash in the sink.

"You didn't drive?" Lee furrows her brows as she puts the spare cookies into a Tupperware container.

"No?" I give her a look. "Shield picked me up."

"Really? Why?"

I pause mid plate scrub. "Didn't you ask him?"

She shakes her head.

That's weird.

"I can give you a ride." Stevie smiles as she comes up next to me to wash her wine glass.

I shoot a desperate glance back at Sydney. I love Stevie, but she really isn't the best driver. Neither am I, but Stevie is arguably worse. She hits objects that aren't even moving.

"We can give you a ride back to yours," Parker offers, sensing my distress.

"Thanks." I turn to give Lee a big hug before saying goodbye.

"We still on for tomorrow?" she asks.

My stomach drops at the mention of tomorrow's horror stream we'd previously planned, pre-swat, and it must show on my face because she gives my hand a squeeze.

"We don't have to if you aren't ready yet."

I shake my head. "No. If I put it off, I'll just keep doing that. Plus, Blade said he would join."

"Okay, love you."

"Love you."

I grab my phone from the bowl in the hallway and rush to catch up to Syd and Parker, who are waiting by the elevator.

"You good?" Sydney gives me a once over as we descend to the lobby.

"Of course." I smile, unlocking my phone and checking for any notifications. My eyes snag on a Discord message from Jackson.

SHIELD

lmk if you need a ride

I check the timestamp to see he sent it a little over an hour ago and gnaw on my lower lip, contemplating whether or not to text him back.

We exit into the lobby and head out into the chilly night air. The valet brings Parker's blue Porsche around, and I stare at it with knowing dread.

"I'm going in the back, aren't I?"

Parker places a hand on my shoulder and gives me a wry smile. "You are the shortest."

I let out a deep sigh as he shifts the passenger seat forward so I can crawl into the obscenely small backseat. Honestly, I don't understand why these cars even bother having back seats.

The passenger seat locks back into place, and Parker and Syd get into the car.

"Comfy?"

I give Parker a sugary-sweet smile. "Positively cozy."

Parker takes off, revving the engine as he races through the streets. Sydney lets out a hiss at his speed, but he just reaches over and rests his hand on her knee.

I look down at my phone again, at Jackson's message. He'd said he drove me because Lee asked him to, but that doesn't seem to be the case. So, why was he there? Maybe he really had been in the area. But that still didn't totally explain everything.

My brain spins, like it's trying to solve a Rubix cube but half the colors are missing.

Parker swings out at the front of my apartment complex and comes to a stop.

He scowls looking up at the building. "I really wish you would move."

"I'm a big girl."

"You're five foot."

"Technically, I'm five four with these heels. Now, let me out of this car." I tap on his headrest.

"Fine," he grumbles, getting out and folding his seat forward. I take his offered hand and try to gracefully crawl out of the car.

"Thanks."

"Text us when you get upstairs," Syd calls from the passenger seat.

I roll my eyes. "Okay, Mom and Dad."

I give them a wave as I walk backward from the car before spinning around. The darkness looming around has me uneasy, but knowing that Syd and Parker are watching settles the anxiety that threatens to bubble up. Once I'm in the brightly lit lobby of my complex, I let out a small sigh.

I'd successfully left my apartment and come back in one piece. I was safe, and honestly, I really didn't need to be that worried about the outside world. I'm just creating monsters in my mind.

My body moves on autopilot until I arrive at my front door. I drop down to pick up a little brown package perched on my rug and tuck it under my arm as I fish out my key and unlock my door.

I toss the package onto my island before grabbing a pair of scissors to slice the box open.

A shiny pink taser sparkles back at me.

Then again, you can never be too safe.

JACKSON

"Thank you."

Savannah smiles up at me through hooded eyes. Droplets of tears bead her lashes after being mercilessly face fucked. I look down at her, but I don't feel the satisfaction or relief that typically comes after our sessions. It has been happening more and more lately.

Which is a pain.

I give her a noncommittal hum as I work on undoing the ropes bound around her plush upper body, signaling the end to our session. Normally, I look forward to meeting up with Savannah. She is the brand director for some fashion company and one of the main investors for Cardinal Club, so it's all high discretion, low commitment with her. But something is off now.

I coil the black rope and place it back in my bag while she stretches out on the bed like a cat.

I don't want to look for a new partner; it's hard enough to find the right person these days. Yes, the Cardinal Club is one of the most exclusive clubs in North America, catering to the sexual needs of the elite, but that doesn't make it any easier.

With all the extra attention The System has been getting lately, I've had to keep a tighter hold on my private life so I don't rock the boat or create any leaks. The Cardinal Club prides itself on discretion, but the right person knows where to look to find the club. There is little you can control once the paparazzi sniff a lead, and I've never liked the idea of being unable to write my own narrative.

I'm not like Parker; I don't relish the media attention. But I also am not like Aleksander; I wouldn't purposely blow the media off, either. Trying to find the middle ground is hard work, and all I want is a little privacy and an outlet for my stress.

I pour Savannah a glass of water and hold it out.

"Thanks," she purrs. I give her a nod and her brow quirks up as she takes an audible sip. "What's wrong?"

"Nothing," I grunt.

"You're quiet. Well, quieter than usual."

"Am I?"

She sits up and cocks her head as she leans forward, bracing her elbows on her thighs. My eyes dip to her massive tits. Even if things are starting to go stale between us, there is no denying that Savannah is sex on a stick.

Ugh. Finding a new rope bunny is going to be more work than I want.

Suddenly another face flashes in my mind. A short woman with fuckable tits and an innocent look that begs to be ruined.

I try to scrub the pink vision away.

"Wow, you're really out of it. I'm not sure if I should take offense."

My gaze snaps back to Savannah's assessing eyes. I open my mouth to bite back but stop. None of this is her fault.

"Sorry," I finally sigh, taking a seat on the edge of the bed next to her.

"It's fine," she shrugs. "You know I don't expect anything outside the session."

"Yes, but you at least deserve my attention while I'm here."

Her eyes soften and she places a reassuring pat on my knee. "Stop. You always treat me well."

When I don't say anything more, she slips off the bed and goes to rummage through her handbag. She pulls out a small purple stick and presses it to her lips, taking an inhale that makes the bottom of it light up blue. When she exhales, a small cloud floats from her lips that smells like grapes. "So, who is she?"

"Who?"

"The girl who's apparently rented an apartment in your brain."

"There's no girl."

"Sure," she drawls before taking another hit. "Is it the one you told me about?"

I stiffen.

"You're the only person I'm involved with."

Surprise ripples across her features. "Since when?"

"I don't know. A while?"

She lets out a laugh. "And you're sure there's no girl you're pining over? Really."

"Savannah," I growl.

Her spine straightens at the warning and her eyes widen a fraction. "I'll drop it."

I grit my teeth together and get up to grab my clothes from the chair in the corner and put them on. The more I think about it, the more it bothers me. I hadn't even realized that Savannah is the only person I've been seeing—seeing being a very loose term—and even this is losing its shine.

I turn back to her, ready to break things off, but she stops me with a raised hand.

"I know." She walks up to me and brushes some lint off the shoulder of my sweatshirt. "I hope you sort things out, Jackson." She gives me a smile before twirling around and heading into the bathroom. "I'm going to have a shower. Make sure you shut the door behind you."

My eyes track her, giving her naked body one last appreciative look as she disappears.

I grab my phone and wallet from the nightstand before throwing on a black face mask and baseball cap. Then I slip on my limited-edition sneakers before picking up my duffle and heading out of the VIP room.

My jaw is clenched tight.

I'm not even in the mood to think about what I am going to do now. Even the idea of trying to find someone to replace Savannah has me annoyed.

Not because of her, but because every time I try to conjure an image in my head of someone new, all I see are flashes of pink.

Which is fucking stupid.

The scrawny guy manning the valet stand gives me a terrified look as he takes my ticket, and I tell myself to stop giving him the death glare. I even fish out a hundred from my wallet to tip him when he returns with my Jeep.

"Thank you," he squeaks out.

I give him a parting grunt as I get into the driver's seat and toss my duffle onto the passenger seat. My eyes flick down to the clock, and I frown seeing that it's only a little after midnight.

My fingers tap on the wheel rhythmically. Savannah is right about one thing, something is off.

I only make it a few streets before the music blasting through my speakers is cut off by an incoming call.

I swear, if one of the guys is—

"Incoming call from unknown number," the robotic voice announces.

Without giving it much thought, I accept the call.

"Hello?"

"Hi, um, sorry to bother you," Deer's voice comes through in that high pitch she typically uses when streaming. "No one else was answering and I had your number from Syd and well, yeah. It's Deer, by the way." Her babbling trails off.

Shock and confusion bubble before annoyance flares in at the offhanded jab that I'm far down her list of preferred people.

"It's fine," I tell her. "I wasn't busy."

"Oh. Okay, cool. Cool, cool, cool."

I wait for her to elaborate, but silence drags on.

"What's wrong?"

"Oh, it's nothing really."

"Really?"

"Yeah, no. Um, I just finished a stream and–" she pauses, cutting herself off "–you know what, I'm sorry. Ignore this call. It's fine. I'm overreacting. Sorry, Shield. Have a good night. Bye!"

"Wait," I call out, but I'm too late. She hangs up and the music returns to my speaker. "Fuck," I curse under my breath as I flick on my blinker and switch lanes before making a U-turn. My foot presses harder on the accelerator as I hit the redial button.

It rings once before she sends me to voicemail.

This woman is going to kill my sanity.

"You have a new text message; would you like me to read it?" my car asks.

"Yes."

"Ok." There's a short pause. "*I'm totally fine. Seriously. Smiley face emoji. Sorry. Praying hands emoji.*" Another pause. "Would you like to reply?"

"No," I grind out as I work my jaw back and forth.

There would be no getting through to her. She is too damn stubborn for her own good. Always hiding behind that perfectly pink exterior.

It takes me twenty minutes, but I finally swing into a guest parking spot beside her apartment complex. The engine barely shuts off before I'm out of the car and stalking to the entrance. There isn't even a doorman at this time of night to stop anyone from coming in.

Fucking bullshit.

I don't even bother waiting for the elevator. I take the stairs two at a time up to the third floor. When I get to her apartment, I rap on the door.

"Deer, open up."

There's no response.

"Deer, I will break this door down if you do not open it. You know I can."

I hear a muffled, "Shit," followed by some shuffling before the door snicks open a few inches.

The buzzing in my ears intensifies as I stare down at the infuriating woman before me. Deer's puffy lips are pursed tightly as she looks up at me briefly before averting her eyes to the right.

"You came?"

"You called."

I give the door a nudge, pushing my way into her apartment.

Deer's pink obsession is a mirror to Parker's love for blue; they both make it their entire personality. Part of me used to think her whole pink thing was just a gimmick, but one look at her apartment—which looks like a unicorn and a fairy had a love child—is all you need as proof that even her blood would run rosy.

"Sure, come in. Make yourself at home."

I turn around to see her fold her arms protectively over her chest, and I force myself to look at her unnaturally blue eyes.

"What's going on?"

"Nothing."

"All right." I shrug before dropping down on her bubbly couch. *Thing is fucking uncomfortable.*

"What are you doing?" Her fingers tighten on her biceps, biting into the fabric of her pastel cardigan.

"Making myself at home." I pull out my phone and swipe it open, aimlessly scrolling.

She lets out an unamused scoff. "Seriously?"

I say nothing and it furthers her annoyance as she stalks over to me.

"No, seriously, what are you going to do? Camp here all night? This isn't funny." Her voice deepens and the ends of her words cut off, her Irish lilt peeking through.

"You didn't call me for no reason, and I'm not leaving until I know why." I look up at her. "Plus, you look like you haven't slept in days."

"Gee, thanks."

"It's not a compliment."

She lets out a frustrated groan and stamps her foot before spinning around and stalking into her bedroom, slamming the door behind her.

Not even a minute later, the door flings back open and she stomps over to me and points a single sharp nail at me.

"Fine, you want to know so badly, Mr. Can't Mind His Own Business? The police called me because someone tried to swat me again while I was streaming."

My blood runs cold as the Antarctic Ocean, and any amusement flees my body.

"What?"

"It's fine. They knew it was a false alarm. It just made me feel a little off, so I called you. But I'm fine."

I fucking hate that word.

Fine.

Such bullshit. She isn't fine. None of this is *fine*.

I stand up, placing myself inches away from her. Deer's eyes flare as she takes a small step back.

"It's not fine. Do they know who called it in?"

She averts her gaze to my chest.

"Deer."

"No," she hisses through clenched teeth. "They still haven't tracked them down. Something about cell tower pinging and stuff."

I sidestep her, making my way into her bedroom. My eyes dart around before landing on the pink suitcase that is still haphazardly full of the random clothes and shoes Lee threw into it two weeks ago. As if I needed another sign Deer isn't doing *fine*.

I throw the lid closed and zip it up before rolling it out of the room.

"What are you doing?"

"You can't stay here."

I move into her streaming room, picking up her laptop and Switch, tossing them into a backpack she has perched next to her desk before grabbing the rest of her gaming accessories.

"Stop!" Her hands close around mine, attempting to pull her headphones from my grasp. It sends a spark across my skin.

What the hell?

I shake it off, tossing her backpack over one shoulder, and level her with a glare. "You have two choices. Either you walk out of here with me, or I carry you."

She's not staying in this apartment for another night. Over my dead body am I letting that happen.

Deer lets out a huff of disbelief, the corners of her

mouth ticking up in a fake grin. "You can't be serious."

"You have sixty seconds. If you need anything else, grab it now."

"Stop," she grits through that strained smile still on her face.

"Sixty, fifty-nine, fifty-eight—"

"Stop." All humor leaves her voice.

"Fifty-five. Fifty-four."

Her brows furrow and her gaze narrows, causing her nose to scrunch up. She lets out an exaggerated sigh but doesn't make a move. So, I continue to count down, keeping my eyes locked on her the entire time. It's not hard, Deer is stunning. She has this soft beauty about her, one that is undeniable even with exhaustion written all over her face.

But I don't let it sway me.

The number "one" passes my lips, and her shoulders tense. When I take a step forward, I see a glimmer of nerves dance across her features, the first sign all night that whatever is going on is affecting her more than she lets on.

"Don't you dare, Shield."

It's a warning.

One that I do not heed.

It only takes three long strides to reach her, and I stoop down to curve my arm around her waist and lift her up. She screeches, trying to reel back from me with a slew of incomprehensible words, but it makes no difference as I haul her over my shoulder. My hand rests on the back of her bare thigh, and the contact has my cock twitching.

"Oh my Gods, stop. Stop! I'm sorry, okay? Put me down. Put me down!" She squirms in my arms, her legs kicking up as her feet threaten to clock me in the head. "I'll come willingly, just put me down. Please."

"You promise?"

"I promise, you insufferable giant. Fucking hell." Her accent cuts through again.

I drop her back to the ground and she glares up at me, her face flushed a bright pink to match her hair. It brings an inexplicable smile to my face.

Deer sobers up and runs past me with a litany of curses, disappearing into her bathroom and returning with a giant blanket and a large pink case of what looks like makeup cradled in her arms. Annoyance bleeds out her eyes.

I hold her front door open, and she clips me with her elbow as she pushes past me. I stifle a snort as I follow behind her, rolling her suitcase across the linoleum.

Her foot taps impatiently as we wait for the elevator, the silver aglet on her pristine white sneakers glinting from the overhead lights. She says nothing, just stews in her thoughts. I can feel the tension radiating off her as we get inside, filling up the small metal box as we descend to the lobby.

She's the one who is being ridiculous. It's bad enough she insisted on staying here the first time around, but I can't believe she was just planning to stick it out after another attempted swatting. What is wrong with her?

If I hadn't picked up, if I hadn't forced my way over here, would she have told anyone what happened tonight?

It doesn't make sense. Why does she try to do everything herself?

Deer stalks ahead of me, burning holes in the ground with every step she takes.

"You don't even know where I parked," I call out to her as she pushes through the revolving doors.

"Maybe I'm walking," she tosses back.

I press my lips into a thin line and pick up my pace slightly. Not enough to make it seem like I'm rushing after her—because I'm not—but enough to make sure I don't lose her to the darkness.

She pauses for a moment, head swiveling until she locates my Jeep parked off to the side. I fish my key out of my pocket to unlock the car, and she doesn't even spare me a second glance before hauling herself onto the passenger seat. I toss her suitcase and backpack into the trunk before joining her.

"What's this?" She holds up my black duffle bag, the one I'd left on the passenger seat.

"Nothing." I pull it from her grip and lob it into the trunk. It lands with a thwack.

I quickly start the engine and turn up the volume on my speakers as I pull away from her apartment.

"You can just drop me off at Lee's."

"No."

"No?"

"No. I don't trust you to stay there."

"I'm not a child."

I give her a glance out of the corner of my eye. "I'd beg to differ. You're being more difficult than my sister, and she's thirteen."

Her lips pop open, forming a pretty O shape.

I ready myself for whatever argument she is going to throw back, but instead she just gives me a curt, "Whatever," before turning away from me. She hikes her feet onto the seat and pulls her knees up to her chest as she stares out the window.

Some unhinged part of my brain is tempted to reach out and rub her shoulder—to comfort her—but I just curl my fingers around my steering wheel tighter. It's bad enough that I keep finding myself interfering with her life, I don't need to make this even more complicated.

By the time we pull into the private garage beneath the apartment complex, it's nearing 3 a.m. Weariness is written in Deer's bones as I watch her slip out of the car at the pace of a snail. It's almost as if by accepting defeat against me, her body has finally begun to shut down.

Silence surrounds us on the elevator ride up to the penthouse, and it's only when the doors open and she steps foot on the shiny black tiles in our apartment that she stops to acknowledge me.

"Where do you want me?"

"My room."

Life sparks in her tired eyes. "What?"

I shrug past her, rolling her suitcase behind me as I turn into the hallway where my rooms are located. I push open the last door on the left and flick on the lights before wheeling the suitcase to a stop.

Deer pauses at the threshold, gaze darting everywhere.

Part of me is a smidge self-conscious, wondering exactly what she is thinking. In comparison to her bedroom, mine is dull. I don't come in here for anything other than sleep, spending most of my time in my streaming room instead. So, other than my bed and dresser, there's just a wall of limited-edition sneakers and a display case in the corner full of vintage horror movies.

I toss my black duffle into my closet before shutting the door, hoping that she won't go snooping.

"There's a fresh towel under the sink," I explain to her as I grab my toothbrush from the bathroom.

It's only when I sling my own towel over my shoulder and pick up my gym bag that she snaps out of her daze.

"Wait, where are you sleeping?"

"Parker's."

"But doesn't he—"

"He's in Bahrain for F1. McKinley Motors invited him and Syd. They won't be back till late next week."

"Oh." She nibbles on her lower lip.

"Need anything else?"

"No." The word is quiet, and it takes me a moment to see the discomfort swimming beneath her skin.

It's not my place to push her, though. I managed to get her here. She's safe. My job is done as far as I am concerned. I don't need to get any more involved in her life.

"'Kay. Night."

"Wait." Her word stops me at the threshold of the door.

I throw her a tired look over my shoulder. "Yes?"

"Do you have tea?"

"Tea?"

"You know, that beverage made when you soak dried leaves in hot water."

"I know what tea is."

"Didn't sound like it."

Brat.

"We have tea." And then, because I can't seem to fucking help myself, I add, "Do you want me to make you some?"

That shine returns to her eyes again. "Yeah, herbal would be great. It helps me relax."

I give her a nod before finally dipping from the room.

I head to the kitchen to turn the kettle on and catch my reflection in the microwave.

How did I get myself into this situation?

Why am I making tea for a five-foot-nothing sprite at 3 a.m.?

I run a hand over my face before dropping a chamomile tea bag into a plain white mug and filling it with hot water. I carefully carry the drink back to my room and find Deer perched on the edge of my bed, fiddling around on her phone.

"Your tea."

"Thanks." She grants me a small smile as she takes the steaming mug from my hands, her fingers grazing mine.

I swallow hard. "Careful, it's hot."

"I know how tea works," she laughs, and the sound settles the brewing storm within me,

"Right, well, night."

"Night, Shield."

I click the door shut but pause outside for a beat.

I wonder why she never uses my name.

I wonder why I've never noticed until now.

I wonder why I even care.

Chapter SEVEN

DEER

The scent of sage, cedarwood, and a hint of something slightly sweet cocoons me. It smells comforting. Safe.

I nuzzle my face farther into the soft pillow and bring my legs close to my chest as I hover in that in-between state of sleep.

Sleep.

I finally slept. I don't know for how long, but I can tell in my bones that it's more than the two hours I've been getting for the last few weeks. The second my head hit the pillow, it was like I blacked out—a total body shut down that I had no control over.

Maybe it's the sleep deprivation catching up to me. Maybe it's the change of scenery. Whatever it is, I'm grateful for it. Not that I'm telling Jackson that. He doesn't need his ego fed, not after he successfully managed to pull me from my apartment.

I knew the second I opened that door to him that I had lost the battle. He has a solid fifty pounds of muscle and an entire foot on me; fighting him was pointless.

That's the only reason why I agreed to leave.

At least, that's what I tell myself. It's not like I actually didn't feel safe in my apartment anymore. It's not like I wanted to escape. And it's definitely not like I was looking for someone to take my choice away and force me to listen to rationality. Nope. I have too much pride to admit that.

I throw my arms and legs wide like a starfish and stretch before throwing the dark charcoal sheets off my body and slipping off the bed. My feet slap against the cold floorboards as I make my way into Jackson's en suite. My giant makeup bag rests on the counter, and I dig through it for my loose toothbrush.

I pause, examining the bags under my eyes and the sallow color of my skin.

Okay, maybe I'd been a *little* too hopeful that just one night of rest would act like a magic potion.

I still look like death warmed up.

However, it is nothing a little makeup can't fix. Or a lot...

I hum to myself as I go about my routine, donning my sparkly eyeshadow, white eyeliner, and bright cotton candy blush before popping in my blue contacts.

Finally, the reflection looking back at me is human.

My gamer persona is my safe space. Deer is a blanket I wrap around myself, one of sunshine and rainbows and laughter. She is a functioning human when I can't be.

I head back into Jackson's bedroom and yank open my suitcase. The lid thunks against the floor loudly and I cringe, my eyes darting to the door. It didn't sound like anyone was awake, but how would I know?

I sift through my clothes, frowning and kicking myself that I didn't pay more attention to what Lee threw in here. It's a weird mishmash of stuff.

After I empty half the contents onto the floor, I settle on a comfy outfit of a pink pleated tennis skirt with built-in shorts and a white athletic tank top before plucking my phone from the nearby charging station.

I'm not too shocked to see that it is almost two in the afternoon.

My heart drops when I see the litany of texts from Rick, worry weaving its way through my veins that something else with the Deer Hunters has cropped up.

RICK

Are u okay?

Seriously??

The police said the swatting issue was dealt with but ur location shows u on the move at almost two?

R u safe? Do u need help??

I see ur at The System's place – pls text me when u see this so I know ur fine

My heart calms when I see that it's just him being concerned and has nothing to do with anything shitty.

ME

hey! sorry!!!!

I'm crashing with the guys >.<

my place doesn't feel safe...

I bite my lip at the admission. I would never tell any-one else this, but Rick knows me, he cares about my se-curity and my brand first. That's why he is my main mod and basically a personal assistant at this point. Seriously, he's the one who deals with everything—like my P.O. box nightmares. I don't need to open another letter that con-tains a used condom.

RICK

thanks for letting me know

I'll schedule accordingly. Need anything?

ME

I'm good for now – ty!

I click my phone off and pad over to slowly crack open Jackson's door, keeping an ear out for any noise. The last thing I want right now is to come face-to-face with either Stevie or Aleks—I don't want to have to explain myself or how I ended up here.

When silence greets me, I take a few tentative steps out into the hallway. I let my feet lead me into the main area of the apartment, squinting at the light flooding in from the floor to ceiling windows.

The System has a gorgeous penthouse. It's an open layout, with the kitchen, living room, and dining room all bleeding into one another. There's a door on the south wall that leads to a massive outdoor space complete with a faux firepit, and there's an alcove built into the north wall that houses a ninety-inch TV connected to a bunch of gaming consoles. The apartment is minimalistic, decked out mostly in tasteful neon signs and video game memorabilia.

It's surprisingly neat for three guys.

I'm ninety percent sure they have a cleaning crew.

I trek across the cool black tiles to the kitchen in search of something to tide over my rumbling stomach when my eyes snag on a Post-it note stuck to the fridge. My name is written in loops and below it is a note instructing me that there are waffles inside and to heat them up for exactly two minutes.

I wouldn't have pegged Jackson as a cursive man.

I pull open the fridge and pause, noting a bunch of Tupperware stacked up with premade meals. Sitting smack in the middle is a plate of what looks to be homemade blueberry waffles covered in plastic wrap.

I guess that's what the sweet smell was when I woke up.

I place them in the microwave for one minute and fifty-five seconds before practically climbing onto the counter to grab a mug from the cupboard. I pop a pod into the espresso machine and then take way too long trying to locate the silverware drawer. By the time I sit my ass onto the chair and take a bite of the warm, sugary waffles, I'm exhausted all over again.

My body is definitely run into the ground, and my

stomach gives up halfway through the first waffle, rejecting the idea of any more food in its dilapidated state.

I slip from the stool, dropping my plate into the dishwasher, and carry my bitter coffee outside.

The early spring breeze whips my hair in a flurry of pink around my face, but I relish the feeling of the world moving around me. My elbows dig into the top of the glass panels fencing in the patio as I slump forward and close my eyes, turning my face up to the sun. I take in the deepest breath imaginable, inhaling the cool air so it fills every crevice in my lungs.

I want to cry.

Reality and everything in between comes crashing down around me. The fear that sliced into my bones and threatened to flay me open when I received that call from the cops last night resurfaces. I finally accept that maybe, *just maybe*, things aren't as peachy as I'm trying to gaslight myself into thinking they are.

But I don't cry, despite the sharp sting behind my eyes.

I haven't cried yet, and I'm not about to start. Those flood gates are staying locked.

"Hey."

My lids fly open, and I jerk, spinning around and almost spilling the remains of my coffee in the process.

Jackson stands in the doorway, strong arm propped against the molding. "You look better."

His gaze burns into me as he slowly looks me up and down, almost like he is trying to memorize every inch of my skin.

"A good night's sleep will do that."

And a fresh face of makeup.

I tuck a stray piece of hair behind my ear.

He hums, walking toward me.

I take a step back, but I just bump against the railing.

Jackson comes to a stop next to me, resting his forearms on the glass as he looks out across the city. His elbow is only an inch away from my own, and I can feel an electric energy vibrating between us. It is like little sparks are jumping off and hitting my skin, as if we can't help but be connected.

I turn around, placing some space between our bodies and mimic his gaze, looking out onto the city skyline.

It's odd to think that the man next to me is the same one who came bursting into my apartment last night.

The man with me now is the Jackson I've come to know; the one who speaks few words and is stoic and grumpy. The fire blazing in his eyes last night was like nothing I'd ever seen before. The control and dominance in his voice had my toes curling, and it makes me curious if maybe he's like me—if maybe he hides more beneath the surface.

"Sooo," I drag out, attempting to fill the silence.

"So?" His voice is deep in contrast with my own as it drawls the vowel out.

I grit my teeth together before taking a sip of my unfortunately plain coffee.

Gods, why did he have to make it so difficult sometimes?

"Whatcha been up to?"

His right brow quirks up and his eyes flick to me briefly, giving me a once over. Then he just shrugs. "Worked out. Ate. Gamed."

"Riveting," I deadpan.

"It's more than you can say, Sparkles."

My lips pucker on the nickname as my hands tighten on my mug.

What a frustrating man.

"Well, I'll be out of your hair soon enough."

This time he turns to face me, and it's everything I can do to keep my focus on the skyline.

"You can't seriously be thinking of going back to your apartment?"

"Maybe."

Honestly, now that I've left, I have no desire to go back. Sure, most—well, all—of my stuff is still there, but the thought of stepping back into the place where I've had my privacy completely violated sends a tsunami of unease through my gut.

My rose-tinted glasses have cracked, and there is no way for me to think of my apartment without seeing all the dangers that truly lurk in the shadows.

"You're more stubborn than I thought."

"Thank you."

"Again, not a compliment."

"Fine," I huff, finally giving him my attention. "Then what's your grand plan?"

"We're setting you up with a place here." He pushes off the glass and stalks back into the apartment.

Great.

"What are you talking about?" I call after him as I'm forced to catch up.

"Parker is putting you up in one of the vacant places here."

"Wait, seriously?" A smile spreads across my face. I'd been thinking of moving here a few months back, but it didn't pan out. This is totally a sign. "Do I get the friends and family discount?"

"The what?" Jackson busies himself by making a coffee at the espresso machine.

I lean against the island and watch him. "Ya know, a discounted rate for the apartment."

"Why?"

"Syd got one."

"'Cause Sydney couldn't afford it. Unlike you." He lifts the tiny espresso cup to his lips and takes a sip. "It's not like this place isn't within your budget."

"And how would you know what my budget is?"

"I've seen your view count."

"Oooh. So, you *do* watch my videos," I croon.

He scowls at my smile, and it just makes me want to push him more.

I pad over to him and lean into his space, blinking up at him innocently. "Are you a secret fanboy? Do you have a shrine to me hidden away somewhere? Is that what's stashed in your closet? Come on, you can be honest with me. I know I'm quite adorable."

Jackson's upper lip pulls back in disgust, but I steel myself, smiling even brighter as I lay a hand on his forearm.

"Don't tell me, your guilty pleasure is playing farming sims? You like to craft teeny, little towns with those big man hands and spend late nights harvesting milk from emus when no one is looking."

Jackson scoffs, shrugging out of my touch.

"Or maybe…" I trail off ominously, waiting until he locks eyes with me. "Maybe you just like to watch me. Is that the sort of thing you're into?"

Instead of turning away again, like I expect him to, Jackson takes a step toward me. He cages me between his body and the island, the cool marble biting into my back. There's a hunger that bleeds across his features, and it makes me feel like his prey.

"You couldn't handle what I'm into." His dark words carry the scent of coffee as he whispers them into my ear. "I suggest you don't go looking for answers unless you want to be responsible for what you discover."

I suddenly become all too aware of the way his body surrounds me. My mind whirls as it starts conjuring up scenario after scenario of his hands moving along my skin. All I want to know is what he hides under that silent exterior. There's no way a guy with all those muscles and secrets isn't concealing something darker under the surface.

Any retort I have gets lodged in my throat as he pulls back and studies my face, a smirk pulling at the corner of his lips. Heat flushes my cheeks at his perusal. I open my mouth to say anything—literally, anything—so he doesn't see the secret want leaking out of my eyes.

"I—" My phone rings out, vibrating against my hip, and I freeze.

"You should get that." He throws me a wink before backing up and strolling in the direction of his streaming room.

My body immediately feels cooler without him near. The clouds fuzzing my brain start to clear, and little pockets of sunshine clarity are peeking through. I take a calming breath before swiping my phone open.

"Hey," I chirp.

"Oh my God, where are you?" Lee's exasperated voice fills my ear.

"Sightseeing in Barcelona."

"Deer."

I roll my eyes. "You know where I am. You have my location."

"I do. The question is, why are you there?"

I groan, which is the wrong response because it just spurs her on.

"Oh God, what happened? Should I come over? I'm coming over. I can reschedule my stream." I can hear a bunch of rustling through the speaker.

"No. It's nothing." I wander out of the kitchen and flop down on the big couch. "Seriously."

"Deer. You can't lie to me."

Sigh.

"Okay, fine. I had another swat scare last night. Nothing happened, but it freaked me out a little." I turn my head and stare at the trophies lining the wall, outlining their shapes with my eyes. The System really are an impressive bunch of gamers.

"That's it. You're moving out. I'll pay to break the contract at your apartment if I have to."

I smile. Lee really is my ride-or-die. There is no doubt in my mind that if I murdered someone, she would be the one rocking up to the crime scene with a bucket of bleach and latex gloves. She also has some of the best knowledge to get away with murder; we don't watch all those crime shows without absorbing some tips and tricks.

"Thanks, but apparently English has it handled."

"Oh?"

"Mmm, he says he's setting me up with a place."

"Stop. At his apartment complex?"

"Yup"

"I'm so jelly! Are you getting a discount?"

I bolt upright. "That's what I asked, and Shield laughed at me!"

Lee begins to giggle, and I find myself joining in. The laughter bubbles out of me, lightening the weight that's been pressing on my shoulders like a backpack filled with bricks.

"Are you sure I shouldn't come over?"

"I'm totally fine, Lee."

"Okay, okay. Look, I have to set up for my stream later, but keep me posted and I love you."

"I love you, too. Bye."

"Bye."

I hang up and fall back on the couch again, staring up at the white ceiling. The easy air Lee had created slowly starts to fade away and I'm left looking at my life—at that kernel of unease that is still festering in my gut.

I need to get my shit together.

I just have to figure out how.

Chapter EIGHT

DEER

66 **W**hat the fuck, Deer?"

I grin, my cheeks splitting wide. "What?"

"You're screen peeking," Aleks huffs.

"I am not."

I definitely am.

"Oh, yeah? Then explain how I just died?"

"Because you're a lousy player, Blade."

"Bullshit."

"Sometimes even the king must admit defeat," I croon, cocking my rifle as I run my character across the map.

"I thought you hated shooters."

"I do. I get performance anxiety; I'm sure you know what that is."

Stevie lets out a cackle, and I let my attention slip as

I turn to give her a conspiratorial smile. Her long legs are strewn over Aleks' lap from the other side of the couch as she sketches in her notepad.

The elevator pings open, but Aleks and I don't move, locked in a stalemate, our eyes focused on the TV screen.

He isn't wrong. I do typically suck at first-person shooter games, and I wouldn't attempt to play *FrozeLine* or *Kill Strike* if my life depended on it. But *Frontline Doom*? I'm not *that* awful at it—I'm actually kinda decent. I just hate playing online 'cause the male population gets weird and judgy which makes me nervous and ends in my own performance anxiety. I don't know how Lee does it as a career, streaming these every day.

But it doesn't matter how passable I am at the game, Aleks is a million times better.

So, yes, I am screen peeking to get an advantage.

Sue me for wanting to win.

My eyes flick from my half of the TV over to Aleks', and I let out a curse as I watch his character headshot me with a pistol.

"Mother fucker."

"For someone so tiny, you have the vocabulary of a sailor."

"Blame my da."

I focus my gaze on the map to find a way from the respawn point back to where Aleks just killed me. This is exactly what I needed tonight—a total distraction from reality. I might be a solo gamer ninety percent of the time, but there really is nothing better than finding a game to play with friends.

"Hi, Jackson." Stevic's lilt pulls me from my focus,

and I turn to follow her gaze.

Jackson grumbles a response as he tosses his keys into the bowl by the elevator and kicks off his sneakers. I trace the lines of his arms as he reaches behind his head to tie his black hair in a knot at the base of his neck.

"Bad date?" She pushes, pausing to look at a fake watch on her wrist. "You weren't gone long."

Jackson remains silent, meandering into the kitchen and opening the fridge to take out a beer.

"Grab me one," Aleks calls out.

Jackson sighs, pulling a second beer from the fridge.

"Oh, I'll take some wine while you're at it," Stevie jumps in.

Which means I obviously have to join as well. "I'll take some wine, too. Or a seltzer."

He levels me a glare, but I just grin even though I'm a little miffed. He didn't mention having a date tonight when I talked with him this morning. I'd thought that since he is the one who stubbornly brought me here that maybe he did consider us friends. But no.

Nope, we aren't even close enough for that.

Jackson plops the two beers, a bottle of white wine, and a cherry seltzer on the coffee table.

"What, no glass?" Stevie cocks her head.

"Do I look like your butler? Get it yourself."

She lets out a tsk and swings her legs off her boyfriend. "Definitely a bad date."

Jackson continues to grumble as he cracks open the beer and takes a long sip. Curiosity gets the better of me.

"She wasn't nice?"

"She was fine."

"She wasn't hot?" Aleks reaches for his beer.

"Aleksander," Stevie chastises, sinking back down on the couch next to him and pouring a healthy glass of wine. "Be nice."

Jackson holds his hand out to me, and I stare at it in confusion. He nods, angling his chin down at the controller in my lap. "The date was fine, she's just not my type. None of them are." The tips of his fingers brush against my thumb as he tugs the controller from my hands.

The boys start a new match, but I struggle to keep my attention on the screen, my gaze slipping to Jackson over and over again.

"What?" His eyes clash with mine.

"That was, like, your fifth date, wasn't it?"

"Didn't realize you were keeping track."

"It's just morbid curiosity, like watching a plane crash."

"Sure."

I take a sip of the cherry seltzer, eyeing him over the can. "It's a pity. All those good looks and you can't even land a girlfriend."

His brows pull together and he starts to open his mouth but Aleks' voice cuts in. "Sucks to suck, loser." Jackson flicks his attention back to the screen, and he lets out a curse as Aleks rains a parade of bullets at his character and continues to mock him. "You're really off your game, bro. Literally and figuratively."

"Let me get one thing straight," Jackson uses the controller to punctuate his words, "I could date any of those women if I wanted to. I just don't."

"Then why bother with the dates?" I ask.

"Because I have to. At least, until my grandmother

gives up."

"Dude, your grandma is even more stubborn than you," Aleks chuckles. "You're going to be stuck going on dates until your dick shrivels up."

"That's not..." he trails off. "Fuck."

"See."

"Why don't you just date one of them for a little while, get her off your back?" Stevie's suggestion turns the fizz in my stomach sour. "You could break up after like a month, but at least it'll show you tried."

"I thought about that," he admits.

"And?" The singular word feels like tar as it passes through my lips.

"And I don't want to lead someone on," he sighs.

"Your funeral," Aleks and Stevie say simultaneously.

"Fuck off," he grumbles, taking a sip of his beer.

And then, my brain malfunctions.

Aliens come down from some alternate universe and zap me, frying any sensibility and making me say something that is so out of pocket that I honestly wish the ground would swallow me up and chuck me on some distant planet to die.

"I'll date you."

Everyone's silent. There's just the sound of the grenade Aleks' character launched exploding.

"What?" Jackson looks at me like I have three heads—which I might, you know, if the aliens are involved.

"That's not a bad idea." Stevie leans forward and curls her hand around my shoulder. "Not bad at all."

"That's a fucking awful idea," Jackson exclaims, and my insides shrivel up and die. He sounds absolutely appalled by the idea, which is just fabulous for my self-esteem.

I square my shoulders, letting his insult roll off my back as I drain the last of my seltzer.

"Rude. I'll have you know that I am a delightful girlfriend."

"Delightfully awful."

"I'm going to be honest, I'm on the same page as Jackson here," Aleks interrupts. "Not the best idea."

I glare at him for the betrayal, but he's still zoned into the game.

"Don't give me that look," Aleks drawls.

Okay, apparently he has the peripheral vision of a freaking shark.

"All right, go on then. Throw in your two cents," I huff.

"You're a little," he tilts his head side to side, "pink."

Jackson snorts and I grit my teeth.

"What's wrong with that?"

This time, Aleks does give me a glance. He even goes so far as to pair it with a weak smile. "I'm not sure dating you would be a solution to the issue. You'd probably freak his family out and make it worse."

"Yeah, Sparkles, you're not really their ideal type," Jackson tacks on.

Okay, I'm a *little* offended.

"Whatever, it was just a joke." I attempt to brush the entire conversation under the rug.

Aleks, however, doesn't seem to get the message.

"Although," he drawls as his gaze returns to the game. Aleks manages to get a few shots off at Jackson's character before losing him to a flash bang. "Maybe if you dated

Deer, your family would be so appalled that they wouldn't care if you didn't date at all, so long as it wasn't her."

And now I'm a little more than a little offended.

"That's also not a bad idea, babe," Stevie chimes in.

"Hey," I counter. "I'm a nice person. People love me. I'm sunshine and rainbows and fucking unicorns."

"You swear in every third sentence," Jackson deadpans.

"I'm Irish, sue me."

"It doesn't matter anyway. I don't want a fake girlfriend."

"Well, I don't want to be your fake girlfriend—even if you beg. Who would want to be tied to your grumpy arse?"

Jackson gives me a once over, the slightest smirk pulling at the corner of his lips. "Sure."

My eyes narrow. "Try me."

He doesn't deign to give me a response, just goes back to ignoring me and playing with Aleks. Frustration bubbles under my skin, uncontained energy coursing through me.

A light tap on my hand pulls me from the death glare I'm trying to laser into Jackson's brain.

"You good?" Stevie mouths to me. Her eyes dip to where my nails are digging into my biceps.

I release my grip, little red crescents marring my pale skin. With a deep breath, I plaster a smile on my face and roll my eyes. *"Yeah. Boys,"* I mouth back.

She gives a light chuckle before holding her wine glass out to me. I carefully pluck it from her grip and take a healthy gulp, pushing my emotions to the side.

But now that the idea is in my head, it starts swimming around, and some strange kernel in my chest lights up.

Jackson's hot. Dating him wouldn't be a chore in the looks department. Plus, I might even feel comfortable enough to leave the apartment with someone like him by my side. He would be like my own personal bodyguard.

Except, the idea seems as appealing to him as broccoli to a toddler. It doesn't matter how good I might be for him; he's just going to push me to the side until someone forces his hand.

Chapter NINE

JACKSON

I stare down at the fairy strewn across my bed sheets. Her head hangs off the side, pink hair dangling to the floor as she watches me upside down.

It's been three days, and I'm seriously starting to question my decision to bring her here.

She is everywhere, even when she isn't. Pieces of her linger around the apartment, and my bedroom is starting to take on her brown sugar scent.

I should've just let her stay in Parker's room.

Out of sight. Out of mind.

But, like every other time I've entertained that thought, my chest swirls with a sourness.

Not to mention, every time I look at her, I remember her proposal the other night.

"I'll date you."

As if that would work. My family would combust at the idea. There is no way they would ever believe it. My auntie already scrutinizes everything I do, the last thing I need is to give her more ammunition for why I'm ruining our family's reputation.

And yet, I can't stop thinking about it.

What a fucking nightmare I've created for myself.

"What do you want, Deer?"

"Nothing."

I look down at her, and for the twelfth time, I have to avert my gaze from her tits that are trying to escape the confines of her tight top. Gravity isn't doing me any favors.

"Do you need a ride to Crime Night or something?" It is Tuesday.

She heaves herself up, cheeks flushed. "Nope, we canceled tonight."

"Really?"

"Lee has a subathon and Syd's still in Europe with Parker, so Stevie wants to take the extra time to work on her new art piece." She shrugs, crossing her legs.

She looks so damn relaxed on my bed.

"All right."

I need to get out of here.

I spent the last two days grinding out hours of gameplay for prerecorded content and slotting in streams, so I haven't seen her much. Deer's been keeping to herself as well, popping in and out of Parker's streaming room, where she set up her stuff in his absence.

There's a small chance he comes back and gets pissed at how things have been moved around, but Parker's a softie, so I doubt it. Even I can't get mad at the way her makeup is scattered around my bathroom or how her clothes litter my floor. She's getting comfortable here, and it makes me feel better after practically dragging her out of her apartment.

But that doesn't mean I'm comfortable being around her. I don't like the way she holds my attention like a moth to a flame. She sets me off, puts me on edge.

"What are you doing tonight?"

Her question makes me pause at the threshold of the door I am attempting to escape through.

Is she...bored?

"Probably playing *Scythe Survival* or something."

"Oh, I haven't played that yet." She looks at me with wide, expectant eyes.

"Did you want to join me?"

She waves her hands frantically. "Oh, no. No, I don't want to bother you."

It sounds exactly like she wants to bother me.

"What else are you planning to do?"

She presses her lips together, drawing my focus to her soft pink mouth. "Mmm, I dunno." She tilts her head. "I was thinking of watching a horror movie. You have quite the collection."

I follow her gaze to the stack of vintage and collector edition horror movies I have displayed in the corner of my room. She slips off the bed and pads her way to the display case, gently opening the glass door. The pink spandex shorts she is wearing barely cover her ass as she leans forward and runs her fingers across the DVDs.

My mind flashes, an image of her bent over, arms tied behind her back.

She plucks a case from the stack and turns around with

a bright smile. "I've been dying to watch this. It's not on any of my streaming services, and it costs like thirty bucks to buy."

Well. Shit.

"That's one of my favorites."

"Really? Well, did *you* want to join *me*?" There's a glint in her eyes as her smile widens.

My lips move before my brain has a chance to catch up.

"Sure."

Guess I'm changing my plans.

"Awesome. Let's get all the goods in order then." She breezes past me, and I'm forced to trail behind her like some giant puppy.

She tosses the DVD on the couch, not stopping her stride as she starts opening cabinets in the kitchen. I lean my hip against the island as I watch her stretch on her tiptoes to grab a packet of microwavable popcorn, her T-shirt riding up to show a sliver of smooth skin. My fingers twitch to wrap around her waist.

Something is definitely wrong with me.

"Do you want a drink?"

I drag my gaze back up to her face. "Sure."

"Perfect, just wait. I make the best drinks."

There's an excitement pouring off her that I've rarely seen before. The bubbly sweetness of her personality doesn't seem artificial but natural. It's refreshing, cute.

A sparkle enters her eyes as she mixes random liquids together, the drink going from purple to pink with a squeeze of a lemon. She crouches to eye level as she begins to pour in the vodka. More vodka than I expect her to pour in.

Fantastic…

The smell of popcorn slowly starts to permeate the air as the pops get louder and louder. Deer frowns as she turns around and eyes a bowl that's just out of reach. The tips of her long, pointy nails tap against the glass rim.

I push off the island and move in behind her, reaching to help her grab the bowl. But just as I position myself around her, she lifts a knee up on the counter and hoists herself up. Her ass presses right against my crotch, almost grinding on it. She gives a surprised yelp, and I hold back a groan. A warmth spreads throughout my body, and my hands close around the bowl as I take a massive step back.

"Here." I hold the bowl out to her, trying to ignore the last five seconds of my life. Trying to ignore the feel of her against me.

She blinks down at me, those thick lashes fanning up and down.

"Thanks." She slips off the counter and takes the bowl from me, filling it up with the fresh popcorn. "Do you mind grabbing the drinks?"

"Sure."

"Ya know, if I hadn't watched some of your streams, I'd think you didn't know how to speak in complete sentences." She gives me the side-eye as she pushes past me to the couch, and I'm stuck trailing behind her again.

"You watch my streams?" I taunt, but it rolls right over her.

"Duh." She shrugs, opening up the DVD and slotting it into the PlayStation.

I fall back onto the couch and watch as she goes around

turning off all the lights before plopping down next to me, crossing her legs. She leaves a healthy foot between our bodies, and I can't tell whether I should take offense to that.

The movie starts up and, while it is one of my favorites, I've seen it enough times that it's easy for my mind to constantly stray to the woman next to me. I keep watching for shifts in her expression so I can gauge if she hates it or not.

I shouldn't care, and yet there is a part of me that is secretly hoping she loves it.

By the time we are halfway through, she's managed to inch her way closer and closer across the cushion. I don't think she's noticed. Her drink sits empty on the coffee table, and there are only sad, unpopped kernels remaining in the bowl she keeps clutched between her hands.

The vodka has started to work its way through my system even though I've only drunk half of what she poured. The girl has a heavy hand. My body relaxes into the sofa, and I let my legs splay open a little farther, so my knee rests only inches from her own.

I watch her jaw drop as the main plot twist is revealed, and her hand shoots out to grasp my thigh.

"No," she whispers. "No!" She turns to me all starry-eyed, a disbelieving smile creeping along her face. Her joy is infectious, and I have to stop myself from smiling back. "I totally did not see that coming." The flash of the TV illuminates her skin, and I can't help but admit she really is a pretty thing.

Her hand doesn't leave my thigh as she turns back to the TV, instead, her grip loosens so it's just lazily caressing. Every once in a while, her hand will twitch, those sharp nails dragging slightly. And I grit my teeth during a particular scene where her thumb presses just a little too high.

And yet, I say nothing. For some godforsaken reason, I say nothing.

Instead, I spend the last twenty minutes of the movie telling my dick to calm down because seriously, who the fuck gets hard while watching a horror movie.

As the final scene comes to a close, she turns to me, her face only a few inches from my own. "That ending was a total mindfuck," she whispers. "Best movie I've seen in forever. Ten out of ten. You said this was one of your faves, right?"

"Yeah."

"Well, what's another?" She leans in closer like she's looking for me to spill a secret. All personal space has been eradicated.

"Another what?"

"Another movie that you like."

I frown. "Why?"

She pulls back and huffs. "Gods, it's like pulling teeth with you sometimes." She swivels her whole body to face me and places both hands on my thigh this time. She is just as bad as Parker. No boundaries. "I'm asking what some of your other favorite horror movies are because you obviously have good taste. So, what do you recommend?"

A jaded part of me wonders if she is fucking with me a little. Maybe it's because I have to drag Aleks with me to the cinema to watch horror movies or maybe it's because Parker will unplug the TV if he comes home and sees one playing. I've never had someone genuinely interested before—and fuck if that doesn't do something weird to my chest.

"Some of the live-action Junji Ito movies are pretty hardcore."

"Oh! His manga are so creepy." Her eyes widen and her nails dig into my sweatpants as she leans forward. "The one with the deer-dude was so screwed up. I couldn't sleep without seeing it every time I closed my eyes. Had to keep the lights on like a wee child."

I can't help the laugh that rumbles out from me when her Irish accent slips out.

It's hard when you feel like there's a part of yourself that no one else relates to. So, when you find someone who seems honestly fascinated by something you like and willing to learn more about it, it creates this sense of validation and partnership that you didn't know you needed. And that's what Deer has managed to do within just a few hours.

"What else?" Her question feels so sincere that a part of me decides to open up—just a little.

"Have you ever watched the *Devil Nun* franchise?"

This time, she slaps her palms against my thigh. "I haven't! You love those movies, right? I think I remember Blade mentioning that."

"Yeah, he's been coming with me to the premieres since we were in high school." Begrudgingly, I don't add. I have to bribe him with chocolate pretzels and ice cream every time I want him to come along.

"Ugh, I love that for you. Lee might share my love for true crime, but she draws the line at gory horror movies."

"I feel that. We can watch the first one if you want? It's still early."

"Totally!" Her smile grows and her hands tighten on my thighs again. As if she just realizes what she's been doing, she blinks down and flexes her fingers. "Gods, your thighs are like steel."

I expect her to take her hands away, but they linger.

"Thanks." I force the word between my lips.

"You're welcome." She gives my thigh a pat and then, *finally*, she removes them, clasping her hands in her lap. She looks at me expectantly and silence stretches between us. Her brows dip. "Are you going to put the movie on?"

"Right," I mutter. "Right." I lean forward and grab the controller, switching out from the DVD to one of the streaming channels. As I mindlessly search for the movie, I attempt to gather my wits.

What the fuck is going on?

I hit play on the movie and relax back into the couch at the familiar opening scene. Deer curls her knees to her chest and places her chin on them.

Her attention stays hooked the entire time, and, once again, I find myself stealing glances at her. I could stare at her all day and probably never get bored; I'd merely get lost in the curves and dips of her changing expressions, committing each one to memory.

I hate to admit it, but I like having her around. It's almost as if I've left the city for the country and looked up at the sky to realize for the first time that there are millions of stars lighting up the night. The thought of going back to the drab darkness is unappealing now that I've seen the sparkle.

We're in the final stretch, only ten minutes left of the movie, when her lids start to flutter shut. Deer's head begins to loll forward before snapping back. She squints her eyes and furrows her brows as she attempts to remain awake and focused on the movie. When the end credits finally begin to load, her eyes close and stay that way.

I let out a deep chuckle.

"Shh," she mumbles.

"Tired?"

"A little." She tips over, curling into a fetal position on the couch cushion.

I reach forward and shut off the TV before giving her shoulder a nudge. "You plan on staying out here?"

"Maybe."

The corner of my mouth quirks up. "Suit yourself."

I begin to stand up when her hand shoots out and wraps around my wrist. "Carry me?"

"Seriously?"

Her hand tightens. "Please," she whines.

I let out a sigh, running my eyes over her body. "Fine." I take a second before bracing my arms and reaching down to scoop her up. Deer snuggles closer to my chest as I carry her to my bedroom.

She is such a princess.

A princess who fits perfectly against me.

The door to Aleks' streaming room cracks open as I pass it, and we both freeze. He blinks at me a few times before his gaze dips to Deer, back up to me, and then down to her again. I open my mouth to come up with something, but he just closes the door.

This will be a pain to explain later.

I pick up my pace, kneeing my door open and carefully laying her on my bed. I reach down and smooth her hair out of her face as she snuggles into the mattress. I hesitate for a second, contemplating tucking her under the duvet, before my brain catches up. Rationality crashes down on me like a piano falling from a building, and I take a step back.

Without another word, I spin around and stalk out of my room. It's only when I'm behind Parker's closed door that I give myself a moment to think.

What the fuck am I doing?

Chapter TEN

DEER

G uns point at me.
　　Empty faces surround me.
　　Closing in.
The room gets darker and darker.
My mouth opens to ask for help, to ask for mercy, but nothing comes out.
　I clutch at my throat, scraping at it, begging it to work.
　The guns cock, the clicks echoing like a death sentence.
　My lips continue to move in silence.
　Desperation clogs my lungs.
　Their hands come around me, gripping me tight.
　I thrash against their hold.
　My limbs fight for release.
　I try to scream and scream and—
My body crashes against the floorboards. Pain rico-

chets through my body. My eyes fly open.

The room spins as I adjust to the darkness, my senses slowly returning to me. I push off the floor, my elbow twinging slightly from the fall.

"Fuck." My voice is raspy as it escapes me.

I kneel on the floor, resting my ass on the backs of my heels, and rub my eyes. Dry mascara sticks to my palm, and I let out a groan.

Right. Jackson carried me to bed, and I totally conked out.

My skin is coated in a thin sheen of sweat, and my makeup probably has me looking like the girl from *The Ring*.

The bedroom door bursts open, and I blink up at two haggard yet alert men—both of whom are shirtless. Jackson holds a baseball bat, while Aleks brandishes a switchblade. Their eyes bounce around the room before settling on me.

Jackson is the first one to breach the doorway, dropping to his knees before me. "What happened?" His free hand twitches, torn between reaching out to me or fisting at his side.

"I fell out of bed."

"You were screaming like a banshee." Aleks cocks his brow as he flicks his blade closed.

"You know, switchblades are illegal in California." My throat burns through the words.

Fuck.

I must've yelled through my nightmare.

Fuuuuuck.

"Don't deflect." Jackson reaches out and grips my chin

101

between this thumb and forefinger, turning my head toward him.

This time, when my throat goes dry, it's not because of the apparent rock metal solo screaming session I had. My focus wavers as I am forced to look into the inky depths of his eyes.

"I'm not deflecting."

"Oh?" He releases my chin and runs a finger up my arm. "Then why do you have the chills?"

"Because you're touching me, you weirdo."

With what little energy I have, I shrug out of his grip and begin to crawl my way to his bathroom. My hazy mind has one clear mission: deny everything.

He lets out a loud sigh. "I'll deal with this; you head back to bed."

"You sure?" I can hear Aleks flicking his switchblade back and forth.

"Yeah, no need for two babysitters."

"Rude," I mutter.

It's only once I cross the threshold of the door and my knees hit the tiles that I force myself to stand, using the counter to support my weight. My eyes squeeze tight as I turn on the lights. When I open them, I catch Jackson's reflection in the mirror as he leans in the doorway.

"Want to tell me the truth?"

"I *want* to take a shower."

"Okay."

I grit my teeth together and let out a groan before summoning all my strength to shove the bathroom door closed. With him comfortably out of sight, I let out a sigh.

It takes longer than necessary for me to remove my

stale contacts and my oxidized makeup. I barely remember to tug on a shower cap before throwing myself under the hot spray of the shower.

My ass sinks to the floor. It's not comfortable; the grooves in the tiles leave imprints on my bare ass. But I don't care. I let the hot water cascade around me as I stare blankly at the glass.

I thought the nightmares had stopped since coming here.

I thought leaving my apartment behind meant leaving my pain.

I didn't count on my ghosts following me.

Dammit.

My knees come up to my chest, and I rest my forehead against them.

I hate it. Hate that it's still affecting me. Hate that it's ruling my life. Hate that I'm still so weak.

Once it feels like my body has successfully turned into a burnt prune, I shut off the shower and cocoon a giant, soft green towel around my body.

My emotional battery is at nineteen percent—definitely in the red.

I lose another two percent of said battery life just applying my moisturizer.

My hand rests on the doorknob and my heartbeat begins to pound in my ears as I slowly twist it open. I only let it crack an inch before peering out. When I confirm there is no Hulk taking up residence in the bedroom, I take a step out and make my way to the bed.

I sit on the edge for a few minutes in nothing but my towel, staring at the ground as a light buzzing runs through my brain, the remnants of the nightmare still wreaking havoc on my nervous system.

Why am I such a mess?

Begrudgingly, I switch on a lamp and try to find my phone.

"Dammit."

I must've left it in the living room.

My head throbs and I contemplate throwing in the towel—figuratively and literally. Instead, I muster up the little energy I have left and poke my head out into the apartment.

All hope fizzles out when I spot a light coming from the kitchen.

I'd really hoped he'd given up and gone to bed.

Maybe, if I walk quietly enough, he won't hear me.

Gripping my towel tighter, I take a tentative step into the hallway. Jackson's back is to me, fiddling with something on the stove. Well, I'm eighty percent sure it is him. Without my contacts in, he looks like a misshapen blob from this far. One of the downfalls of being near-sighted.

I tiptoe my way to the couch and squint, trying (and failing) to make out shapes in the dim light—praying that my phone is somewhere easy to grab.

My jaw clenches as a sweep of the coffee table reveals nothing.

I begin stuffing my hands between the couch cushions, but there is nothing except crumbs and kernels.

Where the hell is it?

I get on my knees, pressing my body flush against the floor as I stretch my arm under the couch as far as it can go without my shoulder dislocating.

"Looking for this, Sparkles?"

I freeze, hoping that if I don't move, I'll just disappear into the ground.

There's a light thud, and I raise my head to see my phone bounce on the couch cushion beside me. The sparkly wrist charm dangles like a taunt.

"Thanks."

I sit up to look at Jackson, but he's already walking back to the kitchen. A river bubbles deep in my stomach at his retreating form, urging me to follow.

"What are you doing?"

"Making warm honey milk."

I scoff. "I'm not a child."

He turns around and looks at me over his shoulder briefly. "Who said it was for you?"

My mouth pops open as a flush creeps up my cheeks.

"Kidding. It'll help you sleep. If you want it?"

My chest sparks briefly, like a match that's too old to truly catch fire.

"I mean, if you've already gone to the trouble." I try to come off nonchalant.

Looping my phone around my wrist, I pad over to the dimly lit kitchen, hauling myself onto one of the barstools.

Jackson grabs a mug from one of the cabinets and slowly pours the saucepan of milk into it. He turns around, and just when I think he is about to offer it to me, he pauses.

The front of his brows pull together in the slightest crinkle, and I see something close to shock filter through his gaze. After a beat, it's gone, and he slides the mug across the counter.

"What?"

"You look different."

My hands halt inches away from the mug and my blood turns to ice. A thousand rocks drop into the depths of my gut. Within mere seconds, I have my hands covering my bare face.

"Oh my Gods."

"I said different, not ugly."

"That's not the point."

I can't believe I slipped up.

Through the slight gap between my hands, I see him come to rest his hip on the edge of the island. He crosses his arms over his chest, but I can't see his face—I can't see his reaction.

Self-consciousness eats away at me like hungry piranhas trapped in an aquarium. I was so caught up in sneaking out to grab my phone that it didn't even click that I'd removed my Deer mask.

Jackson's knuckles knock against my own. "Deer. What are you doing?"

"Hiding."

"Why?"

"Because I don't have any makeup on." I don't afford him any more of an explanation, not when it sounds…silly.

It feels like a million bees are buzzing under my skin as panic begins to take root. He's going to see the truth I hide beneath my carefully painted lies. All my fears will be written in the hazel color of my eyes, the crystal blue barrier no longer hiding me. It's hard to pretend when you're practically naked.

"Your milk's going to get cold."

"I like cold milk."

He lets out a sigh. "I'm not looking at you."

"Promise?"

"Promise."

I crack a peek between two of my fingers, and sure enough, he has turned his back to me. It still feels like a thousand needles are being pricked into my skin, but they're blunt needles now.

My shaky hands grip the mug before me, grateful for some sort of stability. I slowly raise it to my lips and take a sip of the sweet, warm liquid—it tastes like being wrapped in a soft, knitted blanket. It barely scratches the surface of my unease, but it begins to drip into the cracks, filling me with a touch of comfort.

"Do you want to talk about it?" Jackson's deep voice breaks the silence.

"My makeup is like your masks: without it, I'm not Deer."

"I meant your nightmare, but that's a good start, too."

My chest pangs with regret at revealing a shard of myself that he didn't ask for.

It's an effort to keep my grip on the mug when all I want to do is shut down, to sink into the abyss.

"Deer?"

"Yeah?"

"I'm trying here, but I need you to respond so I know you're okay."

"Can't we just sit in silence?"

The sound of me taking another sip of milk crackles through the air as I wait for his response.

"Shield?"

"I thought you wanted silence?"

Annoyance flashes through my veins, but it's quickly

replaced with a short laugh that tumbles past my lips. And though I can't see his face, I can see the way his cheeks move back, almost in a mimicking smile.

"Come on." He pushes off the counter and makes his way out the balcony door.

Like a string is connecting my body to his, I follow the pull and trace his path with my own soft footsteps—careful not to spill my mug in the process.

This late at night, the air carries a bite in the breeze. The hairs on my arms stand up as I'm reminded that, for some Gods forsaken reason, I'm still in my damn towel. I really wasn't thinking anything through tonight.

Jackson leans against the railing, and I come to rest next to him, our position a mirror of the other morning.

The sky is a deep midnight blue, bordering on black, with hazy clouds. The darkness calms my nerves in the knowledge that even if Jackson were to glance over at me, I would be hidden in the shadows.

I can hear a plane landing somewhere, but I have no hope trying to figure out where it might be when I can only see a foot in front of me. The city lights shine dimly in the distance, but to my broken eyes they just look like a muddle of sparkles across the dark expanse.

A cube of ice settles in the center of my chest, slowly melting and dripping into my system. The city is so large around me, and yet I'm stuck in a small corner, refusing to leave out of fear. I can't even begin to understand the person I have slowly become—someone so at odds with who I should be, someone who fears living when they should be thriving.

"I couldn't sleep for a week after we got swatted."

I drain the last of my milk, a thick pool of honey at the bottom coating my tongue as I silently listen to the deep rumble of his words.

"None of us could. I'm pretty sure I made Aleksander watch a million reruns of *FMA Brotherhood* as we survived off delivery pizza and ramen for a few weeks. Parker even flew back to London for a month while we got our security sorted."

"Really?"

"What? You think Aleksander just keeps a switchblade by his bedside for fun?"

"He could be using it as a letter opener."

I feel Jackson give me a look from the corner of his eye, and I bite my bottom lip to stop myself from making any more snarky remarks.

"Point is, you can talk to us."

My nails tap against the ceramic in an odd staccato.

"Or you can just let it eat you alive, up to you."

I pause, pressing my lips together as I glare up at him.

This time, he looks down at me and his stare drowns out all the sound around us. He reaches a hand out, tugging on a loose wave of hair. "There's nothing wrong with wearing a mask. I would know. Just make sure you take the time to breathe because it can become stifling back there, and you don't want to suffocate. Sometimes, you have to let people in so you can take a break for fresh air." He releases my hair and turns to head back inside without so much as another look. "Don't forget to lock the door behind you."

My lips part, tempted to ask him to wait, to stay, but the words get stuck in my throat. I am already imposing on him, living in his apartment, sleeping in his bed. I don't need to take any more from him.

But my guilt is quickly replaced with regret as I'm left standing in the cold, alone.

Always alone.

I feel too exposed out here, awareness prickling its way up my body. But when I head back into the quiet apartment and lock the balcony door, the resounding click echoes in my bones, hollowing me out. My ears hum with the sound of a thousand dragonflies as I stare absently through the glass door, a million thoughts crashing into me at once.

I have no idea what I'm doing anymore.

Everything is going wrong.

My breathing picks up as my brain feels like it is being plunged underwater.

"Deer?"

A strong hand curls around my own, which is still clutching the door handle. I blink and startle back, my shoulders bumping into a hard chest. That strong hand comes up to curl around my bicep and steadies me.

"Are you okay?"

The pure concern in his voice, it's something I've never heard before, and it cracks a shard open within my battered, armored soul.

"No."

The word is barely a whisper through my lips, but I know he heard me because his grip tightens on my bicep ever so slightly. Without saying anything else, he pulls me against his bare chest, his arms wrapping around me.

My brain short-circuits.

His skin feels hot against my cold body, and I let that

warmth seep into me. I let it spread through my system and fill in the broken cracks of loneliness and guilt and fear.

I've always acknowledged that Jackson is massive, but never as much as in this very moment. I feel tiny compared to him, and the way his body cocoons mine makes me feel safe—the safest I've felt in weeks. Which is weird, considering how at odds we normally are with each other.

Jackson and I aren't close, but right now there's a connection in the way my heart begins to alter its beat to match the rhythm echoing through his chest. The steady thump grounds me.

He doesn't say anything else as he rubs soft circles against my skin.

Just this once, I'll let myself accept the comfort.

Just this once.

I'll let someone into my shiny castle to see how it is crumbling inside.

Chapter ELEVEN

JACKSON

MOM

Don't forget your date tonight

It's at Chá House.

Jackson?

??

My phone begins to buzz with an incoming call, and I quickly wipe my hands on a towel before swiping it open. I tuck it between my ear and shoulder as I crack open another egg and separate the whites into the clear bowl before me.

"Morning, I saw your texts. I haven't forgotten."

"Then why didn't you respond?"

"Because I'm cooking."

She pauses before letting out a resigned sigh. "All right. What are you making?"

"Soufflé pancakes."

"I love those!" My little sister's voice trills through the phone. "Why can't you come home and make some for me?"

"Angela." I recognize my mother's warning tone. "*Nei jou gen mut?* Why aren't you dressed yet?"

"I can't find my music book."

"I already packed it in your bag. Now, go put your dress on. I won't have you be late."

I laugh to myself as I begin to beat the egg whites to a stiff peak. I haven't lived at home since the day I left for college, but I still miss being around my family. Thankfully, they only live an hour away, so I'm able to visit them often. I can't imagine living any farther from them—I don't know how Parker does it with his family in England most of the year.

"How are the dates going? I think tonight will be a good one. Everyone at your father's hospital says she's lovely and you know she comes from a good family."

The question catches me off guard and a groan escapes my lips in the distraction.

She turns that warning tone over to me. "Jackson."

"They're going fine." It's not a complete lie. The dates aren't horrible, and the women are fine...just not to my taste.

"Anyone promising?"

"Not really."

I can hear the disappointment in her long, heavy sigh.

"Good morning."

I spin around to find Deer strolling leisurely into the kitchen, her hair perfectly curled and her makeup back in place. There isn't a trace of the shadows that marred her features last night—no hint of the demons lurking beneath the surface. They've been successfully covered with layers of sparkly pink blush.

She hops onto a bar stool with a smile, and I just frown. It's clear she is going to pretend like last night never happened.

My gut roils with a low flame.

"Jackson?"

Fuck. My mom.

"Yeah?"

"Who was that? Stephanie?"

My eyes skate over the sexy spitfire who most certainly is *not* my roommate's girlfriend. The woman I held in my arms last night. The same woman I woke up dreaming about with my cock stiff as hell.

"Uh, yeah. I'm making everyone breakfast, so…"

"Okay, okay. I'll let you go. Just promise me you'll give the girl tonight a proper chance. It's important to your *baba* that you don't mess this one up."

"I promise. Bye."

"Bye."

I toss my phone onto the marble counter and pop an espresso pod into the machine. I can feel Deer's eyes on me, tracking my every movement.

The fuck am I supposed to say to her?

"Whatcha making?"

"Pancakes."

She hums in approval. "Can you make mine with strawberries?"

I glance at her over my shoulder. "It doesn't mix in well with the soufflé mixture."

"Really?" She gives a dramatic pout, drawing my attention to her lower lip. "That sucks."

I can think of something I want her to suck.

Fuck.

No.

I drag my eyes away and turn my head back so she doesn't fill my vision anymore.

This is not cool.

I reach into the fridge and grab the small carton of strawberry milk I bought yesterday, opening and pouring it into a glass mug before dumping the fresh espresso in. I take a metal straw to swirl everything together and then slide the glass across the island to Deer, avoiding any direct eye contact.

"Here."

She blinks at the glass for a second before taking it between her hands. "How'd you know I liked my coffee like this?"

I shrug, turning back to pop a new pod into the coffee machine. "You posted about it."

She chuckles something that sounds a lot like the word "fanboy" under her breath. I'm tempted to look at her, to see what expression she is wearing, but I stop myself. I'm digging myself into a hole, and I need to stop before it becomes too deep and I can't escape.

The sound of the metal straw clinking around the glass echoes into the silence, and I throw my focus into the pancakes, making sure they are perfect, bouncy circles.

Bouncy, like her—

God-fucking-dammit.

"Tastes good."

The corner of my mouth ticks up at her approval.

I flip the first pancake—arguably, always the worst one—onto a plate and set it aside for myself before starting on the second one. While it cooks, I grab some raspberries out of the fridge and drop them in a saucer with some sugar and lemon juice. The second pancake looks perfect, so I plop it onto a new plate and drizzle the raspberry coulee on top with a spray of whipped cream.

I slide the dish over to Deer, who shoots her hand out to curl around mine before I have a chance to let go. Her soft skin teases against my own, and it forces my gaze to meet hers.

"Stop. This is for me?" There's a tone of incredulity that matches the wide saucer look of her eyes.

"We don't have strawberries."

"I—" Her gaze softens. "Thank you. It looks pretty."

She releases my hand and picks up her fork and knife, but I remain glued in my position as I watch her cut a small triangle and pop it in her mouth. Deer squeezes her eyes and lets out a small moan, curling her hand under her chin. "Oh my Gods, that's amazing." She quickly cuts another piece and moans in pleasure as she chews on it.

I hate everything.

I turn around, readjusting my twitching dick in my sweatpants.

"This is the best thing I've had in my mouth. It's like an orgasmic cloud."

I think she's actually trying to kill me. Why does she have to talk like that? It's doing nothing to help my situation.

I busy myself with the next pancake, but my foot starts tapping against the tiles as she continues to moan happily behind me.

"How do you cook so well?"

"My mom taught me."

"Damn, you have to give her my thanks. I'd kill to have this every day. You're gonna make someone a *very* happy girlfriend someday."

There's the word again.

Girlfriend.

I work my jaw back and forth as a scene forms in my mind—one of a woman smiling up at me as I bring her breakfast in bed. Her eyes are a shining blue and her lips a soft pink that matches the color of her hair.

"Something smells good." Aleks' voice pulls me out of my deluded daydream, reminding me to flip my pancake before it burns. "I'll take mine with chocolate chips, chef."

"I'm not taking requests." I turn and glare at Aleks as he rounds the corner and walks towards the kitchen, yawning.

"Come on, you always make mine with chocolate chips. Don't be a bitch, dude."

Aleks claps me on the shoulder, almost making me drop my pancake, before he steals the small mug filled with espresso from the machine.

"That's mine," I growl.

"You going to give me chocolate chips?" He raises a brow in challenge, holding the cup in front of his lips. A smirk curls at the corner of his mouth.

"You don't even like black coffee."

"I don't like plain pancakes either."

He sticks his tongue out, hovering the tip over my precious espresso. My jaw locks and I let out a deep sigh through my nose before opening the cabinet and aggressively grabbing the packet of chocolate chips.

"Knew you loved me." He tosses me a shit-eating grin, placing my mug next to the stovetop.

"Fuck off." I scoop the batter into the skillet, forming two pancakes, and sprinkle them with some of the chocolate chips. I down my espresso while I wait for them to cook, letting the bitterness burn my tongue.

"Here you go, princess."

I slide the piping hot pancakes to my annoying roommate, using just enough force that he has to make a conscious effort to stop them from toppling off the island and onto his sweatpants. He looks up at me and pauses for a brief second before tilting his head to the side slightly.

"What about my chocolate syrup?"

I run my tongue over my teeth before grabbing the syrup from the fridge and slapping it onto the marble.

"You know, he's a big softie," Aleks whispers to Deer as he drenches his pancakes in syrup. "Looks like he's going to rip your head off, but really, he just wants a little tender loving."

"Oh, I know." She nods in agreement.

I cock my head and give them the middle finger with a tight smile before turning back to grab my pancakes.

"Did you know he also cooks for Parker all the time? Makes sure he eats and stays alive. Jackson's almost as much of a mother hen as Sydney is."

"Keep spewing shit and I'll put hair remover in your shampoo."

"Hey, I'm just improving your reputation, man."

"My reputation is fine." I take a seat—reluctantly—next to Aleks and reach across him for the whipped cream. It takes practiced patience to not hit him with the can, maybe knock some sense into him.

"I mean, your rep could be better." Deer sucks on her strawberry coffee. "Syd's been worried."

"What do you mean?"

"She's nervous you're gonna snap on one of these dates. Ya know, like at some point you'll just get so sick of it, and some poor girl will end up crying in the middle of a restaurant and she'll have to chase down the media to kill it."

"This dude? Snap?" Aleks snorts. "Never. Jackson doesn't lose control."

I grunt in agreement, chewing down a piece of pancake.

"Oh, come on. No one's in control all the time."

"I've known him since we were in high school." Aleks points his knife in my direction. "He's a control master, Deer. Disciplined to the bone. Wakes up at 6 a.m. for the gym every day like the good little gym bro he is."

"Gods. No wonder he acts like he has a stick up his ass sometimes," she mutters under her breath.

"No, I don't."

"Sure," she drawls, widening her eyes all doe-like as

she daintily finishes off the last raspberry on her plate. "All that stress is what jacks up your muscles."

"Trust me, I have plenty of methods to relieve my stress other than the gym, Sparkles."

"And plenty of screaming women to attest to that," Aleks chimes in. "Actually, maybe not screaming, considering your methods."

Deer's grip on her fork loosens as a pink flush breaks out on her neck.

Satisfaction fills me at seeing her a little off-kilter. It is so hard to break through that perfectly crafted happy-go-lucky mask she always wears.

I push off the counter and grab her empty plate along with my own, giving her a sharklike grin as I meet her gaze. "I'll spare the details for your delicate ears. Not exactly morning appropriate."

She blinks, those long lashes fluttering against her cheeks before a confident laugh leaves her pouty lips. "You think someone who looks like me is vanilla?" Deer hops off her stool and tosses a lock of hair over her shoulder, pure challenge in her eyes. "Babes, I've tried all the flavors in the candy shop." Without another word, she turns on her heels and disappears back to my bedroom.

"Think she's bluffing?" Aleks asks, sidling up beside me to drop his plate in the dishwasher.

I glance over my shoulder at the empty hallway, a dark curiosity weaving its way through me.

"Guess we'll have to see."

Chapter TWELVE

DEER

"Oh my Gods."

"What?" Lee whips her head around to search the restaurant. When she sucks in a gasp, I know she's spotted the man and woman. "Stop. He brought her here? Fancy." Her eyes are wide as saucers as she turns back to me.

"Agree. It's an intimate choice," I hum, taking a large sip of my second Hong Kong Iced Tea of the night. "Wait, does he even decide the places he goes if they're blind dates?"

Lee's brows furrow. "Good point. Probably not."

I gnaw on the end of my straw as I continue to sneak glances at the couple in the back booth, who were previously hidden by a party of twelve that just left.

"How long have they been here? I didn't see them

come in."

I shrug. "I dunno. He was still at the apartment when you picked me up."

"See, aren't you glad I dragged you out?" She angles her wine glass toward me. "Told you it would be worth it."

"You didn't drag me."

"Mmm, my thirty back-to-back text messages and four voice notes beg to differ."

"You're being dramatic. It was three voice notes, not four."

Lee snorts as she cranes her neck to watch Jackson and his blind date. "What do you think they're talking about?"

"Something boring," I mumble around my straw.

As much as I try not to, I can't help but continue watching them.

"Oh, she's def interested," Lee comments as the girl laughs and tucks a piece of hair behind her ear. "Doesn't he normally dip from his dates within like ten minutes?"

"Supposedly." I blatantly bite down on the straw, grinding it between my molars.

"Death glare, much?"

I release the mangled straw and flick my gaze to Lee who has switched her attention to me. I roll my eyes with a tense smile. "That's my concentration face."

"That is not the face you make when you're trying to decide which villager to live on your island. That's the face you make when the villainess appears in your dating sims."

"Mean."

"Just saying." She reaches forward and tears one of the red bean buns in half before taking a large bite.

I follow suit, ripping open one of the taro buns and

shoving half into my mouth.

My eyes narrow as I watch Jackson nod at whatever the girl is babbling about. I didn't even know he was going out on another blind date tonight.

Not that he owes me that, but you would think it might have come up when I told him I was going to dinner with Lee. He'd grilled me for a solid five minutes about whether Lee's security was coming with us and how long I'd be gone for. He wanted to make sure I was being safe—as if I wasn't already freaking nervous as it was about leaving the damn apartment.

But as always, Lee is my weakness. She's the only person who can get me out of my comfort zone and into functioning society. Plus, this is one of my favorite restaurants, so there is a level of familiarity here that makes me less nervous.

I polish off my drink, sucking on nothing but remnants of ice residue as I continue glaring at the couple. Jackson's attention wanes from his date. He scans the restaurant, gaze colliding with mine. A fleck of ice flies through the straw and goes right into the back of my throat, and I let out a choking cough.

When I look back up, he's still staring at me.

Shit.

His date takes notice, and she swivels her head, her eyes darting around.

Double shit.

I raise my hand to cover my face as discreetly as possible as I turn to Lee.

"What are you doing?"

"They're looking at us," I whisper under my breath.

"Why are you whispering? They can't hear you from here."

"You're whispering, too!"

"Because they're looking at us!"

I spread two of my fingers apart and chance a quick peek. The blood drains from my face as Jackson raises a hand and waves me over. He keeps looking back and forth between me and his date, saying something that is causing her to cross her arms.

Mm. Nope.

I want zero part in whatever is happening.

Taking a deep breath, I sit up straight and allow a tight smile to thread across my face as I raise both hands to wave them side to side in a "no thank you" gesture.

Our silent exchange is blissfully interrupted as our waitress returns to our table.

"Hi, can I get either of you anything else tonight? One last drink, maybe?"

"No!" The word basically catapults out of my mouth, stunning the woman. Shit. I soften my face and give her a placating smile. "Sorry, no. We're good. Just the check, thank you."

The woman nods her head, collecting our empty plates. "Okay, I'll be right back."

I refuse to look back at Jackson's booth. Instead, I busy myself by grabbing my handbag and sifting through it for one of my credit cards.

"Deer."

"Yeah?" I chance a glance over at Lee, who has gone stock-still.

"They're coming over," she whispers through gritted

teeth.

"What?" I'm torn between looking over and throwing my body under the table. "What do you mean?"

"I mean, they are walking over here."

"Why?"

"How should I know!"

Oh my Gods.

Fuck it.

I grab two hundred-dollar bills that are floating around in my mess of a handbag. It has to be enough to cover our meal and drinks.

I slap the notes onto the table and then grab Lee's wrist as I stand up.

"Let's g—" The words die on my lips as my eyes meet a pair of deep black pools.

"Babe." Jackson's hand rests on my right shoulder. His thumb rubs my skin in a weirdly reassuring pattern.

Babe?

His date pops her head around Jackson's giant form, her slick black hair swaying to the side. Her perfectly plucked brows pinch together as she clutches her hands to her chest.

"Hi, I am *so* sorry about all of this. Jackson explained everything."

What?

"I'm Grace." She holds out a hand.

My mind begins to whirl, but I allow myself to slide my mask back on, lifting my chin as a dazzling smile softens across my face. I reach forward and shake her hand.

"Deer."

Her grip tightens as she looks deep into my eyes, sincerity bleeding out. "I completely understand the struggle. I dated my last boyfriend for a year before I told my parents, and they still took forever to accept him. We broke up because he couldn't deal with the pressure from them."

I'm so lost. Why is she being nice?

"I told Jackson he should probably just tell them. It really helps with the stress, and *Lei yi* would have his back. From the way she raves about him, I know she'll get everyone else on board. And you seem really sweet." She pats my hand. "Seriously, there's no sense in Jackson being dragged around on pointless dates when he's already got such a cute girlfriend."

Lee lets out a choking noise.

My. How the tables have turned.

"Thank you," I smile, pulling my hand from her grip. The practiced persona of Deer, the darling of the streaming world, comes spilling forward as I play my part.

I curl myself into Jackson, placing my hand on the center of his chest. The hand he has lazing on my shoulder halts, and I feel the rest of his body stiffen. I stop myself from smirking, pushing my sweetness dial even higher.

"It's been so hard with him going on these dates. Absolutely rips me apart." I raise my head, angling it to look up at him. Gods, why is he so freaking tall? I can trace the entire outline of his jaw from down here. "But I know I can trust him. We just have that bond, don't we, babes?"

Jackson looks down at me, sliding his hand from my shoulder down the length of my arm to rest above my elbow. Goosebumps break across my skin as he gives my arms a light squeeze, something warm stirring low within me. The corners of his lips tilt up in a small smile. And while I know it's just the one he uses in public, it still throws me off-kilter.

"Of course."

I can feel the words rumble through his chest, and I'm frozen, caught in his gaze.

"Well, I wish you guys the best of luck. And don't worry, I'll keep everything above board when I see your dad at the hospital. Promise."

"Thanks, Grace."

"No worries. See you!"

Grace gives a sweet wave as she walks away, and my brain finally starts to come down from the high.

"Okay. What the heck is going on?" Lee pokes her finger into my hip.

"Ow." I step away from Jackson, ungluing my body from his to glare at her.

She cocks her split eyebrow and crosses her arms.

"Ask him." I shrug my shoulder back toward Jackson.

"It's not a big deal." The indifference of his tone matches how cold my skin suddenly feels without his contact.

"Did you or did you not tell that girl that Deer's your girlfriend?" Lee takes a step forward into our space, trying to look menacing. Except we are the same height, and it really doesn't do much to deter Jackson when he is a solid foot taller than both of us.

"I just needed an excuse to cut the date short."

"And you decided to use me?"

"You're the one who offered, Sparkles."

"And you're the one who made it sound like you'd rather throw yourself off a cliff than pretend to date me."

"It was a onetime use," he shrugs.

"Onetime, my—"

"Hi, sorry for the wait. Here's the check." Our waitress finally makes her return.

"Right," I reach for the two bills I'd thrown on the table.

"Here."

I whip my head back to see Jackson tapping his phone on the POS system.

"What are you—"

"Thank you, have a lovely evening." The waitress smiles and leaves us.

Jackson tucks his phone back into his pocket and lazily saunters away in the opposite direction, to the exit of the restaurant.

"Hey, we're not done here," I call out.

He just raises a hand and gives me a pitiful wave.

"Gods dammit," I huff, shoving the money back in my bag and grabbing my jacket as I stalk after him.

"What's he talking about?" Lee jogs up beside me.

"The other day, Stevie suggested he pretend to date someone to get his family off his back. I suggested myself."

"Why would you suggest yourself?"

That's what I would like to know.

I'm just gonna call it a temporary disillusion from being in too close proximity to his hot body. It was easy to distance myself when we only chatted virtually, but now that I am constantly around him, it's making my brain go all mushy.

"Doesn't matter because he said it was an awful idea."

"Clearly, that's not the case."

"Clearly," I mumble.

We catch up to Jackson outside the restaurant, where he has the passenger door to his Jeep open. He nods towards the interior of the car, "Come on. I'm not holding this door open forever."

"What?"

"Home. Unless you've found somewhere else to sleep over the last four hours?"

Gods Dammit.

I shoot Lee an apologetic look. "I'm sorry."

"It's fine." She pulls me into a hug that abates some of my annoyance. "Call me when you get back so we can debrief, 'kay? I'm not letting this go just yet." She waggles a finger before walking off.

"Come on, Sparkles."

I groan, glaring at him before hauling myself into the passenger seat as he closes the door behind me.

How did this happen?

I stare out the window, watching as Lee gets into her own car and wishing I'd made up some valid excuse to follow her. I should've said we were having a girl's night and I was sleeping over.

"Buckle up."

Jackson's deep timbre pulls me out of my haze as he starts up the car.

"Why did you pay?" I ask, fastening my seat belt. "I'm perfectly capable of covering my own dinner."

"Consider it a thank you for your service."

"A service I thought you didn't want to purchase."

Jackson runs a hand down his face, like I'm the one annoying him when he brought me into this whole situation.

"Look, the date was going badly."

"Seemed like she was having a great time," I grumble, remembering the way she had been laughing with him.

"Exactly."

"You've lost me."

Jackson sighs.

"Look, I know you're a man of few words, but I'm really going to need you to spell this out for me, big boy."

"Don't call me that," he grunts.

"I'm waiting."

"Grace works at my father's hospital; I couldn't exactly ditch her in a shitty way. It would've gotten back to them, and I would've been in an even worse situation. The Wangs are close with my family. My mom even called me to make sure I made a good impression on this date and that I not screw anything up." We stop at a red light, and he runs his hands through his hair. "Grace was a little too into the whole idea, and I didn't have many options until you showed up."

"Oh."

"Yeah. Like I said, it's just a one off."

"Sure."

His dismissal burns.

We sit in silence the entire ride back, light music filtering through the speakers as I fidget with the lace on the edge of my skirt. All the while, I can't stop myself from sneaking small glances at him, some part of me disappointed that this is where the farce ends. The same part of me that lit up when he held my arm and pulled me close, that broken part of me that seems to be slowly stitching itself back together the longer I'm around him.

The situation might have been fake, but the way my heart beats is very real.

Chapter THIRTEEN

JACKSON

"Hey, just wanted to let you know I'm popping out for a bit. Ya know, in case you can't find me and think I've been kidnapped by mafia men who helicoptered onto the roof to sell me for ransom."

I swivel around in my gaming chair to stare at Deer. She has one hand braced on my doorframe, the other on the handle, as she leans the top half of her body into my streaming room. A fluffy white purse hangs from one of her elbows, and her pink hair is styled in two elaborate space buns with two small braids framing the front of her face.

I want to tug on those braids, see that frustration light up her eyes. The same frustration I saw last night when I pulled her into my date.

"Where are you going?"

"Nail salon." She releases her grip on the handle and proceeds to wiggle her fingers at me. "They're too long and messing with Parker's keyboard. I was hoping to delay it a little longer, but I'm going to go nuts if I keep accidentally hitting the W key every time I go to tap S."

"Okay, give me a second to save."

I spin back around and pull up the save screen to make sure I save over the right file. I am in the middle of completing a quest and have to make sure I don't save over the wrong file in case things go pear-shaped and I have to revert to a previous save.

I'm surprised to see her going out on her own. The first four days she was here, she barely even left my room. Lee managed to get her out last night, and I guess that's made her feel more comfortable. It's a good thing. I was worried the swatting had really shattered something within her, especially with the way she screamed in her dreams.

"Oh, no need. Syd texted me Francis' number and said I could use him while I was staying here. Said it would be safer than calling a rideshare. Which is kinda valid, as much as I don't wanna admit it."

I frown.

Sure, it made sense to give her access to our private driver, especially since her car was still parked at her place. Syd's been using Francis to get around Cali for years now, but that doesn't make me any less annoyed at the situation.

Quickly saving my game, I turn off my monitor and twist back in time to see Deer tossing me a grin and a half-assed wave as she spins around on a pair of those ridiculously high heels she seems to own a million of and leaves.

"Bye," her voice trills.

"Hang on." I shoot out of my chair and stalk after her with a few long strides. "Are you sure that's safe?"

She cocks a brow up at me. "He's your driver."

"Yeah, but you've been swatted twice in the last two weeks."

"Thanks for the reminder."

"Francis isn't trained to be a bodyguard."

"And you are?" She uses one of her pointed nails to purposefully press the elevator call button.

"I work out."

"And you have the body to show for it, but I don't really care." Her bright blue eyes trail down my bare arms appreciatively. The elevator chimes as the doors open. "Catch ya later, hot stuff."

"Wait." My body moves on its own, my arm shooting out to bar her from entering the elevator.

"Seriously, Shield? I can't be late. There's only a fifteen-minute grace period," she huffs, stomping one of her feet.

"Just give me a second."

"One," she bites out before attempting to duck under my arm. I use the movement to snake said arm around her waist and spin her into me. Her body locks up at the contact briefly before she tries to push away.

"Deer."

"What?"

"I said wait." The bite of my words has her pausing, a flash of heat passing through them so quickly that I think maybe I saw wrong. "I'm putting on shoes and coming with you."

Her lips purse and lids narrow for a beat before she

tsks, her body going slack with submission. "Fine."

I slowly release my grip on her, watching her for any sudden movements. Woman is like a caged rabbit.

I jog back to my room and throw on a pair of Jordans and a hoodie before shoving my wallet into my back pocket with a face mask. When I return, Deer is still there. Her obedience to my words turns over in my mind—a curiosity slowly stitching itself together and causing my dick to twitch.

As soon as I step foot into the elevator with her, she begins aggressively pressing the button for the private garage level.

"You know that doesn't make it go any quicker."

"If I miss this appointment because of you, I swear to the Gods."

For someone who promised sunshine and rainbows, she tosses threats around like free condoms at a college health center.

The elevator rockets down the sixty floors, and Deer practically skips out the second the doors inch open.

"Francis," she chirps with a smile. The spindly man stands by the back door, holding it open for us, and she gives him a giant hug. "Thank you for making time for me."

What the fuck? She's never greeted me with that much enthusiasm.

Francis gives her a brief pat on the head with his free hand. "Of course, miss. I have some peach sparkling water in the center console for you per your request."

"You're the best!" she gushes as she hops into the BMW.

I enter on the other side as Francis gets into the driver's seat and starts the car up to begin the winding exit of the apartment complex.

The sound of Deer popping open her sparkling water cracks against the silence before a quiet fizz hisses out.

"You want some?" She tips the can toward me.

"No."

"Then quit side-eying me."

I let out a huff and turn my body away from her, pulling out my phone and opening a gaming app to pass the time. I don't understand this woman. Her emotions change more often than the wind.

I shouldn't be surprised though. She said her makeup was a mask, and that is clearly the case.

"Hey, what's up?"

I glance at Deer to see her shoving her phone between her ear and shoulder before she riffles through her handbag.

"Mm, I'm fine. Just headed to the nail salon. Thanks for checking in though."

She pulls out a lip gloss and swipes on the sparkly pink color. My attention zeroes in on her plush lips, a thirst growing within me. I don't know what's going on with me.

At first, I thought I was just drawn to her because of a sense of protective duty, like how the guys and I are with Lee—but it's becoming something more than that. She sucks me into her orbit without even trying.

When I look at Deer, there's nothing PG about the way my brain conjures up scenarios of stripping her bare. Even now, I see those lips and instantly imagine the way they would look pursed around my cock.

"I appreciate it, Rick, but don't worry, I'm being safe. Shield is with me."

My hackles rise at the sound of another man's name slipping from her tongue.

Deer laughs at something the person on the other side of the phone says, and my upper lip curls slightly.

I seriously need to get my shit together.

I flip my gaze back to my phone and force myself to get lost in the game, zoning out anything and everything with regard to the woman next to me.

It works for a while, the LA traffic buzzing around me as I focus on shooting my enemies.

That is until a tendril of pink hair suddenly dangles in my periphery.

"That *Kill Strike*?" Deer's sweet tone shatters through my concentration like a hammer on glass.

"Does it look like *Kill Strike*?" My words come off a little gruff, my earlier annoyance still peeking through.

She leans closer, her brown sugar scent cloying the air. There is no personal space with her sometimes.

"Mm, yeah it does."

"Then there's your answer."

"Cool. I'm playing *Love Love Passion School 4: The Idol Chapter*. The mobile version isn't as good as the Switch one, but it's still pretty fun." She moves her phone into my line of vision, effectively blocking my phone screen with her otome game.

I'm stuck looking at some anime dude with red hair and a headset mic.

"This guy is the one I think I want my girl to end up with in this playthrough. He is the leader of the rock band, so he is technically one of the harder characters to win over, but I already have three of the five hearts filled. I'm thinking I'll be able to have his storyline done within the next day or so." She doesn't even take a breath before continuing to ramble. "I read on a forum that there's a secret love interest you can unlock once you win each of the original four love interests on hard mode. I think it's going to be the rival lead singer, which would be cool. Although, winning him over will be even harder than any of the others, but I like the challenge. Hang on, let me see if I can show you…" she trails off, her delicate hands tapping across the small screen until she pulls up some online diary with character profiles. Her nail clicks on the screen as she gestures to the white-blond character. "Ah, there, see? He's the one I think will be the secret love interest."

"Riveting," I drawl, trying to keep up with the bombardment of information she is littering me with.

I like to think I have a pretty good read on Deer; most of the time she is this damn Energizer Bunny, but every once in a while, there is a crack in the wall where I see through to a more muted version of herself. I want to know how much of what she shows to the world is really her. I want to know what side of herself she would show me— just me.

Deer lets out a deep sigh before slumping back in her seat. "You can be a real stick-in-the-mud, ya know. You could at least pretend to be a smidge interested."

"Why?"

"Because you're the one imposing on my nail appointment." She uses her phone to point at me, the little charm attached to the corner swaying. "If you're going to be all

Grumpy Cat, you shoulda stayed home."

I should have.

But I can't stay away.

I'm addicted to her like a finance bro is to his morning coffee.

Fuck. Why do I keep involving myself with her?

"Sorry." The word leaves my lips before I can think better of it.

Deer's mouth closes and her doe eyes blink several times. "It's fine."

"Is it that hard to win the redhead over?" I nod my head toward her phone.

"Aidan," she corrects me before her eyes narrow. "Are you sure you want me to give you the lore? These games get pretty intense. I'm not sure you can keep up; it can be super technical—especially when you play on the hardest mode."

"It can't be that tedious."

She snorts and rolls her eyes. "That's what everyone thinks."

"It's a dating sim." They couldn't be *that* technical, for fuck's sake. You just had to answer the prompts correctly. It was kind of a more basic and less violent version of the choice-based RPGs I've played.

A serpentine smile slides across her face. "Okay, just remember you asked."

She scooches across to the middle seat and proceeds to tuck her left foot under her right thigh, causing her left thigh to plaster against my own. She continues to shift as she gets uncomfortably close, her elbow basically resting against my thigh as she leans over to show me her phone screen.

"All right, so each day is only twenty-four minutes, so you have to try to complete as much as you can within that time. But you only have a certain number of days from when the game starts until it ends. In the case of *Idol Chapter*, there are three months from when the storyline begins until the final concert. Each task you complete takes up time, and even when you move between locations, you lose extra time depending on how far the locations are."

"Currently, I only have a month left until the concert, so I'm a little pressed for time to win those last two hearts from Aidan. The issue is, I can't focus all my time on him because if his bandmates hate me, it causes him to hate me as well. I learned that the hard way during my last playthrough—which I failed," she sighs. "It's why he is the hardest of the four to succeed with."

Deer tucks one of the small pink braids behind her ear before resting her elbow on my thigh, not bothering to hover anymore. At this point, her shoulder is nearly tucked under mine, and there is no discernable space between our bodies.

She might as well just climb onto my fucking lap.

I can barely focus on everything she is explaining, too caught up in the way her fuzzy sweater begins to slip off her shoulder, revealing a lacey pink bra strap and skin covered in a soft smattering of freckles that are barely darker than her skin color—you wouldn't even notice them unless you're this close.

My eyes trace the soft slope of her neck down to the dip at her collarbone. She's wearing another one of those chokers today. This time it has a little metal heart clipped in the center of the black leather.

My dick twitches at the sight of it.

"Don't you agree?" Deer nudges her shoulder backward to get my attention. When it takes more than a second for me to respond, she flicks her eyes up to me and narrows them. "Please tell me you were listening."

"Of course."

The arch of her brow rises. "Oh, really? Then what's your suggestion?"

Shit.

I run my eyes over her phone screen, quickly piecing together the scenario in front of me.

"I wouldn't sneak out to meet him. The note seems like a fake, probably from a rival."

Her eyes turn to slits, and I worry for a second that I read the situation wrong, but she just lets out a disappointed *tsk* and sits up straight. "Yeah, that was my thought."

"We've arrived, miss."

I let out a sigh of relief at Francis' interruption.

I was getting too confused being around her; nothing was making sense anymore. The more time I spend with her, the more sides I get to see, and it muddies the waters of everything I thought I knew about her.

"Thank you, Francis," Deer chirps as we come to a stop in front of a nail salon with a familiar swan logo.

"Of course. I'll be parked here when you need to return."

"Oh Gods, no. It'll be like two hours. Go grab a coffee or something. I'll shoot you a text when I'm almost done." She opens the door and hops out.

"Wait, two hours?"

Chapter

FOURTEEN

JACKSON

I hurriedly exit my side of the car and catch up to her.

Deer heaves open the salon door, causing a little bell to chime announcing our arrival. The chill air inside has a slight chemical scent to it. Several heads turn our way, but Deer doesn't break her stride as she strolls to the station in the back right corner. I avoid all eye contact as I stalk behind like her shadow.

"Amy!" Deer sings as she pulls out a chair and plops into it in front of a short woman, who returns the greeting with a soft smile.

"Hello, Deer. How have you been?"

"Good, good," she reassures, giving the woman her right hand. "Busy, too."

"Mm, I was worried when you canceled last week."

"Oh, no, no. I promise, all's fine. Perfectly peachy."

I genuinely wonder how many times she has spoken that lie these last few weeks.

I wonder if anyone knows just how much she is hiding beneath that sparkly exterior.

Not sure what to do with myself, I hang back and lean against a part of the wall that isn't decked out with various nail polish bottles.

The nail technician pulls out some sort of a drill and begins running it over Deer's nails.

"Do you know what you want to do today?"

"Yeah, I was thinking something kinda like this." Deer pulls something up on her phone with her free hand and brandishes it toward the woman.

"Cute, I like it. Same shape? Or keep it almond?"

"Whichever you think looks best," she shrugs. "I trust you."

Amy nods. Her gaze slips to me, and she gives me a blatant once-over before focusing back on Deer. "Boyfriend?"

Deer frowns before remembering that I'm in the room with her. Her eyes widen as she lets out a small laugh, the skin around her eyes crinkling.

A rock sinks in my gut.

"Well, last night I was his girlfriend, but today he's my purse holder." She lifts the fluffy white handbag off her lap with her free hand and holds it back over her shoulder. "Right, babes?" Her long lashes flutter like butterfly wings as she peers up at me. The honey-sweet voice she uses hides the taunting challenge at the core of her words.

I can feel the other technicians in the salon hushing as they watch the performance Deer puts on.

"Right."

I pluck the tiny bag from her hand and her grin widens. I really shouldn't have come.

"Take a seat," Amy instructs me, angling her chin to the empty chair next to Deer.

I give her a nod before pulling out the seat and sinking onto the soft cushion, the fuzzy bag perched in my lap.

I look like a fucking simp, and I am going to be stuck like this for two hours.

I dig my phone out of my pocket and load *Kill Strike* up, determined to avoid any further temptations of indulging Deer in her tirade of pushing me to the edge. My attention zeroes onto the game. But while it seems to work and deters Deer or anyone else from talking to me, it doesn't stop the fact that I can understand the hushed whispers that float around the salon.

In what alternate dimension did I think this was a good idea?

Tagging along to a fucking nail salon…real smart idea, Jackson.

I'm the only dude in here, minus the guy who is giving an old lady a pedicure, and even he is giving me the occasional glance. I look like a whipped asshole, all because I'm just trying to keep an eye out for her, keep her safe.

My jaw clenches as I attempt to drown everyone out, centering my focus on my phone screen and the game I'm playing.

Deer jostles my leg with the heel of her shoe. "Shield."

"What?"

"Amy asked if you want to get your nails done."

I briefly look up at her before glancing at the woman

and then back to Deer.

"No."

She nudges my leg again. "Come on. You're here, you might as well."

"No."

"Blade paints his nails."

"And that's great for Aleksander."

"I guess you're just not as secure in your masculinity as he is."

I pause my game, giving the brat before me a stern glare. "Be careful."

She purses her lips, cheeks flushing a smidge before turning her attention back to the nail technician. "Just making an observation."

I don't miss the way the other women in the salon are judging me for not entertaining my supposed girlfriend. And I certainly don't miss the way another nail technician slips into the seat across from me and begins setting up various tools regardless of my rejection.

Fucking hell.

I click off my phone and place it not so gently on the table before me.

"Fine." I hold my hands out to the woman whose nametag reads Suzy. "But no color."

"Not even green?"

I side-eye Deer. "Unlike Parker and you, I don't make one color my entire personality."

"Oh, yeah? Then what color are your shoes?"

"Do you always need to have the last word?"

"Depends on the situation," she shrugs.

Suzy takes one of my hands and proceeds to start trimming my nails with a clipper.

"Rough hands," she remarks at the calluses marring my palms—a byproduct of my daily gym grind. "You should do a hand mask."

"Oh, the honey one does wonders," Deer chimes in.

"No," I growl. It's bad enough that I've caved this much already.

Deer reaches out and places her right hand in the middle of my table briefly as she whispers loudly, "I'll pay for it, just ignore him." Her nose scrunches up like she is sharing a secret.

Suzy smiles back.

"Seriously, no," I repeat.

It doesn't stop Suzy from reaching into a fridge behind her and pulling out a small jar.

"No, thank you," I say in Mandarin this time. My family is from the Guangdong province, so we primarily speak Cantonese, but I still learned some Mandarin back in high school to feel confident enough about getting my point across.

Except, maybe not, because Suzy ignores me.

She just unscrews the lid and uses a scooper to remove a large dollop of a light yellow cream. She smiles at me before using her free hand to grip my left hand.

"I only speak Filipino," she muses before slapping the cold cream onto the top of my hand.

A stifled laugh escapes Deer as Suzy proceeds to massage the cream onto both hands.

Unbridled resignation sinks into my bones.

I don't even bother stopping her from slipping a pair of warm cloth gloves on me.

She holds both hands together and gives them a soft pat. "Ten minutes." Then she gets up and leaves me stranded. I can't even use my phone with these damn things on.

Deer has no sympathy for my situation. She busies herself, switching hands as she aimlessly scrolls through her notifications and hearts comments.

I'm stuck watching a TV mounted on the wall that is showing some sort of home renovation show. There's no sound and no subtitles. I just have to use my own deductive reasoning to decipher what is going on—which seems to be a man building what might be either a very small doghouse or an oddly large birdhouse.

I'm annoyed to admit that I get sucked into the show, trying to piece together everything going on and making my own assumptions. I still can't tell whether the hosts are a married couple or brother and sister.

When Suzy returns to wash off the mask and begin my manicure, I let her work in silence. Even Deer just lets me be as she chatters away with her own nail technician. Though, I do see her glancing over every couple of minutes.

"How long have you been dating?" Amy asks her.

"We've been dating in secret for a while now. We have to keep it quiet for his family, ya know."

"They don't approve?" Amy's brows crinkle.

Deer leans forward, and in a not-so-hushed whisper, she says, "He's worried they won't like me."

Amy lets out a tsk, and I suddenly feel very judged for something I didn't even do.

I regret ever opening this can of worms. It seemed like a great idea last night, but now I'm second-guessing everything. I told her it was a onetime thing, but here she is, milking it for all it's worth, like I'm some prized cow she's excited to show off.

"If my son brought you home, I'd be happy. You're such a sweet girl."

"Aw, thank you." Deer looks at me out of the corner of her eye. "Did you hear that, babes? I'm sweet."

"Mm. Yeah, you're the sweetest girlfriend ever." I give her a tight smile, but she just beams back at me.

When she looks at me like that, I start to second-guess my second-guessing. I start to find myself drawn into this game we are playing.

"Jackson?"

My abs contract at the familiar voice.

"Jackson?"

The repetition cements my fear.

I feel like a rusted robot as my head slowly twists to look in the direction of the voice.

"I thought that was you."

"An yi."

My auntie An lays a hand on my shoulder, curiosity glinting through her eyes as she takes in the scene before her. My mother's older sister is a jealous woman and the worst gossip you'll ever meet.

"Did I hear this is your girlfriend?"

Ice washes over my entire body.

"Yes, I am." Deer places a hand on my knee.

"No, she's not." I try to shake her off.

The entire nail salon goes quiet.

"Babe," Deer playfully whines, her brows furrowed in a tease.

Her smile wavers when she looks me directly in my eyes. I'm not sure what she sees written there, but it's enough to bring a spark of concern to her baby blues. Her eyes dart between me and my aunt a few times as her smile slowly deflates. Deer removes her hand from my knee and spins back, returning her attention to Amy.

It just makes everything look more weird, which Auntie An quickly picks up on.

"I was wondering why none of your dates had been successful when your mother totes what a catch you are," she crows. "Who'd have guessed you had a little girlfriend you were keeping secret?"

"She's not—"

"Actually, that would add up with all your other secrets and lies."

My jaw clenches, grinding from side to side.

I am so sick of everyone blaming me.

And I am really sick of everyone trying to control my story.

This is why I kept everything hidden for years so I didn't have to deal with their judgement. They all seem so set on analyzing every detail of my life, making sure that it is up to par with what fits their expectations. They're so afraid I'm going to tip the boat over, and maybe I will.

"I'm not surprised you kept quiet about this." She leans forward, whispering behind her hand. "She's a little much, no? What will your *po po* say if she sees someone like her?"

Deer's body tenses almost imperceptibly, and it feels like the temperature in the room cools by ten degrees. But without missing a beat, Deer flicks her head back around with a perfectly crafted smile, her new glittery nails glinting from the overhead lights as she clasps her hands together on her bobbing knee.

"It's not what you think." Her voice doesn't waver. "I was just joking around. We're not—"

"We're not official yet." I reach over and cover Deer's hands with my own, her leg immediately ceasing its bouncing. "I was waiting to tell everyone."

I can see Deer swivel her head out of my periphery, but I keep my gaze glued to my auntie's, never letting it waver.

"Really?" Her eyes flick up and down as they catalog every inch of Deer's body.

"Really, Auntie." I give Deer's hand a small, reassuring squeeze. "This is my girlfriend."

Chapter
FIFTEEN

DEER

"*This is my girlfriend.*"

Jackson squeezes my hand, and I let his strong grip bolster me.

I don't totally understand what is going on here, but I know it's not the time to hesitate. I can't let myself lag for even a second. I'm going to show this woman why I'm one of the most beloved streamers. This lady is going to get the full show.

I stand up and relinquish my hand from Jackson's, holding it out to his aunt instead.

"I'm Deer, it's lovely to meet you."

Her brows pinch together as she reluctantly places her hand in mine. "Deer?"

I really wasn't racking up any bonus points with this woman, and, in retrospect, this isn't how I would ever introduce myself to my supposed boyfriend's family, but I am grasping at straws here.

One might say this is all my fault because I'm the one who decided to continue this whole ruse, but how was I supposed to know his aunt came to the same damn nail salon? I thought his family lived farther south.

"Yes, it's a nickname."

"I see."

She releases my hand and continues that scrutinous appraisal of my appearance. It doesn't slip past me that she hasn't introduced herself. She doesn't respect me enough for that. I'm beneath her, not worth her time.

A little much, apparently.

I swallow, my throat rough as sandpaper.

I feel more under the microscope now than I have at any gaming convention ever, surrounded by thousands upon thousands of people. It makes me feel like shit. This is what I get for not taking Aleks seriously. He grew up with Jackson. I should've trusted him when he said that pretending to date Jackson wouldn't go well with his family.

Gods dammit.

I need a way out of this, some sort of an excuse that she can't avoid.

I grip my anxiety and keep it locked in my chest, lacing a soft smile across my face as I attempt to smother this cold woman with all my fake cotton candy kindness.

"We're about to head to a lunch reservation, if you would like to join us?"

"I'm afraid I'll have to pass as I still have my appointment."

Thank Gods. That's what I'd been banking on her saying.

I allow my mask to fall into one of carefully feigned disappointment.

"Oh, shoot. Next time? I would love to get to know Sh—Jackson's family more."

I see the moment an idea passes through her gaze with a calculating glint. She turns her thin smile to Jackson, who comes to stand behind me.

"You should bring her to Angela's recital next weekend. I'm sure everyone would be delighted to meet your *girlfriend*." She says the word like it is laced with lies.

Jackson's hand comes to rest against the small of my back, sending a shock through me.

"Of course, that's a great idea." He leans forward and peers at me. "I just paid. We should head to lunch if we don't want to be late."

"Right. Yeah." I nod like a bobblehead. "Can't miss our lunch date."

"I'll see you soon, *yi ma.*"

"It was nice meeting you," I smile back at his aunt as he ushers me out of the salon.

The bell on the door chimes as we exit. My feet continue to move on autopilot, following the direction Jackson keeps leading me in.

"Wait, I didn't text—"

"Miss Deer. Mr. Lau."

I blink up to see Francis opening the back door of the BMW.

"I texted him," Jackson explains as he holds my hand and helps me into the car.

The door closes before I'm able to get another word out, leaving me staring out the tinted window in confusion. The car dips when he gets in on the other side, and it jiggles me out of my stupor.

"What the hell was that?"

"Seriously? You're asking me that?" He crosses his arms.

"You're the one who—wait, oh my Gods, I totally forgot to pay!" I scramble around to grab my phone from my handbag, just to realize I never grabbed it from the salon. My brain feels like someone smashed a dozen eggs and is trying to fry them all at once. "Shit. I left my—"

"Purse?"

Jackson holds the fuzzy white purse out to me, the handle dangling off the end of his pointer finger.

"Thanks." I pluck it from him, uncertainty clouding over me as I look for my phone.

"And I already handled the payment. Did you not hear a word I said in there?"

I pause in my rummaging, my mind taking a second to recalibrate.

Right. Right, he did say that.

"Wait, why did you do that? I told you I was going to pay."

"Because if we spent another second in there, I was going to drown myself with nail polish remover."

"Dramatic."

"Says you."

"At least when I do it, it's on brand."

"This is never going to work." He runs a hand down his face.

"What isn't?"

"Us. Dating."

"Not true." I straighten my spine. "Everyone in the salon believed us. Grace believed us."

"None of those people actually know us." He slumps against his seat. "My family will see right through it."

"'Cause I'm not good enough, right?" I can't stop the venom from leaving my lips.

"No. Because you always argue with me. What couple argues this much?"

"They say it's healthy for couples to argue."

"Who?"

"The internet people."

Jackson groans.

"Besides, this is barely even arguing." I cross my arms and slouch back against my seat.

"I'm so fucked."

There's a hollowness in the words he speaks that catches me off guard. He's normally so gravelly and growly that hearing the misery-laden words causes my chest to clench. I chance a glance over at him and see the way the skin tightens around his distant gaze. I pull my lower lip between my teeth.

I don't want him to feel this way.

"Hey." I reach over and poke his bicep with my freshly pointed nail. "Hey, come on. I'm...I'm sorry."

"Why are you sorry?"

"Because your aunt overheard what I said."

"You only said that because I pulled you into this last night. That was my decision, not yours. I only have myself to blame."

The mood of the car is becoming drenched in depression, a heaviness cloying the air with thick disappointment.

Before I can second-guess myself, I curl my hand around his bicep. His taut muscles are massive beneath my small hands. I give a light squeeze, and Jackson finally tears his eyes away from the window to look at me.

"Let me help you."

"Deer, I don't—"

"I'm serious." I scoot myself over onto the middle seat. "Consider it a repayment for you helping me, for letting me crash at the apartment and stay in your room...and also for finishing off all the sour candies in the pantry."

"You ate all our sour candy?"

"Jackson."

His eyes swirl as his name leaves my lips, but just as quick, they steel up. "This isn't your responsibility, Deer. I can handle it on my own."

"Weren't you the one preaching to me about not being a hero? About letting people help lighten the load so you don't become crushed by the weight?"

"Why do you have such a good memory?" he tsks.

"Come on, trust me. I've got this. I'll be the best fake girlfriend you've ever seen."

"If this doesn't work..."

"It will."

"But if it doesn't, I'm going to get caught up in another lie." Conflict wars in his eyes. "My family will never forgive me. I don't know if I can risk that—I can't risk that."

I reach up and rest the palm of my hand against his cheek. That conflict melts away into shock, his lashes fluttering as he stares down at me. My heart turns to a goopy mess, dripping as I gaze at the man who has always been a pillar of stoic strength but is beginning to crack.

I want to make his struggle disappear.

I want to pull him into a hug.

I want…I want to kiss him.

Shit.

I force a smile onto my face.

"It's up to you. Whatever you're comfortable with, I'll support that. But just know that if you need me to, I'll fake girlfriend so hard, even our friends will wonder what's fake and what's real."

I peel my hand away even though it's hard and shuffle back to my side of the car. Jackson doesn't say anything else, so I just stare out the window, watching cars and palm trees pass us by in a gray tint.

The air in the vehicle is still marked with uncertainty, and I begin to spiral, worried that I totally put my foot in my mouth.

It's only when we pull into the garage under the apartment complex that he speaks again. It's one word spoken so low that it causes my skin to prickle as it rolls over me.

"Thanks."

Chapter SIXTEEN

JACKSON

"**G**uess who's back, losers."

I ignore the noise, centering my concentration as I speed up my car using a rainbow pad. Stevie throws a green turtle shell from her car, but it's easy to dodge. I shoot out a banana peel, but she narrowly avoids it. I'd never admit it, but she's getting a little too good at this game.

"Nice try, but I'm winning this round," she croons.

"We'll see."

I still have a trick up my sleeve.

"Hello? Any of you wankers listening to me?"

"No. Stop distracting me," Aleks clips.

My eyes dip down to the bottom right quadrant of the TV screen to see Aleks riding in seventh place. The corner of my mouth ticks up in satisfaction. Since I met him in high school, he's always crushed me in practically every game we play. It doesn't matter how many more hours of work I put in; he is just a natural at everything—except racing games. They are his Achilles' heel, and I exploit that weakness like no other.

"Come on, come on," Stevie whispers under her breath.

"Sorry, sweetheart." I swerve my car right, angling it into the shortcut hallway. I manage to hit the ramp with enough speed to catapult across the gulf. My car spits back onto the main track, ahead of Stevie.

"Dammit, Jackson."

I grin. Sweet, sweet victory, just seconds away.

I demolished this game.

There's a light chuckle from my left.

My car goes spinning to the side, a giant bullet knocking me completely off track.

"What the fuck?" Stevie and I yell.

It takes me too long to get myself situated again, and by the time I cross the finish line, a third-place banner unfurls across my square of the screen. The quadrant below me is lit up with a first-place trophy.

I turn to glare at the culprit.

"Ooooh, sorry. Did that mess up your winning streak?"

Deer smiles at me, her tone anything but apologetic as her blue eyes gleam with success. My gaze dips to the low-cut top she is wearing, and my annoyance wavers.

"Nice." Aleks leans across me, brandishing his knuckles. Deer knocks them back with her own, the two conspirators gloating.

"Whatever, I still won the most rounds."

"Barely," Stevie huffs. "If I'd won this, we would've

been tied."

"Yeah, but you didn't, so sucks to suck."

"God, you're such a sore loser."

"I'm kicking you all out of my apartment if you don't start paying attention to me." Parker plants himself in front of the TV.

Deer laughs, uncurling herself from the couch and padding over to squeeze him in a hug. "Welcome back."

The fuck?

She's never greeted me with a hug before.

Why do my friends get special treatment?

"Happy?" She releases him and cocks her head to the side.

"I guess," he grumbles, his lower lip pouting slightly.

"Good." She pats him on the shoulder. "Now, where's Syd?"

"Jet lag. She went straight to her place." Parker flops down on the couch, taking Deer's vacant spot next to me. He reaches forward and takes a sip from one of the flutes on the coffee table. "Ugh, what happened to this champagne?" He looks at the glass like it has gravely offended him. "It tastes like ass."

"And you'd know what that tastes like," Aleks tosses, wiggling his eyebrows.

"Fuck off."

"That's 'cause it's not champagne." Deer plucks the flute from his hand and settles herself next to him on the couch. "It's sparkling water, gin, lemon juice, and some sugar."

Parker scrunches his nose. "That's basically a poor person's version of a French 75."

"Sue me for being lazy." She rolls her eyes, taking a large sip of the concoction.

My jaw works back and forth, annoyance brewing as Parker and Deer laugh.

"So, are you and Jackson bunking together?" Stevie tosses her legs over Aleks' lap as she looks at us.

"What are you talking about?"

"You've been sleeping in his room, haven't you?"

Fuck.

I turn to Parker, but he just has his pointer finger pressed on the tip of his nose, "You gotta take the couch, mate."

"What? No. What are you even doing back early? You were due back Tuesday."

"Oh, so you finally realized?"

"Parker," I growl.

"Syd made us come back early because I have a last-minute photoshoot with Health Potionz. You're looking at the new face of HP energy drinks." He leans back, throwing his arms over the cushions. "Besides, it's my room. In fact, it's my apartment complex. I don't need your permission to be here."

"Go crash with your girlfriend."

"No."

"Trouble in paradise?" Stevie jumps in.

"Or did she just get sick of looking at your ugly face?" Aleks laughs.

"Bloody hell. I forgot how awful you lot are," he huffs. "No, she just wanted a night back at her own place."

"I can take the couch." Deer's soft voice slips through the barrage of noise.

"You're not taking the couch," I cut back.

"But—"

"It's not up for discussion."

"Don't worry, Deer. Big guy here can survive on the couch; it's custom made from Norway." Parker slings an arm around my shoulders, a shit-eating grin slapped on his face.

"You better sleep with one eye open."

He rolls his eyes. "Besides, it's just one night. We can get you set up in your place tomorrow, and he can go back to his cave."

"Tomorrow? It's ready?"

Wait. What?

"Yeah, technically. I mean, the paint job was finished up this weekend. Might still smell a little chemically tomorrow but shouldn't be bad enough that you can't move in a few days early."

No.

No, I was supposed to have another few days with her. She wasn't…

This wasn't supposed to be her last night.

"Ohmigods. Yes! I can't wait to see it."

"Great. I'll get the movers to your old place first thing. Syd will drop by and help after our meeting."

"Thanks. It'll be so nice to have my setup again. No offense to your build."

"A little offense. Did you see the res from my graphics card? It's an RTX 4090."

"No, no, it's a sick build. Really. It's just not my style. I have these cooling fans that light up a rotating ombre pink color, and my graphics card is that limited edition Sakura one that has petals falling when it's running."

"Huh. You'll have to show me."

"Sure. I'll have you over once it's all set up." She grins up at him, her eyes sparkling in that way that means she's genuinely happy.

There's a squeaking noise as my molars grind against each other.

"I'm headed to bed."

I push up from the couch, flinging Parker's arm off me in the process. Deer startles, her shoulders pinching back as she makes room for me to squeeze past her.

"What? It's barely midnight," Parker calls out as I stalk away.

"Bed doesn't sound like a bad idea, right, babe?" Stevie purrs.

"Doesn't sound bad at all," Aleks hums back.

"Oh, come on. What did we say about public spaces?" Parker's voice pitches higher, "Seriously! Don't make out on the couch, you guys."

I ignore them all, and trudge into Parker's bedroom to collect my shit. I'd left a fair amount of my gym gear in here, not wanting to bother Deer every morning while she was in my room. I throw everything into my sports bag and zip it up, not really caring.

All I care about right now is Deer leaving tomorrow.

My mind floats back to yesterday: her hand on my cheek, her touch warm and calming.

My jaw twinges as it continues to clench harder.

Maybe this is a good thing. She's making everything confusing. It isn't supposed to be confusing. Life is supposed to be easy, simple. But nothing has been simple since she walked in. She's splattered her whimsy on everything

163

she's touched, and I can't help but find myself drawn to her intoxicating smile.

For the past week, my dreams have been haunted by visions of her. No matter how hard I try to tear her out of my mind, she's burrowed her way in, using those sharp, decorative nails to grip the corners of my sanity. She's an addiction I didn't know I had until it was too late to quit.

Yesterday is only proof of that, of how blinded I've become.

I almost made her my fake girlfriend.

Fuck.

I have to let her go.

Now.

Chapter
SEVENTEEN

JACKSON

I toss for what feels like the fiftieth time in the last hour.

I just can't fall asleep on this fucking couch. I don't care how custom or expensive it is, it doesn't make up for an actual bed. My bed. Which is less than twenty feet away. The very same bed a woman whose face won't leave my mind is lying in.

I flip over, shoving my cheek against the pillow as I attempt to get somewhat comfortable. I've been trying to count sheep to empty my brain, but they just keep morphing from fluffy white animals to fluffy pink ones.

I'm starting to think I might have a serious problem.

A squeaking noise has me pausing, my body locking up as I strain to hear where it came from.

I swear to God, if Aleks and Stevie are fucking again, I'm going to murder them.

Our streaming rooms might be soundproof, but our bedrooms aren't, and the living room echoes sound like a damn canyon.

The noise comes again, but this time it sounds a little different. There's a hitch in the tone.

It...

It almost sounds like someone's crying.

I bolt up, throwing off my blanket. A sinking feeling churns throughout my stomach. My feet slap against the tiles as I make a beeline for my bedroom. There's no light creeping out from under the door, but as I lean my ear toward the wood, I hear muffled wheezing.

My fingers twitch on the door handle, but when a hiccup slips through, so does my resolve. I push the door open.

My room is cloaked in darkness, the only light coming from some charging cables in the corner.

There's a sharp intake of breath, and the entire room feels like it is frozen in time as I move forward. My eyes start to adjust, and I make out her small form huddled in a ball, twisted in the sheets. I'm careful not to scare her as I climb onto the mattress, reaching a tentative hand out to rest on the sheet covering her body. Her breath comes in short, quiet intervals—like she is barely restraining herself from hyperventilating. I'm unable to stop my thumb from moving on its own, rubbing in a slow circular pattern.

I don't say anything and neither does she.

She's been here for a little over a week and this is the second night I've caught her having some sort of a nightmare. My throat thickens as I think about the weeks she spent before coming here when she was holed up in her apartment all alone. How many times did this happen after the incident? How many nights did she cry alone?

No wonder she looked a mess when I picked her up. She'd probably given up on sleeping altogether.

Deer releases another hiccup, but her body begins to relax under my hand. I feel some of the tension ease from the tight curl she's been holding as her muscles start to melt.

Without giving it too much thought, I lower my body to the mattress. I curve into something like a C shape, molding myself into a fence of safety around her. My hand doesn't leave her once in the process, anchoring her to me.

She begins to wriggle, and I spot the tips of her fingers as they emerge from beneath her cocoon. Those pointy nails curve around the edge of the sheet and slowly move it down until her eyes crest. She holds the sheet there, tight against the bridge of her nose as she blinks those puffy doe eyes at me. I don't need light to know that they're bloodshot.

"Hi."

The corners of my lips threaten to quirk up.

Damn, she's cute.

"Hi."

"I'm sorry, I didn't mean to wake you. Again."

I shake my head, bringing my hand up to rest against the crown of her head. "You didn't." The pads of my fingers burrow into her locks as I start to massage her.

Deer's eyes flutter shut as she leans back into my touch. "Thank you."

A golden light warms my chest at her words.

"I told you, you don't need to suffer alone."

Her eyes blink open and her brows pinch. "Practice

what you preach."

"I'm not the one barricading myself in a blanket fortress to avoid my issues."

She lets out a small huff of air and I smile.

Her gaze turns wary, and she grips the edge of the sheet more tightly.

"Do you think…"

"I do think. Maybe a little too much."

I see the corners of her eyes crinkle with a hidden smile. That warmth in my chest spreads.

"Do you think you could stay?"

My hand halts in its path as I blink down at her. Her eyes widen before she pulls the sheet back over her head.

"You know what? Never mind. That was dumb. Ignore me."

"Hey. Wait a second." I grab the sheet near where she has it curled in her fist and tug. "Deer, look at me."

"No." Her knuckles whiten as she keeps me from pulling the fabric back down.

I let out a sigh.

It always feels like two steps forward, three steps back with her. I've never noticed before, but she really keeps people at arm's length. You just never realize it because she always acts so friendly.

I push myself up, resting on my elbows as I search for the corner of the sheet. Once I find it, I slip off the bed.

"Wait!" Deer pops out from her cocoon, pure fear etched into her features.

My chest splits open.

I lift the sheet up and slide under it, joining her in bed. "Shh," I hum. Without giving it much thought, I curl my arms around her. "I'm not going anywhere; I was just getting more comfortable."

Her body stiffens in my hold, and I can feel her heart thumping against the back of her ribs. After what feels like a beat too long, she lets out a breath, her frame slumping. Her breathing starts to regulate, matching my own as she calms down.

"Thank you," she mutters against my chest, her wet cheeks pressing against me.

"You don't have to keep thanking me."

She shrugs and I thread one of my hands back through her hair, pulling her tighter to me.

"Yeah, but you didn't have to come check on me."

"True."

"Except you did because you're a nice person."

"I thought you said I was the grumpiest person you've ever known."

"Can't you let me give you a compliment?"

"No."

She lets out a small laugh. One of her arms unfurls and inches out to wrap around my waist. A thousand lights zap against my skin at the contact. I steel myself as she snuggles closer, unable to ignore the way her breasts are pushing up against my bare chest.

Fuck. Fuck. Fuck.

Come on, Jackson. You're here to comfort her, not to fuck her.

I gulp, my Adam's apple feeling like a thirty-pound rock as I try to center my thoughts. My dick really needs to get the memo that now is seriously not the fucking time.

Except, it seems like the world is hell-bent on making

this hard for me.

Deer shifts, bringing her knees higher to her chest, which causes them to graze against my cock in the process. She lets out a sleepy sigh while I stifle a groan.

Against my better judgement, I let my arm slide down her body until my hand stops at the small of her back. I'm tempted to let it linger lower but stop myself before I do something I can't take back. Just being in here, being in bed with her, is too much.

I shouldn't be holding her like this.

I shouldn't be doing any of this.

She's vulnerable right now, broken. Who am I to take advantage of that?

I'm not that sort of guy.

We're barely even friends.

I look down at her.

Fuck.

I'm so fucked.

Chapter
EIGHTEEN

DEER

66 "Where would you like this, miss?"

"In the bedroom, please."

I smile at the mover even though it feels like I face-planted into a bee's nest. My cheeks are all chubby and pushing against my eyes as I try to make sure the grin doesn't constipated.

I'd like to think I managed to cover up most of the blotchy redness from my tears with the eighty-dollar foundation I slapped on my skin at the ass crack of dawn, but there's nothing I can do about the puffiness other than sticking my face in an ice bucket.

I don't hate myself enough to do that.

Yet.

"All right, that's the last of the boxes." Sydney breaches the doorway, eyes glued to a clipboard in her hand. "Are you fine with them unpacking and organizing, too?"

I look at the mountain of boxes just in the living room. I have absolutely zero motivation to open them. Maybe I should've just thrown everything out and started new. Minimalism is pretty in right now.

"I'm going to take that as a yes."

I give her a half-assed smile, and she rolls her eyes playfully before going to speak with the movers.

Thank the Gods she came to help me out. I'd be seriously lost without her.

Literally. I can't even see over some of these boxes.

I look around my new place, which is a lot larger than I expected. Even with all the boxes piled up, I can tell I lucked out with the stunning open floor plan and two massive bedrooms. When Parker said he was getting the apartment repainted, I thought he meant because the previous tenants ruined the walls. Nope. He'd gotten the entire apartment painted an extremely sheer pastel pink color. He even went so far as to get a doorbell system installed to give me peace of mind. It seems a little much for an apartment on the fortieth floor of a high security building, but it makes me feel better now that I'm living alone again.

I gnaw on my bottom lip as that sinking feeling returns.

It is going to be an adjustment, not having Jackson down the hall. Sure, he's just an elevator ride away, but it's not the same. His body emits waves that calm my nerves, and I just feel safer when he's around.

Point in case, last night was the best sleep I'd had in weeks.

Even though I woke up this morning to an empty bed.

Sure, I mean, I know he goes to the gym at 6 a.m. like

clockwork, but…I don't know.

All my stuff is out of the penthouse now, too. I don't even have a legitimate reason to head back up there unless I want to seem needy or annoying.

My phone buzzes repeatedly, and I pull it out to see a notification from my mod.

RICK

groceries are on their way. Should arrive by seven

and I'm having a sponsored package from that cosmetics company rerouted to ur new place

and don't forget to dip into the Discord tonight

ME

thanks 😊 appreciate it

RICK

do you want me to keep ur stream scheduled this week?

ME

……..I guess

I still have to set up my stuff tho

RICK

k – just let me know

I let out a small puff of air as I weave my way into my new streaming room. I've already begun unpacking in here. I didn't trust Parker's movers enough to handle my set up beyond getting the furniture situated—my PC build alone is worth a couple of grand, and some of the gear is custom. Replacing any of it would be hell.

Trying to distract myself, I begin unboxing all the individual components and cords, setting them up on my desk in just the right way. It's meticulous and keeps my brain focused as I perfect the aesthetic I've spent years curating—which is basically bubblegum e-girl-core.

After what feels like way too long, I plug the final cord into the outlet and watch as the room comes to life. My PC is an ombre pink lightshow, my keyboard sports a flickering rainbow wave, the LEDs lining the ceiling shine a bright magenta, and my gamertag shines on a neon pink sign on the wall. A calm settles over me as my safe haven returns to me.

I hadn't realized how much I missed having my own streaming room. Part of me worried that I would never feel at peace in here again after the incident. Granted, I tweaked the room setup slightly from how it used to be— no sense moving into a new place and creating a mirror of my old one. But still.

I move on to another box, ripping it open to reveal my streaming equipment. My fingers pause on the edges, the contents inside glaring back at me.

I'd taken a bit of a break from live streaming since moving in with the guys. It's not like I could stream from Parker's room without people asking questions. I've just been uploading prerecorded content to my channels. But now that I have my space again…

Come on, Deer.

I take a deep breath and begin lifting out the pieces of my ring light. There is no way I would let this haunt me. The longer I avoid it, the worse it will get. I'm not going to lose my career to these assholes.

"I was wondering where you disappeared to."

Sydney crouches next to me on the floor as I screw my ring light together, her cherry perfume floating into the space.

"I'm sure you had to look super hard."

"I did. You're small and easy to miss."

"Hey, I'm not that much shorter than you."

"Says the person who can buy children's shoes."

My jaw falls open. "You've been spending too much time with your boyfriend. You used to be nicer."

"I won't argue that." She drops to the ground and begins flicking through her phone. "I was thinking we could order in and christen your new place—see if Lee and Stevie are free, maybe?"

Relief floods me at the thought of not having to be alone.

"Sure, let's get Ace Burger."

"Already one step ahead of you." She tilts her phone my way to show the online ordering app.

"Ugh, I love you and all your planning." I turn to give her a genuine smile as I pluck the phone from her.

Syd's eyes flick over my face, her expression faltering for a second. She opens her mouth to say something but ends up just clenching her jaw together.

"What?"

"Nothing."

"It's never nothing with you."

She lets out a sigh.

"Sydney."

"Don't get me wrong, you're looking better than a few weeks ago, but…" She pulls her lower lip between her teeth.

"But."

"But you still look…not…great."

I give her an unamused side-eye.

"Like I said, you're looking better. Seriously." Her smile borders on a wince. "But I don't know. Are you getting any sleep?"

The metal nut I'd been in the middle of twisting slips from my fingers onto my new rug.

"What did Jackson tell you?"

One of her blonde brows rises. "Nothing," she says slowly, carefully drawing out the letters.

Shit.

"Why?"

I shrug, digging my fingers into the soft rug, searching for the nut so I can finish setting up this stupid ring light. Sydney stays silent, and I can tell she wants to push me but is afraid I'll snap back at her. Which I might. I don't want to talk about it. It's bad enough that Jackson knows about the nightmares, if everyone else hears about them…they'll never leave me alone.

And it's getting better. I know it's getting better.

I'm not waking up screaming anymore.

"Yikes, who killed the vibe in here?"

We whip our heads around to see Lee leaning against

the doorframe.

"Hey," I smile. "We were just about to text you about grabbing food."

"Like this?" She holds up two white plastic bags with her left hand, grinning.

"You're a mind reader."

"If only." She laughs and nods her head back. "Come on. I just passed your movers on the way out. We have the place to ourselves, and I'm starving to death."

Syd and I watch as she disappears back into the body of the apartment. I remain rooted to the floor, but Syd gives my knee a pat before she stands up.

"Come on, before she starts whining for us." She holds her hand out to me.

I take her hand and let her pull me up. There's a short pause as that concern returns and flushes over her features again, but she just gives my hand a squeeze before letting go and following Lee.

I close my eyes, imagining all my stress falling off my skin like dripping water. When I reopen them, I feel a little more human again.

Lee has already made herself at home on my couch, her legs kicked under her ass as she fiddles with the remote for my TV.

"The movers didn't hook anything up, so I took the liberty of doing it. You're welcome," she preens, flipping to one of my many streaming services.

"Thank you, Oh Goddess Lee, whatever would I do without you?"

"Why do I have such strange friends," Sydney sighs, settling on the couch next to me.

"Stop, you love us." I blow her a kiss.

She rolls her eyes—she *always* rolls her eyes—and begins ripping open the takeout bags Lee brought. The smell of melted cheese and ketchup wafts around us as we settle in.

"By the way, are you guys busy Sat?" Lee reaches forward and grabs her burger, taking a large bite.

"Why?" I steal a fry from her lap.

"There's this content creator party downtown."

I wrinkle my nose. "Pass."

"Aw, come on. You're not going to make me go alone."

Dammit. See, now *this* is why I always ended up going out. It wasn't because *I* ever wanted to but because I would never let Lee go alone. My sense of Girl Code is too strong, even if my social anxiety pulses like a beacon during a storm at the idea.

"You could always get one of the boys to go with you," Syd offers. "I ended up having to move their streaming schedule around that day so they could have it free."

"Why?"

"Jackson's sister has another piano thing."

My ears perk up, and I try to sound casual as I ask, "Where is that again?"

"The recital? Her high school, I think."

"Back down in Oceanside?"

"Mm, yeah." She pops a fry in her mouth, chewing on it as her eyes narrow. "Why?"

"Just curious."

She holds a limp sweet potato fry out and uses it to gesture at me. "I can smell your lies from a mile away. What are you cooking?"

"Nothing bad. Exactly." I avert my gaze. "Just helping a friend out. Maybe. I don't know. I haven't decided."

Lee's eyes pop wide as a sly smile spreads across her face. "Ooooh. Right."

Sydney whips her head between the two of us so fast I worry she's going to pull a muscle. "Deer, spill."

"No. You might get mad at me, and I haven't even done anything."

A cool wave washes over her features—her publicist persona kicking into gear. "God dammit. What did the boys do?" She tosses her fry on the table and goes to grab her phone. "I swear, they can't let me live in peace for a minute."

"No!" I slap my hand over hers. "No. It's…Gods."

"You better explain or I'm going to call them all right now."

"Fine, fine." I slump back against my couch, and Lee lets out a cackle. "If we're going to point the finger anywhere, Stevie is the one who started the whole idea. Okay?"

Chapter
NINETEEN

JACKSON

need to stop miscalculating these situations.

I am the best game strategist out of the three of us, and yet I didn't foresee the absolute shit show before me.

"What's this your *yi ma* is talking about?" My mom grabs my elbow and ushers me to the side of the auditorium. "She said she met your girlfriend. Since when do you have a girlfriend?" Her eyes dart around as she tries to keep her voice hushed from onlookers. "*Waa ngo zi,*" she pushes, switching to Cantonese.

The recital starts in just a few minutes, and I barely made it in time with all the weekend traffic. I'm hot and gross and don't want to deal with this.

I can't exactly say that Auntie An is lying because that will just earn me more scrutiny. I also can't admit that I was lying because that's just going to land me in hot shit, too. I really dug myself a grave here. If only life was a video game, and I could revert to my last save so I never went to that damn nail salon.

But then I'd still be stuck going on endless dates.

I am beginning to wonder if there is any way for me to win. It seems like every path just leads me to a dead end.

"You can stay silent, but a picture speaks a thousand words, and my sister has the pictures to prove it." Mom pulls out her phone and brandishes a photo my aunt must have taken last weekend when Deer and I left the salon. It's…not great. My hand sits low on her back and I'm leaning down, almost like I'm whispering in her ear. "Your *po po* has seen them." She starts waggling the phone up at me, narrowly missing my chin. "Well? What do you have to say for yourself?"

My mouth opens but I seriously can't think of an excuse to save my life.

So, I just dig my grave deeper instead.

"I'm sorry, I didn't want to tell you until I was sure. *An yi* caught me off guard."

The cold glare in her eyes begins to thaw. "So, you have a girlfriend?"

"Yup."

Nail in the coffin. No going back.

The phone lowers so it's no longer a threat, and my mother gives me a look that teeters on annoyance. "You should have told me." She taps the phone against my arm with a huff.

"Sorry."

The lights begin to dim, and the chatter around us falls to a light hum.

"We'll discuss this later. Come on." Mom takes off without a second glance.

We take our seats in the second row, where Dad has kept our spots. I slide next to my mom, taking my place at the end of the row. It lets me stretch my legs out so I'm not cramped for the next few hours.

My thoughts swirl with the fact that I am now going to have to find a way to keep up this ruse without getting caught.

Angela is the third student to take the stage, and even though I know the lights are blinding, she still manages to search the crowd and find me. I give her a thumbs up, just in case. She takes her seat on the bench, and the audience seems to quiet even further as the first few notes ring out. She plays "Raindrop" without missing a beat, the tune weaving through the air like a swan gliding across a clear lake. When the final note rings out, it bounces throughout the auditorium. The resounding applause is the loudest so far, and I share a look with my parents, pride shining on all our faces.

The next two hours pass by in a blur, and I have to ignore the quiet buzzing of my phone in my pocket the entire time. Whoever is blowing it up better have a good reason.

When it comes time for the adjudicators to award first through third place, my mom clasps her hands tightly in her lap. I reach over and place my hand over hers. The announcer calls Angela's name for second place, and I can feel the dejection ripple out from my mom.

"It's fine," I whisper.

She tsks, her eyes narrowing. "That Han boy shouldn't even be in the same category as her. Everyone knows he is being classically trained; it's not fair. How is Angela supposed to win with him there?"

"Ma." I give her hand a squeeze.

The lights come up and the audience applauds for the three students on stage. Mom plasters a smile on her face as Angela comes down the stairs.

"Great job, Angie." I reach down and scoop her up in a giant hug.

She wriggles in my arms. "Ohmigod, *go go.* Stop, you're so embarrassing."

I place her back down and she makes a fuss of straightening out her black performance dress. I can tell she's annoyed that the certificate in her hand doesn't have a shiny gold circle on it, but at least she seems a little more distracted.

"She should have played a harder piece."

My eyes cut to Auntie An, who appears next to me like a ghost summoned from the trenches. Her words are spoken in a hush, but Angela is close enough that if she decides to pay attention, she'll hear the judgmental tone.

"'Raindrop' was the right choice. I couldn't play it that seamlessly when I was her age."

"That's not saying much."

I clench my jaw to keep from saying something disrespectful even though she deserves it. God, she fucking deserves it. Bitterness stems from my mother's sister like weeds from the crack in a sidewalk.

It's a tradition in our household to learn an instrument while growing up, and both Angela and I had leaned into piano—even though I think our father still wishes one of us had picked up the violin. Still, I was never the most musically inclined. I was better at sports in school—specifically swimming. I won countless medals for breaststroke, but my aunt would always mention how *her son* was stacking trophies at national recitals. Her competitive nature against my mom does my head in, and I hate that I'm dragged into the middle of it time and time again.

"I don't see your little girlfriend." She makes an exaggerated effort to look around the room.

"She was busy."

"Too busy to meet your family? After a direct invitation?" She scoffs. "I would say I'm shocked, but it seems fitting. She didn't exactly look like a respectable woman."

Fire licks at my skin with every word she enunciates, a beast within me stirring awake as she continues to poke at me—poke at Deer, like she has any clue what *kind* of woman she is.

"*Po po* will be disappointed. She was so interested to meet her, and this is not a great first impression."

"I never told *po po* she would be here." The accusation is clear in my voice.

Auntie An raises her thin eyebrows in nonchalance.

I am going to have to come up with a better excuse for this whole situation since it seems like she is dead set on making a fuss about Deer—on making me seem like lesser than her son in the eyes of my grandmother.

For the first time today, I think that maybe I should have brought Deer here with me. It is a lot harder to deal with a fake girlfriend when it seems like she barely exists. She would also know what to say. Deer spends all day using that fake high-pitched voice and putting on a performance for her viewers as The Cozy Deer. I have no doubt that she would be able to spin this story better than me.

"All right, who is ready for dim sum?" Dad comes over and begins to usher us all out of the auditorium, trying to ease the growing tension that is floating around us like a gray cloud.

I take the chance to separate myself from my aunt, getting ahead of everyone so I can retreat to my car without any further questions until I'm trapped at the restaurant. I shove my hand in my pocket, fishing around for my car key as we filter out into the high school's parking lot.

"*Ka-yee.*"

I freeze at my grandmother calling me by my given name.

"*Nei neoi peng yau hai been?*"

Where is your girlfriend?

Shit.

I look down to see my grandmother has snuck her way over to me during the shuffle. She is peering around, not in an accusatory way, but there is definitely a suspicious glint in the way she is taking in the situation. Considering it seems like my supposed girlfriend sprang out of nowhere, I don't blame her. Getting this ruse past her is going to be harder than convincing Auntie An—at least she's seen Deer. My grandmother, on the other hand, is one of the sharpest women I know. The only person who can beat her at mahjong is my grandfather, and that's because she secretly lets him win.

"Your *yi ma* said she was coming."

God damn Auntie An.

"She—"

"Hey, Angela. Congratulations, your performance was

totally magical."

Every bone in my body turns to stone at the words.

I would recognize her voice in a room filled with a thousand people.

I turn around, and sure enough, Deer stands in front of my little sister. If not for her pink hair, I would've needed to do a double take. She's dressed differently than normal— a white sundress that reaches just shy of her knees and a pair of pale pink heels that are nowhere near as tall as the shoes she normally wears. I hesitate to call it conservative because, despite her efforts, the dress does nothing to hide the killer cleavage she is sporting.

She holds out a bouquet of yellow roses, and my sister accepts, a confused smile on her face. Deer straightens and her gaze connects with mine.

I'm once again taken aback. Even her makeup is more subdued, lacking the glitter she typically douses herself in.

The entire look she has going on is so normal that it's abnormal on her. Well, as normal as a girl with pink hair can look.

"Hi."

She smiles at me, and I realize I was wrong. Even when she tries to tamp down her shine, she still sparkles like no one else I've met. Something about her is like cracking open a rock in a mine and finding the most stunning gem- stone inside—it glitters from every angle, no matter what you do.

"Hey."

The air whistles to a stop as she jogs the few feet over to me, and I'm a fucking sinful man watching the way her tits bounce. There is nothing family friendly happening in my brain.

"Are you surprised?"

"Uh…"

Yeah, I'm fucking surprised.

"I'm guessing you didn't see my texts." She rolls her eyes and nudges me playfully. "I know I said I wouldn't be able to make it because of the appointment, but I knew I couldn't miss this, so I found a way to make it work."

"Right."

What?

She bends around me and holds out the second bouquet in her arms, this one made of red roses. "*Nei hou. Ngo giu Deer.*"

"*Do ze.*" My grandmother takes the flowers from her with a smile. "*Nei siu dak hou leng.*"

Deer falters for a second, blinking at my grandmother as her eyes widen a fraction. "I'm so sorry. That is basically all the Cantonese I know."

"I said you have a pretty smile."

"Oh! Thank you." She stands back at my side and leans closer to me. Her arm is barely brushing mine, but it's enough to send a crackle across my skin.

"*Taa han jau ji si,*" *Po po* tucks the bouquet close to her chest and sets off for my parents' car.

She's interesting.

Well, that isn't a bad thing.

With my grandmother's approval, everyone starts moving again, packing into their cars so we can make our drive to the restaurant. It is like a religious practice; whenever we have something to celebrate, we go to this hole-in-the-wall restaurant that's been running for the last forty years—basically since *po po* immigrated here from China with my *gung gung*.

"Should I get in your car?" Deer keeps her voice hushed as she walks alongside me.

"Where did you park?"

"Like over there-ish. Doesn't matter though, I'm getting in anyway. Looks more couple-y."

She waves me off, the charms on her nails glinting in the sun, and makes her way to the passenger side. I can feel everyone's eyes on me as I realize my mistake too late.

Fuck. I should've opened the door for her.

And because I can't seem to catch a God damn break today, the back door opens, and I watch in the rearview mirror as my sister climbs into the back of my Jeep.

"Angela, what are you doing?"

"Mom said I could ride with you." She closes the door with more force than necessary.

Great. How am I supposed to figure out what the hell is going on with Deer when I have Angela in the car? We are about to be surrounded by ten of my family members, and she has absolutely zero prep as my supposed girlfriend.

"So, this is your girlfriend?" Angela leans forward over the center console and peers at Deer without any remorse. "Is he blackmailing you or something?"

Without missing a beat, Deer laughs. "She's funny. Clearly the humor in the family skipped a sibling."

Angela pauses, reassessing her, but I see the way the compliment runs over her and soaks into her skin. She doesn't smile, exactly, there's just a slight twitch at the corner of her mouth as she says "thanks" before slumping back in her seat.

Angela doesn't seem to notice the tension radiating from me or the way I keep sneaking glances at Deer, who seems to be cool as a fucking cucumber while she scrolls through her social media.

"So, how long have you been sucking face with my brother?"

I almost swerve off the road.

Chapter TWENTY

JACKSON

"So, how long have you been dating?"

"Just a few weeks."

It's the same response Deer gave my sister earlier.

Every question that's been thrown at us, she answers before I'm even able to take a breath. Deer is weaving a story, like a spider creating a delicate web in the corner of a dark room. No one knows that she is carefully trapping them in it with every detail she spins.

It helps that the narrative she's crafted runs parallel to our real life—just with a few embellishments.

"I didn't know he was even interested in anyone." Mom hasn't taken her eyes off Deer once since we've sat down. She seems to be analyzing her within an inch of her life.

Then again, everyone is. Deer sits at the round table like a bright pink gumball.

I reach forward and drink what is probably my fifth cup of jasmine tea in the last half hour. It's the only thing I can do to keep myself busy other than stuff my face with food because I don't want to say the wrong thing and screw this up when it seems to actually be working.

"Tell me about it. I've been crushing on him for years and had no idea either. Totally took my chance confessing to him." She places a hand on my forearm.

"You confessed first?"

"Sure did. Jackson's not that forward, ya know, likes to keep his cards close."

My mom nods her head in agreement. "I have always wondered why he's never had a girlfriend before. He mustn't have known how to make the first move."

My left eye twitches. Why does it feel like her narrative is painting me as a loser?

"Nope. Men can be a little emotionally closed off; they're just not as attuned as we are."

"You do seem like you have quite the feminine touch."

"Thank you!" Deer runs her free hand through her hair.

"The pink is *kei gwaai*," *gung gung* frowns.

Auntie An smirks at my grandfather's comment, and it causes Deer to stiffen almost imperceptibly. She might not know what *kei gwaai* means, but she has the social cues to deduce that it wasn't exactly a compliment.

"I don't think it's strange. I think she looks like a doll, and it counteracts your grandson's bleakness." Auntie Lei smiles at us from across the table. "You two make a cute pair." She didn't bat an eye at meeting Deer and has spent the entire meal dropping reassurances, while everyone else keeps their guard up.

Auntie Lei is my dad's younger sister, and she has always been supportive of me. She was the only family member who didn't get pissed off when they all found out I'd dropped out of college and became a streamer—probably because she sees me as a second son since her own son has been studying at an international university in Shanghai the last few years.

"Thank you."

"I'm confused. If you have been seeing each other, why have you been going on the blind dates we've all been setting up?" My uncle frowns, piling more baozi onto his plate.

Auntie An hums in agreement at her husband's annoying observation.

"Like I said, we only just started dating. Shield, I mean Jackson and I wanted to keep our relationship private since we are both in the spotlight. Our careers are super on the up right now, and it's really easy for things to leak, so we thought it was simpler to just to play along. Plus, it helps keep your family's privacy intact as well."

Damn, she is good at this.

"It seems like everything to do with this video game stuff is steeped in secrets and lies." Auntie An narrows her eyes at us. "You said Deer was a nickname, correct?"

Deer's hand tenses on my arm, the tips of her nails pressing into my skin ever so slightly, though her face stays a practiced, placid mask.

"Technically. It's also my gamertag."

"What does that mean?" *Po po* whispers to me, but her

voice carries across the table.

"It's a video game thing," I whisper back.

"You play games as well?" She leans across to make eye contact with Deer.

"I do," she smiles. "I'm not as famous as Jackson, though. He is part of an epic legacy, and everyone really respects him."

She is laying it on thick, but I don't really mind it. It's nice to have someone in my corner who actually understands me, who believes in me.

That being said, she is selling herself short. I don't think Deer realizes how many people adore her content, how she has quickly become a star in the community.

"It's still just playing games," Auntie An chimes in.

Deer tilts her head. "I know a lot of people have trouble understanding the video game industry, let alone streaming, but it is one of the most lucrative spaces to be in. The video game market is worth over two hundred fifty billion dollars and has an expected growth rate of over eight percent over the next few years. The esports industry alone has doubled in the last six years with a viewership of over five hundred million worldwide, and its most popular game, *Gods League,* has a recorded two hundred million hours' worth of streaming watched. The people who own these companies and develop the software are making bank. Sure, there are smaller indie companies and start-ups, but even they have the power to disrupt the norm with the right console or game. And if we look into video game streaming," she lets out a laugh, "wow. People spend more time watching people play video games than playing themselves. You would be shocked to learn the revenue you earn on a video that has over three million views. Sure, not everyone can be in that top percent, but those of us who are make more in a month than your attorney son does in a year."

The table falls to a hum at Deer's speech; there's just the sound of Angela sucking through the straw of her fruit tea.

"That's very impressive to hear." There's an amused glint in Auntie Lei's eyes. "It's lovely to hear about Jackson's success from someone who cares about him so much."

"*Hai meh*? You're just going to believe what she says? *Steven* is successful. *Steven* is dating a lovely girl." Auntie An flicks her wrist at Deer. "We don't even know this girl's real name or what her parents do. How can you trust an outsider?"

This time there is no denying the way Deer's nails dig into my forearm.

No one speaks. They're all waiting to see if she'll answer. My back molars grind against one another as I watch them place Deer under the microscope.

She's not some prey to be cornered, and I'm not going to feed her to the wolves.

"You don't have to answer that." I take her hand that is gripping my forearm and squeeze it reassuringly before stealing a look around the table. "I brought her here to meet you out of respect, not for you to interrogate her and ask private questions."

"Jackson, you can't spring a girlfriend on us and not expect us to ask questions." Mom frowns.

"They're not even hard questions," Auntie An sniffs.

Sure, for normal people—but Deer doesn't fall into

that category.

"Did you get raided by the police?" Angela flips her tablet around, broadcasting to the entire table the *Gamer Weekly* article about Deer's swatting.

"Police?" My grandparents share a concerned look.

"Fucking hell," I mutter lowly as I rake a hand down my face. This is quickly taking a turn from great to awful.

"Egg custard, anyone?" my dad cuts in with a cheery voice.

We all stare at him as he indicates for the server to place a couple of silver platters on the table.

"Honey," mom's warning tone rings out.

My dad waves her off, plucking a custard and putting it on her plate. "It's the first time you've met the girl. You don't want to scare her off when all you've wanted is for him to find a girlfriend." He spins the lazy Susan, bringing the dessert over to me. "Ever had an egg custard, Deer?"

Her shoulders relax slightly, and she smiles. "No, I haven't."

"They're not that sweet, but I think you'll like them." I grab two of the custards, putting one on her plate before popping the other on my *po po*'s.

"Thank you." She picks it up and takes a bite, her eyes widening. "Oh, wow."

"Good?"

"Mhm." She takes another bite, some of that sparkle returning to her eyes.

I smile at her, reaching forward and tucking a stray piece of hair behind her ear. My fingers ghost the shell of her ear, and I freeze, catching myself. My fingers curl back in on themselves like she's burned me.

My other palm starts to sweat, and I realize I'm still holding onto her hand—but I don't let go.

All my wires are getting crossed from this fake girl-friend thing.

The table remains under a hushed silence, unspoken questions floating around us. My aunts whisper to their husbands, while my mom pointedly ignores my dad. Angela is distractedly scrolling through her tablet, glancing up at us every once in a while—I don't even want to know what she is looking up; it will just give me a headache. Overall, everyone seems to have accepted my father bull-dozing the conversation in a new direction.

Po po leans into me and I angle my head down, making it easier for her to whisper whatever it is she wants to say.

"I'll cancel your dates." *Po po* flicks her eyes between Deer and me. "For now."

The smallest sigh escapes me as relief floods my body. I have no idea how we pulled this off, but we did.

"Do ze, po po."

"Don't thank me, thank her." A smile tugs at the corner of her wrinkled cheek. "She cares about you; I see that."

I glance at Deer, at this woman who is slowly turning my world upside down. I'm sure she cares about me as a friend, and I won't deny that I'm protective of her myself. But I'm starting to think that maybe I don't dislike that sugary personality of hers as much as I thought. Maybe I'm developing a sweet-tooth—just for her.

Chapter
TWENTY-ONE

DEER

66 | feel like that went pretty well!"

"It was passable."

"Oh, come on. I'd give our performance a solid B."

Actually, I'd give myself an A and Jackson a C—which is how we average a B. I definitely carried us through that lunch.

"Where the hell did you come from anyway?"

"Well, I went to an international high school in Washington before moving down to Cali. But if you want to get to the roots, then technically Carlingford in Ireland."

"You know that's not what I meant."

I just grin.

He sighs, but I see the way the corner of his mouth ticks up slightly. It's something most people would miss, but I've spent too much time watching him the last few weeks. I've committed every detail about Jackson Lau to memory so that I'll never miss a beat.

"Thank you, by the way. The flowers were a nice touch."

I shrug, sticking my arm out the window so I can play with the wind as he drives us back to the school parking lot. "I told you I'd help. It's no biggie."

Even though I'd spent the extra time looking up the meaning of flowers and their colors to make sure I was making the right impression. Turns out, yellow roses aren't that easy to come by when you're on a time crunch.

"How'd you know where I was?"

"Syd."

In my periphery, Jackson whips his head toward me. "What? Seriously? Sydney signed off on this?"

"Signed off is a bit of a stretch. She wasn't exactly thrilled when I first brought it up, but when I explained it to her, she agreed it was actually the lesser of two evils. She just said we need to keep it on the down-low unless we want a big fuss."

"This is a lot to process."

I use my free hand to reach over and pat him on the shoulder. "Don't worry, big boy. We've got this."

"For the fifth time, I told you not to call me that," he grunts.

I smile up at him. It was definitely a stressful lunch and not something I want to put myself through again any time soon, but it was worth it. The second I showed up, I could practically smell the tension in the air. I like to think I did a pretty good job wafting it away, but his family aren't the easiest to read. Makes sense since I still feel like I've barely cracked the surface with Jackson. But the fissures I've created in his stoic exterior so far have given way to a mosaic, and like a dragon hoarding gold, I'll keep all those shards to myself.

"You look different, by the way."

I catch my reflection in the sideview mirror. "Syd suggested it. Plus, after meeting your aunt, I thought it would be smarter to tone it down. Like Aleks said, I didn't want this to backfire and have them totally freaked, so they push the blind dates harder. That would be really sucky." I look down at the white sundress, smoothing the fabric over my thighs. I'm not going to tell him that I bought it just for this lunch—I think he'll feel bad. Jackson isn't as much of a grump as he makes himself out to be. "What do you think of it?"

"All guys like sundresses." He pauses for a beat, and I think that's all I'm going to get from him, but he surprises me by adding, "I like your normal look, though."

"My normal isn't exactly other people's normal."

"Well, I like it." His gaze lingers on me before turning back to the road, and heat licks across my skin. "I don't want you changing yourself for my family. I would never ask my girlfriend to do anything like that."

A full-on flame bursts in my chest, but I try to tamp it down, mentally imagining a million fans blasting the flush away as I keep my expression wry.

"We'll see if you still say that when I rock up to the next family function in a bright pink mini skirt and go-go boots."

He smirks. "I dare you."

Something about the tilt of his lips has me wanting to lean forward to kiss the corner.

This is *so* not good.

I want to help him out as his fake girlfriend because it is something a good person would do, not because of a crusty old crush that was supposed to have died months ago.

Oh Gods…what if my crush never died? What if it was just in hibernation? What if everything I've been doing has woken it back up?

This is very, very, very, very bad.

Jackson pulls into the parking lot, and I drag my arm back into the car so I can point to where my car is. It's a bit moot since my convertible is the only vehicle left in the lot other than a pickup truck—and it doesn't take a genius to guess which of the two is probably mine.

"I swear, you and Parker are so similar."

"Says the guy with an Army green Jeep."

"It came that way. I didn't pay extra for it."

"What makes you think I paid extra? How do you know mine didn't come that way?"

"It's bright fucking pink."

"So judgy."

Although, I did pay extra for it. Not to get it painted pink but because it was a limited edition and only a few were made. Definitely one of my more questionable purchases, but it wasn't like I couldn't afford it. Plus, despite his jab, I am nowhere near as bad as Parker and his obsessive blue sports car collection.

"Well, this was fun. I'll see you later." I pop the door open and go to hop out when Jackson's hand shoots out to curl around my shoulder to stop me. "What?"

He frowns, staring at his own hand before releasing me. "Nothing. I'll see you back at the apartment." He turns away and begins fiddling with his navigation system.

"Okay. Bye." I slip into my car and shut the door harder than I should.

Here I am doing something nice for him, and yet he still has this layer of ice around his heart. How freaking hard is it to melt that damn thing? I just want him to like me, dammit.

A bone deep awareness sinks in.

Fuck.

Fuckity fuck fuck.

My old crush is definitely out of hibernation.

I groan, leaning my head against the steering wheel. This is going to be a very long drive back to the apartment. A whole hour to stew in my thoughts—just lovely.

I start up the engine and blast my music loudly in an attempt to drown out my brain from straying to thoughts of Jackson. Anything to distract myself right now would be welcome.

As if the Gods hear my prayer, my music pauses to welcome an incoming call from Lee.

I hit answer and keep my voice light. "Hey, hey."

"Hey, I see you're headed back. How'd it go?"

I swear, Lee keeps track of my location like a mom whose teenager just left for college.

"Good, I think. They seem convinced for now."

"Nice, knew you'd pull it off."

"Obvi."

"Think you'll make it back in time for the party?"

I groan.

"Come on," she whines. "Even Stevie said she'd come, and she's been holed up in her place all week prepping for that art show."

"That's great! Means you don't need me."

"No, because Aleks is also coming, and that means that even though she says she's going to keep me company, those two will end up abandoning me to go bang in a closet or something."

"Not if you ask her nicely."

"Deer, pleeease."

"Fine."

Crap. I hadn't meant to say that.

I'm not sure how much social battery I have left. I am already emotionally exhausted from having to play a role for Jackson's family. If I have to go to the party tonight, it means switching myself on for another couple of hours.

"Thanks, you're the best. I'll be over in like two hours, and then we can all catch a ride to the party together, okay?"

"Okay."

"Love you."

"Love you, too."

Chapter
TWENTY-TWO

DEER

"Shots for everyone!" Parker stands on a pool table holding a bottle of very expensive vodka. At least twenty people crowd around him, and he begins pouring the liquid into their mouths.

"Sydney is so going to murder him," I mutter to myself.

Myself, because I have been abandoned. Or, almost abandoned.

Stevie and Aleks are making out on the couch in front of me; the pretty brunette is straddling her boyfriend while their tongues decide to see how far down each other's throats they can go.

Sydney is going to murder them as well.

And as for the lady of the hour? Well, Lee is chatting with a group of lifestyle creators who intimidate the hell out of me. Granted, she keeps glancing back my way, giving me a not-so-subtle thumbs-up to check in every twenty or so minutes. But that's beside the point.

This sucks.

There are too many people, and I am still too sober.

Three shots have done nothing but level out my nerves and put me on the same plane as a normal person.

"Deer!" Parker's British accent draws out the vowels. "Come over here!" He waggles the bottle of liquor.

I don't really want to drink from the communal well of Copper Wolf vodka—even if the bottle is made from crystal.

I swipe my hand in front of my neck, making a cutting motion as I call out, "No thanks."

He pouts because only Parker Covington can make pouting look attractive. But before he can sucker me into taking a shot like I know he will—because I seriously have an issue saying no to people—I push up from my safe little nest in the corner of the room and weave my way through the crowd.

There are way more people here than I expected, and it seems impossible to get anywhere without someone's body touching my own. It's a sensory overload. Especially with all the flashing lights from people taking selfies and videos. This whole party is just a bunch of people trying to use each other to get a leg up in the world. They're wondering whose ladder rung they can step on next to push themselves higher. No judgement on them, it's a tough world out there. I'm just not interested in it.

I spot the door to one of the back rooms and push my way through the throng of bodies until my hand has enough space to reach out and grasp the handle. I push down and practically hurtle my body through the door.

I instantly regret my choice as I watch a guy snort a line of coke off some chick's cleavage.

Mm. Nope.

I swivel on my platform heels to retrace my steps, except a body suddenly bumps into mine, almost putting me on my ass.

"Well, if it isn't the princess."

My stomach curdles at the voice.

"Decker."

"I'm surprised to see you here. Didn't think you left the castle much these days?"

"You know how it is. I like to come down and see how the peasants are doing every once in a while." I give him a dramatic once over. "And now I have, so I'm leaving."

I push past him, and he doesn't stop me. Daniel Decker is one of the most narcissistic streamers I know, and unfortunately someone I had the displeasure of going to high school with. But because our families know each other, it means Decker has some sense of self-preservation and knows not to mess with me. His family has called in one too many favors with mine, so he will always be in my debt and never a true threat to me. Still, seeing him has just made this night all the more lackluster.

I want to leave.

Cementing my choice, I pull out my phone and toss a quick text to the group, letting them know I'm splitting. Parker might be the life of the party right now, but he'll keep an eye on Lee.

I break through the crowd and slam my palm onto the

down button for the elevator. The doors slide open, and a group of girls spill out, giggling and laughing. One of them spots me, her eyes widening with recognition.

"Ohmigod, you're Deer! Can I get a picture?"

"Sure." I plaster on my perfect smile and lean close, throwing up a peace sign.

"Are you leaving?"

"Yeah." I throw on a pout. "I'm not feeling great."

"Oh nooo."

"Yeah." I slip into the elevator and begin pressing the close door button like my life depends on it. "Have a great night, though."

The doors can't close quickly enough as I'm stuck keeping my mask in place with the girl. Finally, the last slivers of flashing lights disappear as the doors clink shut, and I let out a deep breath. The noise of the party fades away as I descend back to the ground.

When the doors open to the ground level, I freeze. There are groups of people waiting to get in as security guards check them over.

Dammit. I should've known this would be the case.

Yeah, it's an invite-only party—but that's never stopped the word from getting out. Everyone wants to be where the limelight shines.

My eyes frantically bounce over the crowd as I quickly map my escape route. Without giving myself time to hesitate, I throw my shoulders back and push through.

I hear a few people call my name, and more than one person grabs my shoulder or pulls on my skirt. But I press one hand to my chest and keep a placid smile on my face as I make my way through the droves of people.

There's too many of them. I need to get away.

More people continue to call my name, and all I can think about is finding somewhere else to go. I break through the crowd and immediately make to cross the street, putting more distance between myself and the party, more distance between myself and everyone else. It's still too much. I feel too exposed. I didn't plan this well at all. I need an escape.

Now.

I spot a couple slipping into what looks like an expensive cocktail lounge, a beautiful red door leading into the black brick building.

Close enough.

I follow behind them, fleeing the outside world for one of hushed music and vanilla-scented air. It doesn't take long for me to notice that there is something different about this place.

The lights are dim, casting a warm glow over the surrounding patrons. The lounge has been designed to resemble an old, prestigious university library. The seats are all jewel-toned velvet, and the tables are a dark walnut. Fake sconces light up the walls, interspersed between bookshelves that are filled with leather-bound tomes and decanters holding whiskey and red wine.

My attention snags as the couple before me flash their phones at the bouncer, some sort of passkey on their screens. The bouncer nods them forward and gestures to the back of the bar. I watch as they bypass all the other patrons and head for another deep red door in the back, scanning their phones again before disappearing.

Shit.

Nerves begin to prick at my skin as I worry about being let in.

"ID?"

I dig around in my purse for my driver's license, holding it out between two nails. The guy angles it up, flashing his light on it before giving me a once over. Once he deems my ID to be passable, he hands it back without a word.

"Thank you."

I try to feel confident as I make my way to the bar, picking a stool off to the side and hidden from anyone who might walk in. It's like I'm in my own little oasis.

"What can I get for you, darlin?" The bartender slides a glass of water and a house cocktail list in front of me. It only takes me a quick glance to land on something.

"The Broken Bombshell, please." I present my credit card to her.

"Open or closed?"

"Closed."

She nods, taking my card and the cocktail list.

I pick up the glass and take a healthy sip of cool water, my body finally calming down and no longer on high alert. Something about this place feels safe.

The red door in the back opens again, two men and a woman exiting this time. The men each give the woman a kiss on her cheek before walking out of the lounge, but the woman doesn't follow. She takes a seat at the far end of the bar, and I watch as the bartender pours her a glass of whiskey without a word. She's stunning, with long dark hair and smoky eyes. The dress she is wearing has a cutout on both sides, revealing a plush hourglass figure.

She catches me staring, and frowns slightly, tilting her

head to the side as she rakes her gaze over me. I fidget with the edge of my dress, worried that she can tell I don't belong. For a second, I think she's about to come over, but a man stops next to her and leans to whisper in her ear. Her eyes widen, some sort of realization glossing over them as she continues to look at me, before a serpentine smile spreads from her red lips. She turns to smooth out the man's tie, murmuring something to him, and then flicks her wrist back to the red door.

He gives her a nod, walking past and scanning his phone before disappearing behind that damn mysterious door.

"One Broken Bombshell and the check."

My daze is shattered as I blink down at the coupe glass filled with a blush pink liquid and topped with a rosemary garnish.

"Thank you." I quickly scribble out my tip and pocket my credit card. I hold out the little clipboard, working up the courage to ask the bartender, "What is that red door?"

A knowing smile crosses her features as she takes the check from me. "If you have to ask, you don't need to know."

That's a little dickish.

I pick up my cocktail and take a sip. The smoky mezcal blends with the fresh strawberry puree and a hint of rosemary. It helps soothe some of the annoyance I'm feeling—but annoyance is better than panic.

When I raise my eyes back to the mysterious woman, I find her chatting away into her phone. Her gaze is still on me, and I have to bite back the instinct to run my fingers through my hair or smooth down my dress.

There's something unnerving about her, like she recognizes me. But it's not the same as when people recognize me from my streams or viral content; she looks at me like she knows me personally.

Minutes pass, and even once she has finished her phone call and begins talking to yet another young man who sidles up next to her at the bar, she doesn't stop glancing my way. I've been bouncing between watching her and that damn red door, but I still can't put the pieces together. The best I've come up with is that there might be some high stakes poker room in the back—like the one I've heard Parker and his friend go to in Vegas.

I'm thinking about this way too much. I should really just go home and call it a night.

I down the last of my drink and pull out my phone, clicking on the rideshare app. The nearest available ride is…

Fifteen minutes away.

Of course it is.

My finger is millimeters away from clicking the confirmation button when I catch the woman moving. My eyes fly up, tracking the foxlike smile that stretches across her red lips as she stares just past me.

In my periphery, I see a man flash his phone at the bouncer before stalking in. The woman gracefully slides off her bar stool, legs eating up the distance as she walks from the back of the lounge to the entrance.

"Took you long enough." Her voice has a sultry pull to it.

"Savannah." The man's voice is deep. Familiar.

"I've kept an eye on her, don't worry." She rolls her

eyes playfully and then reaches out to dust off his shoulder. My vision turns red at the edges, and I have no idea why until the next sentence leaves his mouth.

"Where is she?"

With just three words, I know who it is. I don't even need him to turn around.

"She's right there." Her finger points directly at me, and I freeze like a fox caught in a hen house.

Chapter
TWENTY-THREE

JACKSON

"Jackson?"

Deer's bright blue eyes blink at me as she stares, frozen at the bar of the Cardinal Club.

"What are you doing here?"

She snaps out of her daze, shoulders stiffening as she tilts her chin up. "I wanted a drink."

"Here?"

"Yes. Why? Is that a problem?"

It is *such* a problem. How'd she even find this place? Did she find my duffle bag when she was staying in my room? She never gave off the impression that she was the type to snoop around.

"What happened to the party?"

"It was lame."

"Lame?"

"Yes. Lame."

The videos on Parker's story say the party is anything but lame. In fact, it seemed like it was spawned from the third level of hell—everyone a glutton for drugs, sex, booze, and fame. But that isn't exactly Deer's style.

"Come on, let's get you home." I hold my hand out, but she pushes it aside, looking past me.

"Who's your friend?"

"I'm Savannah." The woman next to me smiles and reaches out her hand to Deer, but instead of shaking it, she places a kiss on her knuckles. "It's lovely to meet you, Deirdre."

All the life drains from Deer's face, her skin turning as white as her eyeliner.

"What?" The word is barely a whisper as it leaves her glossy lips. She scuttles off the bar stool, walking backward until her back hits the wall like a cornered rabbit.

I shoot a look at Savannah before squeezing around the bar. "I thought you said nothing happened?"

Her brows furrow. "Nothing did. As soon as I realized who she was, I didn't take my eyes off her. I'm not sure what's wrong?"

"Deer?" I hold my hands out as I approach her, watching her eyes dart like a ping-pong ball between Savannah and me. I look around myself, trying to figure out what spooked her. "Deer, what's going on, baby?" I lean forward, bracing my hands on her shoulders and giving them a light squeeze.

"Who are you?" Her panic dissipates, instantly replaced with venomous anger. Deer shoves out of my arms, stalking past me until she is chest to chest with a startled

Savannah. "And how do you know my name?"

"What?" Savannah's red lips pull into a tense, confused smile as she frowns down at the petite woman before her.

"How. Do you know. My name?" The words are hushed but laced with a lethal smoke.

"Deirdre?"

Deirdre?

"Yes," she hisses, looking around the lounge like she's worried we might be overheard.

"It was on your license when you came in and logged into the system. I—" Savannah's dark eyes flit to mine with a silent plea for help, except I have no idea what the hell to do. "I'm not sure what else to tell you."

"Oh, I wasn't aware this establishment just handed out private information to all their customers." Deer lets out a laugh, and more than a few heads turn our way.

"Well, they do when you're a majority stakeholder who has heard about a certain pink-haired woman from their good friend before. I was just making sure a lost lamb didn't get eaten by the wolves." Some of that signature fire returns to Savannah. Outside the bedroom, she is a domineering force to be reckoned with. "You should mind your tone."

"And you should watch your back."

"O-kay, ladies," I push forward, placing a hand on each of their shoulders to keep them apart. "Let's not draw more attention to ourselves. Savannah, thank you for your help. I'll take her home."

She holds my gaze for a second, unspoken words swirling between us, but she lets it go, swiveling on her heels and stalking for the club door before disappearing inside—no doubt to let off steam with some poor, unsuspecting soul or souls. When I told her about Deer, I didn't think anything like this was going to happen. It was an offhanded comment I thought she'd forgotten, but I should've known Savannah never forgets the details. Still, I'm grateful.

"I'm not going anywhere," Deer bites out. She's uncaged right now; it's a side I've never seen from her before.

"Yes, you are."

"No." She pushes past me. "In fact, I'm going to see what exactly Miss Majority Stakeholder is hiding."

"No, you're not." I reach forward and scoop her up, maneuvering her until she is thrown over my shoulder in a fireman's carry.

She lets out a string of curses that would cause even the most depraved sinner's ears to heat as she kicks her legs in protest. But despite the amount of damage she tries to inflict, she is still half my size.

My car is running at the valet since I'd only asked for them to hold it while I ran in to grab Deer in the first place. And while the valet attendant is a little thrown off by me carrying an angry pink demon, it's definitely not the strangest thing he's seen come out of the Cardinal Club.

I get her into the passenger seat and lock the door before quickly running to my side of the car, getting in, and taking off.

She's surprisingly silent as I drive home and doesn't attempt or threaten to open the door and roll out, which only makes me worry more.

What the hell happened back there?

I could barely even piece it together myself, so much

of the conversation was unsaid.

Only one thing was clear: she flipped when Savannah called her Deirdre.

As soon as I pull into the apartment complex and park the car, she jumps out and makes a beeline for the elevator. But despite her best efforts at trying to get the doors to close before I mosey my way over, she fails. I stick a hand between the closing metal doors, forcing them to reopen as I take my place next to her.

When the elevator stops on her floor and she gets off, I follow her out.

"What are you doing?"

"Seemed easier to follow you than to try to drag you to the penthouse."

"You didn't seem to have much of an issue manhandling me earlier," she snarls.

"Well, you weren't really open to reason, now, were you?"

She lets out a huff before stalking to her apartment, heels clicking angrily on the floor with each step.

"Seriously, stop." She shoots me an angry glare as she covers her keypad with one hand and inputs her code with the other.

"Can't. Have to make sure you're safe."

And that's when I see it again, the anxious panic bubbling beneath the surface, the stuff she is trying to keep hidden but is struggling to contain as it grows.

Her resolve wavers just enough to afford me the chance to slip through her reinforced walls, and I use that split second to usher her inside her apartment, following closely behind.

But as soon as she crosses the threshold, every string that has been keeping her upright snaps. The familiarity and safety of her apartment strips away her hard shell, and I watch as her steps start to drag as she trudges into her bedroom, failing to slam it closed.

I close the door behind me and head to her fridge, pulling out her water filter and pouring us each a glass.

When half an hour passes, I begin to wonder if she's actually going to come back out or just leave me here...I wouldn't put it past her.

I raise my knuckles to her bedroom door and give it a short rap.

"What."

"I brought you water."

There's a beat of silence before the door cracks open. I hold the glass out to her, and she takes it between her hands, cradling it to her chest as she peers up at me.

"Why are you still here?"

"Because I didn't want you to be alone."

She lets out a sigh and opens the door fully before turning to head into her bathroom. I take a seat on the footboard bench, watching her.

"You feeling better?"

"I feel like I'm going to throw up."

"Okay."

She eyes me through the reflection in the mirror, her nails tapping rhythmically on the marble counter. "Do you have any other questions?"

"I do."

"Are you going to ask them?"

"Would you answer them?"

She slumps forward onto her elbows, dropping her head so her pink hair creates a curtain around her face.

My body moves on its own, unable to watch as the cracks in her armor begin to bleed. I wrap my arms around her, lightly pulling her into my body.

"Have a shower. Take a breath. I'll be here when you're ready."

"Promise?"

"Promise."

I place a kiss on the top of her head—not giving it much thought—before letting go and shutting the door behind me. It only takes a few minutes before I hear the shower start up, and it helps calm the tapping of my foot on the carpet.

I have questions. Of course, I have questions.

Like who the fuck is Deirdre? Are her eyes blue or did I imagine them a different color? Does she feel safe in her new apartment? Has she had any more nightmares? What's her favorite season? Did she actually enjoy watching *Devil Nun*? Who are her parents? Does she have any siblings? What's her favorite Pokémon (I think it's Togepi)?

I don't know my fake girlfriend, and it's driving me up the wall because for the first time in years, I find myself actually wanting to get to know someone. Deer has found a way to get under my skin, and now I'm determined to do the same. I want her to think about me just as much as I think about her. I can't be the only person in this relationship who feels like their entire world is slowly tilting.

The bathroom door opens and a cloud of steam wafts out. Deer hugs her fluffy pink robe close to her body as she makes a beeline for her walk-in closet. She finally emerges in an over-sized anime T-shirt and micro shorts.

Fuck me.

When she looks up, one of my questions is finally answered.

"Your eyes are brown."

"Biologically, yes."

She throws her robe haphazardly into her bathroom and then pads over, crawling onto her bed. I turn around and face her as she gathers up the blanket on her bed and scrunches it into a ball close to her body.

"I thought it was a trick of the light the other night."

"Nope." She avoids looking at me directly. "No one else knows."

"So, I'm special?"

"Hardly. It's just hard to keep the contacts in when taking off my makeup; they get all cloudy."

"Sure," I grin at her excuse. "Brown eyes are cute."

"Yeah, well, they don't work." She squints at me. "You're blurry unless you stand close to me."

"Oh?" I shift from the footboard to her mattress. "How close?" I continue moving across the bed, closing the distance between us.

Her hands tighten on her blanket, but she says nothing until I'm mere inches away. I drink up the way her cheeks are flushed red from the shower. Her skin is covered in a smattering of very pale freckles. I reach out and cup her jaw, running my thumb over them.

"Too close." She pushes me back with more force than I expect from her tiny body. "My vision is not that messed up."

I lean back on my forearms, tilting my head as I watch

her draw her knees to her chest.

"What's going on in that mind of yours, Sparkles?"

A haunted look passes through her eyes. "Why haven't you asked me?"

"Asked you what?"

She lets out a light huff that borders on an almost self-deprecating laugh. The small smile that pulls at the corners of her lips is sad and her lids lower with a look of defeat.

"What happened back at the club, Deer?"

Her sadness muddles into confusion. "Club?"

And now it's my turn to avert my gaze. "How about this. You tell me what happened, and I tell you what's behind that red door."

Some of the tension leaves her shoulders, and she gnaws on her lower lip before nodding.

"You do have to go first," I push, nudging her foot with my own.

She lets out a tsk, but when her eyes meet mine again, I see a fire building. She opens her mouth, and that fire promptly snuffs out. "I'm going to be sick." She drops her forehead to her knees.

I'm so lost. I don't want to push her; I don't want to hurt her...but something tells me I need to. That whatever is haunting her is something she wants to share but is terrified to. Whatever weight she is carrying, I just want to be able to lessen the load even if it's just by the smallest fraction. Deer is always determined to be the knight of her own story, but even the strongest warrior needs backup.

So, I don't move. I sit and wait, and wait, and wait, until she finally comes to terms with herself.

"My name is Deirdre."

Deirdre.

"Sounds very…Irish."

"I know." She lets out a sigh, raising her head.

As someone who also kept their real name a secret for years, I know just how much this means. That she is entrusting me with a very fragile piece of her soul, and I can't afford to let it shatter. Everyone has their own reason for creating an alternate persona online. For Parker, it was so he didn't involve the reputation of his famous family name. For me, it was because I knew my family wouldn't approve and I wanted to keep my privacy. I want to know what Deer's story is.

"Your gamertag makes more sense now."

She smiles briefly. "Everyone called me Deir growing up."

"Washington, right?"

"Kinda. My mam and da moved us here when I was ten, but they moved back to Carlingford when I graduated high school."

"You don't have to answer, but why all the secrecy?"

"Cone of silence?"

I nod my head, and she slumps back against her headboard.

"Honestly, there's many reasons. One of them being that I do value my privacy. You've seen how it is for Lee. People love to invade the lives of female streamers, and they can be creepy about it. I've received some weird messages over the years. Having an alternate personality makes me feel safer, makes me feel like nothing will happen…although the swatting kind of murdered that hope."

"We'd never let anything happen to you."

"I appreciate that, but you guys can't be everywhere. You can't stop the creeps who flood my streams with sexual innuendos, or who DM me all the stuff they'd like to do to me if we ever met, or who mail used condoms to my P.O. box."

"Are you serious?"

She winces. "Yeah. It got bad, which is why I have my moderator handle it all—especially the fan mail and packages—to keep me safe."

"Shit. I'm sorry."

"It's not your fault." She sighs. "And then there's the Deer Hunters."

"The Deer Hunters?"

"The people who swatted me. They're dead set on freaking me out. I can't tell if it's because they hate me or are obsessed with me. Either way, I can't imagine how much worse it would be if they had access to my personal information."

"Why didn't you say this sooner? I thought it was just a random swatting."

My blood heats under my skin. How long has she been dealing with this? No wonder she has so much anxiety in public if she feels like there is a group of people out to get her. If I'd known, I could've…I could've done something. Anything.

"You can't do anything about them, Jackson. I've tried."

"Well, I have a Parker."

"And?"

"And there aren't many places his family can't reach. We're ninety percent sure his sister has something to do with MI-6."

"Parker isn't the only person from an affluent family." She bites the inside of her cheek. "That's the second reason I've kept everything secret. My name's Deirdre Malloy."

I frown.

I'm not really sure where this is going.

"My da's name is Cathal Malvin Malloy." She pauses. "CM Malloy."

"Wait. As in *the* CM Malloy? The dude who founded *Gods League*?"

She nods.

Holy fuck. Deer is a legacy. Hell, it wouldn't be a stretch to say she comes from video game royalty.

"I knew it wouldn't take long for people to figure it out if they knew what my name was. I mean, look at Lee; you can find her entire family history on Wiki. I didn't want people to think my entire gaming career was based on who my family is—it's hard enough to get taken seriously as a female gamer."

"But you don't even play *Gods League*."

"Yeah, for a reason."

"Does this mean you're secretly super OP? Have you been holding out on us?"

She rolls her eyes. "I'm still not as good as Aleksander—and I don't want to be—but I could crush Parker."

"Anyone can crush Parker in *Gods League*."

"Fair."

"So, no one knows? Not even Lee?"

She shakes her head. "No. It all seemed too risky."

"But you're telling me."

"Well, you are my fake boyfriend, and I didn't have

much of a choice after Savannah." Her upper lip twitches. "I didn't count on my ID being logged into a system, I thought it was just a normal bar."

"I'm sorry about that."

"Will...will Savannah say anything?"

"No." I reach my hand out and lay it on her knee, giving it a squeeze. "If anyone knows discretion, it's Savannah."

"How do you know her?"

Here we go.

Chapter
TWENTY-FOUR

DEER

"Savannah?"

"Yeah, the beautiful woman who seemed *well* acquainted with you."

The words leave me easier now. Everything feels easier now. It doesn't feel like there are a set of claws gripping onto my shoulders, crushing me in on myself and making me crack under the pressure. The Category Five hurricane in my stomach has also calmed down, and I'm no longer at risk of upchucking the entire contents of my digestive system.

Granted, there was a moment there when I really thought I might just pass out from the sheer panic of it all. But I've gotten pretty good at quelling my anxiety attacks in the last couple of weeks—nightmares aside.

My head is still spinning from the fact that my secret

is no longer my own. I'm not alone anymore. Sure, Jackson is my fake boyfriend, my fake partner—but he is my partner, nonetheless. And it feels so fucking good to have someone in my corner who understands me.

I just hope I won't regret it. Especially since my heart is becoming more and more invested as I remain in his orbit. There's something comforting about him that makes me feel protected.

"I met her through the club."

"You keep saying 'club.'" I raise one of my hands in air quotes. "But you're not really giving me much to go off."

He lets out a barking laugh, running his hand through his long hair. His smile is uninhibited, one I've rarely seen, and Gods damn if it doesn't make him look even more attractive.

"What?" My hackles rise, feeling like there's some inside joke I'm not privy to. It's the same feeling I got when I saw Jackson with Savannah.

"No, it's just—" he leans back on his forearms, "let me start at the beginning."

"That does tend to be the ideal place to begin."

"The cocktail lounge you were at, do you know the name of it?"

I close my eyes, trying to recall what the sign outside said, but all I can see is the red door. I don't even remember the bill I signed having any name on it.

That's odd.

"No, I don't."

"The lounge is technically open to the public, but it mainly serves as a foyer and decompression zone from the actual club within. It also adds an extra layer of privacy for its clientele. Which is why, technically, it's called *The Foyer*—it serves as a front if you ever need to search the address online."

This is starting to sound kind of suspicious.

"But when you enter that red door in the back, you find yourself at the Cardinal Club."

"Cardinal Club?"

"It's a membership-only place."

"What kind of membership?"

"The depraved kind."

"It's a sex club?" The words fall off my tongue before I can think of a better way to word them.

A crooked smile spreads across Jackson's face, his eyes turning even darker than normal.

"For lack of a better term, yeah. But it's also more than that. It's also a discretionary place for any high roller to use. One of Parker's friends turned me onto it after he heard about all the NDAs Sydney was dishing out to keep my sex life out of the press."

"I see."

My brain whirls, trying to slot all the pieces into place. What sort of person is Jackson behind those dark red doors? What side of himself did he show to those women?

My skin heats up as I imagine him in a dim room, removing each layer until just his muscular body was left on display.

Would he wear his hair loose or would he tie it up?

Jackson did say that I wouldn't be able to handle what he's into…is this what he was talking about? If it is, then he was totally wrong. Everything I'm hearing is pulling at my deepest fantasies.

And I want, no, I *need* to know more.

My lips part to ask, but I don't know how to weave the words together without giving myself away.

Oh, fuck it. I'm not some pansy. And at this point, Jackson knows basically everything else about me. What's a little more ammunition in his pocket?

"Is that all it is for you? A discretionary place?"

"No. They also help pair people up, depending on their tastes."

"And what does your palate include?"

"Do you really want to know?" Jackson sits up, bringing himself closer.

"Yes."

He continues to move closer until his hands come to rest on the top of my headboard, gripping the metal as he leans in. My breathing shallows, pulse racing through every inch of my body. Jackson's cheek brushes mine, and I feel the ghost of his breath on my neck right below my ear.

"I love my women tied up. I like to take my time threading my ropes around their naked, wanting bodies. It's calming, having them in the perfect little package for me to play with. I could edge you for hours, and you would just be squirming against my holds."

My breath hitches, images of just that flashing through my mind.

He pulls back and smirks. "Is that what you would like, my dear Deer? Would you like to be completely at my mercy, tied up with those fuckable tits and pretty pussy on display for me to do whatever I want with? Would you like to submit yourself to me so I can fuck you like you've never been fucked before?"

My core tightens, his dirty words turning my insides to liquid.

Jackson releases one of his arms from caging me in and presses his thumb against my lower lip, pushing it down. "Just think how pretty this mouth would look with a gag in it."

I've tried many things before, even had a girl who used to love using handcuffs when we fucked, but never anything like what he is suggesting. I've definitely watched pornos with Shibari, but this would be experiencing it first-hand—and fuck me if he didn't make me want that.

The idea of submitting to him, of giving him control, glows over my skin. My mind is always racing at a mile a minute, everything in my life is so highly curated. I would love to be able to just shut off and give my body over to him.

My thighs clench at the idea of him controlling me with those degrading words.

Fuck it.

I dip my head, taking his thumb in my mouth and sucking hard.

Jackson's eyes flash with surprise.

I grin. "Don't tell me you're all talk?"

"You better watch that mouth of yours."

"I think you'd be pretty impressed with what this mouth can do."

Then, without giving him time to back out, I surge forward, claiming his mouth with mine. His lips are softer than I imagined they would be, almost like a girl's.

He doesn't immediately kiss me back, and I suddenly

worry that he actually *was* all talk.

Shit. Did I just screw this all up?

"Dammit, Deer," he groans against me.

Jackson's hand curls around the nape of my neck, pulling me toward him, deepening our kiss. My hands circle around his neck, and I kiss him like my life depends on it. Every breath I breathe gets lost in him, and I become dizzy, lost to the spell he seems to have me under.

My knees splay open, making room for Jackson to press himself closer. I slide farther down the headboard, almost horizontal on the mattress now. Jackson drops the arm that's been clinging above us, but I still feel completely surrounded by him.

His tongue swipes against my lips, and I open up to let him in, allowing his taste to mingle with my own.

That free hand of his begins exploring, trailing down the side of my body. I feel the heat of his fingers through the thin fabric of my T-shirt. He reaches the edge, and I let out a moan as his hand dips underneath. His palm caresses my ribs, but there is no mistaking the feeling of his thumb skimming the bottom of my breast.

"This okay?"

"Yeah," I nod like a damn bobblehead.

"Hell, Deer." His hand comes up to squeeze my boob, and my back arches off the bed as I yearn for more. "I've dreamed about fucking these incredible tits."

"You should try the real thing."

He pulls back, grinning at me. "Such a dirty girl." His fingers find my nipple, and he gives it a roll before pulling with just enough force to elicit a short gasp. "I wonder if you'll make that same face when you're full of my cock."

I don't know who I was fooling.

I should've known a man like Jackson could ruin me with just his words.

My ankles hook around the backs of his knees, and I use my arms to pull him back down to me, desperate for another taste. I lose myself to the tangle of our lips, letting everything else slip away until all that's left is the feel of him.

I let one of my hands loose and rake my nails down his back, pressing the tips of my claws hard enough to elicit a deep groan from Jackson's lips. His hips jerk forward in response, and my eyes pop open when I feel the hard press of his length.

He tries to pull back, but I lock my ankles tighter around his thighs. I feel his responding smirk as he whispers, "So greedy." His hips buck again, and I let out a soft sigh as his length presses against my core.

Heat pools, and I want nothing more than a release from the pressure that has been building.

"More," I moan.

Jackson kneads my breast and begins rocking his hips rhythmically against me as I squirm against him, desperate for pleasure. His lips trail down the side of my neck, peppering me with hot kisses down to my shoulder. His tongue slides across the length of my collarbone, and my pussy clenches at the sensation.

"More," I beg, my voice all breathy. "Please."

Jackson's hand leaves my breast, and I let out a whine of protest until I feel it trail down my stomach, coming to a stop at the band of my shorts. My hand tangles in his hair as my hips lift off the bed, encouraging him to explore further.

"So hungry for me, aren't you?" His hand slides over the fabric of my shorts and cups my center, two fingers pressing against my entrance. "Fuck, I can feel how wet you are." His head dips, forehead resting on my chest as his fingers rub me through the fabric.

Holy hell.

I can feel myself becoming wetter and wetter, and when he presses another biting kiss to my lips, I all but start grinding myself against him.

"Dammit, Deer."

Jackson dips his hand beneath my waistband, and his fingers slip between my folds, gliding against the clear proof of how much I want him.

It feels so fucking good, but it's not enough.

I shift my hips, pushing myself against him, chasing his touch.

Jackson leans back, and we stare at each other, chests heaving. He removes his hand from my pussy, and I'm about to complain until I see his lips curve up in a smirk, head tilting slightly.

"Open up for me, sweetheart."

Lost in his eyes, I do exactly as he says.

He slips his fingers into my mouth. "Now suck. Taste how much your greedy pussy wants me. How much you want me."

My lips close around his fingers, and my tongue presses up to suck as he slowly pulls back out. I taste myself on him, my salty need for him clear as day.

"That's my girl, so obedient."

I smile at the praise.

"Can you follow the rest of my instructions?"

I nod because words won't work right now.

"Good." He leans back on his knees, eyes raking over me like I'm a meal he is about to devour. "I want you to reach down and remove your underwear." My hands scramble to lift the hem of my T-shirt before hooking into the band of my shorts. "Ah—just your underwear. Keep the shorts on." I frown momentarily but do as he says, hooking my legs one at a time through the material.

I hold the pink satin in my hand, an obvious dark spot marring the center.

"Thank you." He plucks the thong from my hand. "Now, I want you to go to sleep."

I blink at him a few times. "I'm sorry, what?"

"And don't think about touching yourself or making yourself come. I'll know." He pushes off the bed.

"Jackson."

"I'm serious. You said you could follow my instructions, didn't you?"

"Yes," I say slowly.

"Good." The grin on his face is anything but kind as he watches me squirm on the sheets. "Then I'll see you tomorrow, Sparkles. Thanks for the gift." He holds the thong up in a salute before strolling out of my bedroom. I hear the front door click as he closes it behind him, but I don't move, completely at a loss as to what the hell just happened.

I sit up, flushed and aching.

Fuck that.

There's no way I'm about to just lie here and fall asleep. I reach over into my bedside drawer and dig around until I find what I'm looking for. My hands close around the rose suction device, and I fumble to turn it on.

A quiet buzzing fills the room, and I quickly peel off my shorts, throwing them across the room before bringing the device to my clit. The relief is immediate, and I quickly increase the speed of the vibrating suction, my thighs quivering with each second that passes. It takes no time before I feel my orgasm crest. I squeeze my eyes shut, images of Jackson burning themselves on the backs of my eyelids.

A pang of guilt spears itself in my stomach at the knowledge that I'm defying his command. This inherent need to follow his rules and heed the submission brands itself on my skin.

"Fuck," I groan, pulling the toy away.

The wave falls, my orgasm sinking back. I shut the damn thing off and throw that across the room as well. My thighs clench together as I roll over in the sheets, groaning again.

He is going to pay for this.

Chapter TWENTY-FIVE

JACKSON

"Fuck."

I fist the soft fabric over my cock. The wet sheen of her arousal mixes with my precum. My head falls back against the wall as I continue pumping, images of Deer's pouty pink lips parting in a gasp urging me on.

My balls tighten and my brain blanks out as I come in thick hot jets all over my hand and her panties.

I should feel a little bad that I'm up here getting myself off when I expressly told her to just suffer in want. But I'm greedy and the temptation was just too much to deny.

I'm lucky I could control myself enough not to fuck her right then and there.

That was *not* how I saw my night going, but I don't have any regrets.

Although, this might pose a small issue considering we have been in a fake relationship for less than twenty-four hours and I've already had my hands on her pussy.

But fuck me, what else was I supposed to do when she seemed so eager to explore exactly my kind of kink. It's not every day the woman you've been unintentionally fantasizing about offers to become your next rope bunny.

I'll have to ease her into it though. I'll have to ease her into everything.

That's part of the reason why I edged her tonight; I had to make sure she really meant what she said—that she would be the type of sub to follow my rules.

Part of me does wonder if she'll keep her word.

Deer can be the defiant type, but I don't think she's a brat.

She can be stubborn at times and rigid in her ways, but it's that tightly wound and heavily curated persona that tells me she craves a release from the gilded cage she's crafted around herself. I've always had this desire to protect her, and that's no different than my want to care for her as a dom.

No, I have faith that while she is probably cursing me out right now and wishing I'd bang my hip on the corner of a counter, she will keep her hands far away from her wanting pussy no matter how much it pains her.

Such an obedient girl, deep down.

Just my type.

I grab my phone with my clean hand and open to an app, scrolling until I find the perfect gift for her. A reward for following my instructions. Something she'll look so fucking delectable in when I finally fuck her.

Chapter
TWENTY-SIX

JACKSON

66 *know you're there,"* the creepy voice echoes.

I pause at the door I was just about to open and instead opt to look through the peephole. Everything is a little distorted, kind of like looking through a fish-eye lens, but it's enough for me to determine whether the culprit is actually outside the room or just fucking with me.

When I confirm that there's nothing out there except the flickering wall sconces making the decrepit hotel hallway look even shittier than it is, I say, "Fuck it."

I open the door and step outside, looking both ways.

Left or right?

Left or right...

"All right, chat, left or right?"

I probably should've asked them this before exiting

the room so I'm not standing here like a sitting duck in a haunted hotel where any number of fucked up creatures could come out and kill me at any moment, but we can't win them all.

The chat seems pretty split, but I feel like I see more people opting for left.

"Left it is," I confirm into the mic.

I make my way down the hallway, scanning every inch of it.

I come across a dumbwaiter in the wall about two-thirds of the way down. There's a fifty percent chance I open this thing and some headless creature comes rushing at me, and a fifty percent chance nothing happens.

I steel myself and click on it.

"Come and play with me," a childlike voice echoes as the dumbwaiter creaks open.

"Mm. Nope. Not fucking with that."

I promptly shut the dumbwaiter and turn around, only to see what looks like a giant spider with legs made of human limbs crawling toward me.

"Shit," I yell, my heart lurching. I spin and run. "What is that? Bro, I can't even tell what that is."

There's no way for me to check how far behind me it is without losing speed. I'm just going to have to ride it out.

I come across another door and run through it. There's writing on the wall, but I don't have a chance to read it before I spin back around and lock the door behind me. I wait a beat until I'm sure the creature won't follow me.

My chat is blowing up with a bunch of skull emojis and RIPs.

Dread settles in my gut as I turn around and look at

what is written on the wall.

Don't lock the door.

Of course.

And of course, it's written in blood.

And of course, a bunch of bloody handprints start appearing all over the wall, a squelching noise accompanying each one.

And of course, when I turn around, the door won't let me reopen it.

A pair of bloody handprints squish onto my screen and I think that's the end until a bloody, peeling face jumps into the frame.

"Jesus fucking—" I grit out with a sigh as my screen goes dark.

I run my hand down my face.

"All right. That's got to be my fifth death in the last hour. I'm calling it a night." I click out of the game and switch my stream to just my camera. "Thanks for watching me suffer. I'll see you guys next week. And if you're coming to Ani-Con this weekend, say hey. I don't bite." I smirk at the screen before hitting the END STREAM button.

Immediately, a notification pops up in the corner.

NIGHTBLADE32

we're playing FL join

SHIELD3D

you stalking me

NIGHTBLADE32

always bbygrl

I snort, clicking on my Discord and scanning my friends list. Seems like everyone's on and playing *FrozeLine*.

My eyes catch on Deer's pink avatar, a little green circle showing she's also online. She's not playing with the rest of the crew though—she's playing one of her cozy games, *Moonstone Valley*.

Curiosity gets the better of me, and I pull up her stream.

Her laughter rings through my headset and my monitor fills up with her 2D pixel cloud streaming design, her screen capture center stage and her little video in the top left corner.

She makes idle talk with her viewers as her character interacts with a bunch of pixelated pigs, cows, and what look to be two ostriches.

The chat moves quickly, thousands of people trying to get her to see their messages all at once—each of them clamoring for her attention. Some of them send little virtual gifts and coins, causing their names to pop up in the middle of the screen. Deer takes the time to thank as many of them as she can while still pursuing her gameplay.

One sub donates a thousand dollars, telling her that she is gorgeous.

"Aw, thank you, DMan1989. I actually tried out a new blusher today." She frames her right hand under her jaw all cutely. "I think I'm going to keep it because the color turned out really nice."

I've dipped into her streams before, but I've never really paid too close attention to her chat or anything. Now that I am, there are more subs than I realized who comment on her looks and praise her for her general beauty. Deer refers to her fanbase as fawns, and that moniker couldn't be more accurate with the way they fawn over her.

Another sub donates five hundred dollars; this time it's accompanied by a shower of hearts that rain down the screen.

She giggles, thanking them.

My jaw ticks.

"Oh! Look at that—a Void egg! Sweet. It's taken forever. I was beginning to think the witch wouldn't drop one and that I'd have to spend five thousand gold. My patience was seriously running thin." She starts humming along to the game's background music as she harvests eggs from inside the chicken coop before placing the Void egg into an incubator. "Once we get a Void chicken, I can start getting more Void eggs and continue my seduction of Sebastian."

She continues to hum all cutely, and I find myself smiling as I watch her.

"Ugh. Why are you all obsessed with me seducing Marie instead? I married her daughter in my last run-through; I want Seb this time. He looks yummy."

The chat fills with a litany of comments, but I don't miss the ones that filter in saying that Deer can seduce them any day. More and more tiny donations filter in, little emotes popping up in the corners. It's not abnormal—the guys and I get the same thing happening to us all the time. But something about all of it is pissing me off slightly tonight.

My fingers twitch over the chat bar.

Even if I were to type something, the odds of her seeing it among all the comments spamming in are slim.

But maybe…

I hit the donation button and submit it.

SHIELD3D has donated $100,000

Little sparkles spray out from the text notification on the center of the screen. Deer pauses, her face going through ten stages of confusion. Those crystal doe eyes blink wide as she looks directly at the camera.

"What?"

The chat begins to fill with her subs freaking out over the fact that I'm among them.

"Sorry, fawns. One second." She twists in her chair, seemingly checking something on her other monitor. Her jaw drops in disbelief, and she shoves off her headset and mutes the stream before bringing her phone to her ear.

My phone begins to buzz.

"Yes?"

"What is wrong with you?" she hisses out under her breath.

"What?"

"A hundred thousand dollars, Jackson?"

"You're welcome."

"Are you nuts? Everyone's going to be talking about this."

"Good. I had to show those fanboys of yours that their money isn't worth shit compared to me. I'm the one who knows what you taste like, not them."

I watch the way my words set her even further off balance.

"I, I don't…" she stammers.

"You should really be paying attention to your stream, Sparkles, but don't stop thinking of me. Bye." I grin before hanging up and clicking out of her stream, pulling up *FrozeLine* instead.

The second it loads, a party request comes in from Aleks and I hit accept, shifting my headset back on.

"I'm shoving a number two pencil in your dick hole," Aleks barks.

"Is that foreplay?" Parker taunts.

"Am I interrupting your date?" I muse.

"Hey, mate. Nah, Aleks is just bitching 'cause I got more kills than him."

"Only because you fucking stole half my kills."

"Testy."

I snort. "All right, boys, let's do this."

Chapter TWENTY-SEVEN

DEER

DEERHUNTERR192302

CAN'T WAIT TO SEE YOU THIS WEEKEND

I stare down at the screenshot Rick sent me, my head still ringing.

They started spamming my DMs after the stream.

I'm just grateful it wasn't during the stream itself because then Jackson might've seen it and he would've lost it. Although, it would only serve him right after pulling that stunt. Seriously, I can't believe he did that.

Was it kinda hot and possessive? Sure.

Was it also totally excessive? Yes.

Am I totally confused about my feelings? One hundred percent.

Still, I don't need him to know about this and be even more worried about me this weekend than he already is. I'm already nervous as shite, and these comments are not helping.

It's my first time going to a convention since the swatting incident, and yet the Deer Hunters just had to go and make it worse. I'd barely been able to have fun at the last gaming tournament I went to, because of them, holing myself up in The System's green room when I wasn't having to make appearances.

A lot of people attend these events, and it can be overwhelming to deal with them. Because of the way I look, people automatically think they can touch me. Maybe it's the anime-pink hair, maybe it's because I'm so small, but regardless of the reason, they feel like I am up for grabs, and I hate it. It's nice being called cute, until they think being cute gives them a reason to touch you.

I feel like I'm treated like a small and fluffy white dog on the street—people walk past and automatically think they can pat you without asking permission because you seem like a toy.

The lack of consent from strangers makes me want to hide away from the world and stay in my own little protective bubble.

I hate letting that fear rule me.

I want to actually be able to walk around this time and see the different booths. I want to experience the con and not hole myself away from society. There is a fan artist from Canada attending I would die to buy an expo-exclusive art piece from for my new place, and this guy who makes these really cute *Passion School* varsity jackets that

I have to snag for my collection.

The only issue is, as much as I want to do all that, I don't know how to quiet the noise in my head. The thought of wandering through the crowd alone with all these threats around me is something I'm still struggling to push past. I don't want to take an entire security detail with me because that will just draw more attention and really make me feel like everyone is watching me.

I groan, slumping backward on the hotel bed and watch the ceiling fan twirl around for a minute. My eyes track the monotonous spinning, using it to calm the nerves that are constricting my throat.

Knock, knock.

"Hey," Lee's voice calls out. "Want to help me do my makeup?"

I flop right back up and slide off the mattress, moving to crack open the door. Lee grins at me, bare faced. I brace my forearm against the frame, and give her a look.

"You know we have to be downstairs in twenty."

"And?"

"And what if I said no?"

She rolls her eyes. "As if."

"I could've still been getting ready."

Lee nudges the door open and slips past me. "Yeah, yeah. When have you gone to an event and not had your hair and makeup done like hours in advance?"

I can't argue with that. Getting ready before an event is how I calm myself down and allow my public mask to slip into place—it's an entire therapeutic ordeal.

"You have to tie me into my corset as payment," I call after her, following her path to the bathroom.

"Deal."

I pat my hand on the counter, and she hops up, dangling her legs as I sift through my makeup bags.

I take a quick look at her outfit: low-rise black cargo pants, a cropped fishnet top with a white bandeau underneath, and a pair of Swarovski-covered platform sneakers—in other words, her usual color palette of black and white and nothing in between.

I, on the other hand, am cosplaying as my own farmer from *Cherry Farm* for the first day, which isn't that different of an outfit to what I usually wear to cons. It's a custom pink corset dress; the bodice part is hand stitched with strawberry vines, and the ruffle skirt hits just an inch or two below my ass—which I make up for with sheer white thigh highs and a pair of special-order strawberry-bejeweled heels.

Lee pulls up some music on her phone, and I hum along as I begin painting her face.

"I'm glad they put our meet and greet lines next to each other."

"As if you'd let it be any other way," I snort.

"Well, duh."

She doesn't say it, but I know it's so her security team can keep an eye on both of us at the same time instead of having to split their efforts.

"I forget, are you doing the showcase tomorrow?" I grab one of my thinner brushes to contour her aegyo sal before digging around for the right liquid glitter shadow.

"Nah, just the guys are doing that. I do have to be at the *Gods League* booth for a signing, though. You?"

"Nah, they have me adjudicating the cosplay competition tomorrow."

"That'll be fun, though."

"True. Now, stop moving and look at my right shoulder." I pick up a set of false lashes with my tweezers and carefully line the band up to her lash line.

Thankfully, other than the meet and greet both days and the competition tomorrow, I don't have any other obligations during the expo. I would be drained as it was. All five of us do have a brand party tomorrow night, but that's way later and I'll probably find a way to dip early.

"Okay, close your eyes." I grab my setting spray and douse her with a heavy layer. "Beautiful."

Lee blinks her eyes open and grins at me before spinning to look at herself in the mirror.

"You're a miracle worker."

"I can't help that the Gods gifted me with this talent." I spin around, brandishing the ribbons from my corset. "Now, tie me up."

"Kinky."

Thank fuck I'm facing away from her because I do not have it in me to school my expression. Flames lick their way through my body, combing deep in my center as my mind whirls back to the other night with Jackson.

The man still owes me an orgasm.

It's been two days, and I'm wound tighter than a clock.

If he'd just let me cum, maybe I wouldn't have so much of this anxiety bottled within me.

Lee must use every ounce of strength in her body when she pulls the ribbons tight because within point five seconds, my lungs become the size of peanuts.

"Oh my Gods," I wheeze out. "Gonna let a girl breathe

maybe?"

"Beauty is pain."

"I hate you."

"You love me." She gives me a tap on the butt before walking out of the bathroom "Come on, let's go."

This line is never-ending.

"Wow, you are, like, even prettier in person."

"Aw, thank you."

"Okay, and smile," the photographer calls out.

I turn toward him, throw up a peace sign, and smile. The girl next to me does the same just before the flash goes off.

"It was lovely meeting you."

"You, too!" She waves emphatically as she is ushered out of the meet and greet area.

I turn to receive the next person.

"Hiya." My smile never leaves my face.

"Hi, ohmigosh, it's so cool to meet you. You got me into playing video games."

"Aw, really? That's awesome. Do you have a fave?"

"I love *Moonstone Valley,* but," she gestures to my outfit, "I'm also a fan of *Cherry Farm.* Super cute, by the way."

I give her a curtsey. "Thank you."

"Okay, and smile," the photographer calls out, again.

Bless. If it weren't for him, I wouldn't be able to move

through the line as quickly as I am; it's hard to end conversations when the fans are chatty without feeling like the bad guy. They're the ones who paid to be here, and I don't want them to feel shorted.

I repeat my same pose for the camera, and the girl moves on.

"Hi!" I say to the next person.

"Um, hi." They're also in cosplay, but theirs is from an anime.

"Cute cosplay."

"Thanks, I made it myself." They shuffle up next to me and start to smile slightly for the camera. I take their cue and follow suit. Not everyone is a big talker at meet and greets; for some people, it's an overwhelming experience.

Hell, it's overwhelming for me, and I've done this dozens of times. The only way I'm able to get through it is by remembering that I'm Deer, not Deirdre, and Deer can do anything.

"Bye." I wave.

And on and on it goes. I twist back and forth like a spinning wheel, repeating the same motions over and over. My knees start to hurt from standing up for so long, but I push past the pain, making sure that everyone gets the same experience, making sure they all get to meet the Deer they expect.

"Hiya, how're you doing?"

"Good. You're beautiful."

"Aw, thank you."

I have no idea how many times I've uttered those three words today.

I try not to make it sound like I'm just on repeat, but

it's kinda hard to come up with new things to say when you've seen over three hundred people.

"Really, you look amazing." His gaze lingers a little too long on my breasts, but I brush it off. It's not like it hasn't happened a bazillion other times today. With how tight Lee made the corset, my tits are kinda unavoidable. But also, people are pervy at these conventions.

"Thanks, are you ready for a photo?"

"Can I get a hug first?"

My smile freezes, my brain whirling for a response. It is explicitly stated on the signs at the start and end of my line that I don't do hugs. It isn't that I hate them, it's just the fact that for every fifty respectable people I hugged, there would be that one person who'd take advantage of it. And the last thing I needed was a repeat of Anime Expo, where someone's hand basically squeezed my entire ass cheek.

"No, hugs." One of Lee's security team steps in.

The man eyes him with a frown but takes his place stiffly next to me and smiles for the photo.

"Lovely meeting you." I try to put as much warmth in my voice as possible.

"Yeah, you, too."

I make eye contact with the bodyguard and give him a subtle nod, which he returns before stepping back to his post. They really do make me feel a lot safer. So far, nothing has gone wrong, and no one has been overly aggressive or leery. But that Deer Hunter comment still floats in the back of my mind—anyone in this line could be a potential threat.

My brain begins to scream, and I lock up, reality slipping through my fake façade.

Breathe, Deer. Breathe.

"Next," the line attendant calls, and I quickly harden my mental walls as I turn to grin at the next person in line.

Again, and again, and again.

It's right at the end of the event when everything starts to go downhill.

"Okay, and smile," the photographer calls out.

My hand automatically shoots up in a peace sign, and the perpetual smile that's been on my face doesn't falter.

Gods, I hope my makeup still looks good after four hours of this.

The fan I'd been pleasantly chatting with snakes a hand around my waist and I jolt. Within seconds, they've pulled me into their body and their fingers are gripping tightly right below the edge of my corset. Their other hand has gripped my arm, and it's digging into the soft flesh at my elbow to keep me from moving.

My body turns to stone.

"Sir, please take your hands off the lady." The same bodyguard has stepped forward again.

"I just want a picture."

"There's no touching for the photos." He squares up. "If you do not remove your hands, I am going to have to remove you from the area, without any photo."

The fan's grip tightens in response.

Shit.

Shit shit shittttttt.

"You're kinda hurting me." My voice comes out all high-pitched as I try to keep my smile straight.

"I don't want to hurt you." I feel nauseous at his words.

"I just want a picture."

The bodyguard grips the fan's shoulder with one hand and has his hand on his holster with the other. "I will forcibly remove you if you do not let go in the next five seconds."

"What the hell, man." The fan begins to panic and tries to shrug him off, which causes his grip on me to somehow tighten even further. His nails dig through the soft ruffles of my skirt.

I can't help the wince that escapes.

"Is there a problem here?"

The area falls silent at the commanding words, and I look up into the faces of three men—well, "faces" is a stretch.

The three masked men push their way into my meet and greet area.

Aleksander's red mask is just as menacing as always, and he uses that to its full effect as he squares up with the fan, tilting his head to the side. Parker and Jackson are right at his back—Parker looks almost lax with his posture, but Jackson's arms are crossed over his chest, highlighting his muscles in a way that poses a threat to anyone nearby.

The effect of these men is immediate.

The fan lets me go and basically pushes me aside. The bodyguard is quick to restrain him now that I'm no longer in the way and at risk of getting hurt further.

But I begin to trip over my heels at the sudden jostle, and my frozen mind takes too long to think of a way to stop my fall other than with my face.

A hand shoots out to stop my fumble. The only issue is they grab me right where the fan was gripping me, and this time I can't school my face as it scrunches at the pang.

Jackson's hand quickly releases from my arm, and instead he curls me into him, cradling my shoulders. I look up into his deep green mask and my heartbeat starts to slow. Jackson holds my wrist delicately, stretching out my arm to study it.

"Fuck, you're red," he growls. "I'm going to punch that—"

"Let's not make a scene." Parker's blue mask enters my field of vision as he places a few light taps to Jackson's pec. "My girlfriend will remove our dicks if we do anything in such a public setting, and I personally don't want to lose the big guy."

"He's being escorted out of the venue." Aleks pushes his way to us, and I spot the bodyguard and some of the expo's security guards dragging the guy off the show floor through the gap he creates. "You good, Deer?"

"Yeah."

"Come on, let's head back to the suite. Lee's team is going to bring her to meet up with us when she's done— but she's safe, no incidents on her end."

Their red, blue, and green lights surround me as beacons of safety, blocking out everything else, and it allows my mind to clear slightly.

"Wait, there are still more people waiting to see me." My eyes break past their barricade to look at the small line of people that still remains, no more than fifteen or so.

"Deer," Jackson warns. "You need to rest."

"No." I shake out of his arms. "No, it's not fair to them. They didn't do anything wrong."

"We can let them join the line first tomorrow," Aleks

tries to barter.

"They've been waiting for hours." I fold my arms over my chest. "Would you guys leave them?"

I can't see their eyes, but I know I've struck a chord because each of their shoulders droop ever so slightly.

"Fine, but we're staying." Jackson shifts off to the side and rests on the metal bar that separates my area from Lee's. He looks like a gargoyle standing watch, and I can't say that I hate the way it makes me feel to have his protective presence.

Aleks joins him, leaning on the metal rail as well. Parker, however, drops to the ground and pulls off his mask. Aleks kicks him and Parker rolls his eyes before sliding the mask back on and standing with them too.

It makes me laugh.

I lock my eyes with Jackson's mask and give him a small nod of my head, which he returns.

Then, with a deep breath and new smile on my face, I turn around and greet the next person in line.

Chapter

TWENTY-EIGHT

JACKSON

I've never been a violent person.

But right now, it's a struggle to keep myself in check as I look at the way Deer's arm is still marred with dots of red where that asshole's fingers gripped her.

The door to our suite beeps open, and Lee comes running in. Her stride doesn't break as she beelines for the armchair Deer is curled up in.

Reading her best friend, Deer unfurls her body and holds her arms out so Lee can crush her in a hug. Although, considering they're both five foot, crush is a bit of a stretch.

"Are you okay? They wouldn't let me come over, safety and all that blah blah." Lee grasps her jaw with both hands and starts looking her over.

"It's fine, I—"

Lee gasps, holding out Deer's right arm. "Fine? That

is not fine."

My fists clench and I have to look away before my blood begins to boil again. I've barely got it simmering beneath the surface.

"I bruise easily."

"Nolan never should've let it get that far. He's going to get an earful from me." Lee stalks past me, and Aleks shoots up to grab her by the waist.

"Not so fast." He lifts her up and promptly plops her onto the couch between him and me.

"Your team followed protocol." Parker looks up from the floor where he is playing *Kill Strike* on his phone. "But I already spoke to the company; they're sending over some extra people for tomorrow. We're also going to give Deer one of our personal detail for the meet and greet."

"We should've done that earlier," I mutter.

I'm kicking myself. The boys and I don't need the same security attention as the girls do. We know how people get at these events when it comes to them, and we let our guard down.

I let her down.

"Coulda, woulda, shoulda." Deer stands up and crosses in front of us, propping her hands on her hips. "What's done is done. Let's move on, please."

Lee opens her mouth to protest, but Aleks squeezes her knee.

"Fine, for now." She slumps back against the couch.

"Thank you." Deer curtsies. "Now, I'm drained. I'm going back to try to get some sleep before doing this all again tomorrow morning."

"But the room service hasn't arrived yet," Parker

chimes in.

"Just have it sent over. I'm across the hall." She picks up her phone and gives us all a twinkle of her fingers.

My body follows her automatically, standing up to trail behind her.

"Jackson." Aleks' voice is blunt.

I look at our leader, but he just raises his brows and shifts his eyes from me to the couch and back again.

Fine.

I'll stay until the food arrives, then I'll head over.

I slump back down on the couch, and Lee nudges my knee with her own. *"Curse?"*

"Sure," I sigh, pulling out my phone and loading *Gods League: Titan's Curse*, the mobile version of the acclaimed game.

"I'm not joining," Parker defends.

"We didn't ask you." Aleks flicks his bottle cap at the blond and downs the last of his water before getting his own phone out.

We start playing a few rounds, and honestly, considering it's a 4v4 version of *Gods League,* it would be better if we had a fourth team member to collude with rather than some random who could be halfway around the world.

I bet I could have convinced Deer.

I haven't seen her play before, but after everything she told me about her family, she must have a dummy account.

Fuck.

Now, I'm thinking of her again. Her and all the secrets she's been letting me in on…all the trust she's been giving me.

But what is that trust worth if I can't do anything to

protect her?

"By the way, what happened to the guy? Was he banned?" Lee breaks me out of my spiral.

"What guy?"

"The creep from her signing line."

The doorbell rings and Parker stretches up. "I dealt with him; he won't be back."

"Still the Covingtons' golden child, aren't you?"

"You bet, baby," he winks before heading to the door and letting room service in.

One of the security team accompanies the hotel employee, and I can see it makes them all nervous with the way their hands shake lifting the silver cloches onto our table.

"Tower down," Lee nudges me.

"Copy. Coming up mid."

When the round ends, we all click off to grab our food—although Parker has already popped a bottle of champagne and is sipping on a glass as he waits for us.

"Want any?" He tips his glass a fraction as we gather around the table.

"Sure!" Lee plops down next to him and holds out a glass for him to fill.

I don't bother sitting down.

"I'm just going to bring Deer her food."

"Already sent it over, mate."

"What?"

"I already had them bring it to her." Parker glances up at me mid-pour with a frown. "What? You wanted it to get cold while you finished playing?"

I clench my jaw and take a seat, grabbing my utensils

and ripping into my steak.

No, I didn't want that. What I wanted was an excuse to go over there to see her, to make sure she's doing okay because I know that she was putting on a brave face earlier. She always does that, always tries to make sure she is keeping the peace and causing minimal interference. She's small enough as it is; I don't get why she always insists on making herself smaller to not disturb those around her.

It's a fucking pity because, when she shines, she's the brightest person in the room, but everything going on lately has put a damper on her light. She might be out there throwing around her smiles, but I caught the way she was picking at the skin around her ring finger with her thumb nail in between greeting fans.

My steak turns to poison in my stomach as I imagine her alone in her room, slowly spiraling with no one to ground her.

Fuck this, I can't wait.

I push away from the table and pocket my phone, abandoning my food as I stalk to the door.

"Where are you going?"

"Air."

"Whe—" Aleks' voice cuts off as I slam the door behind me.

The six bodyguards in the hallway flick their eyes to me, but I just grunt and head across the hall and to the left, knocking on Deer's door.

My foot taps on the carpet as I wait.

What's taking so long?

Is she having a panic attack? Did she pass out?

I knock again, louder this time.

"Oh my Gods, I'm coming. Seriously," she shouts.

My tapping stops and I hear some disgruntled muttering as the deadbolt clicks free and the door swings open.

Deer's eyes pop wide, and I drink her in. She's wearing a lacy pink camisole set, one that does nothing to hide the swell of her breasts. My dick twitches in response, but I rip my eyes away as I nudge past her and enter her hotel room.

"Yeah, sure. Come on in." The deadbolt clicks back into place, and she trails after me. "Do you ever wait to be invited inside?"

"No."

My eyes land on the plate of pasta she ordered. It looks hardly touched.

"You didn't eat."

She lets out a huff, squeezing past me. "I'm not that hungry."

I follow close behind as she shuffles through the suite to the bathroom, turning on the sink.

"You interrupted my nighttime routine." She uses her knuckles to remove those bright blue contacts. "And don't make that face."

"Looks uncomfortable."

She snorts, tossing her hair up in a messy bun. "Don't worry, I've had a lot of practice."

"Well, I do worry. About you."

Deer's hands freeze for a moment before she resumes lathering a white foam and massaging it onto her face. A silence stretches out between us, just the sound of running water filling the space. She lets down her hair and grabs some lotion, smoothing it over her hands. A deep brown sugar scent fills the air, that very same one I always smell around her.

I lean flat against the doorframe as she dips past me, her skin grazing mine as she goes to crawl onto her mattress.

"Do you plan to keep watch over me all night, Batman?"

"Maybe." I move to sit on the edge of her bed.

She runs her tongue across her top teeth, staring at me under her lashes before letting out yet another sigh. "Fine." She lifts the comforter and wiggles down, getting herself all situated on the side farthest from me, with her back turned.

"I just wanted to make sure you were okay."

"I'm fine. It's not the first time something like this has happened."

"That doesn't make it any easier for you."

"No. It doesn't." She lifts her head and looks at me over her shoulder. "But I can't let it stop me, either."

"You're pretty strong, you know that?"

She smiles. "Pretty? Yes. Strong? Not the first word that comes to most people's minds when they think of me."

"I beg to differ." My hand itches to reach out and touch her. "Will you be okay tomorrow?"

She turns her entire body to face me. "Honestly? I want to cancel the whole damn thing and just hole up in my room."

"You could camp out in our green room; it's right by the stage the cosplay competition is on."

She frowns. "How do you—"

"I looked it up. Wanted to make sure you had somewhere safe nearby to decompress if you needed it."

She lets out a short laugh and props herself up on one of her elbows, her other arm coming out to tap the space on the bed next to her. "You're making me uncomfortable looking at you over there like that. Come lie down."

It's the same arm with the marks, although they've calmed down a fair bit—just a faint pink now.

Deer catches where I'm glaring and quickly shoves the arm back under the comforter. "My offer expires in five seconds. Either you move your butt over here, or you can leave."

"Wow, no middle ground." I kick off my shoes and climb over, lying on top of the comforter next to her with my shoulder braced against the wall.

She matches my movements, fluffing the pillow behind her back and propping herself up.

"I'm serious about the green room; you know you can always use it."

"I know." She begins fiddling with strands of her hair, smoothing them down rhythmically between her fingers. "But there's stuff I wanna do. I don't want to hide away."

"Mm. Like what?" I reach out and calm her hand, taking it in my own. I press my thumb softly into her palm at intervals, massaging it like my mom did when I was a kid.

"Um, well." She swallows, eyes glued to our hands. "I sorta wanted to see this artist who's selling these retro anime art prints."

"Really? That's cool."

"Yeah."

"And? What else?"

She purses her lips together, and it's fucking adorable.

"Come on, what else?"

"There's this jacket I want."

"What kind?"

She whispers something under her breath, and I don't really hear it.

"Going to have to repeat that for me, Sparkles."

"A Love Love Passion School varsity one."

I let out a chuckle, and she snatches her hand back to her chest, glaring at me with the fierceness of a kitten.

"See, I knew you'd laugh."

"Hey, no. Not making fun of you. I did spend like an hour in the car with you playing it. I respect the grind."

She narrows her eyes like she doesn't believe me.

"Really. In fact, I even downloaded it just to see for myself."

"Seriously?"

"Yup, but if you tell anyone, I'll deny it."

"I don't believe you."

"I just finished the part where I picked to go to the aquarium instead of the skate park."

"Oh my Gods. You actually downloaded it."

"Yup."

"And you're doing the Kenji route, interesting. Although, I guess it makes sense that you'd go for the smart and sensible love option."

"I feel like you're judging me."

"I'm not. It's actually pretty sweet." She risks a glance at me and pauses for a beat. "You know, if you want, we could maybe visit the booths together tomorrow? No pressure, but if you think you'd be into that I wouldn't mind the company. I'm not totally into the idea of going alone after today."

I have to tamp down the giant grin that threatens to spread across my face. I'd steal any chance at spending time with her. It's not hard to make the choice to ditch everyone else just to gain an extra second in her company.

"Sure, how about after your competition? Our showcase ends at the same time."

"Okay." She smiles and shifts closer to me but quickly winces when her elbow squishes against my chest.

I reach over and gingerly hold her wrist, stretching her arm out. When I look at the four pink dots at her elbow, I no longer see a haze of red. Instead, it's like a boulder crashes into the pit of my stomach.

I lean down and place a soft kiss on the first mark.

Deer sucks in a breath.

"I'm sorry." I kiss the second mark.

"It's not your fault," she whispers, peering up at me through her lashes.

"Doesn't matter." I kiss the third mark.

"Really, it's not something you need to take responsibility for."

"It is." I kiss the fourth mark.

"No, it's not."

"Yes, it is. You're my responsibility, Deer."

"Oh? And how is that?"

"Because you're my fake girlfriend."

She gives me a pitying smile, pulling her hand free from me. "I'm just your fake girlfriend when your family is around."

"And what if I said I wanted you to be my fake girlfriend all the time?"

I need more than just a temporary fix. Ever since she

moved out of the penthouse, the apartment has felt empty. Her presence is one that I've come to crave, and I don't care what I have to do to keep her near—even if it's taking this ruse one step further than necessary. I need an excuse to keep her close without scaring her off.

"Why?"

"It would keep the creeps off you for one. So shit like this doesn't happen again."

She shakes her head. "I don't know. That sounds messy."

"It got messy the moment you licked your pussy juices off my fingers."

"Oh Gods, do you have to say it like that?" She covers her face with her hands. "Juices is so, ugh."

"Don't get shy on me now." I lean forward and nip at her fingers. "Would it be that bad to spend a little extra time with me?"

Those honey-brown eyes peek back at me through the gaps.

"We're playing a dangerous game here, Jackson."

"Yeah, but it's our fake game. I won't let you get hurt."

"Promise?"

I reach out and hold her hand in mine, kissing her fingers. "Promise."

DEER

I'm a goner.

Deep, sultry onyx eyes. A gruff yet sexy smile. Smooth skin corded with thick muscles. Strong hands and wicked fingers. Gods, fingers that touch and tease and taunt as they curl inside me.

A hand traces lightly up my thighs, and I arch into the feeling, inhaling the delicious scent of sage and cedarwood floating around me. Four strong fingers grip my ass as the thumb swirls lazily around my hipbone. I swing my leg up, bringing the body closer to me. My pussy brushes against something hard, and I rock into it. The friction between that and the material covering me hits a spot of aching tension that's been present for days now.

More. I need more.

My hips continue to move, grinding for release. That

grip begins to tighten, kneading into my ass. A deep groan reverberates against my chest, and it sends a shiver through my psyche.

"Dreaming about me?"

The words are whispered in my ear, the voice low and gravelly, making me even wetter.

Dammit, why is Jackson's morning voice that hot?

Wait.

What?

My eyes pop open

Fuck.

FUCK.

"Oh my Gods, I..." My brain fights to piece reality back together as I scramble back. Except my legs are tangled with Jackson's body, and I just end up hitting myself in the eye with my flailing arms. "Fuck."

I blink, blurry vision struggling to focus on everything around me.

Hotel. Jackson. Talking. Sleeping. Sex dream.

SEX. DREAM.

I would've rather had a nightmare and woken up screaming in his face than this.

"Good morning."

I will the heat in my cheeks to go down as I attempt to glare at him, which is kind of hard to do because every time I shift, I feel a Gods damn wet patch on my underwear, reminding me of exactly what just happened.

"This is your fault."

"Oh?" Jackson grins at me with a stupid, sexy smirk. "How, sweetheart?"

"Because you," I poke his chest with my nail, "haven't

let me orgasm in days, asshole."

"So, you did listen."

"Of course I did."

"Technically, I only said you couldn't orgasm that night." He reaches out and twirls a piece of my hair around one of his large fingers. "But for your extra credit, I suppose I can give you a *reward*." The word is laced with hot honey that heats up my skin.

"Reward?"

"Mm." He reaches behind his neck and pulls off his T-shirt, tossing the material aside. "Would you like that?"

"Yeah." It comes out all breathy as I drink him in, every inch of bare skin. Damn. I want to climb all over this man, touch and lick every inch to claim him as mine.

He shifts in front of me onto his knees and reaches for my hips. He grips and pulls me forward, my knees bunching up before him as I slide down the bed.

Jackson loops his fingers between my shorts and skin. He gives my ass a light tap, and I automatically raise my hips. With a deftness that shouldn't surprise me, he slips my shorts and panties off in a smooth motion. He nudges my knees, and they fall apart at his touch, laying me open for me.

"You know what, Deer?"

"What?"

"I have to say, I'm quite hungry this morning." Jackson's eyes leave my face as he stares down at me, a dangerous grin forming. "And this pussy looks fucking delicious." He reaches down and runs a finger up my core. "So wet already." He holds his fingers up to the sliver of light peeking through the curtains before popping them in his mouth and sucking.

My breathing pauses, air trapped in my lungs as I watch the display, unable to deny that it's just making me wetter.

Shit. I take it back. This is a *great* way to wake up.

Jackson pushes up and begins to slip off the bed.

I jerk up on my elbows. "Wait." The word is laced with pure desperation as my eyes plead with him.

"Don't worry, I'm not leaving. I'm just grabbing a little something." He leans around the bathroom door, fiddling with something, and I bite my lip.

I probably would've gotten on my hands and knees before letting him leave me high and dry again. Well, dry is the exact opposite effect he has on me.

Jackson dips back onto the bed and crawls next to me. I watch as he dangles a long white strip of fabric from his hands—the tie from the bathrobe.

"You said you'd used handcuffs before, right?"

I nod.

"Words are important here, sweetheart."

"Yes, I've used them before."

He stretches the fabric between both hands. "And what if I tied this like handcuffs? Interested?"

Want churns in my core, fantasies I've dreamed of rising to the surface. The closest I've successfully gotten to bondage was an ex who used his suit ties to secure me against his headboard and his belts to bind my wrists. A bathrobe belt is definitely new—and a lot closer to the ropes I've always wanted to try.

Newfound hunger surges through me, the prospect lighting me up.

"Yes." I bring my hands forward and brandish them

toward him.

He smiles, his eyes lighting up with mischief. "All right, hands behind your back."

I shift to follow his instructions and watch him as he gets to work, feeling the fabric thread around my wrists.

"If it ever gets too tight or you feel like you want to stop, just say 'red.' That will be your safe word."

"Okay."

It's not my preferred safe word, but it would work in a pinch, and I didn't feel like getting into the details right now. All I want is Jackson to finish what he started the other night.

I glance back and trace his face with my eyes. He has a strong jaw. There's no sign of any stubble, no moles or beauty marks on his skin, kind of like someone drew him on paper—perfection.

With a final tug, the fabric tightens, and my hands attempt to move on reflex only to be met with resistance. But there's no panic, just a sense of relief that travels down my chest. I feel secure around Jackson; his domineering aura calms the storm within me and just lets me be present.

This is what I crave—the feeling of safety and being looked after. The ability to find someone I can trust to just take over and let me feel.

"Perfect." Jackson places a kiss on my jaw as he presses my chest back until I'm propped against the padded headboard.

I follow the way he shifts down on the bed and his hands grip my thighs, spreading me wide. He leans down and blows a stream of cold air against my pussy, causing my body to shiver.

"I love how responsive your body is." I suck in a breath as his tongue finally traces up my center, coming to rest on my sensitive clit, circling it. "So fucking wet for me."

"Oh my Gods."

His tongue dives in and my hips buck off the mattress for a split second before he pushes them back down, keeping me rooted as he eats me out. The sensation is all-consuming, and when he lets go of one of my thighs and replaces his hand on my clit, rubbing rhythmically, I let out a moan.

I feel him smirk briefly before he picks up the pace. My hands pull at the ties as my fingers scrunch out looking for something, anything, to grab onto. The pressure is coiling, squeezing tighter and tighter with every passing second.

My heels dig into the mattress, fighting for purchase as they keep slipping with all my squirming.

The pressure. Everything. It's too much.

"You can take it."

I blink down, realizing I must've spoken aloud. Jackson looks up at me, and fuck me if the look of him grinning up between my thighs doesn't almost send me over the edge.

"Next time, I'm going to have to restrain these legs of yours." His eyes glint with the promise, and then his fingers dip inside me, curling.

"Oh, fuck," I cry.

"That's it, baby. Scream for me. Show me how eager my little slut is."

His other hand continues its ministrations of my clit as he adds another finger inside me, stretching me even further, filling me so completely with him. I can't stop the gasps that strangle their way out of my throat.

"Yes. Let everyone know how fucking desperate you are for me."

"Jackson." I barely get the moan out of my mouth before it's lost in another gasp.

That coiling building inside me is strangling me, pressing on me and making it hard to even take a full breath. I've never felt anything like this before. My hands try to find purchase again, only to drag against the belt binding them. I can't escape, trapped at his mercy as he keeps pushing me closer and closer to the edge.

And then his fingers hit me just right, pressing that little button that releases the dam, and I tumble, eyes squeezing shut as his name rips from my throat in a crying moan. It feels like the entire well inside my body is emptying as his fingers continue to milk me through the orgasm, like it's gushing out of me the more he pushes.

"Oh, fuck." I distantly hear Jackson growl before his fingers pull out, replaced by his mouth.

My body spasms as his tongue licks over my sensitive pussy, and when he nips at my bud, my thighs clamp shut to escape the sensation that is sending me into overdrive.

It's like my brain is forty thousand feet in the sky, floating with the clouds. Even with how spent I feel, my throat sore and legs a numb mess, I can't stop myself from saying, "More."

"What?"

"Jackson, please. Want you."

Chapter THIRTY

JACKSON

66 **Y**ou're going to kill me, Sparkles," I groan, palming my dick through my pants.

She grins up at me, high on her orgasm. "Not a bad way to go?"

"Fuck. Look how hard you make me, baby."

"Then fuck me."

"Such a dirty mouth on you." My smirk turns to a sigh. "I don't have anything, though."

Because I honestly didn't come over here last night thinking I was going to fuck her. I didn't even think I was going to spend the night.

Deer purses her lips

She pushes herself up and leans forward, showing off her cleavage with a grin. "You said I had fuckable tits, right?"

My dick twitches. "Be careful what you say, Deirdre."

"Offer stands."

Well, shit, I'm not so self-sacrificing that I'm going to pass that up. Not when I've been imagining my dick running through those tits more times than I care to admit over the years.

"Turn around."

I move behind her and make quick work of the fabric around her wrists, undoing the knot. Her wrists are a little pink but not bad—should fade in less than an hour. I give them a brief massage before setting her free.

Deer immediately peels off her night shirt, giving me full view of her porn star tits. Those dusty pink nipples stand out against her pale skin, and I just want to run my tongue over them.

I fist my dick again. "Is this what you want, baby?"

"Give it to me," she nods, reaching up to knead both her breasts.

I make quick work taking off my pants and briefs, my cock springing free. Deer's lids become hooded as I run my hand over the tip, giving it a quick pump.

"I'm going to fuck those tits, and then I'm going to cover that pretty face with my cum." I swirl the bead of precum over my tip. "Gotta lube up first, though."

"Oh, I don't hav—" She sucks in a breath as I reach down and run my hand over her pussy, taking her release and using it to coat my dick. I groan at how good that feels.

So fucking dirty.

So fucking hot.

I swipe through her again, teasing her swollen clit.

"Jackson," she twitches, legs clenching.

Fuck, I love hearing my name pass through her lips.

"Lie back for me."

Obedient as ever, she lies flat on the mattress and grabs her tits, pressing them together.

I straddle her, gripping the headboard with one hand and guiding my cock between her breasts with the other. I curse under my breath. Her wetness makes it easy for me to slide and begin pumping.

After everything we've done this morning and spending all night next to her, I'm hanging on by mere threads.

"Massage them while you squeeze," I instruct.

"Like this?"

She starts kneading her breasts as she squeezes them.

"Just like that," I groan, throwing my head back as I continue to rut into her.

Without me even having to tell her, she angles her chin to her chest and opens her lips so the tip of my cock hits her warm mouth. I look down to watch the way I move between her tits, mesmerized by the view. And when I push my cock a little farther so she can suck on the head before it pops back out, I lose it. The dual sensations have my balls tightening, and I know I only have a few seconds.

"Fuck, I'm going to come."

Deer squeezes her eyes shut but opens her mouth, sticking her tongue out, and just that pushes me over the edge, white hot cum covering her chest and mouth, like a pretty fucking picture. I'm going to burn this image in my mind and file it for later.

I reach down and swipe some of the cum off her chest and drag it along her tongue. Her eyes pop open and, like a good girl, she closes her lips around my fingers and sucks, sending a latent jolt to my spent cock.

"It's like you were made for me."

She laughs, that twinkle that does something to my insides, twisting them all gooey. I turn to stare at her, taking in that raw beauty.

I flop onto the bed next to her. "Just give me a second and I'll clean you up."

"Mm, take your time. I like having you on me."

"Fuck, baby." I use the last of my strength to turn on my side and place a deep kiss on her lips, drinking the taste of myself on her tongue.

Knock. Knock.

Our eyes pop open, alarm mirrored as we turn to look in the direction of the door.

"Was that—"

"Hello?" Sydney's voice rings out.

"What is she doing here?" Deer's eyes widen.

"Her flight must have gotten in," I whisper back.

"Yes, but why is she at *my* door?"

"I don't know."

"Jackson. I can't answer the door looking like *this*." She tugs her hands free and gestures to the white cum all over her chest as her voice pitches higher.

"Fuck. I'll grab something."

I'm halfway off the bed when Sydney calls out, "I know you're both in there."

My foot gets caught in the sheet and I barely manage to get my hand out in time to stop myself from completely eating shit. I brace myself on the wall and look back at Deer who is scuttling off the bed.

"How does she know that?"

"It's Sydney. What doesn't she know?"

"Oh my Gods," she whines.

I place a kiss on her forehead. "It's fine. Hop in the shower. I'll deal with her."

"But—"

"Shoo." I give her ass a tap before reaching down for my briefs and hopping into them as I make my way through the hotel suite.

I hear the shower turn on just as I get to the door. With a deep breath, I pull it open.

The grumpy blonde publicist is furiously tapping on her phone. Her eyes flick up before quickly falling to take in my lack of clothing. She brings a hand to rest on the space between her brows, massaging it. "Seriously?"

"'Sup." I rest my arm against the doorframe and give her a chin nod.

"Oh my God," she groans. "What is this?" Sydney waves the hand holding her phone at my chest before pushing past me into the suite.

I shut the door behind her.

"Deer said you approved."

"Of you *fake* dating," she hisses. "Nakedness does not seem very fake. You know what? This is my fault. I should've seen this coming." She paces back and forth, tapping the back of her phone against her palm.

"How'd you know I was here?"

"The security team saw you enter last night."

"Right."

"And then you never left."

"Riiight."

"Where's Deer?"

"Shower."

She lets out a sigh. "So, what's going on? Are you still fake dating? Is this real dating? Do I need to get out a statement? Lay it on me."

"It's complicated."

We're teetering the line of fake and real, and I'm not sure where we are going to land. We're still a fake couple, but part of me keeps questioning why it needs to be fake at all?

Sydney stops pacing and gives me a *look*. "Fine. Whatever. We'll deal with this later. I need you back in the suite and getting ready. You've got the showcase this morning before the meet and greet in the afternoon; it's a tight schedule."

"Okay, okay. I'll just say bye, and then I'll be right over."

"I'll wait."

"Why?"

"So, you don't get distracted."

"Come on, Sydney. It's me."

"Mm, no. Hurry up." She makes a shooing motion before going back to her phone.

I jog back to the bedroom, taking a second to collect my clothes and throw them on before ducking my head into the bathroom.

"Hey, I have to head out."

Deer rubs her hand against the shower glass so I can see her through the steam. "How's Syd?"

"Confused, but it's fine."

"If you say so," she sighs. "I'll see you later."

Some base instinct inside urges me to kiss her goodbye, but I shove it deep down—that would definitely tip us over the line, and we are straddling the gray area as it is.

I shut the bathroom door and return to a waiting Sydney, who already has the front door open to usher me through.

"See, no distraction."

She just shakes her head and stalks across the hall to scan into our suite, leaving me to trail behind her.

The security team in the hallway keep their faces straight, but the one nearest to Deer's door makes eye contact with me before quickly looking away. Something tells me that maybe these walls are a little thinner than I'd assumed.

"Yo, where were you all night?" Aleks comes out of his room and slings a hard arm around my shoulders as soon as I enter the suite.

"I was with Deer."

Aleks' brows rise. "Huh. Thought you might give me a little more run around than just coming clean."

"Do not mention this to your girlfriend. I don't need her getting ideas in her head."

"Oh, dude, too late. We spent half our video call last night speculating. Stevie has all the theories."

I groan.

Parker comes darting out of his room, socks sliding on the shiny floorboards, wearing nothing but his briefs.

"Thought I heard you." He grins, throwing finger guns at me. "Busy night, huh?"

"Parker." Sydney's admonishment breaks through. "What are you doing? I told you to get dressed fifteen minutes ago."

"I got a little distracted."

I snort. "And you were worried about me."

Sydney glares at the two of us.

Parker walks over and drops a kiss on the tip of her nose. "Don't worry, love, I'll be on time."

"All of you, to your rooms. Meet me back out here in thirty to go over the schedule, otherwise I'm placing you all in tech isolation when we get back. I'm serious, we can't get behind today."

"What? But I'm ready," Aleks protests.

Sydney pops her hands on her hips and speaks lowly, "Now."

Parker puckers his lips and waits until she lets out a huff and kisses him back. I hold up my hands in surrender and turn to escape back into my room.

"Jackson," she calls out.

I poke my head out of my door. "Yeah."

Her storm-gray eyes lock with mine, "Don't hurt her."

Deer is too kind for this world, I knew that, and I'd do whatever I could to keep her safe from any harm. If we were trapped in a sinking submarine, I'd sooner give her the breath in my lungs than let her suffer.

"I won't."

Chapter
THIRTY-ONE

DEER

"Okay, and—last one—smile!"

I throw up my peace sign, grin, and pause for the pop of flash.

"Thank you so much for waiting," I tell the fan.

"Thanks for coming, you're awesome." He gives me a wave. "And you crushed the cosplay competition this morning."

I wave back, but the second he leaves the meet and greet area, my hand drops, exhaustion wrapping around me like a blanket. But with that comes a small slice of relief because nothing has gone wrong all day. No one being touchy, grabbing where they shouldn't, and no one claiming to be part of the Deer Hunters threatening me. I am still a little on edge, but it isn't half as bad as yesterday. Although, that may partly be because of the killer orgasm

I had this morning. I could've easily gone for round two in the shower if Syd hadn't shown up.

The only issue is, even after last night's conversation, I'm still unsure where we stand. I agreed to extend this whole fake dating situation because I was feeling greedy in the moment. I wanted more of Jackson—more of his time, more of his touch, more of his attention. But now that we've added orgasms to the mix, it feels like it's gotten complicated all over again.

"Would you like us to escort you back to the green room, miss?"

One of the new security members comes to stand next to me, pulling me from my spiral. He's the addition from the boys' personal team, and I'm a little surprised by how young he is. I crane my eyes past him to look over at Lee's line. I'd guess she has a solid fifty or so people to go through before being done.

"Are the boys still going?"

"One moment." The man presses a finger to his ear and speaks softly.

As I wait, I grab my phone and blue HP energy drink. The convention staff provided it to me at the start of the event, but I've hardly had any time between people to take a few seconds to even rehydrate. Probably not super smart on my behalf since I skipped lunch and am feeling a little lightheaded. This photo op, paired with the cosplay competition this morning, has left me socially drained—I have no idea how I'm going to make it to the brand party tonight.

"The System are finishing up shortly."

"Okay, I'll head back to the green room to wait."

It's closer to the artist booths anyway.

The security team creates a square formation around me. They're efficient as they guide me through the crowds, not allowing anyone to stop in our path. It kinda feels a little excessive—drawing way more attention to me than normal, and that's saying something.

I hope Jackson will let us ditch them when we explore the show floor later; I wanted to enjoy it without all the fuss of me being, well, me. I even stashed a change of clothes in my bag to switch into so I could be more discreet.

We reach the room in record time, and I immediately make a beeline for my backpack and tug out a black hoodie and skirt. Two of the security team follow me inside while two stand guard. I'm really not used to this. I normally have one person on me at events unless I am with Lee or the boys. Then again, after everything, I suppose it isn't unwarranted. Maybe I wouldn't be in these situations if I'd upped my security ages ago.

"Do you guys mind turning around?"

The security men nod, giving their backs to me. I unzip my skirt, letting it pool to the ground. I'd specifically worn something easier today for this exact reason. I step into the black pleated mini skirt, zipping it up before grabbing the black hoodie and slipping it on, tucking my pink hair into the hood.

"Okay, done."

I move to the mirror and check myself out, confirming everything looks good before collapsing onto the couch.

I don't move for a solid minute, letting my weary bones settle before forcing myself to sit up.

I grab my phone and check my notifications. There

are hundreds, people tagging me in all their pictures from the meet and greet yesterday. My mods will go through it all and make sure there's an emoji commented on each of them for me, but I still like to pop in and interact when I can.

I swipe out and pull up my text messages.

A wave of nausea rolls over me, making my lightheadedness feel even worse.

RICK

Hey, just wanted to let you know we've had a bunch of new DH accounts spawn this morning and they're all commenting on your recent post at the con. Nothing threatening tho

Yeah, Rick, not threatening at all.

I guess, in the grand scheme of all the stuff they've done, it is the least creepy?

ME

Thanks for flagging it. Keep me posted if anything else crops up.

RICK

of course. Don't forget to eat and stay hydrated

ME

I knowww

There are only a few more hours. I just have to get

through it.

The door to the green room opens, and the three guys burst in, all of them immediately ripping off their LED masks, with Sydney hot on their heels.

I'm quick to school my face, reaching forward and grabbing my HP energy drink to twist it open and take a sip to hide my unease.

Parker tosses his mask on the coffee table and launches himself at the couch, causing the blue liquid to slosh around mid-sip. The drink goes down the wrong way and I choke on a giant mouthful.

"Parker," Syd warns.

"Sorry, Deer." He reaches up and pats between my shoulders.

I swipe the back of my hand across my mouth. "It's fine."

"Damn, my face looks sexy on that." He eyes the energy drink with a grin. The bottle has his masked persona plastered on one side of the plastic branding band and his gamer signature printed next to it. I have to give Syd credit; it's a killer sponsorship.

"Is that your way of asking for a sip?"

"Maybe."

I hand the drink over and he takes way more than a gulp, downing half of it—classic dude move.

"Looks like you're ready to go on a stakeout." He nods to my outfit as he hands it back.

"I'm going to visit some of the booths."

"Incognito, nice."

"Alone?" Sydney's voice carries an edge of worry.

"I'm going with her." Jackson's protectiveness rings

out.

I catch his eyes as he peels off his T-shirt. The giant tiger tattoo on his back shines against his otherwise bare skin. He gives me a smirk, flexing his bicep slightly before reaching for his hoodie. I roll my eyes but don't stop my smile from spilling over either.

"If I didn't already know you guys banged, I'd know for sure now."

"What?" I whip my head back to Parker. "We did not bang."

"You don't need to deny it." He gingerly pats my knee. "We're happy for you."

"We did not have sex," I protest.

"So, you're saying Jackson didn't introduce you to his ropes and whips last night?" Aleks' takes a seat opposite us, wiggling his dark brown brows.

"Whips?"

Parker throws out his arm, pointing at me, "Aha! She didn't deny the ropes."

My cheeks heat. "What? No. I—"

"Oh, fuck off, guys," Jackson cuts in. "Leave her alone."

I chug the rest of the blue drink to keep my mouth busy and avoid incriminating myself any further.

"Aw, come on, mate. I'm just teasing."

"Yeah, and I'm just going to tease my fist up your ass if you don't shut up."

"I am an ass man."

"Okay, all right. That's enough." Syd steps up and places one of her heels on the coffee table. "Both of you, leave the two of them alone."

"Love, you're supposed to be on my side."

Sydney's professional mask cracks slightly, a slight flush pulling at her cheeks.

"Come on." Jackson reaches a hand out for me. "Let's escape while we can."

I smile, taking it and letting him pull me away from the lion's den.

"Wait," Syd calls out just as we open the door. "Take one of the security team with you."

"But—"

"Just let them trail behind, for my sake. Please?"

I sigh, "Okay."

Jackson gives my hand a squeeze, and it brings the grin back to my face.

"Here." He pulls out a black face mask from his pocket.

"Ooh. You came prepared." Reluctantly, I let go of his hand so I can loop the mask straps around my ears. "Good?"

He finishes putting his own mask on and then reaches forward, tucking a stray piece of pink hair back under my hoodie. "Good. No one will know."

As soon as we step onto the show floor, the noise returns full force. The constant chatter is a crackling buzz around us, and it takes me a second to acclimate as the crowds return, bodies everywhere I look. Now that I'm actually on the main floor and looking around, I realize just how busy the event is. It was easier to ignore it when the security team blocked it all from my view and I was kept safe in my designated areas.

My feet begin to lag, refusing to listen to me as that exhaustion creeps back with a vengeance. I shake my head a little, trying to clear the growing fog.

Maybe this is a mistake…

"You okay?" A strong, calloused hand grips mine, and Jackson pulls me close to his body.

His touch centers me, grounding me back in the present. And when I look up into his gaze, it helps turn some of that noise to a quiet hum.

"Yeah, I'll be fine."

He squeezes my hand, and though I can't see it, I know he is smiling at me from the way his eyes soften and the skin around their edges crinkles slightly.

"Come on, I mapped out where the booths are so we won't get lost in the crowds." He starts walking at a slower pace for me, and my chest warms.

"Really?

"Yup."

Jackson really must have studied the hell out of the convention center because it takes us less than ten minutes to find the artist's booth. That and because of his massive frame, the crowd basically parts and makes space for him to stalk through.

I should bring him more places; he's quite efficient. If I'd been left on my own, I think it would've taken me a solid thirty minutes to get here…if I even made it at all.

"My lady," Jackson gestures dramatically at the booth, and I giggle at him before taking a look at the booth and letting out a small squeal.

It's so adorable!

All the art prints and merch are set up on the wall behind the artist, and I'm at a loss for exactly which one I am going to purchase. She has this really cool nineties shoujo manga art style that just melts my heart.

"Hi."

"Hi." I give her a small wave.

"Just browsing?"

"Oh, no! I'm totally here to buy. I'm a huge fan."

Her face pulls in mild shock before she looks away. "Oh, wow. That's…thank you." She clears her throat. "The large prints are twenty and the standard ones are fifteen. Here, you can flip through this book if you need a closer look." She hands a binder to me. "I also have some stickers that are three for ten dollars, plus keychains for six."

"Awesome." I flip through the binder, trying to decide which I want. The prints are a little blurry in my vision, almost like my contacts are giving out. I squint my eyes, focusing on them until I land on the ones I want to buy.

"Can I do these three? Large, please."

"Sure, that'll be sixty. I can take cash, card, or you can tap."

"We'll do cash." Jackson holds out three twenty-dollar bills.

The girl takes the notes before I have a chance to stop him.

"What are you doing?" I whisper, softly nudging his arm with my shoulder.

He pulls his mask down and smirks at me. "Treating you."

I roll my eyes, but when the girl hands me the plastic bag with the prints all neatly packaged together, he grabs that as well and a small part of me is a little giddy over the fact. I make more than enough money myself, and anything less than a hundred dollars doesn't really blip on my radar—I know it's the same for Jackson. Which is why it kind of matters even more; he's not trying to be showy by flinging his money around or expecting me to front it because I have the capital, like other guys have done in the past.

He's doing it because he knows it's something I actually care about.

I bite my lip to stop my smile, afraid he'll be able to read my emotions even when they're covered.

"Come on, the jacket place is on the other side of the Artist's Den."

He grabs my hand again, and it really just reinforces the fuzzy feeling going on inside that's making me feel a little weak in the knees.

Or maybe…a lot.

I only take a few steps before almost tripping, my knees giving out temporarily. Jackson's other hand shoots out to grab my elbow and steady me.

"Whoa, you good?"

My brain starts to feel all throbby, but I can't really place what's wrong.

It doesn't feel like one of my panic attacks.

Is it because I haven't eaten enough?

I thought the energy drink would've fixed that.

"Yeah, sorry. A little lightheaded, maybe low blood sugar or something."

"Do you want to head back?"

"No! No, I'll just grab a snack, but I want to keep going."

A deep frown mars his forehead. "Fine, but if you get any worse, I'm taking you back. This jacket isn't worth you passing out."

"Ah, that's because you haven't seen it."

Instead of holding my hand, he loops his arm around my back, his palm coming to rest just above my hip. I try not to, but my body leans into him, seeking support as we continue weaving through the booths.

The farther we walk, the worse everything gets. It really feels like someone stuck my head underwater; everything's kind of in a big bubble. And all these people? They're fish in the sea. Swimming past me. Why are there so many fish?

"Deer, baby, seriously. Are you all right?"

I slowly blink up at Jackson.

Wow. He's sexy as fuck with that commanding tone.

"Deer?"

"You're hot." I reach up and touch his face. "Like reeeeally hot." My tongue feels thick in my mouth, so it takes me a second to get all the words out.

I dig my hands into the mask covering my face and pull, welcoming the cooler air on my face.

Much better.

The humming around intensifies.

Jackson's definitely saying something to me.

I'm looking at him, but I'm not looking at him because there's two of him, and that's weird.

Why are there two of him?

Everything feels like a sparkly dream.

Except my tummy. That feels kind of sick.

I feel like I should be worried, but I can't remember why.

I think I'm sitting on the floor.

Nope, not on the floor. I'm moving too much to be on the floor. The colors around me are spinning, like a Tilt-A-Whirl ride.

They spin, and spin, and spin, and spin until all the colors come together and turn…

Black.

Chapter
THIRTY-TWO

JACKSON

cradle her in my arms, running through groups of people, not caring who I push out of my way.

"I'm confirming that emergency services have been called," Derrick, one of the security team who has been shadowing us, says as he jogs up beside me.

"If they're not here by the time I get out there, I'm taking a car myself."

"I advise against that. We should wait for medical personnel."

"I'm not waiting if she'll just get worse," I bark.

Deer stirs against my chest, but when I glance down, her eyes are still shut.

"Deer, come on, stay awake."

She mutters something incoherent, lips barely moving. She's like a ragdoll; there's no conscious thought in her.

"Fuck, this is not good."

I push my legs to move faster, ignoring the burn and instead using it to fuel my muscles. The pain in my body distracts me from the pain in my heart.

I don't understand what happened. One minute she was fine, the next it was like someone accidentally kicked the power cord and her entire body shut down.

She said she was tired. I should've pushed her to stay back.

But I was excited to spend time with her.

God, why did I have to be so selfish?

"I have confirmation that the ambulances are just down the street."

"As in more than one?"

Fuck. They must think something is seriously wrong with her if they've sent multiple. My heart begins to crack.

"No, there's, well." Derrick clears his throat.

"There's what?"

The guy is a lot fitter than I gave him credit for; he's in a full suit and keeping pace with me without breaking a sweat. It's impressive.

"I'm not sure it's appropriate to tell you, given your current mental state."

"Well, my mental state isn't really going to matter if you're fired. Now, is it?"

I take it back. It isn't *that* impressive. We can replace him.

"A second ambulance was called for Mr. Covington."

My steps falter on the last step I'm climbing, but Derrick anticipates my reaction and reinforces my weight by grabbing my elbow. I stop, facing him.

"What do you mean?"

"It appears he is also unwell."

"Is it the same as Deer? Is he conscious?"

Was there something in the food? No. No, she didn't end up eating last night. Maybe it was something from today? But that wouldn't make sense. Our schedules didn't sync up; she had the cosplay competition, and we were at the showcase for a few hours before the meet and greet.

"I don't have the full information yet, but Mr. Knight is escorting him."

"Shit."

I pick up my pace again, really sprinting this time. It isn't that much farther to go now.

As soon as I break through the doors to the valet circle, I see Sydney burst out on the opposite end.

"Everyone, move out of the way." Her voice explodes over the people crowding the ambulances. "Move, or so help me God, I will do everything in my legal power to make you regret it."

Aleks comes jogging out with Parker on his back. He is definitely awake, but I wouldn't go so far as to say he's lucid. Parker looks the same as he did two years ago when he made a bet that he could drink an entire magnum of champagne in under an hour.

I'm torn, wanting to check on him and see what the situation is, but also, I'm not going to leave Deer's side. Parker is my brother, but Deer is something more.

"Is this the other patient?" The emergency responder meets me halfway.

"Yes, she's going in and out of consciousness."

"For how long?"

"I want to say the last fifteen minutes or so, but she wasn't well a bit before that."

Another responder comes to remove her from my arms, but I can't bring myself to release her.

"Sir, I need you to let go. We need to move her into the ambulance for transfer and to check her vitals."

I relinquish my hold, passing her to the waiting responder.

"Can I come?"

The first responder hesitates, looking me over.

"I'm her boyfriend."

"Fine, you can sit in the passenger seat."

I want to argue, want to sit in the back so I can hold her hand, but I don't want to push and get banned entirely. So, I give her a terse nod and slip into the front where the driver is waiting.

I peer over my seat through the grates, watching as they load Deer onto the gurney and push up the sleeve of her sweatshirt so they can take her blood pressure.

They're trying to speak to her, trying to get her to respond, but they only manage to pull a single moan from her before she's out cold again.

"You said symptoms only began fifteen minutes ago?" The first responder glances up at me.

"That's when she started to get really bad, but," I try to think back, piecing together every little detail, "she didn't seem well for the last half hour or so."

"Can you elaborate? Was she feeling nauseous, dizzy, sluggish? Maybe having difficulty remembering things?"

"She was dizzy and tripping over things, said it was just from being tired." My voice cracks a little as guilt rears its ugly head.

I watch as they shine a light in her eyes.

"Does your girlfriend wear contacts?"

"Yes."

It takes them a second to remove them before they shine the light again. The entire time it feels like there's a hundred elephants stampeding all over my chest, crushing me over and over again.

"Has she taken any drugs today?"

"No."

"Are you sure?"

I mean, I wasn't with her all day, so no, I wasn't one hundred percent sure. But I've known Deer for years. She doesn't even smoke weed, as far as I know.

"Sir? You won't get into any trouble. I just need you to tell me the truth so I can help her."

"She doesn't take drugs."

The two responders give each other a look.

"What? What's wrong?"

The second responder keeps monitoring her, but the first one comes closer to the grate, using a voice that would almost be soothing if it didn't feel like I was about to jump out of my skin. "Is there any chance someone could have slipped her drugs?"

"What?"

Ice rains down on me, causing every nerve to go haywire.

"I'm just trying to check each possibility. It could have been in a drink or maybe even food? Can you think of anything?"

"I—I wasn't with her all day, I don't know."

"Okay." She nods her head and returns to her colleague, with a hushed tone. "Call ahead and get them to prep for a tox screen. This stuff metabolizes fast."

Positive.

The toxicology screen tests positive.

It takes six hours before Parker is coherent again, although the effects are still wreaking havoc on his body.

"This is the worst bloody hangover I've had in my life," he groans.

Deer, however, is still asleep in the bed opposite him. Because of how much smaller she is, they think it's going to be another couple of hours until the drug flushes from her bloodstream enough for her to come to. Lee is also out cold, sleeping in the armchair as it's well past 1 a.m.

I continue rubbing my thumb over Deer's knuckles, needing to remind myself that she's here, that she's not in danger anymore.

"Here, drink some more water." Syd pours Parker what has to be his fourth cup in the last hour.

"No, I feel sick."

"You need to stay hydrated."

"That's what the IV is for, love."

I watch her hand grip tightly around the glass, and Parker reaches out to steady her.

"Come on, join me on the bed."

She puts the glass down on the side table and crawls

onto the bed.

"You know, this is quite the déjà vu. Two emergency hospital visits in less than six months. Maybe I should see about the family buying up one of them so we're not giving all our money to the Harts."

"This is serious, Parker."

His face sobers and he squeezes her hand. "I know. I just—"

"I know." She cuts him off and kisses his cheek. "I know."

They rest their foreheads against one another's and speak in hushed voices. All the while I'm here with my heart bleeding on the floor. The police came in to take Parker's statement earlier, and it seems like they might have a few leads, but until Deer wakes up, we're in a holding pattern.

Because it's most likely that she was the target, and Parker just got caught in the crossfire.

It makes me want to smash something.

The door to the hospital suite swings open, and Aleks walks in, running his hand through his hair—which is basically standing straight up at this point from the number of times he has made the motion.

"Any news?"

"Maybe. We still have to wait for Deer's statement before we can confirm."

"So, they have something?"

"Maybe."

I stalk over to him, getting right up to his chest. "Don't fuck with me, Aleksander."

"I'm not." He takes a step closer. "But I'm not telling you shit before it's verified because you'll go fucking apoplectic."

"She was fucking drugged," I growl. "Under our watch."

"Boys," Sydney's cold voice cuts through. "You will not argue in this room."

"Well, this seems like a party," a feminine English accent drawls. The owner of the voice places her hands between Aleksander and me, not so gently pushing us apart so she can walk between us. "Hey, lil' bro."

"Pheebs." Parker sits up, eyes lighting up as his eldest sister strolls over.

"You look pretty shit." She ruffles his hair.

"Gee, thanks." He bats her hand away. "What're you doing here? I thought you were headed to London."

She scoffs. "I had the jet turn around and reroute here. You're all over the news. I mean, really, Parker, you think people wouldn't notice a Covington being rushed to the hospital?"

"Wow. I apologize for the inconvenience."

"It's fine, Dad's handling my stuff." She rests her hip on the metal bedframe and runs her sharp blue gaze over the rest of us. Phoebe Covington has a perpetually icy aura around her, one that screams 'don't fuck with me.' "There's quite the army of reporters outside."

"I know," Sydney groans, running a hand down her face. "They weren't appeased by my statement."

"I can get rid of them."

Syd looks like she is about to refuse, but her shoulders droop. She's been awake for as long as I have, and the exhaustion has spawned dark circles that make her gray eyes look even more haunted. "Only if it's not a hassle."

"It's not." She whips out her cell and starts tapping away.

Over the last year, Parker's sister has fixed our issues in more ways than I can count—from blackmail, to scandals, to stalkers. She might be the current Chief Financial Officer for the Covington conglomerate and the heir to the entire company, but that woman has connections all over the world that surpass even her family. I've learned not to look too closely at how blurry the line she walks is.

There's a short knock at the door, and Aleksander and I spin around. A man I don't recognize steps into the room, and while I go on high alert, his demeanor has me hesitating. The security team outside wouldn't let just anyone enter this room; they were under explicit instructions.

Phoebe glides past us and the man leans down to whisper something in her ear. Her eyes narrow to slits. She pulls him closer to the door and they continue to exchange hushed words.

It sets off a million alarm bells in my mind.

Without ever speaking to us, the man leaves. The room rests in silence as we turn to Phoebe.

She walks calmly back through the room, her designer heels clicking across the floor as she makes her way to Deer's bed. She perches on the edge of the mattress and reaches a hand out, picking up a lock of Deer's pink hair and studying it thoughtfully as she runs it through her fingers.

"Seems like someone is gunning for you, little one."

Chapter
THIRTY-THREE

DEER

S omeone is using my brain as a gong, hitting it over and over so the pain reverberates through my entire skull, bouncing off the bone and turning everything inside to mush.

Using all the energy I can muster, I force my eyes to open.

Why is everything blurry?

I frown, trying to make sense of my surroundings. It's pretty dim. I can gauge what seem like two lamps lighting up the darkness.

When I shift my arm, a heavy weight in my hand stops me. Squinting, I make out Jackson's palm gripping mine as he hunches over, asleep by my knees. I don't recognize these bed sheets. I continue tracing a path up my body, clocking an IV poking out of my elbow before catching the

303

light blue gown that covers me.

A hospital?

Why am I at the hospital?

My brain is all foggy. I don't remember anything to do with the hospital.

Why can't I remember?

The monitor next to me starts beeping faster.

"Deer? Are you awake?"

"Parker?" I can't keep the panic out of my voice.

I look toward the voice, but I can't fucking see anything but blurry shapes. I could see earlier. What happened to my contacts? Oh my Gods. My eyes. They can all see my eyes.

I pull out of Jackson's hold, gripping my head. My breathing comes faster. I don't even know who is in this room. I can't see them. I don't like it. I don't like it at all. It doesn't feel safe. I'm not safe.

"Deer," Jackson's gravelly voice blasts through the ringing in my mind.

But I can't stop the panic that is causing my lungs to constrict.

His strong hands grip my face, and he brings himself into focus. His black eyes are bloodshot, and for the first time, I can read his emotions clear as day. Worry and relief twine together, rippling over his features. Jackson's thumbs rub over my cheeks affectionately, the motion centering me.

My hands drop, releasing their grip on my hair, as I automatically reach out for him.

The bed dips with his weight as he settles next to me and pulls me gently into a hug. I might not understand anything that is going on, but I do understand him. I know that Jackson is safety. As long as he is here, it can't be that bad.

"Shh, I've got you."

My face is wet with tears that don't make any sense.

"I've got you. I'm so sorry."

I shove my face farther into the crook of his neck, letting his scent drown out the antiseptic smell of the room.

My breathing starts to even out, and I relax into his body.

"I heard the patient is awake?"

I still at the foreign voice.

"It's fine," Jackson soothes, pulling away and rubbing my shoulders. "It's the doctor."

I look past him and can kind of make out the white coat on the person standing at the foot of the bed.

"I can't see," I whisper to him.

He frowns before understanding dawns. "Shit."

I reach out and squeeze his forearm. "Who else is in the room?"

"Just Parker. Sydney took Aleks and Lee back to the hotel for the night. I'll get her to bring your contacts when she comes back."

"What happened?"

Jackson's lips turn into a thin line. "You should speak with the doctor first."

My lower lip trembles. "Okay."

The man asks me a few simple questions, checking that I'm cognitive and that my reactions are fine. When he shines the light in my eyes, I wince a bit because it makes that pounding headache feel so much worse.

"Am I okay?"

"Your symptoms are what we would expect after what you've been through. That headache should clear in the next day or so, but you can take pain relievers to deal with the worst of it."

"And what did I go through?"

He pauses for a beat before answering, "One moment, let me get the officer so she can hear your statement."

"Officer?"

The nausea returns like a whirlpool in my stomach as the doctor quickly shuffles out of the room. I try not to let the panic resurface, focusing on breathing steady inhales. My hands seek out Jackson's again, and he cups them together, steadying the sea inside me. The doctor returns with a fuzzy blob next to him, and I'm starting to get seriously frustrated that I can't fucking see them properly.

"Hi, Deirdre, I'm Detective Layton."

I stiffen at my name.

How many people know?

"Hi."

"Can I ask what the last thing you remember before waking up is?"

I squeeze Jackson's hands, running my fingers over them nervously. "I went back to the green room after the meet and greet, and then Jackson and I went to explore the show floor."

"Okay. Anything else?"

I frown, trying to remember what happened, but there's a giant hole. I can see myself leaving the green room, but that's it. I try to focus. I can see myself holding Jackson's hand but...

I groan, bringing my fingers up to my eyebrows, and

begin massaging them. "That's it. That's the last thing I remember—going onto the show floor."

Why is my brain blanking?

"Really?" Concern laces Jackson's voice.

"Mr. Lau," the detective reprimands.

"Sorry."

"What did you consume today, food- and beverage-wise?"

That's an easier question. "Rick, my mod—well, PA—set Lee and me up with bagels and coffee for breakfast. I didn't have lunch because I was too nervous between the competition and the meet and greet."

"Nothing else to snack on or drink at all?"

"No. No snacks." I almost had some gummy worms but... "Oh. I had an energy drink after the meet and greet. Although, Parker drank, like, half of it." I wave a hand in Parker's general direction; I wasn't sure where he was sitting.

Somehow, the room gets even more silent. It's like I can feel it, crawling along my skin.

I said something wrong.

"Where did you get the drink?"

"The meet and greet." My words are hesitant; I feel like a kid who's been brought into the principal's office.

"Did someone hand it to you?"

"One of the volunteers."

"Did you recognize them at all? Do you remember what they looked like?"

"No, I—I'd never met them before. And kind of? I mean, I saw a lot of people today, so I don't really remember."

"Male? Female?"

"Female. White. She had brown hair." But I can't picture her face or anything else. "Why? What's this have to do with everything?"

"Deirdre, it appears you were roofied."

My stomach bottoms out.

"What? Why?"

"That's what we will try to find out. From this conversation, we can confirm that it was from the contents of the sports drink, as that is something you and Mr. Covington shared in common."

"What do you mean? What does Parker have to do with this?"

"Mr. Covington was also roofied."

My head snaps to Parker, and—Gods fucking dammit—I'm going to cry again because I can't even make out his face. Is he mad at me? Does he blame me? It's all my fault. Of course, he would blame me. He drank *my* drink.

"Parker?" My voice cracks as I desperately search him out.

"I'm fine, Deer. Just feels like I went on the piss." His voice is gentle in response.

"But—"

"Really, it's okay."

"I'm going to be sick. Like, now."

There's a bunch of shuffling, and by the time I get to the bathroom, I'm just dry heaving. Makes sense. There's nothing in my body except the fucking drugs.

"We'll let you get some rest." The detective stands awkwardly in the doorframe. "We're going to continue running down leads and will look into the woman you mentioned, see if she has any connections to you or your recent incidents." She means the swatting. It always comes back to haunt me. "We will be in contact if anything comes up."

The doctor and detective leave the room, and I just slump against the toilet. I don't feel well enough to risk abandoning it yet.

Jackson runs his hand up and down my arm. I'm not sure he knows it, but his constant contact is my lifeline. He's my lighthouse, keeping me steady throughout the storm, letting me know that I'm safe and that he's here.

I hear the door creak open and let out a pitiful groan. I don't want to deal with more people.

"Thank God, you're awake."

Unless it's Sydney.

She crouches down on the bathroom tiles and gives me a hug. I feel bad; it's definitely not the best position to be in nor the most ideal location.

"Oh." She blinks at me, and I see the surprise when she takes in my noticeably brown eyes. "I thought it was weird I could only find colored contacts in your toiletry bag. I figured maybe you'd run out of normal ones, so I brought your glasses."

Ugh. I hate these things. I never wear them unless I am feeling seriously lazy, but I don't have much of a choice now.

Everything just keeps getting worse.

Sydney holds out my designer black frames, and I reluctantly slide them on. My surroundings come into focus, and I startle when I notice a woman standing behind Sydney and Jackson. She looks familiar, but I can't quite place it.

"Jesus, Phoebe." Jackson follows my gaze. "Give us a heart attack, why don't you?"

Ah. She's one of Parker's older sisters.

I saw her…

Last time I was at the hospital…

Wow.

My luck has not been good these last few months.

"This is some déjà vu, shit," I mumble.

"That's what I said!" Parker yells.

Phoebe tilts her head, her short blonde hair dusting over her shoulders with the movement. Her crystal blue gaze runs over me like she is analyzing every inch of my body and using it to connect dots on a map I can't see.

"Let's talk, Miss Malloy."

Chapter
THIRTY-FOUR

DEER

I throw up, for real this time, and Jackson all but shoves Phoebe out of the hospital room. He tells her she isn't to come back until I'm feeling better. She wasn't all that thrilled about him telling her what to do, but Parker stepped in to back him up. I feel a little bad because, while she kinda sets me on edge, I could tell she didn't mean any harm.

Now, eight hours, two panic attacks, and one mandatory therapy session later, we're on our way to the airport to get on the Covington jet. Since Phoebe's been waiting to talk to me since last night, she offered to take us all back to California.

I'm secretly grateful because the idea of going to an airport and being around people...

Nope. Not going there.

Dammit.

I grip my seat belt harder.

Just when things were starting to look up. Just when I was all excited and ready to get back out there, *this* just had to happen. It's like the universe wants me to be a recluse.

Maybe I should just move back to Ireland, visit dear old Da in all of his retirement.

Shit.

He is going to kill me once he finds out about this. The only good thing is that my da hates social media, fame, and the like. It's why he stepped down as CEO once *Gods League* really took off and moved back to Ireland with my mam. He loves the game, loves what he created, but he doesn't want that to get mixed up with all the stuff online. It's also how I was able to become Deer without anyone really knowing who I am unless they gain access to my legal name. He kept me out of the limelight; just a few baby pictures turn up on search engines if you really know where to look.

I ended up having to put Sydney in contact with my moderators. She's working with them to deal with my social media while everyone is still speculating about why Parker and I went to the hospital. In return, Sydney put me in contact with her therapist. I'm not exactly looking forward to it. I've been dealing fine on my own.

Kind of.

Not really.

"You're sighing an awful lot over there. You okay?" Jackson rubs my knee as we pull onto the tarmac and drive up to the coveted Covington jet.

"Yeah, I'm just ready to be home."

"I know."

Jackson holds his hand out to help me out of the car. I don't know why they make Escalades so high off the ground.

There's ruckus from the other vehicle. My gaze strays to Parker as he leaps out of the car and throws his arm around Aleks, giving him a noogie, to which Aleks elbows him in the gut and tries to push him off. Syd rushes forward to break them apart, but the two boys just start laughing at one another.

I don't get how he is handling this so much better than me.

The truth is, if Parker hadn't drunk half my drink…I would have been in way worse condition.

"You'll sit opposite me, right?" Lee comes up on my left as we walk to the stairs.

She's still upset she wasn't at the hospital when I woke up even though I know she had been there the entire day.

"You can sit next to me."

"I appreciate the offer, but I don't want to spend the entire flight with the Hulk glaring daggers at me." Lee's gaze flits to the man beside me.

"Fair," I chuckle.

I clock Phoebe the second we enter the jet. She sits on a seat in the back right corner, a man in a black suit next to her. She looks up briefly, glancing over me before returning to her laptop. Her stoic expression never shifts.

I'm terrified about what she wants to talk about.

It's bad enough that, at this point, I'm pretty sure everyone knows that I've been keeping more than a few secrets from them. Something tells me that my cauldron has been bubbling too long and that everything is on the verge of spilling over.

I take the seat farthest from Phoebe that faces away from her. I know if I have to look at her throughout the flight, I'll drive myself to an early grave.

Jackson takes up the seat next to me, and Lee, true to her word, sits opposite me. Parker, Syd, and Aleks mimic our seating arrangement on the opposite aisle.

I try to distract myself, pulling my Switch and headphones from my handbag. I allow the music to drown everything out as I start up *Moonstone Valley*. I've been practically glued to my comfort game since I woke up, losing myself in another world is the only way to prevent my mind from overthinking everything that's happened to me.

I vaguely feel the jostling of the jet as it rolls down the runway, and my stomach does a little flip when we go airborne.

I'm so focused on trying to woo this damn village doctor to marry me that it takes a second for me to realize Lee is nudging me with her foot. I look up and raise one of my brows at her. She makes a drinking motion with her hands and then points to her right.

The stewardess stands there with a couple of water glasses and champagne flutes on a platter.

My stomach drops again, and not from the altitude.

Jackson must notice me tense up in his periphery because he looks up from his laptop. I'm not sure what he sees in my face, but he lifts one side of his headphones and says something to the stewardess that makes her blanch.

She comes back with a water bottle, which Jackson inspects before cracking it open and taking a sip. He then holds it out to me, and I can't help feeling a little embarrassed. But that embarrassment doesn't overshadow my relief at his gesture. I mouth "thank you" to him as I tentatively accept the bottle.

I know now that the reason why I couldn't detect the roofies was because the damn sports drink was blue, which hides the way the tasteless little pill tinges drinks a blue color.

Everyone keeps saying it's not my fault, but I can't help feeling like I should've known better. I mean, come on, you don't just accept drinks from people—not if you're someone in my position, especially with everything that's been happening. Sure, she seemed official because she was a volunteer with the expo…

I take a sip of the water, and my nerves scream at me even after I've gulped it down. Out of everywhere, this is one of the last places my drink could be spiked, but my brain doesn't seem to understand that. It makes the liquid feel like fire clogging my throat, but I try my best to push past it.

I return my attention back to my game, forcing myself to forget everything.

Until Lee nudges me again.

I glare up at her. I had just died in the mines, and— even though I am dating the town doctor—he is still charging me a thousand gold to revive me. Asshat.

Lee bites her lip and points.

I follow the direction of her finger to where Phoebe has slipped into the seat next to Lee. She has her legs crossed at the ankles and is fiddling with her gold watch. My annoyance dissipates, turning into a cloud of ugly dread.

I pause my game and slip off my headphones, the deep whooshing hum of the airplane coming back into focus. The anticipation in the air crackles around us like electricity, setting everyone on edge as we wait for Phoebe to speak. All I want is to put my headphones back on, to drown out the ambient noise and return to my little mind palace.

Phoebe opens her mouth, but when her eyes finally rise to meet mine, I see something shocking: a flash of sympathy. I don't think anyone else notices because she quickly steels her resolve, her shoulders straightening just a little bit more.

"I have my contacts looking into your case, Miss Malloy, since I doubt it's something the local detectives will be able to piece together when they don't have the full story to go off of."

"I'd prefer if you called me Deer."

"I can, but I think, for the purposes of this conversation, it is a little moot."

I press my lips together.

She tilts her head. "We can continue our chat somewhere more private, but considering the situation, you're going to have to tell everyone here sooner or later. You pose a security threat to them all until this is sorted."

I kind of hate her.

And I definitely hate that what she's saying makes sense.

Everything is getting so messy, and I am having trouble keeping track of all the webs I have woven. Jackson already knows everything, Parker will find out from his sister, and Sydney knows my eyes aren't blue. There are hundreds of little cracks in my armor. Do I really want to continue wasting my energy keeping it together when it is so obviously about to crumble?

"We can talk to her in the bedroom?" Jackson rests his hands on mine.

I let out a sigh. "No. She's right. It's a pointless fight."

My gamer identity was supposed to be my safety blanket, keeping me warm and protected. But all the threats around me are like someone throwing gasoline on the fabric, and at any moment it could go up in flames. It is no longer shielding me; it is putting me in more danger.

I maneuver my hands, so they're clasped with Jackson's, and raise my gaze to Phoebe, not shying away from her arctic eyes.

"What do you want to know?"

The smile she gives me is borderline villainous as she raises a hand and motions behind me. The man who had been sitting next to her comes forward and slips into the spare seat next to Aleks, pulling out a tablet and keyboard.

"Let's start with the beginning. When were you first approached by the Deer Hunters?"

This is going to be a long flight.

I take my time, explaining to her how they were just spam comments initially. That the group seemed like just a bunch of trolls until the comments started getting a little more aggressive. That they hadn't done anything outright threatening for the first couple of months, so I'd brushed it under the rug. They'd made me uncomfortable, sure, but a lot of comments and DMs made me uncomfortable, and at least these hadn't been sexual in nature. And that my moderator took charge of fielding it all once it became apparent that they were set on me.

When I tell her that they started to insinuate they had my address, I feel Jackson tense up beside me. There was a scare at Halloween a few months earlier that had me worried they were stalking me. I explain that I'd begun taking a few more precautions after all that, that I stopped going out so much or posting where I was until after I'd already been somewhere. The more I speak, the more I realize that it was a mistake to keep this hidden for so long.

Phoebe asks for the details of all my moderators so she can fact check, wary that they might have hidden details from me to keep from making me even more worried. It's that realization that causes a chill to break over my body, puckering my skin.

I gloss over the swatting, knowing that all she has to do is look my stream up online to see how that went. I don't need to choke myself up with that again.

When I tell her about the message before the expo and the odd comments that cropped up during it, I find myself wincing. It was such a clear sign, I'd known that, and yet I'd refused to fully acknowledge it.

Phoebe's gaze never strays, not once. And what first seemed like a cold and emotionless stare I'm learning is actually her version of determined and calculating. It almost becomes comforting because she is so unwavering and there is no hint of judgement or pity.

"I just don't get it. What have I done to warrant all this?" My throat is dry from all the talking.

Phoebe sighs. "I don't like to make speculations."

"But if you had to?"

"If I had to, I'd say someone's obsessed with you. It's

not unheard of when it comes to public figures."

Obsessed.

"Look, honestly, Deer, I'm not sure I understand why you don't just come clean?"

"You mean dox myself?" My voice pitches higher.

"Yes." She holds her hand out like she's holding a platter, gesturing across the aisle to Aleks and Parker. "It worked for them."

"Because they were being blackmailed."

"And it made the blackmail go away."

"I'm not being blackmailed! I'm being stalked." The words wrench themselves from my throat with the sting of a thousand razorblades.

Phoebe must be nuts. The Deer Hunters have clearly veered from online trolls into stalker territory—revealing who I truly am would just put me in more danger, and that makes me want to throw up. Actually, it makes me want to buy a private island and escape off the grid.

The last thing I want is to make myself more of an available target for them.

"We would take measures to keep you safe."

"No."

"It's going to come out someday."

"How? My parents don't live in this country anymore. I have no family here they could track me to. I went to an extremely private and prestigious high school and never went to college." I check each point off on my fingers. "My entire look is different to how I was three years ago. No one would see me and go, 'Oh, lookie here, that's Deirdre Malloy.'"

"Your legal name is still your legal name."

"So? I rarely travel, and if I do, I use private companies. My car is registered under Rick, and my new apartment is under your family's name."

Phoebe's eyes flick to her brother. "I know."

"I'm careful, Phoebe."

"Fine." The word is curt, cut with glass through slightly clenched teeth. "Fine. We'll do this the hard way. I'll work to make sure your life continues as it is and try to root out this poison, but just remember I advised you otherwise."

She's giving me what I want but makes it feel like she's handing me a death sentence.

I can only hope she is wrong.

Chapter
THIRTY-FIVE

JACKSON

"Are you sure?" I hold my hand against the elevator door to stop it from closing.

"Yeah, I'm just going to go rot in my bed for the next twenty-four hours. Not exactly fun stuff."

"We could just cuddle?"

"This is so weird." Parker stares at me like I'm an alien.

"Shut the fuck up."

"That's more like it." He shoots a set of finger guns at me.

"Go. I'll text you later. Promise." Deer perches on her tiptoes and I lean down as she presses a kiss to my cheek. "Seriously, go." She grabs her giant pink suitcase and wheels it away.

I want to go after her, but I don't want to suffocate her. If she needs some time, I'll just have to deal with it.

Somehow.

"Dude, let go of the elevator." Aleks nudges his foot into the back of my knee, causing it to fold.

I glare at him but pull back, allowing the elevator to continue its ascent to our penthouse.

"So, you and Deer?" Parker rocks back and forth on his heels.

I ignore him.

"Oh, come on, mate. You're not going to give us anything?"

The elevator doors open, and I grab my bags, exiting first.

"You can't seriously tell me that after the last seventy-two hours there's nothing going on," he calls out.

There's nothing for me to say because I'd never gotten a chance to talk to Deer about it; *because* of everything that had just gone on, there had been no time.

"Stevie said they're fake dating."

"Fake? *That* is not fake. *That* is territorial wolf mate shit."

He's right. This whole fake-dating thing is hanging on by a thread. A very thin gossamer thread. It didn't have much of a leg to stand on in the first place, and now everything seems so much bigger than it.

She's mine, no question about it.

I stop short of my room and toe off my sneakers, picking them up and carrying them and my bag inside, shutting the door behind me. I toss the duffle on the ground and then place my sneakers in their proper spot on my sneaker wall.

Maybe Deer has the right idea; the last few days have

really zapped my energy. I collapse onto my bed, staring at the ceiling for a moment before pulling out my phone and tossing her a text.

ME

How's the rotting?

DEER

Commencing shortly. I had to prep first

ME

u have to prep?

DEER

duh

blankets, games, food, drinks, the works – all within three feet of me

if I have to leave my bed at all, I'll cryyyy

THAT'S A JOKE BTW

ME

lmao well if you need any room service...

DEER

oooh what're u offering?

ME
what do u want?

DEER:
 I can think of a few things

ME
naughty girl

DEER
:P

There's a knock on my door.

I stare at it curiously. Parker doesn't knock. Aleks would knock, but then he'd walk straight in, not even waiting a beat after warning me.

"Yeah?"

"Come out, we need to talk."

Phoebe?

I sit up and quickly change into a more comfortable pair of sweatpants before opening my door. She's not standing there, so I head into the main area of the apartment.

Aleks is sprawled on the couch, and Phoebe is leaning against the wall next to the TV with her arms crossed. She doesn't look mad, just bored.

Parker is pulling an HP energy drink out of the fridge, and he gestures to me. "Want anything?"

"Seriously?"

"None of this is the drink's fault."

I sigh, taking my place next to Aleks.

The man who has been accompanying Phoebe this entire time seems to materialize out of thin air, rounding the corner as he continues to survey the apartment. Strange dude.

"Parker, hurry the fuck up."

"Chill, sis." I hear the cracking of the can before Parker takes a loud sip.

He takes his sweet time walking over to the couch and sitting on the far end, tossing Aleks a bag of chocolate pretzels in the process.

"You may proceed."

She rolls her eyes at him, letting out a deep huff before standing straight. "After thinking it over, I figured it was best to wait to give you all this news separately so as not to alarm the girl."

That doesn't sound good.

"There was mirroring software on all of Deirdre's devices."

"What?" Parker sits up.

"Yes, I had my people go through her belongings after Sydney handed them over, and they found traces everywhere." She tsks. "I mean, really, it was quite a pathetic show."

"So, you think this is linked with the drugging or the swatting?"

"I'm not one hundred percent certain because when we tried to track the malware, we ran into issues, and I can't exactly push the boundaries more than I already have without it becoming flat-out illegal." She sighs, like this whole situation is a giant inconvenience. "But it's my best guess that it's all linked."

I clench my teeth together as my fists ball up at my

sides. Phoebe follows the movement but doesn't show any change in her emotions.

"So, what does this mean?" Aleks leans forward.

"Well, while the local detectives are still looking into that girl from the expo, I already found her. I mean, I guess it's better to say he did, but, same-same." She throws her hand to the side, signaling to the man who has been following her like a shadow. "Anyway, we're going to do our own deep dive into her—but it seems she's been brought into the whisper network of Deer Hunters, based on what we've found so far."

"Fuck," Aleks sighs. "How many people are there?"

Phoebe tilts her head to the side, a slight wince pulling at her lips. "A lot. That's why it's taking a little longer to get to the bottom of it without it being, well, really illegal. Paige keeps reiterating that the evidence needs to be clean to convict once we find the instigator."

Paige Covington, the middle child and softer sister, is one of the top lawyers for the Covington conglomerate.

"So, where does that leave us, Pheebs? What do you need us to do?" Parker has that serious glint in his eye that he rarely lets out, the one that makes you realize why he was the original Covington heir.

"I need you to keep acting normal. The closer I get to the head of the snake, the more likely it is to retreat. We don't want to tip them off."

"You want us to do nothing? Fuck that," I bite out.

She must be joking. Does she expect me to sit here and listen to how the Deer Hunters are a much larger threat than I ever imagined and then just go about my daily life? As if my girl's life isn't in danger?

Yeah, right.

"I contemplated not even telling you." Phoebe's eyes cool as they slide back to me.

"Her life is in danger, Phoebe," I growl.

"And this apartment complex is well fortified; my little brother made it so. Plus, we're adding extra security personnel downstairs."

"You want to keep her trapped in the building until this is dealt with? She's not fucking Rapunzel."

"I mean, she's the stubborn one who is determined to keep her identity a secret."

"Don't put this back on her."

The corner of her mouth kicks up in a smile. "You really like her, don't you?"

"Of course, I do."

She nods her head, that smile widening. "Cute."

"God, you Covingtons are all the same."

Phoebe moves forward and perches on the edge of the coffee table, crossing her legs at her ankles and leveling with us. "Look. This is messy as fuck, and I have other things my time would be better spent on. But I'm doing you a favor because that little knobhead over there is one of two people in this world I can't say no to."

Parker blows her a kiss.

"I'm handling it, and I'll work with Sydney to make sure things stay clean, but I came here to warn you to be extra vigilant. I know you can't keep her locked in this building—although I wouldn't be surprised if she did that willingly, looking at her track record—so just stick with her and help her through it."

"You don't have to tell me twice."

"Good." She stands up and makes her way to the bar cart opposite the kitchen and pulls out a bottle of whiskey, pouring herself a good three fingers.

"Hey," Aleks shoots up. "That's my good stuff."

"That's why I'm drinking it." She takes a sip. "Ah, that hits the spot."

My phone buzzes.

DEER

I've thought it over

i wouldn't mind some room service brownies

preferably chocolate-raspberry flavored

<3 <3 <3

I'll protect this woman at any cost.

Chapter THIRTY-SIX

DEER

pass by an open door and peer in.

There looks to be something human shaped curled in the corner.

"Well, this is probably a bad idea."

I walk into the room only to have the door lock automatically behind me. Yeah. Shoulda seen that coming. Some weird chanting noise starts up, and the closer I get to the burnt body, the louder it gets.

"What's it saying?"

I try clicking on the body, but nothing happens. Its charred face keeps following me around the room. I strain my ears to make out what it is saying while not letting it out of my sight.

"Live. Live. Live. Live."

"Well, guess that's a good thing, right?"

My eyes flick to the chat, only to see that everyone else seems to think I am in a deep load of shit. I click around the old bathroom, trying to see if there's anything else in here, but come up empty.

"Can I leave?" I walk up to the door and try clicking on it.

The door swings open.

A scream leaves my body.

And a giant blob-shaped fleshy *something* attacks and kills me.

My screen goes fuzzy with the words SIGNAL LOST splayed across it.

"Great. What even was that?"

My stomach rumbles, and I reach for my phone to check the time, only to remember I left it in the other room since I'm filming and didn't want another repeat of Jackson distracting me with his dirty texts.

I've been streaming for a solid two hours this afternoon, which is pretty damn impressive considering that last week I barely managed an hour before my anxiety began to spike and I quit. Maybe I should just call it while things are still going well. My fans are happy just to see my spontaneous streams; I doubt they'll be annoyed that it's on the shorter side again today.

The spontaneous streaming is Aleks' idea. He figured if I don't outright announce when I'm going live, there is less of a chance any of the Deer Hunters could preplan something. So far, it seems to be working. Rick hasn't flagged any suspicious behavior recently, and the streaming has helped curb the rumors around my mysterious hospitalization.

"Okay, fawns. I'm logging off for the day, but thank you for tuning in." I curve my hands into a heart shape and smile. "Thanks for all your love and support, bye!"

I turn off the stream and remove my headset before I begin the process of shutting down my PC. I push back on my chair and stand up to stretch.

Ugh, my shoulders are all tight because of how tense I was playing that game. I'd seen Jackson play *Haunted Huntings* a few weeks ago and thought I'd try it out for myself. Fuck, the jump scares are on another level—but that's a good thing because my brain gets so focused on surviving the game that I'm not able to think about surviving real life. It's better to feel scared over some mysterious creature popping out in a game than to sit in the corner of my room and panic that a person will stalk out of the shadows to murder me.

I hold onto my trap muscle, massaging it as I pad into my kitchen. My fridge is dismally empty minus the most recent batch of Oreo brookies Jackson made me the other day. I take out the container and carry it to my couch, flopping down and opening it to remove one of the brownie-cookies.

Damn, that man can bake.

I devour it with no shame, happily grabbing a second one...and then a third...and then the fourth and final one. Part of me suspects he puts some kind of hex on these things. They are devilishly addictive.

A loud banging reverberates through my apartment. The Tupperware container clatters to the ground as I jerk up, my heart rate catapulting to new highs. I can't even get my legs to function properly as I tumble off my couch and crawl on all fours across my living room, hands slapping on the floorboards with every move.

Where's my handbag?

I spot the heart-shaped purse on my kitchen counter and reach a hand up, hooking the nail of my pinky finger around the handle and tugging. It topples to the floor, contents spilling out—but that's fine because it makes it easier to spot what I was looking for.

Gripping the item in my hand, I continue with a slow crawl to the door. My free hand splays against the wood, and I use it to help me stand on shaky legs.

My eyes catch on the doorbell camera Parker installed, and I still. Cold embarrassment washes over me.

Gods dammit.

I should've checked the camera first before going all panic mode.

With some strength in my legs now, I stand a little more confidently and undo the deadbolt on my door before opening it.

"Hi."

Jackson looks me up and down with a frown. "Is that a pink taser?"

"Yes."

"Cute and dangerous, just like you."

I roll my eyes but smile, stepping back to let him in. He places a kiss on my forehead, and I feel something press in just below my chest. My grin widens when I see a new Tupperware container in his hands.

"More room service?"

I am getting a little spoiled. Jackson has been over every other day the last two weeks with a new sweet treat.

Part of me has been tempted to ask if he would bake in my apartment so it could smell like fresh brownies instead of me just burning artificial candles to fill the hole.

"Strawberry cheesecake blondies." He places the glass container on my counter before taking a seat on my couch. He picks up the empty brookie container off the floor by my coffee table. "Please don't tell me that my baking is all you've been eating?"

"Fine. I won't."

"Deer."

"I haven't been that hungry." I bend down to pick up the spillage from my purse, shoving it all back inside before setting the bag on the counter. And because I actually haven't been eating anything but his baking, I open the new container and pull out one of the blondies. I really should ask Rick to restock my fridge, but I don't have the energy to cook anyway.

"You haven't left the apartment since we got back. You even had Lee move Crime Night to your place."

"So?" I take a bite of the blondie and—oh my Gods, how is it so good? I moan around the bite. It tastes like heaven. Well, if heaven was filled with strawberry clouds and vanilla bean rivers.

"Don't try to distract me with that moaning of yours."

"It wasn't on purpose but," I grin, "if it works."

He grabs me by the waist and pulls me down so I'm seated across his lap.

Our relationship is…weird. Part of me feels like I should bring it up because we're currently living in this gray area that is getting murkier with each passing day. With everything going on, I'm sure playing this game with my heart isn't the smartest idea—but I'm more worried that I'll lose him, and I can't afford that. Jackson is my sanity; if he leaves me, I will fall right back into the dark smoke that curls around me and threatens to swallow me whole. I need my lighthouse to see clearly, to know that there are no monsters.

"So, I wanted to ask you something in person because I thought you might shut me down if I just texted it."

I still around my next bite of blondie.

There's no way he can read my mind...can he?

"Okay."

"You know how the new, unrated director's cut of *Devil Nun 5* just came out in theaters?"

"Yeah, you sent me a link."

"I was wondering if you'd come with me to the movies this afternoon?"

"You mean like a movie theater."

Suddenly, the blondie doesn't seem so appetizing. No, that's a lie. It still looks great. It's just that the idea of taking another bite conflicts with the way my stomach is now collapsing in on itself.

"Yeah, the one on Roland Street by the ice cream place."

"Oh."

No. That sounds awful. Movie theaters mean people. Lots of people. Random people. And while Dr. Ainsley says that I need to start trying small things—like even a walk around the block—I'm not that keen. I'd figured they'd all be happy enough that I'm not hibernating in my bed twenty-four seven, but apparently the bare minimum isn't appeasing them.

"Deer?"

"I don't know."

"If you don't come, I'll have to drag Aleksander. And I'd much prefer you because you're prettier than him, more fun, and actually care about the movies."

"But—"

"Do you trust me?"

"Yes." The response is automatic, and I know in that moment that I'm going to go. Because I do trust him. Even when it seems like the world is aiming a thousand arrows at me, I know Jackson will step in front of me with his shield to prevent it from hurting me.

"Then let me take you to the movies. It'll be safe."

"Promise?"

"Promise."

Chapter THIRTY-SEVEN

DEER

I regret this.

Jackson parks the car, but I don't make a move to get out or unbuckle my seat belt. I just stare straight ahead at the movie theater. The tinted glass makes it impossible to see inside.

There could be dozens of people inside. They could recognize me. Take pictures. Post them online so anyone can come find me. So *they* can find me.

I really regret this.

"Deer?" Jackson's voice breaks through the hum as he opens my door and leans over me, unbuckling my seat belt and grabbing my purse. My body stays stock still—I just look at him out of the corner of my eye. "Come on." He takes my hand and gives it a squeeze. My traitorous body seems to not be communicating with my brain because it follows him out of the car.

"Jackson," I whisper, grabbing his bicep with my other arm. I'm clutching onto him like a small sugar glider that's staring wide-eyed at its surroundings and shaking from the potential predatory threats. "What if people recognize me?"

"They won't."

I scoff. "You can't guarantee that."

"Trust me, they won't."

As we walk up the stairs, the tinted doors swing forward, a man in a suit holding it open for us. My steps falter as I take his large frame in, but my nerves steady as I realize I've seen him before. He's one of the security members from the expo.

I give him a small nod as we walk inside, my nails gripping Jackson's arm even harder as I wait to see just how busy it is.

"In and out," I mutter to myself, taking controlled breaths through my nose like the therapist instructed me. The smell of buttery popcorn and salty pretzels wafts around me and I look up.

It's…empty.

I mindlessly follow Jackson as my eyes dart around the theater foyer. There are two employees, one at the ticket office and one by the concession area. I note three more people in suits stationed throughout, whom I'm assuming are extra bodyguards.

I know it's a Tuesday afternoon, but I still thought more people would be here. Maybe all the other movies just started…

"What do you want to snack on?"

"Hmm?" I blink up, noticing he's led me right to the concession counter. "Oh."

Candy, popcorn, pretzels, pizza, chips, slushies, ice cream, curly fries, mozzarella sticks, chicken tenders…my Gods, there are a lot of options. When did movie theaters get so complex? It is like a drive-through in here.

"A pack of fruit gummy worms and a large salty popcorn."

"Drink?"

I hesitate, looking at the fountain machine. It's not like someone could put something in that without drugging the entire theater. That's what my rational brain tells me. I, however, am unable to listen to it.

"Nope."

"Not even a bottled water?" He points to the mini fridge on the ground next to his feet that houses a few bottled beverages.

"Fine."

I won't drink much anyway—I hate getting up to use the bathroom at the movies—but this will appease him enough.

Jackson also orders himself popcorn plus a pretzel and then pays while the employee scoops up the buttery popped kernels and drops them into a plastic bucket.

"Here." The girl's smile is sweet, and she has blonde hair, not brown, but it still sets me a little on edge.

"Thanks." I take my bucket and gummy worms, trying to smile back because I don't want to seem like a bitch when it's just my anxiety talking.

Jackson flashes his phone at the employee at the ticket office, and they instruct us to head to theater seven.

I scan the movie posters lining the walls as we walk to the theater, but once we get to the set of double doors with a bright, glowing seven above it, I halt. We haven't seen anyone else so far, and it just makes me worried that everyone is already in the theater, crowding it with their bodies in the dark room.

Jackson opens the door, and I step in, bracing myself as I walk up the ramp. The theater is still dimly lit because the movie itself hasn't started yet, so I'm able to run my eyes over all the seats.

It's…also empty.

"What time does the movie start?" I'm not sure why I'm whispering when there's no one else here.

"In a few minutes."

I frown, following him to our seats smack dab in the center, sinking down when he motions to the correct ones. This must be one of those fancier movie theaters since the chairs are all plush with black leather and extra cushioning around the headrests.

"I thought this movie just came out?"

"It did."

"Then where are all the people?"

Jackson shrugs, ripping off a piece of his pretzel and eating it.

That's when I hear the doors open.

I knew it.

I whip my head around, ready to see a herd of people rushing in at the last minute.

My shoulders droop.

It's just another bodyguard…

I turn back, slumping into the chair. Confusion rattles

me as I rip open the packet of gummy worms and dump them into my popcorn bucket before giving it a careful shake to distribute them all.

"What are you doing?"

"What?"

"You just put the gummies in your popcorn."

"I did." I reach in to pick one out, popping it into my mouth. The chewy gummy is coated with some of the salty butter, making it delicious. "Want one?" I hold another one out for him.

Jackson stares down at me with uncertainty but opens his mouth. Surprise ripples through me, but it is laced with a small kernel of fire. My heart pounds loudly against my chest as I slowly bring the piece of candy closer.

He looks right at me as his lips close around my fingers, and it sends a bolt of lightning right to my core. The room feels like it notches a few degrees higher as we lock in place. But the heat in his eyes quickly dies as he continues to chew on the gummy worm, his jaw tensing up with every bite. I stifle a smile. It wouldn't take a rocket scientist to know that he is not a fan of the flavor combo.

"Is it bad?"

"Well, it's not good."

Laughter spills out of me as he immediately twists open his water and takes a chug. I give the bucket another shake.

"Ya know, if you let it marinate for a little longer, the popcorn takes on some of the sweetness from the gummies as the heat melts them."

"No thanks. I'll just stick to my normal popcorn."

The lights start to turn off, and I give the room another

once-over to see if I missed anyone else entering while I was distracted. But nope. No one.

The trailers begin rolling, and as each minute ticks by without some last-minute viewer rushing in, my nerves begin to calm. And by the time the movie starts, I'm able to tune out and just focus on the screen before me.

Around halfway through the movie, Jackson lifts the armrest separating our seats and pulls me into him. I snuggle against his side, relishing in his warmth as we watch the Devil Nun eviscerate one of the witch hunters in the underground catacombs. This unrated version really is taking the gore to a whole other level.

"That was interesting," he mutters under his breath as one of the hunters gets bitten by the nun, the wound quickly turning a poisonous purple.

"What was?"

"That. It wasn't in the theatrical cut." He looks down at me, the lights shifting on his face and highlighting the strong cut of his jaw.

A horror movie isn't supposed to feel intimate, but with each passing minute, I find myself sinking deeper into the man next to me. His calloused fingers rub circles on my arm, causing my attention to split between the movie and him.

"What?" He gives me a wry smile.

"Nothing." I try not to grin back, but I can't help it, the apples of my cheeks tightening.

"Nothing?"

"Nothing."

Our smiles continue to grow, matching one another beat for beat until I have to bite my bottom lip to stop it.

Jackson's lids go hooded at the action, gaze flicking from my mouth to my eyes. He brings his hand to rest beneath my chin, thumb brushing over my bottom lip.

I take in a stuttering breath, completely mesmerized by him.

Jackson dips down, closing his lips around mine. His hand comes up to cup my jaw, and it angles me right into him. I reach my arm out, searching for purchase, and land on his shoulder, using it to pull myself closer to him. When I'm with him, it's like nothing else exists. He quiets the hurricane in my mind, soothing it into a gentle breeze that licks over my skin.

Kissing Jackson feels like looking through a telescope for the very first time and noticing all the stars in the sky—it's bright and all-consuming, drowning out the world around me. His tongue dances with mine and I moan into it, craving more.

We're like teenagers, our hands swimming over each other's bodies, desperate for touch as our panting gets louder and kisses more frenzied.

"The things you do to me, Deer," he growls against me.

I love the way he talks; it makes me feel like the most desirable woman in the world.

His hand palms my breast, and I arch into him, wishing there was no fabric separating us. I trail my hand down his chest, letting my fingers rake across his T-shirt until I hit his jeans. I tamp down my smirk as I continue going lower, my hand rubbing down the hard evidence of his want.

"Someone's playing naughty," he grins against my lips.

"Oh?" I grin back, giving it a light squeeze before I continue to rub up and down.

He groans. "You better stop doing that unless you plan on taking responsibility for it."

My stomach swoops. "And what if I am?"

He pulls away, eyes darkening as his hand rests on mine, and he pumps us together along his length. "You want to suck this cock? Then beg me for it."

"Please," I breathe, slipping off the seat and onto my knees. "Please let me suck your cock."

I fumble a little in the dark, working to get his jeans unbuttoned. My fingers close around the band of his briefs, pulling his cock free. His hands close around his length, and he looks at me as he pumps himself.

"Open your mouth."

My lips part, and he guides himself into my mouth. The tip of his cock hits my tongue, and I taste that salty bead of precum, my eyes lighting up.

"Now, suck."

I close my lips around him, letting my tongue mold against his dick as I suck. My cheeks hollow out and I look up at him, watching his reactions as I begin to bob. I move one of my hands to his base, twisting it in motion with my mouth. Jackson's brows crease and he threads a hand through my hair, gripping it lightly. A thrill shoots through me as his force increases, and he uses me to pump a steady rhythm as he begins to fuck my face.

"Such a good little cocksucker, aren't you?" His deep voice courses through my blood.

Jackson's hips buck up, and it pushes his cock even farther down my throat, causing my gag reflex to kick in. But I refuse to stop, eager to please him. His grip around my head tightens as I choke, taking him deeper and deeper with every bob of my head. Tears begin to bead and then fall free, trailing across my cheek.

"Look at those pretty tears slipping down your whore face as you choke on my cock."

I've been with some men before who used degradation, but none like Jackson. The way he utters those words has my pussy clenching and aching, desperation leaking free.

I work faster, suck harder, not caring about the sloppy noises that only seem to spur him on. He lets out another groan, his hips lifting again, and I move my hand to cup his balls, giving them a light squeeze.

"I'm about to come."

His words fill me with satisfaction, and I swirl my tongue, letting him thrust against me until he groans. He lets his grip loosen just enough so I don't totally choke, his hot cum shooting down my throat. "Fuck," he breathes, pulling back to look at me. And the post-orgasmic adoration in his eyes as he swipes a thumb across my cheek to clear my tears has my heart skipping a beat.

He tucks himself back away and guides me onto my seat. I squirm a little, clenching my thighs together at the tingling that won't go away. Jackson rests his hand on my thigh, his fingers squeezing in a way that only exasperates the sensation.

"If you can wait, I have a gift for you later."

"Gift?" I tilt my head.

"Yes. The fun kind." There's a dark promise in the way he raises his brows and smirks, and I can't help my curiosity.

"I can wait."

"Are you sure?" His fingers trail higher.

"Yes," I hiss, trying to ignore the way I want to shift my hips so his fingers can give me some relief.

"Good." He removes his hand, and I'm both grateful and woeful for its loss. Jackson tugs me closer, nestling me against his chest. "I can't wait to see how pretty you'll look."

The words themselves sound innocent enough, but the wicked gleam in his eyes vows depravity.

Chapter
THIRTY-EIGHT

JACKSON

I push her against the wall of the elevator, diving into her sweet kiss. A guy could get drunk off the taste of her.

The doors open to the penthouse, and I pull back, raising one finger to my lips as I grasp her hand with my other. None of the main lights are on in the apartment, and I can't hear anything coming from either of the guys' rooms.

"Come on." I tug her along with me as we quickly slip through the quiet to my bedroom.

I take the time to make sure my door is locked before spinning to face Deer, my hunger growing with every second.

"Ready for your gift?"

"Yup." She perches on the end of my bed, clasping her hands in her lap as she waits and watches me.

I open my closet and pull out my duffle bag, sifting

around until I find the floral pink box. I hand it to her wordlessly, and she holds it, hesitating for a second before popping it open with a gasp.

I can't tell if it's one of shock or reverence, and I shift on my feet as she removes one of the bundled ropes from the kit.

"They're so pretty." She smiles up at me, running her fingers over the cherry blossom pink jute ropes in a way that has my cock twitching in my pants.

"Mm, they'll look even prettier tied around your body."

Her eyes flash with molten heat, and she places the rope back in the box, holding it out to me.

"Show me."

I smirk, leaning forward to take the box and place it next to her on the bed. Looking at her directly, I tilt my head as I ask, "Show me, what?"

"Show me, please?"

"Good."

I cup her jaw and bring her into a heady kiss, nipping at her bottom lip and drawing out a gasp. Her hands loop around my neck, and I move to place my knee between her legs on the bed. My other arm snakes around her ribs, and I lay my palm flat on her back, drawing her near.

She tastes sweet and salty—and I continue to kiss her, searching for more of that deliciousness. Her hands shift, her nails digging into my back. Fuck, I love that feeling, the pain she draws out while being so soft and supple beneath me.

I reach down and grip the bottom of her top but pause, reconsidering.

"Take your top off."

Her hands scuttle to the hem, and she pulls back for a moment to rip it off before crushing her lips back on mine. Fuck, it fuels me how needy she is.

"And the bra."

She peels off the lacy fabric, tossing it aside. I reach down and give her breasts a squeeze, loving the way her soft skin feels against my rough fingers. I could spend all day worshipping them.

I run my thumb over her dark pink nipple as it stiffens, waiting until just the right moment to give it a pinch. Deer sucks in a short intake of breath, her eyes popping open.

I smirk, moving to her other breast and showing it the same attention. I lean down and give her nipple a suck, circling it with my tongue and running my teeth over the hardened peak teasingly. This time, when I give it a tug, she moans, her hands threading through my hair and tightening. She starts to squirm under me, her legs shifting and clenching. Right where I want her.

"I could spend all night on these," I murmur before pulling away.

"But—" she starts to protest until she sees me pick up the pink box.

"Why don't you go ahead and take off the rest of those clothes?"

She quickly stands up, looping her thumbs in her skirt and pushing the material down along with her panties. I spend a moment admiring the way her breasts hang as she bends to step away from the pooling fabric.

She promptly sits back on the edge of the bed, looking at me for further directions.

Perfect.

"I need you to follow my instructions carefully, all right?"

"All right."

"Once I have these ropes bound and for as long as they stay on, you are mine. Mine to use, fuck, and pleasure however I please. But, if it ever becomes too much and you need me to stop, use your safe word. Remember?"

"Oh, can we not do red? I like to use 'poppy.'"

My jaw twitches at the reminder that she's been with other people, but I push that jealousy aside. It doesn't matter. She is mine now.

"Okay. Poppy. As soon as you say that I'll stop. No questions asked. Understood?"

"Understood."

"Good, now be a pet and raise your arms over your head for me."

I hold the rope and use a lark's head knot to tie two parallel lines across her chest, one above and one below her tits, before looping it over her shoulder and bringing it back to weave through the middle of her chest and then back over the other shoulder. I finish tying the basic harness and admire the way her perfect tits are caged by the rope. I run my finger down the center before sweeping under her breast, toying along the material as my dick continues to harden.

"Lie back on the bed and bring your knees to your chest."

She blushes as she follows my order, and that pinkness intensifies when I reach down and spread her knees farther apart, putting that pretty pussy on display.

I take her wrist and position it just above her ankle, tying two column ties so her arms are restrained to her legs. It's a simple crab position, nothing too excessive in the grand scheme of Shibari since she can still move around a fair bit, but it does leave her in a very vulnerable position.

I grin down at Deer, running two fingers up her cunt.

Fuck. She's already so wet.

I reach back and pull off my shirt, tossing it on the floor. Deer angles her head up, watching me as I unbutton my jeans and slip them off along with my briefs. Her pupils widen, taking me in as I fist my cock.

"Do you think you're ready for this?"

"Yes."

"I don't know." I take a few steps forward, continuing to pump myself lazily. "You don't seem nearly desperate enough."

"I am, I swear. Please, Jackson." She shifts in her ropes, fingers stretching out for purchase that she won't find.

I run my thumb over the bead of precum, swirling it around my head with a groan.

"Jackson," she whines.

I love it when she sounds needy.

But as much as I want to fill her with my cock right now and watch the way her eyes roll back as I fuck her senseless, I want to have some fun first.

I head back to my duffle, searching around until I find a satin bag and pull the item free. As I stroll lazily back to Deer, I see her trying to angle her head so she can get a look at what I'm holding behind my back. I rest my knees on the edge of the bed, pulling her close to me so her legs are forced open around me.

The sound of buzzing fills the room.

Deer's doe eyes widen as I bring forward the wand and slowly run it up her pussy. A sigh of relief escapes her as the truth of her dirty need spills across her face.

"Shit," she breathes out, her hips wriggling, searching for the friction.

Her brows furrow as I hold the vibrating head over her clit, increasing the intensity of the vibrations. Her small moans fill the room as I tease her. I watch the way her pussy clenches, like it's desperate for my cock to fill it.

"Oh, fuck," she gasps, her hips bucking. "Fuck, it's too much."

"Too much? Baby, it's not enough."

I up the intensity again, and she lets out a cry that has me smirking down at her. Her ankles dig into my thighs as she struggles against the restraints, her body getting desperate for some sort of relief.

I keep a close eye on her expression, noting the way her brows pinch just a little bit tighter and rise a bit higher.

I rip the vibrator away, and she gasps, staring at me like I've just committed the gravest sin possible.

"But-but I was just about to—"

"Come? Did I say you could?"

"No."

I shut off the vibrator, tossing it toward the head of the bed as I go to my side drawer and pull out a condom. Tearing the foil, I wait a second, giving myself a few pumps as she squirms before me. Deer clenches her thighs as close together as she can while tied up, trying to relieve that pink pussy from all its throbbing.

I roll the condom on, positioning myself back between her legs. I lean down, giving her a soft kiss right as I push myself inside her.

Fuck.

We both let out matching moans. The sensation of finally being inside her is fucking heaven-sent. I've been thinking about this for weeks now, and nothing could have prepared me for the feeling. I tense up, reminding myself not to come even though it's the only thing I want.

My mind reverts to its basest instincts. I thrust into her, rough and hard. The force makes her tits bounce between the bindings, and the vision just spurs me on. *Mine. Mine. Mine.* I continue to pump into her, gripping her thighs to keep her from moving back. She lets out a cry as I angle her hips slightly, giving myself more leverage to sink deeper.

"Keep up those noises, Sparkles, and I'm going to have to gag you. Can't have the whole apartment hear how sexy you are when you scream."

She bites down hard on her bottom lip, eyes squeezing shut as her arms tug against the restraints.

I reach down and rub my thumb over her clit, massaging it and feeling the way her cunt clenches around my cock in response.

"Oh my Gods. Jackson. Please. I'm going to come."

Her eyes plead with me, short gasps spilling from her mouth as I fuck her hard. Just as I feel her pussy clench again, I pull out.

"No!" she whines.

The absolute wanton desperation on her face is a beautiful sight.

"You don't get to come until I say you do."

I run the head of my dick up her slit, watching the way she whimpers. Then I grab her hips, flipping her over so she's face down on the mattress, and kneel behind her. She barely has a moment to adjust to the change in position before I tighten my hands around her and push back into her hot pussy with a groan.

My patience isn't going to last much longer.

I've wanted this too much.

I piston my hips, relishing in the way her ass slaps against my skin with every thrust. My nails dig into the flesh around her hips, pressing just enough to leave crescent indents. I let go and slap my hands back down, eliciting a deep moan that turns into garbled pleading.

"You want to come?"

"Yes. Please."

"Well, too—" *thrust* "—fucking—" *thrust* "—bad."

Her keening whimpers fill the room, and it is music to my ears.

"Does my little slut like when I fuck her like this, from behind like a fucking dog?"

"Yes," she cries out. "Please, Jackson. I can't. I can't keep this up."

She's right on the precipice, her entire system going haywire. Tears start streaming down her face as her pussy quivers, fighting for its release.

I fucking love it.

"You can come."

With just those three words, her body goes slack, the tension she's been coiling to prevent herself from coming unfurls as her orgasm crashes down. Her pussy gushes, milking my cock for all it's worth.

"Fuck," I groan as she lets out a strangled sob.

I continue thrusting, drawing out her release as she

continues to mutter praises to the Gods in between all her whimpering. I pull out, tearing off the condom, and run my hand over her release before using it to coat my dick. I only last two pumps before I'm coming—my release painting a beautiful picture over her ass and back. I can't help it, my eyes squeeze shut as I continue lazily fisting myself through what seems to be the best never-ending orgasm of my life.

"Fuck." I rest my hand on her ass, breathing heavily as I open my eyes and admire the way she is covered in my cum yet again. "I have to say, Sparkles, white looks good on you."

She laughs, smiling half deliriously up at me.

I make quick work of heading into my bathroom and grabbing a soft towel, dampening it with warm water before returning to clean her up.

She whimpers when I run the material across her sensitive folds, and even though I'm fucking spent, I still feel my dick twitch at the sound.

I'm careful as I begin untying the rope from her wrists and ankles, taking my time to massage the pink skin. It seems she tugged a little harder than I expected. Nothing bad, but it will take at least the night for the indents to go down.

She stretches her body out like a cat, and I continue to massage her legs to press out the tension that's built over the last hour. Deer hums, still lost in a daze from the sub drop. I pick her up and carry her into the shower, taking my time lathering her body with my soap and washing her hair.

I grab the pink robe I bought for her and wrap her in

it. When I think she has enough lucidity to stand, I rest her against the marbled sink counter and pull out the hairdryer I rarely use and softly dry her hair.

"Can I dry yours?" Her eyes sparkle in that way I love.

"Sure."

I hand her the black appliance and kneel on the bathroom rug so she doesn't have to stretch up. Her nails lightly graze my head as she weaves her hands through my hair.

It's nice. Calming.

By the time we crawl into bed, I'm all but ready to crash, fatigue wrapping its way around me.

"Jackson?"

"Yeah?"

"I really like this." Her voice is soft and drowsy as she snuggles closer to me.

"Me too," I whisper back. "Me too."

And I can't help but notice that us falling asleep together is beginning to become a pattern.

But it's a pattern I don't want to break.

Chapter THIRTY-NINE

DEER

Waking up to an empty bed is not ideal.

Waking up to the smell of what is most certainly breakfast? That I can accept.

I stretch against the charcoal sheets; my muscles are still a little sore from last night. I give my wrists a roll, noting that the pink markings have all but faded away.

Raking my hands through my hair, I search the ground for my abandoned clothes only to find them neatly folded in the corner with my handbag perched on top.

How sweet.

I dig around for my half-dead phone, noticing a few missed texts from Lee and one from my da.

DA

Everything okay? Saw the news

ME

yup!! Don't worry 😄 just overworked

I had to hope the excuse would hold up. I'd been lucky enough that it had taken him this long to notice anything was wrong. The odds of him clocking my lies at this point had to be nonexistent.

I eye my discarded clothes, quickly dropping the idea of putting them back on and instead opening Jackson's closet to paw through it for something to wear.

It only feels fitting to settle on a distressed *Devil Nun* T-shirt I find tucked away in the back. Although, I thought that it would at least hit mid-thigh, but with my boobs, it rests a few inches higher,

I kind of wish I'd stashed some clothes here before I moved out.

Maybe I could go across the hall and see if I can snag something of Stevie's?

The second I pull Jackson's door open, Aleks' door opens at the same time. The stunning brunette blinks her caramel eyes at me—dressed in only a NightBlade32 fan T-shirt, with tousled hair; we look like a mirror of one another.

Speak of the devil.

She smiles like a snake, her cat eyes narrowing as she realizes she's caught me.

"Well, good morning." She slings her arm around me and any chance I had of escaping back to Jackson's room disappears as she pulls me along with her into the kitchen.

Jackson stands at the stove, his bare, tattooed back to us as he fiddles with what smells like eggs. Aleks is also shirtless, pulling a carton of creamer from the fridge. He turns our way as Stevie announces, "Look who I ran into."

"Oh." He gives me a knowing grin. "We were wondering who was making enough noise to rival us."

My cheeks flush even though I will them not to.

"Aleksander, really?" Stevie rolls her eyes before releasing me and padding over to him.

"Hey, we're all friends here." He wraps his tattooed arms around her and gives her a quick peck. "I'm just finishing up your coffee. Take a seat, babe."

Jackson's heated gaze falls on me, tracing from the bottom of my feet to the top of my head.

"Morning," his deep voice rumbles as he walks over, spatula still in hand. He places a kiss on my cheekbone before whispering in my ear, "Guess we should've used the gag."

My toes curl, and I bite my bottom lip to keep my smile from being too obvious as I whisper back, "There's always next time. Maybe you can get me a pretty one?"

His eyes flash, and I all but melt into the floor. My heart is becoming a mess over this man.

"Hop on a stool, I'm almost done cooking." He gives my ass a quick tap before returning to the stove.

I climb on the seat next to Stevie, trying to ignore the way her eyes are silently watching me with a million loud questions. All the girls are going to seriously dig into me now.

"Your coffees, miladies." Aleks slides the glass coffee mugs across the island to us before continuing to pour what looks like a gallon of chocolate syrup into his own.

"And I thought my coffee order was weird," I tease,

taking a sip of my strawberry concoction.

"You both have the worst sweet tooth." Jackson rolls his eyes as he starts piling plates of bacon, eggs, toast, and hash browns onto the marble counter.

"Damn, I love your breakfasts." Stevie immediately snags some hash browns and douses them in maple syrup.

"Oh, but that's not all, Stephanie." He leans down, opening the oven. A sweet berry aroma floats out, mingling with the unmistakable scent of freshly baked gooey banana. "Raspberry banana bread." He flips the pan over and plops the most delicious looking loaf I've ever seen right in front of me.

My fingers itch to cut a piece.

"Give it a second, it's hot," Jackson warns, somehow reading my mind as he takes his seat next to me and cuts me a slice.

There's commotion at the sound of a door flinging open, and a mostly naked British man comes sliding across the floorboards. "Is that brekkie I smell? On a weekday? What's the special occasion?" Parker skids to a stop just shy of crashing into the corner of the island. He looks me over with a grin. "Oh, I see. Impressing your bird."

This is so embarrassing.

Sydney comes strolling out, a pair of blue sweatpants in her hand that she throws at him before opening the fridge and taking out a jug of some green-looking juice. "Full house this morning." Her gray gaze glints as she pours herself a glass.

"Banana bread's vegan, Sydney." Jackson nods at her.

"Ooh, thanks."

Compared to the rest of us, Sydney looks the most

put together, wearing a blue silk night set. She and Parker take their places on the last two stools that curve around the side of the island, the latter still not having put on any more clothes.

"Where'd you go last night, by the way? We were playing some rounds of *Zombies* and wanted backup," Aleks asks Jackson, forking a bit of banana bread—that he has also topped with chocolate syrup—into his mouth.

"Movies."

"Movies? To see what?"

"Devil Nun 5."

"Didn't we see that a few months ago?"

"Yeah, but they came out with an unrated director's cut."

His face drops. "And you went without me?"

"You don't even like it."

"That doesn't matter. I always go with you. It's our thing." His cutlery clanks down as he leans forward to give Jackson a pained look. "Wow. This is such a betrayal."

"Seriously?"

"I'm dead serious, bro." He clutches a hand to his chest. "Why would you go alone?"

"Never said I went alone."

"Oh?" Stevie perks up, eyes bouncing between us. "Did you guys go on a date?"

"Yeah."

I almost choke on my coffee.

Date?

My stomach floods with the feeling of a windstorm picking up a pile of leaves and swirling them around and around. But it clashes with the fact that my brain becomes a loading screen, trying to process the idea as I sit here blinking. I see Jackson smirk out of the corner of my eye, and it just furthers my brain melting.

Stevie claps her hands together. "Ah, I love that for you guys!"

"Wait, you left the apartment? How was it?" Sydney interjects, eyes dancing between us. "There weren't too many people, were there? Did you take precautions? Bring security? I can't believe I didn't know this." Her love for me bubbles with concern, and I adore her for that.

I clear my throat, gathering all the mental marbles I just dropped. "It was fine. I was a little nervous, but the place turned out to be practically empty."

Plus, I wasn't able to really worry about anything with Jackson's dick in my mouth—but no one needs to know that.

"That's good." Syd smiles. "Proud of you, girl."

"Really? Whenever we go that place is packed," Aleks mutters, still a little annoyed. "What'd you do, man? Rent the thing out?"

"Actually, yeah."

"What?!"

We all turn to stare at him as he continues to eat his eggs like he didn't just storm through a perfectly crafted sandcastle and reduce it all to waste.

Except for Parker, who just praises him with a "Nice one, mate."

"Are you for real?" I lay my hand on Jackson's wrist.

"Yeah."

"W-why?"

He shrugs, placing his hand on mine. "Thought it

would be less stressful for you and safer if we had it to ourselves."

"So, you rented out the theater for me?"

"Yeah."

"As in the whole thing? Not just the auditorium?"

"Yup."

"Oh my Gods. Why didn't you tell me?"

It's the second largest movie theater in the whole state, which for Cali is pretty freaking huge. It would've cost him several thousands of dollars, and he did it for me—for my comfort.

"Because it's something you needed to conquer up here." He gives my temple an affectionate tap.

That's it.

I'm done.

I'm in the gutter, being swept away downstream by this man without any hope of going back.

All my life, I've hidden my struggles, kept them trapped deep within me so no one saw them buried beneath my light. Not Jackson, though. He understands me down to the center of my fractured core and doesn't shy away. He sits there with glue and helps me fill the cracks so that I can become whole again.

I slip my hand onto his thigh and lean forward. "Thank you."

"Anything for you."

"Please don't start making out. It's bad enough that we have one exhibitionist couple in this household."

Jackson grabs a piece of crust and throws it at Parker who narrowly dodges it.

"What the—did you just throw bread at me?" He blinks

in offense before grabbing a slice of banana bread and reeling his arm back. "You wank—"

"Oh, no, you don't." Sydney's hand shoots out to stop him. "Seriously, are you both five?"

"He started it."

"Really?" she deadpans.

Parker juts out his bottom lip in a pout, and it fractures her mask, pulling a smile at the edges.

Jackson's phone begins to ring on the table, and I spot an image of his parents on the screen.

"Hang on, I have to take this. You knuckleheads clean up." He pushes off the stool and gestures to Aleks and Parker before heading in the direction of his room.

"Do you see the way he treats me?" Parker grumbles.

"I can help?" I offer.

"Nope." Stevie puts a hand on my shoulder. "Apartment rules dictate that Aleks and Parker have to do it themselves if Jackson cooked. We're exempt."

My own phone starts buzzing on the counter, and I flip it over to see Lee blowing up my messages.

LEE

GIRL????

STEVIE SAID UR AT THE BOYS APARTMENT

SHE SAID U SLEPT THERE

AS IN SLEPT THERE SLEPT THERE

PICK UP UR PHONE NOWWWW

Lee's face immediately fills my screen as her call filters through.

I glare at Stevie, who gives me a not-so-sorry smile as she clasps her hands back in her lap.

Dammit.

"Hel—"

"What the hell, Deer?" she whines. "As your best friend, I am seriously butt hurt right now."

"Sorry, I—"

"Did you sleep with Jackson? Wait, no. Don't tell me. He's like a brother. I don't want the details."

"Then why'd you call?"

"Because I feel left out." She lets out a loud huff, and I can imagine her pouting in my mind. "Are you guys dating?"

"That's kinda hard to explain."

"What do you—"

I frown, looking down at the totally black screen.

Shit.

I never charged it last night.

Lee is going to chew me out later.

"I need to go plug this in." I wave my phone at the girls before slipping off the stool and padding over to Jackson's bedroom.

Are you guys dating?

At this point, I have no idea what's going on between Jackson and me. We're sitting in this gray area that just gets murkier and murkier with each passing second.

How am I going to explain this to Lee when even I don't understand what's going on?

I stifle my groan as I twist the handle to his bedroom.

"I'll have to ask Deer, but I can't make any promises."

I freeze.

Jackson switches to Cantonese, but there are a few English words peppered throughout. I try to weave together what I can, but it's no use.

"Just tell her I'm sorry and that I'll try, all right? Okay. Thank you. Bye bye."

He hangs up, and I take that as my cue.

"Hey."

"Hey." He gives me a quick once over. "How much of that did you hear?"

"Mm." I walk over to his bedside and plug my phone in. "About as much of it as I could make out in English."

Jackson sighs, sitting on his bed.

I plop down next to him, resting my head against his shoulder. "What's going on?"

"Angela has an audition for one of the summer music camps this weekend, and my parents wanted to see if we were free for dinner while they're up here."

"Oh. That's sweet of them."

"They have reservations at The Bay. You know how busy that place can be."

True. It is the best seafood restaurant in town. A lot of big names dine there, so it is never short on customers. Not only that, but it would mean being in a place where I have no control. Any of the servers could be a potential danger, someone planted there to spike my drink again or something worse.

The premise sounds less and less nice the more I think about it.

But still…

"I don't want to disappoint your parents."

"It's not disappointing them. They know you were in the hospital a few weeks ago."

I let out a sigh. "Can you put me down as a maybe?"

"I can, but I don't want you to force yourself. You did really well last night as it was."

"About that…" *This. This is the time to ask him.* "Last night was a date? Like, a *date* date, not a fake date."

"Depends."

"On?"

"On if the idea of it being a real date freaks you out?"

"Doesn't freak me out." I try to keep my voice neutral because I am freaking out—but in a good way. My hopes start to rise higher and higher.

"Then, yes. It was an actual date."

The apples of my cheeks puff up as I grin.

"I take your smiling to mean that's a good thing," he teases.

"I guess." I look away, biting my lips together to tamp down my excitement.

"And why's that, Sparkles? You becoming attached to me?"

"Hey, you're the one who called it a date. That makes you the attached one."

"True. I was getting quite sick of the whole fake dating thing."

My heart leaps. "Huh?"

"I'm saying, I'm quite attached to you. Nothing fake about that." He tucks a stray piece of hair behind my ear, and his touch lingers, caressing my cheek. "You don't exactly rent out a theater for someone you don't like."

"You like me?"

"I think I've liked you since that night we stayed up watching *Devil Nun* and you made me carry you back to my room."

His confession rocks me. "That was weeks ago while you were still refusing to even consider fake dating me."

"I like playing hard to get."

"Jackson."

"You ever noticed that you stopped calling me Shield?"

"What?" My smile drops as the realization crashes into me.

"Yup. Something tells me you like me as well."

"Just a little." I avert my gaze.

"A little?" He tugs me so we fall back onto the bed, and he pulls me into his arms. "You sure about that?"

I snuggle against his chest, listening to his heartbeat.

"Fine, maybe more than a little."

"How much more?"

"A lot more." So much more—it feels like my soul is becoming one with his.

"Good, because you're on my mind every second of every day. You've infiltrated my life for the better, lighting it up where it was dark, and there's not a moment that goes by when I don't crave you near me." He squeezes me tightly, and all of his emotions flood into me. "You make me whole, Deer, and I don't think I can let you go."

"Then don't. Keep me."

"Yeah?"

"Yeah, I'm yours."

Chapter
FORTY

JACKSON

We pull up to the restaurant and I'm thinking more and more that this isn't a good idea. My hand rests on Deer's knee, but no matter how much I try to soothe her, that knee just keeps bouncing up and down. One of her long pink nails twists between her forefinger and thumb.

The bodyguard we brought with us exits the passenger seat and comes around to open Deer's side. She stares past him at the revolving restaurant doors where patrons are flowing in and out of the renowned establishment.

There's a sharp intake of breath. And then another. And another.

Each one comes faster and faster.

Deer's knee finally stops moving, but now her chest is heaving in short bursts.

"Close the door," I command the bodyguard. "Francis—"

"Yes, Mr. Lau." Our private driver immediately takes off, putting distance between us and The Bay.

"Hey, Sparkles, look at me." I give her shoulder a squeeze.

She turns, crystal blue eyes melting from wide panic to misery as I rub my thumb in calming circles over her skin.

"I-I'm sor-ry," she hiccups between breaths.

"It's fine." I press my forehead down to hers. "Just breathe with me."

We spend the next few minutes going through her exercises, and eventually she evens out. She slumps farther forward, squeezing her eyes shut and cussing. "Fuck."

When she opens them again, shame is written all over her features—from the furrowing of her brows to the clenching of her teeth. I dig around my pockets for my phone.

"I'll call my parents and—"

"No. I want to go back."

"Deer, you don't have to push yourself for me."

"I'm not. I want to try again." She turns to Francis, placing a hand on the center compartment to get his attention. "Take us back to The Bay, please, Francis."

"Yes, miss."

She sits back in her seat, collecting herself. I watch the way she steels her gaze forward and rests her palm on her chest, breathing slowly.

As soon as we pull back up to the restaurant, she's up and out of the car before I get a chance to ask her again if she really wants to go through with this. The bodyguard we left behind watches her closely.

"Okay, let's do this." She smiles and anyone else looking at her would think that she is completely fine, except I can see that the sparkle in her eyes is missing. The light just doesn't quite reach the surface; it's left bubbling underneath, suffocating under the cloudy water.

My heart clenches, guilt squeezing it as I follow suit and get out of the car.

I hold my elbow out for her to hold onto, and when she does, there's no hiding the way her hand tremors slightly.

I moved my parents' reservation from the main dining room to one of the private rooms at the back of the restaurant. Normally, it would take months to get this particular reservation, but Parker's grandfather knows the owner and was able to pull some strings to get it switched around. I don't like asking for favors, but for Deer, there's nothing I wouldn't do to make sure she feels her most comfortable.

My mother's eyes light up when we enter the room, and Deer's entire demeanor changes into a practiced persona as she gives her a hug, exchanging greetings, before handing her a small black box wrapped with a white ribbon.

"For me?" My mother's eyes widen as she pulls out the pair of Chanel earrings, holding them up to the light. Try as she might to hide it, I can see how impressed my mom is by the gift.

"Of course. I saw them the other week and just knew they'd look perfect on you."

My girl knows what she is doing.

Angela tries not to appear overly enthusiastic about seeing us, but I can see the quiet awe in her eyes whenever she looks at Deer—it seems she's also taken a real liking to her since their first meeting.

Dad watches us all with a knowing smile, and I take my seat next to him, Deer on my right.

We fall into easy chatter, with Deer leading most of the conversation as she asks my parents a litany of questions about themselves while also making sure Angie doesn't get left out. Her voice never wavers; it's that same practiced tone she uses when she streams.

You wouldn't be able to tell how anxious she is just by looking at her. No, the only way to realize it is in the way her eyes dart every time a server walks into the room, tracking them, and how her shoulders stiffen whenever a loud noise from the main restaurant bangs too close, or if you somehow glimpse the fingers of her left hand tapping silently in a wave motion on her knee under the table.

It takes me a second to realize that throughout the meal she has been artfully weaving all conversation away from herself—never outright denying any questions but skirting around them in a way so she can always redirect. She keeps talking so that no one notices that she isn't eating much of the food, moving the truffle shrimp on her plate in subtle intervals.

"Here, let me show you." My mother searches her handbag for her wallet and proceeds to pull out a small, two-by-two-inch passport photo of my chubby five-year-old face. "Look at him!"

I groan.

"Oh my Gods, stop." Deer carefully plucks the photo from my mom and holds it reverently. "You're adorable." She turns to me with a grin, and for the first time tonight, I see those sparkles gleaming in her eyes.

"Sure, sure. Let's put that back." I gently knock her hand away.

"No, look at you. Those cute little chubby cheeks." She tilts her head. "What happened? How'd ya get all scowly?"

"It's called resting grump face, RGF," Angela chimes in.

My phone begins to buzz in my pocket, and I feel around for the power button to reject the call while still keeping my attention on the table.

"RGF? I like that." Deer winks at my sister before handing the photo back to my mom. "Did you come up with it yourself?"

"Yup, I did."

"Impressive."

"Thanks, my friends even use it, too. We have this history teacher, Mr. Jefferson, and he has RGF. Last week…"

My phone begins to buzz again, and I fiddle to hit the decline button again.

Within seconds it starts to buzz for a third time.

Seriously. Who is this persistent?

I try to discreetly pull it out without anyone noticing, my attention no longer on the conversation around me.

I glance at the caller ID, freezing.

"Sorry, but I really need to take this." I give everyone an apologetic smile, trying not to let the wariness show on my face.

I swipe accept as I make my way out of the room and off to the side so that I'm out of ear shot but still close enough to keep my eye on everyone.

"Hel—"

"We have a problem," Phoebe interrupts.

"That sounds bad."

"It is."

Fuck.

"Okay, so—"

"Is Deirdre on her phone?"

"No. It's—"

"Good. Keep her off it."

"Wh—"

"How many bodyguards came with you to dinner?"

Is this woman going to let me get a fucking word in?

"Two," I grind out.

"Seriously, Jackson? Two? You brought an entire horde to the movie theater where no one else was present, but you bring *two* to one of the most popular dinner restaurants in all of California?"

I work my jaw back and forth, not wanting to raise my voice. "Get to the point, Phoebe."

"I'm sorry." Her voice softens on the words, and it just makes me all the more nervous. "I told Paige we needed to be quicker about all of this, but she wouldn't—"

"Phoebe."

"You need to get her out of there now, Jackson. She's been doxed."

Chapter
FORTY-ONE

DEER

I keep my lips carefully tilted in a soft smile while making sure that I'm nodding as I listen to Jackson's sister chatter away about her new friend at school and the history teacher they both dislike.

All night it has felt like there are beetles crawling across my skin, and I've had to use every ounce of mental willpower to not fidget every five seconds. The mask I'm wearing to keep my cool is fracturing around the edges, and I'm just praying it stays together until the end of the meal. The very same meal that sits like lead in my stomach.

I believed too much in myself and am falling short. My sanity is splitting at the seams, and I'm just trying to prevent the frays from completely unraveling. I should never have agreed to this, but I was so worried that his parents would judge me for not showing up, that they'd think I was unreliable and not good enough for him. I just wanted them to approve of us as a couple.

Gods.

I want to bury my face in my hands and slump against the table. My mental battery is reaching a critical low.

"Sorry, but I really need to take this."

I glance up as Jackson quickly dips from the table, phone in hand.

All those nerves dancing across my skin suddenly pause, and the hairs on my arm stand on high alert as I keep my gaze locked on him.

Something's wrong.

I can tell by the way he's tensed up, and it doesn't help that his eyes keep flicking over to me.

"I'm sure everything is fine, honey."

I smile at Jackson's mom, but I know it doesn't reach my eyes.

"Yeah, it's just…do you mind if I check my phone for a moment?"

"Not at all," she waves me off.

"Thanks." I reach under the table and pluck my purse off the bag hook. The second my hands touch the soft leather I feel the vibrations. My fingers quickly unclasp the gold Dior closure, and I pull out my phone, which is buzzing with such ferocity that the damn thing feels like it's a million degrees.

A premonition of sickening dread crashes over me as I swipe it open.

"Deer, wait." Jackson's hand lands on my shoulder as he snags the phone from my hands, but it's too late.

The news alert sears itself into my eyes.

BREAKING: POPULAR VIDEO GAME STREAMER "THECOZYDEAR" DOXED ON MAJOR SOCIAL PLATFORM.

My entire body is dunked in an ice bath, and frost works its way through my bloodstream, freezing me in my tracks.

What.

The restaurant chatter that's been steadily streaming around us turns into a cacophony, beating against my ears and drowning everything out.

No. I must've read it wrong.

"I'm sorry but there's been an emergency, and we have to leave." Jackson announces to the table as he pulls me up, arm around my waist to support my failing body. "I already paid the bill, but—shit, we really need to go."

I follow his eyeline to the bodyguard who stands at the door to our private room.

"Mr. Lau, we have to go out back. Reporters are beginning to gather out front."

"All right."

Reporters? Already?

How did they even know I was here? Are they tracking me?

I barely process the restaurant as we move through it, past the dining patrons and behind the kitchen.

Everything's too much. The lights are too bright. The noise is too loud. The air feels too hot.

My head swims and the little food I just ate churns in

my stomach. I'm trying to keep it together, I really am. But I'm suffocating.

The second we step outside, and the balmy night breeze licks my sweaty skin, the contents of my meal make a violent reappearance.

I vaguely feel someone holding my hair back so it doesn't get caught in the mess.

Gods, I really hope there are no reporters back here or else this is going to be front page news.

Once it feels like the entire menu of The Bay has exited my body, Jackson lifts me into a waiting Escalade. He takes care of everything, buckling me in, cleaning me up, giving me water, and holding my hand.

"How?" I croak.

"I don't know yet. I didn't have long enough to talk to Phoebe."

My body feels all gross and clammy, and my mind is spinning like a roulette wheel, going round and round and round. This is a fever dream, driving me to the very brink of madness.

I'm living in a haze and everything is blurry. Time passes fast and slow, and nothing computes in my brain.

"Deer, baby, I need you to breathe for me." His voice sounds all muffled.

"What?"

"Breathe, you're hyperventilating. You'll pass out if you keep it up."

My awareness starts to trickle back drip by drip, and I hear myself, hear the sharp intakes of breath that aren't enough to feed any real air into my lungs.

Jackson puts a hand on the center of my chest, trying to

get me to slow down, but it's no use.

I can't. I can't. I can't.

Little black dots poke at my vision, like a screen going static.

And still, I can't stop.

I can't stop.

Not until my body gives out.

The world swims around me, like I'm underwater but my goggles have a crack, and everything turns murky as the salt assaults my eyes.

I can tell that I'm cradled in someone's arms and they are carrying me somewhere.

Where?

Panic begins to claw at me like a tiger trapped in a cage, and it's ripping my insides to shreds. I beg my body to move. I beg and I beg and I beg.

My leg kicks out and hits something metal, pain ricocheting up my shin.

"Fuck. Deer, stop."

The voice settles over me like a blanket.

"Can someone please hit the penthouse button. I need to make sure she doesn't hurt herself."

The voice continues to calm me, allowing the rational side of my mind to creep back in piece by piece.

Elevator. Jackson. Bodyguards. Me.

The elevator's ascent sixty stories into the sky doesn't

really help the nausea that seems to have returned, but I pray to myself to hold it in. I squeeze my eyes shut, the fluorescent lights assaulting my senses.

Nothing seems real. Jackson's touch on my skin feels like a ghost, and whatever words he is speaking sound like they are spoken through cotton balls in my ears. Denial slots itself like a sheet over my brain so I don't process what just happened.

We start moving again, and I risk opening one eye to see the boys' familiar apartment. People rush around me, but Jackson doesn't stop until he gets to his room and lays me on his bed.

He reaches down and moves my hair out of my face, running his thumb down my temple. His inky stare holds me true, and I use what little strength I have to hold onto his forearm in a silent plea.

He crawls onto the mattress next to me, giving me a life raft in the middle of the churning sea. I grip onto that safety for dear life, begging it not to leave me.

Jackson lets me curl against him. My hands grasp the front of his sweater as my head rests against his pec. I seek out his heartbeat, that steady thumping a thread of sanity in the madness pouring through my mind.

"I've got you," he whispers, lips on the crown of my head. "I've got you. You're safe."

Except, I'm not.

My physical being may be safe right now, back in the confines of the high-tech apartment building. But my mind? My mind is not safe. It is seconds away from a gust of wind coming in to knock that sheet of denial away and reveal all my weaknesses. My mental barriers that I've spent so long trying to build up to keep me protected just keep getting beaten over and over, and the boards I've put up to stop the cracks are coming loose.

It's everything attacking me simultaneously.

It's the Deer Hunters tormenting me.

It's the nightmares that won't let me sleep.

It's the SWAT team invading my apartment.

It's the sports drink that left me roofied.

It's the messages I pretend I don't see telling me I shouldn't exist.

It's the DMs I try to ignore with gross, sexual fantasies.

It's the world outside that doesn't feel safe.

Everything, everywhere, all at once.

I'm not sure how much more I can take before I'm split wide open.

My head begins to pound, like someone has placed a nail on the back of my skull and is trying to hammer it in. I squeeze my eyes shut tightly and dig my forehead into Jackson's chest, trying to get the pain to go away.

But it won't.

The pain, the terror, the dread just burrow deeper until they take root, like a poisonous plant latching on and becoming part of me, and I worry it's too late for me to survive as it begins to feed off the light inside me, dimming my sparkle with each passing second like a vampire draining a human of blood until I'm nothing but a lifeless husk.

Chapter
FORTY-TWO

JACKSON

A knock at the door has Deer shooting upright and out of my arms, her head narrowly missing my chin.

Dammit, right when she'd finally drifted to sleep after tossing for the last few hours.

Her sharp nails dig into me as she stares owl-eyed at the door, her breathing coming in shallow pants. She looks absolutely terrified, and my heart cracks, leaking in agony.

"Hey, it's me," Aleks calls out. "If you're awake, come on out—the sisters are here."

"Yeah, one second." I shift, placing my hand on Deer's as I speak to her in a hushed tone. "Hey, it's okay." Her fingers only seem to tighten. "It's okay," I repeat, giving her hand a squeeze.

She finally looks down at me, her consciousness returning bit by bit. Slowly, her grasp loosens enough that I'm able to peel her fingers free and sit up.

"Do you want to join or…" I trail off, leaving it up to her.

"I—" She bites her lower lip. "I don't know. Are there a lot of people out there?"

"Why don't I go check?"

She nods her head.

I lean forward, placing a soft kiss on her temple before slipping off the bed and cracking the door open. Looking down the hallway, I spy our friends with just the addition of Paige, Phoebe, and that shadowy sidekick of hers.

"You're good, just the usual misfits." I turn back and offer my palm to her.

She takes her time, padding softly across the floor until her small hand latches onto mine. I lace our fingers together as we head to join everyone.

Deer startles, pressing herself closer to me when we pass the elevator alcove and notice two new bodyguards standing watch.

Lee and Stevie huddle around Deer as soon as we get close, pulling her into one giant hug. I step back and let them coo over her, checking and doing their own things. Sydney stands, her face a little paler than normal. Parker looks up at her, worry etched on his face. She gives him a smile before taking a deep breath and joining the girls, her smile growing wider, but her gray eyes remaining a cloudy haze of worry.

"Okay, kids, let's take our seats." Phoebe is perched on the coffee table, as usual. She seems to like placing herself there so she can look at us as we all sit on the couch.

Paige, the middle Covington sibling and all-star law-yer, leans against the wall, tapping away at her phone in a pale pink suit. She is the opposite of Phoebe; her blonde hair reaches her waist, in sharp contrast to Phoebe's chic bob, and her heart-shaped face has a softness to it compared to her sister's ruthless edge. Yet whenever you have the Covington siblings in a room together, there is never any denying that they come from the same model-blessed genetic pool.

"You should start. I'm still waiting on something," Phoebe nods to her sister.

"Sure. Sorry, I was just checking in with the detectives." Paige gives us all an apologetic smile as she tucks her phone into her pocket. "How are you holding up, Deer?"

My girl shrugs, and I tug her closer to me, wrapping her under my arm.

"Right, yeah. I'm sorry."

"It's not your fault."

"Kind of is," Phoebe mutters.

Paige glares at her sister. "I am doing everything within the law that I am capable of, and the law takes time. We have to follow protocols and get court orders signed in order to gain access to information to keep digging." She looks at Deer. "I'm making sure this is done right so, whoever the culprit is, they are dealt with to the full extent of the law."

"I appreciate that."

"So, are there any leads?" I push.

I don't think they would've come all the way here if there wasn't something they wanted to tell us.

"Well," she starts, and it sounds like the answer is no, "we're looking into the doxing. While I hate to say it, it does help our case because we can add it to the other criminal offenses they've committed so far, like the harassment, infliction of bodily harm, incitement to violence, the—sorry, I'm not meaning to freak you out."

"It's fine." Deer gives a watery smile.

"That's not to say we didn't try to kill the identity leak, but the internet is a hydra—you cut off one head and two more grow," Phoebe sighs.

"Right," Paige nods. "I mostly just wanted to apologize that it got this far before we could do anything and to let you know that we are taking your case seriously. I also thought that maybe you and I could sit down and go through some documents."

My attention shifts as I catch the mystery man—whose name we really should fucking know at this point—pulling out his phone and striding over to the back wall. I keep one ear on the conversation around me as I watch him, but there's never a shift in his expression. He calmly strolls back over and places a hand on Phoebe's bicep before he leans down and whispers in her ear.

Whatever he says has her eyes widening, something like satisfaction slashing across them.

"What happened?" Deer asks what we are all thinking.

The blonde attempts to steel her gaze, but there's a slight crease between her brows she can't seem to smooth away.

"We might've figured out who it is."

There's a beat before the room erupts, everyone clamoring for information.

"Hold on. Give me a second." She gets up and heads to the glass door that leads to our outdoor patio and steps outside, gesturing for her shadow to follow.

The air instantly falls to a deathly quiet as we watch them through the glass, but they turn their backs to us so we can't see their expressions. The seconds trickle by as we wait.

"Dammit," Paige breaks the silence, the frustration clear in her voice as she glares down at her phone. She pushes off the wall, her heels pounding on the tiles as she stalks over to her sister. But despite her clear determination, she doesn't make it there before Phoebe is already at the door and stepping back inside.

The elder sister tilts her head. "What?"

"Where did you get this lead of yours?"

Phoebe blinks and then sidesteps Paige, heading back to where the rest of us wait, without giving an answer.

"Phoebe."

"The team found him." She waves her hand dismissively.

Him.

"Team?" Paige's voice rises. "If it was the team, then where's my notification?" She comes trekking back, shaking her phone in the air.

"What does it matter?"

"It matters because I told you everything had to be done legally. Le-gal-ly."

"Stop," Parker barks. "Both of you, seriously."

The two sisters whip their heads to their younger brother, the ice in their eyes cold enough to freeze a lake. Parker flinches back like a wounded dog at the sight.

Aleks sighs, standing up and placing himself between the sisters. "He has a point. Your arguing isn't helping any of us." They begin to protest, but he holds a hand out, giving them his signature *don't fuck with me* look that has them both hesitating. "What's done is done, and we'll deal with the technicalities later. Now, tell us who the fuck it is."

"Floor's yours, sis." Paige gestures patronizingly to Phoebe.

She gives herself a second to roll her eyes before slipping back into that cool composure she normally has. Phoebe perches back on the edge of the coffee table.

"Rick Adley."

Who?

"What?" Deer blinks in confusion.

"That's who we traced it back to."

"No." She shakes her head, laughing through a tight smile. "That's not possible. Whoever it is must be framing him."

"Who's Rick Adley?" I ask.

"He's her lead moderator," Phoebe states.

"What? Her mod? Why would he do this."

"He wouldn't. It doesn't make sense." Deer shoots out of my grip and begins pacing around, folding her arms across her chest. "You're wrong."

"My source is never wrong," Phoebe drawls. "That's why they cost a pretty penny."

"Please, don't say that where I can hear it," Paige reprimands.

"Well, they're wrong this time. Rick's been working with me for years. He's the one who's been stopping all the

Deer Hunter stuff on my streams and socials. Why would he do that if he was the one doing it in the first place?" Deer is spiraling, her fingers raking nervous red marks down her arms.

I walk over and place my hands over hers, stopping her from hurting herself.

"Deer, baby, take a beat."

"No!" she screeches, pushing me back. "Where's the evidence, huh? What did they find that makes them so sure it's Rick?" She throws her anger like an axe at Phoebe.

"He watched you."

"What?" Deer freezes, her flame of fury flickering with uncertainty.

Phoebe sighs, walking past me and resting her hand on Deer's head, stroking it like a mother does to her child. "After the drugging, we dug into your system and found some inconsistencies. The screen-mirroring software we initially uncovered seemed a little odd, so we kept looking. That's when a certain someone who shan't be named for legal reasons noticed that your webcam was being remotely accessed."

"I thought I'd just been leaving it on." Deer's whispered words lance through my heart like a spear made of ice.

This asshole was watching her.

He was fucking *watching* her.

A smokey red haze seeps into my vision as I think about how this fucking man whom my girl trusted, whom she employed for years, took her vulnerabilities and twisted them for his own sick benefit.

"Why?" Her breathing starts ramping back up, those

short, little inhales as her brows pinch together.

"I mean, I'm no psychoanalyst, we won't know his motives until we get a hold of either him or hack into his devices—"

"Do not do that," Paige interrupts.

"I won't if your people get their shit done in a timely manner."

Deer's legs give out, and I barely manage to reach past Phoebe to grab her before her knees crack on the tiles. The shock seems to be shutting her body down. All the feral anger from earlier has extinguished into a shattered cry.

"No, I—" She pulls her elbow free and continues stumbling backward. "I can't do this." She turns tail and runs to the elevator, slamming the button until it opens.

"Wait, Deer. Where are you going?" I follow after her.

"Mine. I need—I don't know. I just." She's barely able to string her words together, everything coming out in broken, breathy pants.

"Fine," I soothe, placing my hand between the elevator doors to stop them from closing. "Fine, we'll go to yours."

"No. No. I need to be alone. I can't—I can't think. I need to be away. I need space." Her hands keep shaking as she scuttles into the corner of the elevator.

My heart cracks at her rejection.

I'm watching her break apart before me, cracks of herself are falling off as she keeps deteriorating with the growing panic. She shouldn't be alone—I need to be with her. I can help her, stop her from completely unravelling.

I take a tentative step forward. "Sparkles—"

"Stop," she shrieks, pure terror leaching out of her. I halt, watching as she slides to the bottom of the elevator.

"Please, Jackson. Just stop," she begs, gripping her head and scrunching her hair between her hands.

Phoebe places her hand on my bicep. "It's fine, we already have bodyguards stationed at her apartment. Just give her some time to calm down."

No. This is all wrong. She's hurting, she needs someone with her, someone to support her as the darkness closes in.

"Jackson." Phoebe pushes, forcing my hand to let go of the elevator.

I just stand there and watch as the doors close and a part of my heart runs away.

Chapter
FORTY-THREE

DEER

I don't know how much time passes.

At least a day or two from the way the light shifts on the ground beneath my curtains, a thin line of sunshine appearing only to be replaced by the blackness of night, plunging my room into a sanctum of stars over and over again.

It's a cycle that shows the world is still spinning even though it feels like it's stopped.

I unplugged my Wi-Fi—ripped it from the wall, to be more specific, since I'd yanked hard enough on the ethernet cable without unscrewing it that the entire socket wrenched itself from the plaster.

It doesn't matter though. The point was to disconnect me from the outside world, from any threats, and I'd done just that.

No one can watch me.

My streaming room is trashed, my webcam smashed to pieces on the floor.

My phone is…somewhere. Dead, probably, at this point.

A good thing.

It stops me from going back through every message I've ever exchanged with Rick over the years. But it doesn't stop my mind from running through the memories. From questioning why? Did I do something wrong? Was it me?

I spend most of my time sleeping or just lying in bed, staring at the wall, cycling through an endless cavern of self-destruction and self-pity.

Sometimes, like now, I'll find my way into my bathroom and stick my head under the sink faucet for some water. There's still some part of me, I guess, that reminds my body it has to live.

I wipe my mouth with the back of my hand, risking a glance in the mirror.

Haunted desert brown eyes stare back at me.

Live isn't the right word.

Survive is more fitting.

That's what I'm doing, surviving.

A knock at the front door echoes through my shell of an apartment.

I stop breathing, body frozen midstep back to my bed. I strain my ears, but all I can hear is my blood pumping. It's only when my lungs begin to burn, and my vision goes double that I inhale. The sound of my sharp breath forces me back into action and I scurry onto my bed, crawling back under the covers and squeezing them tightly around myself.

I'm broken—a butterfly that's gone into a cocoon to become a caterpillar.

I don't care who is at the door. I don't want to think about the world outside this room, the dangers. If someone like Rick could turn on me, who is to say someone else won't? I trusted him, he seemed fine…normal.

You can't trust anyone.

The world isn't safe.

Nowhere here is safe.

I'm not safe.

There's a resounding bang, almost like my front door was flung open so hard that it hit the wall.

On instinct, my body shoots up, my eyes flying open to search for the threat.

Someone's here.

Is this how it ends?

No.

There's still a small spark inside me, a little star that is twinkling fiercely, trying its hardest not to be engulfed by the darkness. It's that little sparkle that has me reaching to grab my taser from my side table, brandishing it like a sword at anyone who comes in.

"Deirdre?"

I suck in a breath.

"Deirdre? Where are ya?"

I suck in another breath, but it quickly turns to teary hiccups.

"Da?"

My bedroom door pushes open, and a man with red hair streaked with gray and a weathered but kind face comes trudging in. His presence is an instant shot of relief to my haywire system.

"Oh. Oh, my little princess." He takes three strides to my bed, reaching out to pull me into him. "You gave me half a fright."

My hiccups quickly transcend to full-blown sobs, the taser slipping out of my hands as I dig my fingers into his sweater.

"Da," I continue to cry.

It's the only word I seem capable of getting out.

"I know. Let it out." He cradles me against his chest, whispering soothing words as he runs his hand over the back of my head.

It's the first time I've cried since everything happened. His familiar woodsy scent is a signal to my system that I'm safe, and the floodgates just won't stop.

"Come on, I've got you." He begins to lift me out of the bed.

"No!" It comes out as a guttural screech. "I'm not going anywhere." My body scrambles, trying to escape from his hold.

"Deirdre Maura Malloy." His tone is deep and commanding.

I look up at him like a cornered rabbit.

"I'm not trying to bite yer head off. It just breaks my heart seeing you like this." His hard hazel eyes soften as he sighs, running a hand along his beard. "Why didn't you say nothing?"

"I don't know. I—I thought I could handle it."

"Doesn't really look like you're handling it."

I press my lips together.

"What're you gonna do? Stay cooped up in here forever?" He makes a show of looking around my musty room.

"No."

Yes.

"Yer coming home."

"Home?"

"Carlingford. I'm taking you back to Carlingford."

I'm about to protest, tell him there's no way, but…

Why not? No one's going to come looking for me there. Da's kept the location hidden from the public with countless security measures. The house is secluded, even for a small village like Carlingford, and the townsfolk protect the privacy of their own.

It's not safe here, not even in my room—it's why I can't sleep, it's why I can't breathe, it's why I can't live. I'm doxed. My information is out in the world for anyone to find. A selfish bubble in my chest pops, leaving a hollow cavern inside. I want to run. To leave. To escape.

I want out. I want the noises in my head to stop. I want to feel safe.

Can I feel safe?

"It's not up for discussion. Your mam's worried sick about you, and reporters are queuing outside your apartment like it's the last Sunday service. Safety comes first."

"They are?"

My mind conjures up images of people gathering outside the complex, of them storming past security and convening at my door, where they'll hound and hound and hound until they break me down. I'm not safe.

I'll never be safe.

"Come home, child. Take a break. Enjoy some fresh

country air."

Within my fractured soul, there is a churning whirlpool of guilt and shame trying to fight my selfish cowardice. It swirls with the reminder of my friends, with the reminder of the man who has stayed by my side this entire time and fought to help me. The man who has been my protector and who promised me the world.

My heart beats for him, but my heart is damaged. And while there is a part of me that yearns for him, that loves him, it is struggling to win out over the part of me that is dying, the part of me that just doesn't care.

My mind is a mess of anxiety, fear, and depression.

I'm a forest that's been put under a curse. My trees are withering, the air is turning poisonous, and the animals are morphing into monsters.

He calls me Sparkles, but my light is waning and soon all I'll be is a speck in the dark.

What good am I to him like this?

What good am I broken?

I raise my phantom gaze and open my lips.

"Okay."

And I fall deeper into the abyss.

Chapter
FORTY-FOUR

JACKSON

Maybe today.

I load my latest batch of brownies into the glass Tupperware container, hoping that when I go downstairs that the container from yesterday isn't still sitting outside.

It's killing me.

She's not replying to any of my messages, and all my calls are going to voicemail—there's been nothing but radio silence. Every fiber of my being wants to break her door down and force myself inside so I can hold her. I'm not sure how much longer I can respect her healing process until I force the master code from Parker and let myself in.

My fingers tighten on the container as I steel myself and head to the elevator, ready to try again, to knock again and hope maybe today I get some kind of response.

"Hey, you bringing those down to Deer?" Parker wanders up beside me.

"Yeah."

"Can I do it today?"

"No." I punch the elevator button.

"Aw, come on. Let me give it a try. You know I have the golden touch."

"No."

The elevator doors begin to slide open, and Parker's arm shoots out across the frame to bar me from entering.

"What the hell are you doing?"

"Just let me take them down."

What is with him?

"I said no."

I push his arm out of the way, but then he just sticks his leg out, creating another barricade.

"Please."

"Fuck, dude." I reach out and grab him by the shirt, forcing him aside as my patience runs thin. "Stop."

"Come on, Jackson."

It's then that I catch it—a desperation wavering through his eyes.

My grip tightens.

"What happened?"

His easy smile twitches down ever so slightly before he catches it. "What do you mean?"

"I mean, what are you hiding? *What happened?*" I push him against the elevator.

"Chill for a second." His eyes flash with that rare heat and he puts his hand on my chest, applying a quiet force.

"Parker," I growl out.

"What the fuck are you two doing?" Aleks stalks over and tugs Parker out of my grip. I've known Aleks long enough to know when not to put up a fight. I might be stronger than him, but he plays dirtier.

"He's hiding something." I point a finger at the platinum blond, who's shifted behind our mediator and out of my reach.

Aleks lets out a loud sigh, turning to raise his brows at Parker, who in turn just points a finger back at me—or, more specifically, my container of brownies. Aleks' face neutralizes, eyes flicking up to mine.

"You going to see Deer?"

"Yeah."

He looks back at Parker briefly before placing a hand on my shoulder to guide me back into the apartment.

"I need to talk to you first."

"But—"

"Jackson." My best friend gives me a look that causes a rock to drop into my gut.

We sit on the couch, and he takes the Tupperware container from me, placing it on the coffee table.

"There's something we need to tell you."

"What?"

"Deer's dad flew in last night."

"Oh. Okay." Shit. I would've gone down there and been caught completely off guard. I've been going there each day in just my sweatpants. Not how I would've wanted to meet him for the first time. "Thanks for the heads-up."

"No, it's," he pauses, looking to Parker again, "it's more than that."

"Al," I deadpan, "you're killing me here."

"Her dad came and took her home. He thought may-be—"

"What do you mean *home*?"

"I mean Ireland."

No.

No, there's no way.

"You're lying."

"I'm not. She's gone."

"No." I shake my head, pushing up from the couch and beelining for the elevators.

"Jackson," he calls out.

They both follow me inside the elevator, and I hit the button for her floor over and over and over until the doors close. A gentle hum begins to build in my ears. My foot taps against the cold floor as I try to swallow down the knot in my chest, trying to make it go away.

Aleks stands silently in the corner, watching me. Parker nervously spins his cartilage piercings, looking anywhere but me.

They're wrong. They have to be.

The doors open, and before I realize it, I'm running, sprinting down the hallway to her apartment. My steps falter when I notice the Tupperware container is missing.

"Deer," I yell, rapping my hand against the hard door. "Deer, baby, just let me know you're in there." My knuckles smash on the wood again and again, but the pain is nothing.

Come on.

Come *on*.

"Deer!" My voice cracks, the fear leaking out.

"Jackson," Aleks whispers.

"No," I snarl, spinning to face him. "No, she's in there."
My eyes zero in on Parker. "What's the master code? Let
me in." I stalk over, scarlet clouding my vision.

Parker raises both of his hands, palms facing me. "Hold
on, mate. Give me a second." He treats me like a rabid dog,
speaking slowly as he carefully circles me.

He presses a code into the electronic lock, and it makes
a light chiming noise before he reaches over and pulls
down the door handle, flinging it open and stepping aside
so I don't barrel into him.

The apartment is dark, blinds closed, lights off—not
even the magenta hue from her streaming room shines
through. I can feel it in my bones, the emptiness, the lack
of life inside.

"Deer?" I call out hesitantly.

Her bedroom door is open.

A stampede of animals is thudding inside my chest,
knocking against my ribcage with each silent step I take.

I swallow, trying again, "Deer?"

My feet breach the doorway, and the world falls out
from under me at the sight of her empty bed, the sheets
strewn haphazardly. My nose pricks, and I clench my teeth
at the pressure building behind my eyes.

I dive into her closet, trying to find her favorite suitcase, but it's not there.

"No."

All the hesitation leaves my body as I begin running
around, checking every room, calling out her name. I
kneel on the floor to look under the bed and couch. I lift
each blanket and pillow I can find. I open every closet and
drawer, no matter how small.

Somewhere.

She has to be somewhere.

"Jackson." Aleks' voice tries to break through the blood rushing in my ears.

I can't stop moving, can't stop checking each room, over and over and over again. Her streaming room is trashed; webcam smashed, ring light in pieces on the floor. The gaming chair has been flipped over and the LED lights that lined the walls have been ripped off. Her router's been torn from the wall, chunks of plaster marring the plush rug.

Seeing everything in ruin forces the poisonous truth to the surface.

"Jackson." Aleks' hand lands on the middle of my back, palm pressing between my shoulder blades.

It debilitates me, sending me to the floor, knees crashing—his touch forcing me to accept reality, forcing me to accept that she isn't here.

My heart fractures in two, splitting open and leaving me empty.

"No." I look up at him, tears quickly filling my eyes. "No." I shake my head, causing them to spill over.

He kneels on the ground next to me, his hand returning to my back.

"I'm sorry."

Those two words snap the final thread, and I fall apart. Beads of tears tumble down my cheeks as I squeeze my eyes shut against the pain strangling my chest.

I'm not sure how long I sit there, how long I grieve the loss of her, but eventually the tears dry up and that sharpness in my chest turns to a spark. I feel it inside me. I feel that sparkle of *her*. Deer might be gone, but I still carry her with me. If I search through the shattered pieces of my heart, I can find that sparkle, and I'm going to hold onto it.

I'm going to hold onto her.

I'm going to find her.

My hands push on the ground as I leverage myself to stand. The guys steady me, sharing worried looks.

"I'm going to Ireland," I tell them. My knees ache with every step I take, but I push through it.

"Shit," I hear them mutter before their hurried feet catch up with me.

"Mate, you don't even know where she is." Parker jogs ahead, turning to walk backward as he tries to reason with me.

"I don't," I pick up my pace, looking him square in the eye as I stalk past him, "but you do."

Parker sighs. "You need to give her time. You can't go barging over there when she clearly needs her space."

"You don't know that." I pull my key fob out and scan it at the far elevator bank that connects to our private lift and press the button. "You don't know her—us."

He doesn't know how I held her in my arms as she slept, chasing away her nightmares. He doesn't know every time I came running when she felt scared. He doesn't know that I love her.

He doesn't know.

I know.

"Look, I'm just saying—"

"I don't want to hear it!"

The elevator doors open, and I stalk inside, slamming on the button for the penthouse. They follow in quietly, still sharing that apprehensive look.

"I'm going to Ireland."

"Then you're *going* to be wandering around like a child because I'm not giving you her address," he pushes back.

"Parker," Aleks warns.

"Really?" I get up in Parker's face. "You really want to try that?"

His eyes burn icy blue as he stares at me quietly.

"What if it were Sydney?"

That burning wavers.

"What if she were hurting and she ran back to Missouri; would you not follow her?"

He looks away, fingers coming up to twist the twin studs in his ear. "I—"

"And you," I spin on Aleks. "Don't tell me you wouldn't do the same for Stephanie." My teeth clench as a I spit out, "Don't even fucking *try* to tell me you wouldn't go to the ends of the earth for her if she up and disappeared."

He opens his mouth but just sighs.

The elevator doors open, and I turn my back on them, leaving them behind as I head for my bedroom—tunnel vision blocking out everything except the fact that I need to throw a few things into a duffle and leave. It doesn't matter what, I just need to get on the first flight out.

"You're not going anywhere."

I spin to find Sydney leaning in my doorframe.

"Yes, I am."

"No, you're not."

"No disrespect, Sydney, but we pay you. If I say that I'm taking some time off and going to Ireland, I'm doing that."

"Don't be an asshole." Her eyes narrow, and it's then

that I realize they're rimmed with red and slightly puffy. She sighs, walking in and perching on the edge of my bed. "Sit." She pats the spot next to her.

I slam the T-shirt I've been holding into my duffle with a huff before trudging over. While I might be behaving like an ass, I'm not one—the guys and I have always respected Syd, always trusted her.

"I'm hurt that she left as well, but I get it."

"Get what?"

"That she needs the space to heal. What she's going through is traumatizing, and up until now, all she's done is ignore her trauma and shove it aside, time and time again. At some point, all that pain is going to poison her from the inside out. It's what happened to me when my brother died."

"But she doesn't have to do it alone."

That's what hurts the most.

"Actually, she does. Until she decides to heal, it doesn't matter how much anyone around her says otherwise. She needs to make that mental choice for herself. Once she takes that first step, then, yeah, we can help her. But she has to start the journey on her own two feet first."

"I can wait. I'll go to Ireland, and I'll wait."

"I know you can, you have the patience of a saint. But you're not going to Ireland—you won't if you want to keep her safe. Rick is in the wind, so the rest of us are grounded. Deer's family is going cold until he's in custody. Do you understand what I'm saying?"

I want to fight her on it, but I can't when the reasoning is Deer's safety. That's all I want, for her to be safe. And if it means I have to stay here and feel like my heart is being run over by a truck every five minutes, then fine, so be it. I'll endure that pain so she can heal from hers.

But I won't give up. I'll never give up.

Deer is my star, and without her, the night sky is but an empty void. So, I'll wait until the time comes for her to return and light up my world with her sparkle.

"Fine."

"Thank you." Syd chuckles softly. "It's funny how love changes people."

"What do you mean?"

"I mean you, you big oaf. I can practically hear your heart beating from here. It's going D-Deer, D-Deer, D-Deer."

"Shut up." I nudge her with my shoulder before flopping back on my bed.

Except, she's right.

Deer owns my heart, and I'm going to keep it safe until she returns.

Chapter FORTY-FIVE

DEER

I wake with a scream.

My hands tear at the sheets that are stuck to my clammy skin, ripping them away as I struggle to take in a breath. Raw terror crawls over me like hundreds of tiny spiders, and I can't shake them off, no matter how hard I try.

The room is cloaked in darkness, and I don't recognize it.

Something is in the corner watching me—someone.

Not safe. Never safe.

My breaths come shorter now; I can hear them wheezing out of me.

I need air.

My body tumbles off a bed that is too high, and I thump onto the carpet below. The pain of my knee hitting the ground at a weird angle brings some sliver of aware-ness back.

I'm at my parents' house.

The shape in the corner is nothing more than a lamp.

I curl up on my side, hugging my knees to my chest as I bury myself against the carpet.

I hate sleeping because the nightmares are always floating nearby, a daemon ready to grab me from the shad-ows and strangle me with the fear that is eating me alive. I hate being awake, the memories of the man I left behind haunting me everywhere I accidentally look for him.

The bone-deep fear morphs into a guilt-laden sorrow, and I cry until my body gives out.

JACKSON

My phone smashes against the wall.

I can't keep doing this.

I'm driving myself to the brink of madness.

I sink down next to my bed. My hand reaches behind me until it lands on a bundle of soft material, pulling it down and clutching it to my chest. I inhale the brown sugar sweetness of her scent on the blanket I stole from her room—my reminder of her.

My chest pangs, ringing out in the empty cage that once held my heart.

I want to go find her.

I want to see her.

"Jackson," Aleks calls out.

I ignore him as I continue to wallow.

"Jackson," he yells a little louder, his tone curt.

"What?"

He doesn't reply.

Are you fucking serious right now?

"What?" I shout harder.

Still nothing.

I'm going to strangle him.

I push to my feet, stalking with the wrath of an angry god through the apartment.

"What is it?"

Phoebe perches on one of the bar stools, legs crossed and head tilted as she casts her eyes over me. "Well, aren't you just a peachy lad?" Her lips twist up in a smirk, and it causes mine to curl.

"Pheebs." Parker gives her a pleading look.

"What? Looks like you could roast a marshmallow on all the fire coming off him."

I scoff at her. "You know, Phoebe, you're here so often, we're going to have to ask you to start paying rent."

Phoebe lets out a sigh as she gracefully steps down. She walks over to me with measured steps, heels pointedly clicking on the tiles. She stops three feet away and just stares at me, expression bored.

Seconds pass, and just when I'm about to burst out of my skin, she smiles—but it isn't a kind smile, it's that of a deadly shark facing down its prey.

"You know, Jackson, I wouldn't threaten the person who comes bearing news you so desperately want."

"What?" All the anger drains from my body, replaced with a rush of desperation.

She smirks, turning her back to me and strolling away, waving her hand lazily in the air. "Contrary to your complaining, I never show up without a purpose. I thought you would know that by now."

"I don't care. Did you find Rick?"

She tsks, taking back her seat at the island. "No." The annoyance is clear in her voice. "Paige is being anal about keeping it all above board, so my hands are tied."

"Then what's the news?"

"Well, they were able to raid his apartment before he had a chance to clear it out."

"And?"

"And it seems like Rick developed an unhealthy attachment to Deer. Based on the files they found and his prior actions, the profilers don't believe his intention was ever to harm her but more so to scare her into a dependent state and cut her off from the world for just himself. Sort of like a superfan gone wrong."

"What, they don't consider the roofies harm?" Aleks scoffs.

She shrugs. "They think it was just another fear tactic, to make it so she couldn't trust anyone. It backfired when it pushed her to spend more time with Jackson." She looks me up and down. "He had a lovely picture of you with a dart through it, by the way."

"Seriously?"

"Mm, quite cliché." Her lips curl like she just smelled rotten fish. "This guy really is pathetic; it's doing my head in that he slipped through the Feds hands."

"Wait," Aleks frowns. "Could he be coming after Jackson then?"

"Possibly, but probably not. Like I said, the profilers think he's one of the more nonviolent types. But it's why we had Sydney ground you boys, just in case."

"If he fucking tries to come after me, I'll—"

"Do nothing, because murder charges are a bitch to magically disappear. Not even I have the resources for that. Do we understand?"

"Whatever," I huff. "So, that's it? Your news is the confirmation that Deer's moderator is a delusional, obsessed stalker, who isn't going to hurt her but maybe wants to hurt me?"

"Yes."

"No other updates?"

"No."

"Fuck, are you serious right now, Phoebe?" I run my hands through my hair.

"Watch your tone, Lau."

"No. You're telling me that you have no other leads, nothing. My girl is all the way in Ireland, cut off from the world—from me—and I'm stuck here because he's still on the loose."

"What do you want me to do?"

"Find. Him."

Chapter
FORTY-SEVEN

DEER

I stare out the bay window at the dark green hills in the distance, my forehead resting on the cool glass and my knees curled against my chest. It's windy today—the trees in the distant forest are swaying more than usual. I raise my hand to the glass, tracing my nails down as if to reach into the open fields.

It's so empty out there.

Peaceful.

"Deir, it's me," my mam announces. "You decent?"

"Yeah."

The door clicks open, and I hear her soft footfalls on the carpet.

"I brought you some tea."

"I'm not hungry."

She lets out a sigh, the sound of whatever she brought

in clacking onto my coffee table. Well, calling it mine is a stretch. I hadn't been back to Carlingford in three years, not since my channel started to really take off.

At first, I'd been too busy—putting out a new video every day, researching new games and perfecting my persona—and then, I'd been too scared. That fear kept compounding more and more until the idea of the outside world became a living nightmare I refused to step into.

The more time that passes here, the more I realize my new therapist is right.

"You need to eat." Mam takes a seat next to me. "Here—a slice of coffee cake, fresh from the oven."

My eyes flit to the baked goods, and my heart plummets.

Jackson used to be the one bringing me desserts. He was the one who would take the time out of his day to bake me something new just so I'd have something to eat. Even when I'd stopped opening the door, he'd still tried. And I just left him—like a coward.

"Oh!" Mam hurries to put down the plate and reaches out to wipe a stray tear. "Oh, now why'd that make you cry?"

I can't tell her it's because I'm pretty sure I'm in love with a six-foot-something grumpy gamer whom I just left high and dry back in America without any warning, and that he probably hates me now as a result, which is causing my heart to bleed like someone removed a brick from a dam and the water is gushing out. That it should be so easy for me to pick up my phone and just send him a message, that I could type out two simple words—I'm sorry—but that every time I get close to grabbing my phone, a wave of nausea overtakes me, and so I just keep avoiding it because avoiding is what I do best. Because there's a man out there who is trying to hurt me, and I don't want to put Jackson or anyone else in danger.

"Maybe we go and get you some fresh air?"

I stiffen in her hold. I've barely left my bed let alone my room since arriving.

"Not into town or anything," she's quick to add, "but just outside." Her voice is hesitant, testing the waters.

But the storm inside me hasn't calmed; the waves are still crashing.

"No thanks."

Her hand strokes down the back of my head in a soft, soothing motion. "Dr. Ainsley said you need to try. Even if it's just sitting on the back porch swing for a few minutes."

I know that.

"I'm still not ready."

She sighs, pulling back. "Look out there, Deirdre, and tell me what you see." She nods out the window.

"Trees. Some wildflowers. The field." A swallow dives across the sky. "A bird."

"Any houses?"

"No." We own the entire twelve-acre property. There isn't anyone for miles, and it takes twenty minutes just to drive into town.

"Then what out there—" she taps on the glass "—is scaring you?"

"Life."

I know it isn't rational, I know there isn't anything out there, but there's this little voice in my head that says *what if?* What if he's somehow found out where I am? What if he is watching me from a satellite, waiting until I leave this house? What if there's a drone hidden somewhere to stalk me?

"Please. I promise it's safe."

Promise.

The word makes me think of Jackson again.

How he also promised he wouldn't let me get hurt. How he promised to help me. How I abandoned those promises.

If Jackson were here, would he take my hand and lead me out into the sunshine?

I blink out the window, my mind hallucinating a couple in the field, holding hands.

Mam must see something pass over my face because she stands up and lightly tugs me out of my huddle, and my body seems to comply for once. My legs unfurl until my feet touch the carpet, and I hold onto my mother's hand as she slowly leads me out of my bedroom.

The house is quiet save for the light piano music that seems to always be playing. Still, I keep glancing around in case someone comes slinking out from the shadows, my hand gripping the balustrade as we wind down the staircase.

My steps begin to slow as we approach the double set of back doors. The buzzing of a hive hums against my ears, and my heart begins to shake in response.

Mam squeezes my hand, looking back at me with a smile as her warm brown eyes crinkle with hope.

"Breathe."

My head moves in short nods as I try to do just that.

In. Hold. In. Out.

In. Hold. In. Out.

"Good."

She turns the doorknob, and that hive of bees makes its way into my lungs, filling them with their hurried agitation.

I can't breathe.

I can't do this.

I start to pull out of her grip, but then the door tugs open and the crisp air whisps around me, sending my pink hair in a flutter. On instinct, I inhale. Cool, clean air fills my lungs, and suddenly that sparkle that's still buried deep within me begins to flash brighter.

"Just one step." She runs her thumb over my knuckles.

I take another breath. A little bit of salt from the bay carries on the wind, and I use it to ground myself.

One step.

I move forward to the threshold, my toes curling around the edge.

One step.

But even though I keep telling myself that, my legs don't seem to move.

I gaze out into the lush fields, tracing the dips of the hills in the distance before searching higher into the sky dotted with clouds. Searching for something to get me to take that one step.

Distantly, the piano music filters back into my consciousness, and it chimes like a bell in my mind. My brows pull together as I focus on the sound, trying to figure out what about it is niggling at me.

A chord of notes plays out, and that sparkle briefly shimmers again.

It's the same song I heard Angela play at her recital.

Memories of that day come trickling in.

How I held his hand for the first time. His smile teasing me as I wove the delicate tale of our secret romance. The way his fingers traced reassuring patterns on my thigh as we banded together—partners.

"Oh, Deir." Mam hugs me. "I'm so proud."

I shift in her hold, feeling something soft under my feet.

Grass.

My toes scrunch against the blades, curling them against my skin as I blink the world back into focus. She lets go and smiles—she smiles because I am smiling.

And then, I take another step.

Chapter
FORTY-EIGHT

JACKSON

My knee taps up and down as I try to focus on the game at hand. I'm driving in fourth place with Aleksander somehow making a rogue comeback in fifth, tailing my ass like a dog sniffing out a bone.

But my attention keeps slipping because Paige's phone rang twenty minutes ago and she flew out onto the rooftop patio like her house was on fire. She said they were closing in, that there had been some developments overnight, but that we still shouldn't get our hopes up too high.

"You did not just banana peel me." Phoebe glares at her younger brother, who just laughs maniacally.

"Tough luck, sis."

The patio door slams open, and we all turn around to stare as Paige runs inside.

"We got him."

Hope coils in my chest. "Really?"

"Yes." She smiles as she snatches her purse from the island. Her heels clack on the tiles as she beelines for the elevator. "I have to go meet with the prosecutor and then head to the airport. He was in Wyoming." She presses on the elevator panel, and the doors open.

"How'd he slip up?" Parker calls out.

"He didn't; it was an anonymous tip. I'll call later," she shouts back as the doors close.

The boys and I turn to stare at the woman who never once flinched during that exchange and has proceeded to take first place in the round.

"What?" Phoebe doesn't take her eyes off the screen.

"Anonymous tip?" The insinuation in Parker's voice is clear.

"It wasn't me."

"Okay. Then you know who it was."

She crosses the finish line and looks over at us, raising a brow. "Do you really want me to tell you?"

"No. I'd rather not get caught up in your weird SIS shit."

She scoffs. "If I were using the agencies, it wouldn't be considered illegal, now would it?"

"Stop." Parker places his hands over his ears. "I won't be implicated in your activities."

"You're the one who asked in the first place."

I toss my controller on the coffee table and make a beeline for my bedroom. The duffle bag that's been sitting on my dresser for the last two weeks shines at me like a beacon. I quickly check it over, making sure my passport is in place before slinging it over my shoulder and grabbing a pair of sneakers from my wall.

Aleks waits for me in the hallway, following me as I head to the elevator alcove and sit on the footstool to slip my shoes on. He hits the button for me and leans against the wall.

"What's the plan?"

"I'll catch the first flight out, find her, and bring her home."

"And if she doesn't want to come?"

"Then I'll wait with her until she's ready."

"Good luck, brother." He claps me on the back.

Chapter
FORTY-NINE

JACKSON

I stare at the woman sitting alone on the end of the pier. Her pastel pink hair is the same color as the sunset that is trying to peek through the cloudy sky. The bay is still busy, the town going about their end of day activities, but no one bothers her—not even the seabirds that squawk at every passerby.

The salty breeze brushes around me, and I reach back with shaky hands to tie my hair in a half knot.

"Come on, man," I whisper to myself.

Before I end up standing here all evening, I force my legs to move forward. The worn planks beneath my feet creak slightly, and I know that the closer I get to her, the more likely she is to sense my presence.

My heart beats out of my chest, butterflies swarming my stomach and rising up to escape. The noise from the

421

town gets quieter the farther out I go, replaced by the soft waves of the sea and occasional bird call. It makes my steps sound louder and louder until I'm a few feet away and watch the woman's shoulders stiffen. Her freezing is brief—her hands sliding to the heart-shaped handbag at her side and opening it up to slip something out.

"I'd appreciate it if you didn't taser me."

She stops moving, head tilting slightly before it slowly twists around. Those honeyed doe eyes crash into mine.

"Jackson?"

"Hi, Sparkles."

She lets out a gasp, dropping the taser as her hand comes to clasp her mouth. I pick up my pace, jogging over as she scrambles to stand up. I reach out to lift her against my body, spinning her around and holding her as close as I can.

"Oh my Gods," she whispers.

I carefully lower her back down, and my heart begins to slowly stitch itself back together now that I have her again. Her hands come up to cup my jaw, and she looks at me like I might be a figment of her imagination—bewilderment and hope shining true.

"Is this for real? You actually came to Ireland?"

"I did." I lean into her touch. "I missed you."

"You're not mad?" Her voice cracks on the question, and glistening tears start leaking down her cheeks.

"What? No, why would I be mad?"

"B-because I left," she sobs. "I left, a-and I didn't say anything. I abandoned y-you." Her hands fall to my chest, and she fists my shirt. "You're m-my rock, and I tossed you aside like a random pebble. I thought you'd never sp-

speak to me again."

"Oh, sweetheart. Come here." I hug her to my chest, feeling her tears dampen my shirt as she buries herself against me and continues to cry. "I could never be mad at you. I won't lie and say I wasn't hurt when I found out you'd left—it felt like someone took a pitchfork and stabbed me right in the chest. Every day I spent without you, without speaking to you, that pain got worse. There wasn't a second that passed when I didn't think of you and wish I was holding you in my arms, but I understood why you left. I understood even though it killed me not to run to you.

"Because more than anything, I missed you. I missed your brown sugar scent and how your nails trace along my skin whenever we're cuddling. I missed the way you bite your lip when you're focused while playing games and aren't afraid to crack back at the guys when we play. I missed how you moan when you taste my food even though it has my dick hard at the worst of times. But most of all, I missed the way you laugh because it sounds like a symphony of angels and makes your eyes sparkle in this way that not even the most expensive diamond could compare to. And I wouldn't have been able to hear that laugh or see that sparkle until we caught that son of a bitch."

"Promise?"

"Promise." I pull back and smooth her hair behind her ear as I gaze down at her. "The only mad I am is madly in love with you."

I knew I was the moment I found out she was gone, but the second she turned around on the pier, there was no denying the fact that my heart only beats properly when

I'm near her.

"Good," she sniffles. "Because I'm in love with you, too. Even in my most desperate hours when it seemed like I was on the edge of a cliff and about to sink into the abyss, there was one thread that kept me from tumbling off, and it led back to you. As terrified as I was about facing the world and living in it, I was more scared that I had lost you."

"You'll never lose me. I'm not leaving your side again."

I lean down and kiss her, and everything clicks. That final thread stitches into place, connecting the two halves of my heart together again. I taste the salt from the bay on her lips as I drink her in, savoring the feel of her against me. Deer sighs, her body softening beneath me as our tender kiss deepens.

It's been so long that I can't help myself. The more I kiss her, the more desperate I become. This woman before me has me wrapped around her finger, and she doesn't even know it.

"I forgot to say that I missed these lips as well," I murmur against her.

She smiles and pulls back, rolling her eyes. "Of course you did. How'd you find me here, anyway?"

"Well, I went to your house, and your mom told me."

"You met my mam?"

"She said I was very handsome."

"Of course she did."

"Once I got down here, it wasn't that hard to look for the girl with pink hair."

I tug on a strand, and she bats my hand away before smoothing her hair back down. I catch sight of the goosebumps on her arm.

"It's getting a little chilly; do you want to head back?"

"Sure."

I thread our hands together, not ready to let her go. As our steps creak along the pier, I study the way she stares out at the town, cataloguing the people nearby.

"Jackson."

"Yeah?"

Her brows crease, and she chews on her lower lip. "I—uh. How long are you staying for?"

"Depends. However long you're here, I guess."

"What?"

"I told you, I'm not leaving your side again. So, I'll stay for as long as you're here, and when you're ready to leave, so will I."

"What if"—she looks down at the ground—"what if I'm never ready?"

"Then I'll probably need to start looking into how to obtain Irish citizenship."

"What? Jack—"

"But I don't think that will be the case." I stop walking and turn to her. "I know you, Deer. You have a lot of resilience in that pint-sized body. You'll be ready someday. And when that day comes, I'll be ready to bring you home."

"Thank you." She looks up at me, some of that sparkle back in her eyes, and I know that I would wait until the end of the world for her.

She is the spark that makes my heart beat, and I would be lifeless without her.

DEER

ONE MONTH LATER

"Are you fucking kidding me?"

"What's wrong?" I frown as I focus in the mirror on slotting another pin into the left space bun I twisted atop my hair.

"He rejected me!" Jackson shouts incredulously from the bedroom. "I spent the last six hours wooing this man, doing all the little things he likes—including wasting one of my days helping that annoying band camp chick—and he just rejects me? What a fucking douche."

I stifle my laugh. "Let me see."

He hops off the bed, stalking over as I tuck the last flyaway behind my ear.

"Look." He holds out the Switch like he's presenting a badge.

426

I turn and squint at the screen, looking at the different statistics of Lucien LaRue, one of the conquerable love interests in *Love Love Passion School: Summer Session.*

"Ah." I tap the screen with the tip of my nail. "You're half a sun rating off."

"What? I thought you said it only mattered what the heart ratings were."

"Yes, on normal mode. But you're the one who insisted that he was too good for that, picked hard mode, and then said you didn't want any help because that was *cheating.*"

He tsks.

"I told you that hard mode is no cakewalk; those men are a finicky lot."

"Whatever," he huffs.

He is such a sore loser, but I have to admit it has been funny watching him these past few days trying and mostly failing to win some of my otome games.

Since he arrived here four weeks ago, Jackson has helped me ease my way back into gaming. No streaming or content filming—nope, he just lies next to me on the bed as we both play our Switches, or he sits next to me when we're on our laptops. He gives me commentary on when he thinks I'm picking the wrong villager to woo or animal to invite to my farm. Thanks to him, I now have this ugly octopus resident on my *Cherry Farm*, and it looks like I'm going to marry the hot florist girl in my new *Moonstone Valley* save file.

He's helping me see the world as fun again, and I couldn't be more grateful that he has stuck by my side. He hasn't wavered once, encouraging me and letting me take my time but still pushing me when he knows I can handle it—even when I doubt myself.

Which is why today is so important.

"You look cute." Jackson gives me a knowing smile, eyes lingering on the way my breasts aren't exactly hiding in my House of CB pink floral sundress.

"Thank you." I grin, cupping my hands under my chin in a V shape and wink at him.

Over the last few weeks, I've gotten more and more back to myself, back to being Deer. The excitement I used to feel at picking out my outfits for the day has returned piece by piece—a skirt here, some heels there. I am able to face myself in the mirror now without seeing a zombie staring back. My naturally flushed cheeks have returned, bringing color to my still pale skin—because Ireland is not the place to live if you hope to get any sort of tan.

"Let me get my sneakers on and we can head out." He drops me a quick kiss.

With his back turned, I take a deep breath, fisting my hands at my sides. I close my eyes, letting that breath sit in my lungs as I center myself.

I can do this.

"Ready?"

I open my eyes.

"Yup."

My hands tighten on the steering wheel the closer we get, and I can't stop my gaze from constantly flicking back and forth between the road and the GPS—watching as the kilometers slowly tick down. I'm pretty sure my neck is going to be stiff as a tree trunk by the time we get there.

Less than ten kilometers now.

Jackson reaches down and places his hand on my left thigh, calming the way it jostles up and down. It happens every once in a while, and he always seems to notice, even when he is deep into playing games on his phone.

I focus on my breathing as the traffic gets a bit more congested. I'd thought that by picking a weekday it wouldn't be so busy, but it is Dublin after all.

I've spent the last month and a bit building up to this, learning to calm my anxiety. From walking around the empty fields at the house, to sitting at the pier and listening to the fishermen go about their days, to venturing into the town itself and slowly staying longer and longer each time. Last Thursday, we'd spent the entire day out, and then we'd gone to the Sunday market, which is the busiest place in town, and I was there for three hours before I needed to get out of the crowds.

Today, I am taking the next step. I know if I can do this…

I smile to myself, that sparkle of hope shining within me.

We cross the threshold of River Liffey into the main city center, and it takes us a solid thirty minutes until we're able to find a place to park the car. I press the stop button and wait as the music in the car switches off and the quiet rumble of the engine disappears. All that's left is the noise of the city around us.

I can do this.

I'm safe.

There's no one here out to get me.

Rick is behind bars, awaiting his court date. Paige has been working with the prosecutor's office and says the case they have is iron clad.

Unbuckling my seat belt, I reach for the door handle and open it before I can second-guess myself. The chatter of the street becomes louder without the walls of the car to muffle it—but the market on the weekend prepared me for this.

Jackson quickly rounds the car and comes to my side, offering me his hand. I take it, feeling his warmth as he gives me a reassuring squeeze.

"Well, here we are."

I take a deep breath, looking around. "Yup, here we are. We are here. In Dublin. Very cool."

Jackson chuckles at my nervous babbling, and I shoot him an annoyed pout.

"Come on." He smiles, tugging me onto the sidewalk. "What are you going to show me first?"

I perk up. "St. Stephen's Green."

We begin walking down the brown brick street, and he lets me chatter away, chuckling while I talk nonsense.

As we near Grafton Street, the prattle around us gets rowdier and the road begins to cram up with more bodies. It's the most touristy path in town and mostly stacked with chain restaurants and shops. My palms start to sweat as my attention bounces between all the people walking near us.

I veer us onto Wicklow Street, which is still busy but not as stifling. It's lined on both sides with three- to four-story red brick buildings. People walk on both the sidewalk and the black stone road, filling up the entire path as they wade through. They pass in and out of shops, and I'll admit, what is supposed to be a ten-minute walk ends up taking us close to twenty because my feet drag a little slower.

It's one of the things that is most confusing. You would think because of how alert I am about my surroundings and the way my heart is beating a few ticks higher, that I would be trying to rush through, but it's the opposite. I lag, constantly cataloguing everything around me.

The crowds start to thicken again as we near the park, the clear skies and gentle temperature bringing out everyone in a fifty-mile radius. It seems like everyone is watching me, and I make eye contact with more than a dozen people, only confirming the feeling. That telltale crawl of ants over my skin starts to appear, and I step a little closer to Jackson while fortifying my mental walls.

He squeezes my hand, bringing me out of my head, and I realize I've been quiet the last few minutes.

"Sorry."

"Don't be. How're you holding up?"

"Fine. It's just," I swallow, "there are a lot more people staring than I expected."

Jackson hums. He doesn't try to tell me I'm just imagining it, that people aren't ogling us as we pass. Instead he says, "Well, that's what happens when you're gorgeous."

"Or when you look like a walking pink highlighter," I counter.

"Then you're the most high-end highlighter a stationary enthusiast can purchase."

"Thank you?" I laugh as the ants on my skin trickle

away, replaced by the mild warmth of the sun shining down.

He cringes. "I spent too much time around Parker when you were gone. Don't tell anyone I said that."

"Or what? You'll gag me?"

His eyes heat and he leans down, lightly gripping my chin. "Oh, I'm going to do that anyway, Sparkles. That's a promise."

My thighs squeeze together, his words igniting that need deep within me. I push past the flush that's creeping up my cheeks and raise my brow, taunting him. "Promises, promises. I'll believe it when I see it."

He smirks before catching me in a quick, blinding kiss, his tongue snaking past my defenses and sweeping inside me with a moan. My mind swims all dizzily as he pulls back and snakes his arm around my ribs, tugging me close, his thumb grazing the fabric beneath my breast.

My body is like a marshmallow on fire, melting under his hot touch.

Being with Jackson is an easy distraction from all my worries. There's no one else on this earth, in this universe, who is able to clear my mind like he does.

We continue wandering around the park, stopping a few times to take pictures and lingering on the bridge to watch the way the stream bubbles, before we make our way to Dublin Castle.

The gray stone former medieval fortress is less packed than usual, and we're able to take our time exploring all the history. We head down to the cooler Subterranean Chamber, where all the original fortifications are preserved, before trekking back up to get some fresh air in the gardens.

As we amble over to St. Patrick's Hall, where the ceiling is covered by three large canvas paintings by Vincenzo Waldré, I can't help but think of Stevie, how she would love this.

I miss my friends.

By the time we leave the castle, my social battery begins to wane again. Being around large crowds for the last few hours has drained me more than I realized, but not once did I feel like I was going to have a panic attack.

That knowledge brightens the sparkles within me, and I know I'm about to make the right choice—that I'm ready for that choice.

We head to a hole-in-the-wall pub on the outskirts of town to grab some pints and food. It's one that's dotted exclusively with locals who know the area well enough to find it. The chatter in here is low and the lights are a dim orange. It gives me some space to think and breathe as I prepare myself.

The butterflies brewing in my stomach aren't from nerves but excited anticipation.

"You've been smiling at my beer for a couple of minutes." Jackson nods. "You good?"

I look up and lock eyes with him.

"I want to go home."

Jackson pauses mid-sip, putting his pint down. "All right, I'll go get the bill. Are you fi—"

"I don't mean Carlingford."

He tilts his head.

"I mean *home*."

"To Cali?"

"Yeah."

"Really?" He smiles but then schools it. "You're sure? You're not just saying that? Because I have no issue staying longer if you're not ready. I like Ireland, lassie."

I snort at the awful Irish accent he tacks on at the end. He really is too sweet to me.

"Really. I'm ready. I miss our friends. I miss free two-day delivery. I miss my nail technician. And, Gods, I miss having our own space where we can, ya know, without worrying about my parents."

He smirks, nodding his head. "You make a fair point. It's hard to fuck you right when you scream so loud."

I duck my head, glancing around at the nearby tables as I hiss, "Really?"

He reaches out and takes my hand; it's a little cold from the beer. "If you're ready, then, okay, let's do it."

I smile. "Let's go home, Jackson."

Chapter FIFTY-ONE

DEER

"Are you ready, ma'am?"

No.

In fact, I think this might be a horrible idea—one of the worst I've ever had.

"Yes."

The guard opens the door at my confirmation, and I take one step into the concrete room. My eyes scan each of the cubicles until they land on a young man.

Yup, this is definitely a shite idea.

I take steadying breaths as my platform heels carry me across the room to where he is sitting. My focus is just on the silver chair, my goal: getting to it without panicking.

In and out.

In and out.

I tuck my dress beneath me as I take a seat, but it doesn't

stop the cold metal from biting into my thighs through the thin fabric. With a hand that shakes slightly, I pick up the phone attached to the partition. Once the plastic hits my ear, I steel myself and turn my gaze forward.

"Hi, Rick."

"Deer." His gaze slides over me like slime oozing down my skin.

I'm struck by how different he looks.

When I'd first hired Rick as my moderator, he was a shy, skinny guy with a mop of brown hair and gentle eyes. He'd been subbed to my channel from the very beginning, always commenting positively and encouraging me. When I started live streaming, he was there in the chat bolstering me along as I played my first run-through of *Cherry Farm: Beginnings* and sending me virtual gifts. I still remember the day he emailed me asking if I needed someone to moderate my comments—it was right after I'd worn this cute sailor corset and some person in the chat kept writing lewd remarks throughout the stream until I'd paused to remove them. It had seemed like such a no-brainer to accept Rick's help. He wasn't asking for payment or anything; he just genuinely wanted to help me succeed and prevent any trolls from derailing that.

His background check had come up clean—just a comp sci student with some spare time on his hands as he was job hunting.

As the weeks went on, he started doing more and more outside of the streams. Offering to help moderate my comments and DMs on social media, manage my emails, and even set up a P.O. box for me where he would vet the mail to make sure it was safe for me to open. So, I had him become a pseudo-assistant. He knew privacy was the most important thing to me, and he made my life less stressful by ensuring I was always safe. It helped decrease my anxiety significantly, and I'd been so grateful for that.

I just never noticed how he was using all of that against me—taking that weakness and exploiting it until he became so woven into my life, I couldn't see the translucent webs he was spinning around me.

At some point, he turned into the man before me—pale skin, hollow eyes, and black buzzed hair.

"I knew you'd come for me." He grins like he just won a prize. "You even dressed up."

"Actually, I'm headed to the Streamzies after this."

It's going to be the first gaming event that I've attended since the convention months ago. I'd made a slight detour to come here today, without telling anyone, and depending on how this went...

I shake myself, halting the potential spiraling of my thoughts.

Rick's face immediately sours. "You can't. It's not safe."

"So long as you're behind that glass, I'll be fine."

"They're lying to you. You need me. You've always needed me."

My free hand fists my dress, bunching the material as tight as possible.

"No, I don't."

"Don't play games, Deer. I'm your protector."

He manipulated me, day by day.

He'd smashed me like a vase, making it so only he could pick up the pieces.

But I can see through the smoke now. The forest view is clearing, and I can easily find the hole he dug in the ground, hoping that I would fall in while blinded, running from the fire that he kept stoking.

I just need to hear it from him. I can't move on until that last puzzle piece slots in. I've tried—tried to heal without speaking to him. But the nightmares are still gripping me with their talons, they're still ripping screams from my throat and coating my sheets in sweat.

So, here I am, facing my demon.

"You were *supposed* to protect me. I was supposed to trust you, but you broke me. You harassed me online, had me swatted, roofied."

He scoffs. "Because you were slipping away."

"What?"

"You were mine until you met them."

"Them?"

"The System," he spits out. "They took you out to clubs, and parties, and conventions—they were endangering you. You broke your routine for them. And the more you hung out with them, the further you got from me. I've been with you from the start, Deer. I'm the one who looks out for you. And you were throwing that away for these flashy guys. It's your own fault. I had to save you from yourself and remind you it isn't safe out there." He raises a hand to the glass. "You know you're only safe with me."

Had I created this monster?

Was it my fault?

That sick anxiety swirls in my chest, spinning guilt and fear together. He isn't wrong. Before Lee introduced me to the guys, I was a homebody. My life was game, stream, sleep, repeat—with the occasional shopping spree and anime binge-watching thrown in here and there. Meeting The System changed everything. I started to live life again. And then as Jackson and I started to become closer and closer...

Am I to blame for pushing Rick to the side? For making him hit a breaking point?

No.

No, this is all him, all his own twisted perception. I'm not going to let myself get warped by his words again. I'm not so fragile anymore that his manipulation can shape me as he pleases. I've become stronger. I've worked so damn hard on myself these last few months to heal my wounds, and I won't let him reopen those scars—he doesn't have that control any longer.

"I'm sorry that things turned out the way they did." I raise my hand to his on the glass. "But I'm going to continue living my life. I'm not hiding in the shadows from monsters."

"You think you'll be safe out there? You'll learn. You'll learn just how wrong you are, how the world will eat you alive. There's no one to save you."

"I don't need someone to save me. I saved myself."

I hang the phone up and watch as an ugly fury swirls in his eyes. He shouts at me as I get up on trembling legs and turn away, leaving him behind.

Chapter
FIFTY-TWO

JACKSON

"And the award for Hottest Streamer of the Year, as voted by you, the fans, goes to…"

We all lean forward on the table, watching as Andy—also known as the top streamer Celery-God—opens a slim black envelope.

"NightBlade32!"

"Fuck yes." Aleks fists pumps before turning to give Parker his middle finger. "In your face, bitch boy."

"Fuck!" Parker barks.

Stevie plants a kiss on the side of his mask before he stands up and jogs to the stage, enthusiasm flowing from him in waves. He's never been this excited to win an award in the entire time he's been streaming—not even when he was given the Golden Vizor last year.

He takes the award from the award girl and gives Andy

a clap on the back before taking his post at the microphone. His red mask tilts as he looks over the audience and says, "Let me give you all a look at the face you voted for," before tugging it off.

A series of whoops and cheers ring out, including a wolf whistle from the brunette at our table.

Aleks give zero fucks as he smirks, hyping everyone up. "I would just like to say thank you to everyone for voting for me as the hottest streamer. You see, a certain British fuck—" Sydney grimaces across the table "—has spent the last eight months since our face reveal insisting that he would win this award, even going so far as to bet his beautiful Aprilia if he lost."

He pauses, and the cameras switch to one that zooms in on Parker as he tears off his own mask and reaches forward to drain his champagne flute with one hand and flip Aleks the bird with the other.

"Today, I can claim not only the title of the most attractive member of The System, but also that stunning motorcycle. So, thank you and good night." He gives a dramatic bow and a wink before being led off stage.

"He's going to be insufferable for the rest of the night," Lee whines as Aleks comes running back to our table with a shit-eating grin on his face.

I reach up and remove my own mask—no sense keeping it on when the others are done for the night. The annual Streamzies award ceremony will be ending soon, and we've won more awards this year than any other year.

"Get ready to pay up." Aleks slaps Parker on the back before taking his seat between Stevie and Lee.

"How about another bet?"

"No," we all shout at Parker.

"Just accept the loss, hon." Syd places her hand on his thigh. "You don't even use it."

"Yeah, because you won't ride with me on any of my bikes," he pouts.

"And I never will."

"Whatever." He turns away from her, still sulking.

"Hey, you guys coming to Electric Tyger for the after?" Wylder bounces over to our table, resting his hand on the back of Aleks' chair.

Parker immediately perks back up. "You got a table?"

"Castle got a bunch."

"Ooh," Lee croons. "We're down."

I slide my hand under the table and grip Deer's hand with a small squeeze. "What do you want to do?"

"Hm?" She blinks those unnaturally ice blue eyes up at me.

Even though this is the first event she's gone to since everything went down with the doxing, she's been quieter than usual tonight.

"Wylder invited us to the Electric Tyger after-party that Castle is having. Do you want to go?"

"Oh."

"We don't have to."

She smiles and shakes her head, the sparkly glitter on her cheekbones shining in the light. "No, I want to."

"You sure?"

"Mhm. You'll be with me."

"You're fucking right I will be."

Everyone is sloshed.

"I am not *that* drunk," slurs Parker as he pushes out of the elevator and almost trips.

Syd, the only completely sober person, shoots out to grab her runaway boyfriend. "Sure, you're not."

"You are so beautiful." Parker reaches down and cups her face between his hands as she laughs at him. "How'd I get so lucky?"

"Because I love you."

The rest of us file out of the elevator behind them. Deer stays tucked close to my side, her fingers rubbing circles on my bicep where she's holding onto me.

"Night, guys," Stevie calls out as she and Aleks disappear into his room.

"What about you, babe?" I peer down at my girl.

"I kind of want some air. The club was stuffy."

"Okay, come on." I tug her toward the outdoor patio.

We step outside and the breeze immediately picks up, slicking its cool air over us. Deer reaches up to curl her arms around herself.

"Cold?"

"A little."

"Give me a sec."

I run back inside to my room and grab the package that's been hidden in my closet for the last week, ripping it open. When I come back outside, I find her pressed up against the glass railing as she peers out at the city.

I slip the jacket over her shoulders.

"Thanks." She starts to thread her arms through the sleeves but pauses with a frown. She takes it off and holds it in front of her, jaw going slack. "Oh my Gods." Her head swivels from the varsity jacket to me and back, again and again. "What?"

"You like it?"

"Are you kidding? I love it." She hugs the jacket to her chest. "How did you even get this?"

"I sent a message to the owner after the convention."

Despite everything that had gone wrong that day, I hadn't forgotten how much Deer had wanted to go see the booth that sold the custom *Passion School* varsity jackets.

She throws her arms around me and snatches a quick kiss. "Thank you."

"Come on," I chuckle. I take the jacket from her hands and hold it open so she can slip her arms into the sleeves. Once she's all bundled up, I spin her and wrap my arms around her chest as she leans her head back against my pecs.

"I went to see Rick today."

Her sudden words freeze the world around me.

"What?"

"Rick. I went to the prison to see him."

She only had two drinks tonight, both canned seltzers that no one could've tampered with, and yet the words she is saying make no sense. I twist her around to face me, her back pressing against the glass.

"You went to go to see Rick Adley at the prison, alone?"

"Yep."

"Did something happen? Are you okay?" Panic ricochets through my veins. My hands move on their own, touching all over her arms as I search for an invisible wound.

"Nothing happened, I just needed to see him—to face him." Her hands come up to rest on mine, keeping them grounded to her shoulders.

"Why didn't you tell me? I would've come with you."

"I know you would've. You're my protective grumpy bear, and I love you for that." She tilts her head, so her cheek rests on our joined hands. "But I had to do this myself."

"Why?"

"Because—" she taps my right temple "—I had to conquer it up here, remember?"

Absolute pride and adoration fill my chest.

"You're the strongest person I know, Sparkles. You know that?"

"Yeah?"

"Yeah."

She smiles. "I love you, Jackson. Thank you for never giving up on me."

"I wouldn't ever dream of it. *Mou baan faat jung ci jyu lei jing jung ngo deoi nei ge oi.*"

Words cannot describe my love for you.

I pull her into a kiss, tasting that brown sugar sweetness on her lips. For as long as I live, I will be the lighthouse that guides her home and keeps her safe even when the world goes dark.

She is my sparkle, and I'll always help her shine.

THE END

BONUS SCENE

DEER

Excitement thrums through my veins as I hold my phone out to the black box beside the red door to scan my membership ID. There's a faint beep, and then I place my hand on the ornate gold knob and twist, pulling the door open.

I take my first step into the dimly lit hallway. The floor is made up of black marble tiles, while the walls and ceiling are all painted a deep scarlet red. My heels click softly as I take my time, the noise of whatever lies ahead getting louder. I push aside a black curtain and come face-to-face with the true identity of the Cardinal Club.

It's an intimate, chic bar adorned with red velvet chairs and couches, with black tables dotted throughout. The walls here are painted black, but what catches my eye is the stunning art on the wall—they're depictions of naked bodies painted in shimmering gold.

"Hello, Deer."

I startle, looking up to find Savannah next to me, with a martini glass in hand.

"Hi."

She smiles at me, her gaze lingering on my body for a beat too long and causing me to flush. She finally turns away and takes a slow sip of her cocktail. "Welcome to the Cardinal Club. What do you think?"

"It's beautiful. Different from what I was expecting though."

"Mm? What, did you think people would just be fucking right when you got in?"

Yes.

My thoughts must be transparent on my face because she chuckles. "We do have a room for that, for people who like to watch or be watched."

"Oh. Okay."

"Come, let me show you where you can find him. Can't have a lost deer among all these bears."

I trail after her as she moves through the bar to one of the many doors that line the far wall.

"Down here." She opens a door marked with a gold feather. "Use your membership card to scan you into the correct room."

"Thanks."

I step into yet another hallway, and the door clicks shut behind me. I take slow, measured steps, eying the numbers on the doors as they increase. The want in my core begins to heat up, the anticipation growing as I finally come to a stop. The golden number eight gleams back at me, and I pull out my phone to check the time.

9:59.

I pause in front of the door and wait, watching the screen until the number changes again.

10:00.

With a deep inhale, I scan my phone on the round circle above the door handle and wait for the beep before wrapping my fingers around the cold metal and pulling it open.

The moment I step into the room, my breath leaves me in a reverent exhale. Like the rest of the club, the walls are painted black, but the floor here is gold. A beautiful king-size bed rests in the center of the room, and next to it is a beautiful man clad in nothing but a pair of slacks.

"Don't you look stunning," his deep voice rumbles. "Although, I can't wait to see what's underneath."

"I think you'll be pleased."

He smirks, walking over to me in just a handful of long strides. The hunger in his eyes has me frozen in anticipation, but I melt the second his lips lock onto mine.

I don't think I'll ever get tired of kissing Jackson.

My hands wrap around his neck, and he reaches down, hooking his hands under my ass to lift me up. My legs part, the slit in my dress allowing me to wrap around his waist.

His cock is already stiff against my core, and I smile against his lips as he walks us over to the bed. He sits on the edge, and the position gives me stability on his thighs. I use it to my advantage, grinding myself against him.

"Someone's hungry," he mumbles before dropping kisses down my neck.

I squirm against the feeling, his hot tongue sending shivers straight to my center. His hands toy with the thin straps of my dress, slowly pushing them off my shoulders until the entire top half of the silky material tumbles down, revealing my bare breasts.

"You listened."

"Don't I always?"

He cocks his head at my haughty response, and I press my lips together to stop from smiling. He gives my breasts a squeeze, and I love the feeling of his calloused hands on my soft skin.

"Arms up."

I lift my arms, watching as he reaches for the pink rope

that is coiled at the head of the bed. My body relaxes as he winds it around my breasts before finishing off the harness around my shoulders and tying it in front.

He gives my tit a slap, fingertips brushing my nipple, before he gives in to a tender squeeze. "Fuck, I love these." His praise of my body warms me. "But let's make them prettier."

He lifts me off his lap and places me on the edge of the bed before walking over to the side table and grabbing a set of pink nipple clamps that are connected with a thick chain.

I straighten my shoulders, pushing my breasts higher as he clamps the silicone-coated tips around my delicate nipples. The pressure is minor until he clamps the second one and lets go—the weighty chain connecting the clamps hangs down and tugs my nipples, creating a tension that is delicious.

I freaking love it.

"Look at you, smiling at your tits like a filthy whore." Jackson smirks down at me. "I bet if I run my tongue along that pussy of yours, I'll find you already wet."

Without giving me time to register, he pushes my shoulders back so I fall flat on the mattress. I tilt my chin to my chest and watch as he quickly drops to his knees and loops his hands around the backs of my knees, pulling me forward before laying them to rest on his shoulders.

His tongue slides up my slit, and my head lolls back. The hot, wet pressure against my throbbing core is a relief. "Oh my Gods," I moan as his tongue dips into me. He eats me out like I'm his last meal, and I lose myself in the feeling, my heels digging into his back until I'm basically suffocating him with my pussy.

Pain lights up my nipples, and I gasp as Jackson quickly tugs on the metal again. It does nothing but stoke the fire building within me. He loops the center of the chain around his finger, a devious glint in his eyes as he gazes up at me from between my legs. This view alone could have me coming.

Jackson tugs again, and my hips buck in response as I moan his name.

He releases the chain, his hand coming down to my clit and swirling the sensitive bundle of nerves. My pussy clenches, my orgasm building dangerously high now.

"More, more, more," I plead.

He pulls back, and I whine as his tongue leaves me. But he proceeds to bite the sensitive flesh on the inside of my thigh as he inserts three fingers inside me, and a high-pitched gasp breaks free from my throat. My brows furrow, fighting against the pressure that grips me like a vice.

"Are you going to come for me?"

"Can I?" I ask through the haze.

"Yes."

And like a dam breaking, my release flows out of me. Pleasure courses across my skin and lights up my body.

He pulls his fingers free of my pussy, and I mourn the loss, feeling empty without him there. He taps the side of my hip, and I feel my release sticking to my skin.

"Sit up."

I fight against the groan, forcing my limp body up on weak arms.

Jackson reaches next to the bed and brings out a pink ball gag, the sight of it injecting a dose of clarity into my orgasm-haze brain. Without him even telling me, I open my mouth.

He chuckles, the corner of his lips pulling up in a smirk. "Such an obedient slut."

He positions the ball in my mouth before buckling the leather behind my head. My tongue automatically runs along the bottom of the silicone, feeling it out.

"Go lie in the center of the bed, arms and legs out."

I follow his instructions, pushing my body to crawl to the middle and spread like a starfish. My nails hit something hard, and I frown, flipping my hand around and curling my fingers around what feels like a bar. I twist my head just as Jackson comes to rest on the mattress next to me—having taken off his slacks, leaving his glorious cock on display. I watch as he takes my hand and buckles a soft cuff around my wrist before attaching it to the bar that seems to be strapped at the head of the bed. He repeats the process on the other side, rendering my upper body useless. But he doesn't stop there. Jackson pulls out another set of cuffs and buckles them around my ankles before attaching them to another bar located toward the bottom of the mattress. There's nothing stopping the dripping between my legs as I'm spread wide

"Look at you," he mutters to himself as he stands next to the bed, pumping himself slowly. "Completely at my mercy."

My mouth waters at the sight of his cock.

He leans down and blows cold air on my pussy, and I clench in response, my sensitive folds still tingling from my last orgasm.

"Please," I beg, but it just sounds like a moan.

Jackson crawls over me, his strong frame caging me in with one forearm next to my head. His other hand trails languidly down my body, sending sparks along my skin. His lips hover a hairbreadth from my skin, trailing softly along my jaw. The subtle sensation is so distracting that I can't help but gasp when he suddenly pushes in.

His cock fills me completely, slipping through my wetness with ease.

"Such a wet slut."

Jackson pulls back with a smirk as he begins to fuck me. His hips smack against my thighs with each strong push, forcing his cock so deep that his balls slap against my ass. The brute strength of this man is overwhelming, and I love the way it completely consumes him.

"I fucking own this pussy," he growls, using me for nothing else but his own pleasure.

It's relentless.

I scream as my orgasm builds again, but the gag turns it into a muffled garble. I try to bend my knees, but they only lift slightly before the bar prevents them from going any farther. A frustrated moan leaves me as I struggle against the pressure building in my core, wanting nothing more than to wrap my legs around him.

My breathing comes faster, wheezing against the plastic in my mouth. I strain against the cuffs, my wrists pulling to no avail. The more I try to move, the more desperate I become—it's a cycle that viciously feeds my desire.

"Oh my Gods, oh my Gods, oh my Gods," I chant, but it comes out more like a garbled gasp through the gag.

"Don't you fucking come yet," he warns me.

Jackson reaches under my thighs and loops his hands

around my hips to lift my lower back off the bed. The new angle has his dick pushing even deeper, and stars start to speckle my vision.

He pumps into me with no breaks, and it feels like I'm about to explode as he winds me tighter and tighter.

Shit.

I can't do this. I can't last.

Strangled sobs leave me as I try to stave off my release, but it bites at me like a vicious dog on a leash that just wants to be let go.

"Come."

And like a dog, I do.

My second orgasm crashes over me like a tornado landing in a field, ripping me apart. I lose all sense of the world around me and just fall.

"Fuck," Jackson groans, his hips jerking with more force as my walls clench around him. He pulls out, and jets of white hot cum spurt over my stomach as he fists his cock.

"Beautiful," he smirks, and I stare at him dazedly, admiring the way he paints me.

This man has ruined me for anyone else.

Thank you for reading Fake Game!

Curious about how Jackson proposes to Deer?
Download the **bonus content** by, visiting:
https://BookHip.com/FGQDJRT

***

If you haven't read the rest of *The System*, check out
Aleks & Stevie's romance in **Good Game** or Parker &
Sydney's story is **Forbidden Game**.
www.authormadisonfox.com/books

Thank you for reading, *Fake Game*.
If you enjoyed this book, I would be grateful if you could leave a review on the platform(s) of your choice. Reviews are one of the best ways to support an author!

Kisses,
Madison Fox

ACKNOWLEDGEMENTS

I can't believe it. I finished my very first complete romance series!!! The past twelve months have been an absolute journey, and I have been grateful for every single moment. There have been lots of moments of learning and—let me tell you—juggling a writing career while working a day job (which is practically a 24/7 on-call job for me…haha…ha), trying to maintain something of a social life, and not just drowning has been hard. BUT I DID IT! And for anyone who aspires to publish their own book, take this as your sign that you can do it. It might be a struggle, but I believe in you.

To every human who has read my book, THANK YOU. Just by picking up my book and reading a few words, you have supported me on this journey, and I am so grateful that you have given my books a chance.

I just want to give a quick shout-out to all the cozy gamers out there. I grew up heavily obsessed with *The Sims*, but always being told that wasn't "real gaming" *insert eyeroll* Which is why I was so determined to write Deer's character. I wanted to showcase the most cozy gamer-y girl I could possibly create and shove it down everyone's throats. Plus, I secretly wish I had her aesthetic. Additionally, I put some of my own experiences with anxiety into Deer. There are plenty of people who present themselves one way online or even in real life but are really masking something deeper that can truly debilitate them at times. We are always taught to put on a smile, but eventually the pressures cause you to crack. I hope everyone who has even felt a fraction of the way Deer did can find their Jackson who will hold their hand.

I want to make one quick note on doxing and swatting. These are very real and serious issues that afflict the online world, but especially the streaming community. It is extremely dangerous to dox or swat a person and is not something to take lightly. People can be severely hurt, and undergoing these experiences is very traumatising.

Okay, now onto my people.

THANK YOU TO TATE JAMES FOR BEING A TOTAL BABE. Also, for being the reason the Cardinal Club came to be while we were driving around this past summer.

As always, thank you, Cat, for creating two gorgeous covers for me. You are my personal sparkle, and I adore the heck outta you.

To my amazing editor Katie K! You've been with me throughout this series, and I really could not have done it without your amazing editorial support. You always make me smile with the comments you leave.

Thank you, Alyssa, for formatting my books even though our day jobs are crazy as they are.

Alexandra, your proofreading has been an absolute gift! Thank you for catching all the little hiccups that pass by everyone else. And also, for loving all the spicy scenes between Jackson and Deer.

Thank you, Jenn, for always being my number one alpha reader. I always drop these manuscripts on you with such little notice, but you are my rock and are always prepared to drop everything to give me that first round of feedback when I feel like what I have written is total garbage.

To my beautiful sensitivity reader, Aurora, who has adored Jackson from the moment she met him on page,

MWAH. And thank you to Meaghan (thecozylibrary_) for helping me with my Cantonese translations.

Thank you, Becca, for always dealing with my absolute madness as a human. And Jade, thanks for always accepting my random texts that really make zero context.

I can't believe I'm typing this but…thank you, Katie, for helping me with my big titty committee short girlie questions.

LASTLY, THANK YOU TO ME, FOR DOING THIS.

FOLLOW ME ON SOCIAL MEDIA FOR ALL THE FUN!

I post fun updates on my socials pertaining not only to my upcoming releases, but also my life in general and the books that I am reading. I would love to connect with you

<3

authormadisonfox.com

ABOUT THE AUTHOR

Madison Fox was born and raised in Australia but currently resides on the West Coast of the USA as a cat mum to Zelda (yes, based on the video game). She grew up obsessed with reading and collecting books, which fuelled her to write her debut romance, *Good Game*. When Madison isn't writing a new book, she can be found drowning in one of her other obsessions, such as k-dramas, anime, video games, and espresso martinis.

Milton Keynes UK
Ingram Content Group UK Ltd.
UKHW021934201124
451474UK00014B/1084